These special c
authors Marion L
capture the
two surprise

Enjoy our new 2-in-1 editions of stories
by your favourite authors—

for double the romance!

with

CLAIMED: SECRET ROYAL SON
by Marion Lennox

EXPECTING MIRACLE TWINS
by Barbara Hannay

Dear Reader

We hope you like our new look and format!

We want to give you more value for your money—and the same great stories from your favourite authors! Now, each month, we're offering you two Mills & Boon® Romance volumes. Each volume will include two stories. This month:

Follow the first steps and first smiles
of bouncing babies and their proud parents in…

CLAIMED: SECRET ROYAL SON
by Marion Lennox
&
EXPECTING MIRACLE TWINS
by Barbara Hannay

* * *

Add a trip to India and an invitation
to a glamorous ball to your itinerary in…

A TRIP WITH THE TYCOON
by Nicola Marsh
&
INVITATION TO THE BOSS'S BALL
by Fiona Harper

For more information on our makeover, and to buy other Romance stories that are exclusive to the website and the Mills & Boon Bookclub, please visit: www.millsandboon/makeover.co.uk.

The other titles available this month are: **KEEPING HER BABY'S SECRET** by Raye Morgan and **MEMO: THE BILLIONAIRE'S PROPOSAL** by Melissa McClone.

Best wishes

Kimberley Young

Senior Editor, Mills & Boon® Romance

CLAIMED:
SECRET ROYAL SON

BY
MARION LENNOX

MILLS & BOON®

All the characters in this book have no existence outside the imagination of the author, and have no relation whatsoever to anyone bearing the same name or names. They are not even distantly inspired by any individual known or unknown to the author, and all the incidents are pure invention.

First published in Great Britain 2009
Harlequin Mills & Boon Limited,
Eton House, 18-24 Paradise Road, Richmond, Surrey TW9 1SR

© Marion Lennox 2009

ISBN: 978 0 263 86964 4

Set in Times Roman 13 on 14¼ pt
02-0909-49845

Harlequin Mills & Boon policy is to use papers that are natural, renewable and recyclable products and made from wood grown in sustainable forests. The logging and manufacturing process conform to the legal environmental regulations of the country of origin.

Printed and bound in Spain
by Litografia Rosés, S.A., Barcelona

MARRYING HIS MAJESTY

She'll be his bride—by royal decree!

The crowns of the Diamond Isles are about to return to their rightful heirs: three gorgeous Mediterranean princes. But their road to royal matrimony is lined with secrets, lies and forbidden love…

This month
CLAIMED: SECRET ROYAL SON

Next month
BETROTHED: TO THE PEOPLE'S PRINCE

Nikos is the people's prince, but the crown of Argyros belongs to reluctant Princess, Athena—the woman he was forbidden to marry. Can Nikos finally persuade her to come home? Because together they can create a truly modern royal family.

And in November
CROWNED: THE PALACE NANNY

For Elsa, nanny to the nine-year-old heiress to the throne of Khryseis, Zoe, there's more in store than going to the ball. This Cinderella is about to win the heart of the new Prince Regent.

Join Marion Lennox on the Diamond Isles, for three resplendent royal romances!

To Sheila, who makes my books better. With gratitude.

CHAPTER ONE

'WAKE up, Lily.'

There were two doctors and four nurses gathered by the bed. This had been groundbreaking surgery. Heroic stuff. If Lily hadn't been close to death already, they'd never have tried it.

After the operation she'd been kept in an induced coma to give her damaged brain time to recover. They'd saved her life, but would she wake up...whole?

The junior nurse—the gofer in this small, exclusive French hospital—had nothing to do right now and she was free to think about the patient. She'd seen this girl come in a month ago, deeply unconscious, drifting towards death. Rumour said she was related to royalty, but no one came near her.

A nurse was supposed to be objective. She wasn't supposed to care.

There wasn't one person around this bed who didn't care.

'Wake up, Lily,' the surgeon said again, pressing his patient's hand. 'The operation's over. It was a huge success. You're going to be okay.'

And finally Lily's eyelids fluttered open.

She had dark eyes. Brown. Too big for her face. Confused.

'Hey,' the surgeon said and smiled. 'Hello, Lily.'

'H… Hello.' It was a faint whisper, as if she'd forgotten how to speak.

'How many fingers am I holding up?'

'Three,' she said, not interested.

'That's great,' the surgeon said, jubilant. 'You've been ill—really ill—but we've operated and the tumour's been completely removed. You're going to live.'

Lily's gaze was moving around the room, taking in each person. The medical uniforms. The eager, interested faces.

And then, as if she'd remembered something really important, her eyes widened. Fearful.

'Are you in pain?' the surgeon asked. 'What hurts, Lily?'

'Nothing hurts. But…' Her hand shifted, slow from disuse, and her fingers spread over her abdomen.

'Where's my baby?'

CHAPTER TWO

'I, ALEXANDROS KOSTANTINOS MYKONIS, do swear to govern the peoples of the United Isles of Diamas—the Diamond Isles—on behalf of my infant cousin Michales, until such time as he reaches twenty-five years of age.'

Alex's black uniform was slashed with inserts of crimson and richly adorned with braid, tassels and medals. A lethal-looking sword hung by his side, its golden grip emblazoned with the royal coat of arms. His snug black-as-night trousers looked sexy-as-hell, and his leather boots were so shiny a girl could see her face in them.

If she got close enough. As once she'd been close.

Lily could barely see Alex's face from where she watched in the further-most corner of the cathedral, but she knew every inch of his hawk-like features. His brown-black eyes were sometimes creased with laughter, yet sometimes seemed so severe she'd think he carried the weight of the world on his shoulders.

It had been wonderful to make him smile. He'd made her smile, too.

He'd melted her heart—or she thought he had. Love was all about trust, and trust was stupid. She'd learned that now, but what a way to learn.

She watched on, numbed by the day's events. Shocked. Bewildered. Trying desperately to focus on what was happening.

The ring, the glove, the royal stole, the rod with the dove, were bestowed on Alex with gravity, and with gravity he accepted them. This coronation ceremony was as it had been for generations. Alex looked calm, assured and regal.

The last time she'd seen him he'd been in her bed, leaning over her in the aftermath of loving. His eyes had been wicked with laughter. His jeans and shirt had been crumpled on the floor.

Alexandros Mykonis. Successful landscape architect, internationally acclaimed. Her one-time lover.

The new Prince Regent of the Diamond Isles.

The father of her baby.

'Doesn't he look fabulous?' The woman sitting next to her—a reporter, according to the press pass round her neck—was sighing mistily as Alex knelt to receive the blessing.

'He does,' Lily whispered back.

They watched on. He was well worth watching.

The blessing over, Alex rose and proceeded to sign the royal deeds of office. Trumpeters, organist and choir filled the church with triumphant chorus, but there was room within the music's shadow for talk.

'There's not a single woman here who doesn't think he's hot,' the reporter whispered.

Lily hesitated. She should keep quiet, but she was here with a purpose. If she were to get her baby back she needed all the information she could gather. 'It's a wonder he's not married,' she ventured.

'He's not the marrying kind,' the reporter told her, sighing again with the waste of it. 'Though not for want of interest. There's always been some woman or other. My guess is he's disillusioned. His father, King Giorgos's brother, disobeyed royal orders and married for love, but the marriage caused nothing but grief.'

'Why?' she asked, but before the reporter could answer they were distracted.

The Archbishop, magnificent in his gold and white ecclesiastical gowns, had handed newly signed documents to an elderly priest.

The priest, a bit doddery and clearly nervous, took the documents with fumbling fingers—and dropped them.

'That's Father Antonio,' the reporter whispered as the old priest stared down at the scattered papers in dismay. 'He's been the island's priest for as long as I can remember. The Archbishop didn't want him to be part of this ceremony, but Prince Alexandros insisted.'

The old priest was on his knees, trying to gather the scattered documents, clearly distressed. Instead of helping, the Archbishop looked on with distaste. Following his lead, the other officials did nothing.

It was Alex who came to his rescue. As if this pomp and ceremony was an everyday occurrence, he stooped to help gather the papers, then helped the old man to his feet.

Then, as the old priest's face worked, trying desperately to contain his distress at his clumsiness, Alex set his hands on his shoulders and he kissed him. Once on each cheek, in the age-old way of the men of this island.

It was a gesture of affection and of respect.

It was a gesture to restore dignity.

'Thank you, Father,' Alex said simply, his deep voice resonating throughout the church. 'You've looked after the islanders well during my whole life. You baptised me, you buried my parents, and now you do me honour by being here. You have my gratitude.'

He smiled, and almost every woman in the cathedral sighed and smiled in unison.

'See, that's why the islanders love him,' the reporter whispered, smiling mistily herself. 'That's why the islanders would have loved him to take the throne himself. If only this baby hadn't been born. Who'd have expected the old King to get himself a son at his age? He only did it to block Alex from the succession. His marriage to Mia was a farce.'

But Lily was no longer listening. That smile… that gentleness…

She'd forgotten, she thought, blinking back involuntary tears. She'd forgotten why she'd lost her heart.

She was being dumb. Emotional. She needed to gather information and move on. She needed to stay detached.

Impossible, but she had to try.

'What happened with his parents' marriage?' she managed.

The reporter was gazing adoringly at Alex but she was still willing to talk, and she hadn't lost the thread of their conversation.

'Horrid story,' she said absently. 'Alex was their only child. Because his father was Giorgos's brother and Giorgos was childless, until this baby was born Alex was heir to his uncle's throne.

When Alex was five his father drowned, and Giorgos banished his mother from the island. But because Alex was his heir, he kept him. He didn't care for him, though. Alex was brought up in isolation at the castle. When he was fifteen rumour has it that he stood up to his uncle—I have no idea what he threatened him with but it worked. His mother was allowed back. She and Alex went to live in their old home but she died soon after. They say Alex hated his uncle for it—they say he hated everything to do with royalty. But now he's stuck, minding the throne for this baby but with no real power himself.'

Suddenly the reporter's focus was distracted. Some angle of light—something—had redirected her attention to Lily. A glance become a stare. 'Do I know you?' she demanded. 'You look familiar.'

Uh-oh. She shouldn't have talked. Not here, not at such close quarters where she could be studied. 'I don't think so.' She tugged her scarf further down over her tight-cropped curls and pretended to be absorbed in the proceedings again.

'I'm sure I know you.' The girl was still staring.

'You don't,' she said bluntly. 'I only arrived this morning.' To shock, to heartache and to confusion.

'You're a relative? A friend? An official?' The girl was looking at her clothes. They were hardly suitable for such an event. She'd done her best, but her best was shabby. She'd gone for a plain and simple black skirt and jacket, a bit loose now on her too-thin frame. Her only indulgence was her scarf. It was tie-dyed silk, like a Monet landscape, a lovely confection of rose and blue and palest lemon.

She knew she didn't fit in with these glamorous people from all around the world. How anyone could link her with her older sister…

'You look like the Queen,' the girl said, and it took all her control to stop herself flinching.

'I'm sure I don't.'

'You're not related?'

She made herself smile. 'How could you think that?' she managed. 'Queen Mia is so glamorous.'

'But she's abandoned her baby,' the reporter whispered, distracted from Alex's romantic background and filled with indignation for a more recent scandal. 'Can you imagine? The King dies and Mia walks away with one of the world's richest men. Leaving her baby.'

Her baby. *Her* baby!

But still the girl was staring. She had to deflect the attention somehow. 'I'm here in an official capacity,' she told the reporter bluntly, in a voice that said *no more questions*.

She fingered the gilt invitation in her jacket pocket. When she'd arrived—in those first few dreadful minutes when she'd realised what Mia had done—she'd half expected to be turned away. But Mia had invited her and apparently she was still on the official guest list. Alex had probably long forgotten her existence. Her papers were in order. Her invitation was real. There was no problem.

Ha! There were problems everywhere. Where to go from here?

A trumpet was sounding alone now, a glorious blaze of sound that had the congregation on their feet, applauding the new Prince Regent. Prince Alexandros of the Diamond Isles swept down the aisle, looking every inch a monarch, every inch a royal. Looking worlds away from the Alex she'd fallen in love with.

He was smiling, glancing from side to side as he passed, making eye contact with everyone.

He'd be a much better ruler than the old King, Lily thought, feeling dazed. He'd be a man of the people. Others were clapping and so did she.

His gaze swept past her—and stopped. There was a flicker of recognition.

His smile faded.

She closed her eyes.

When she opened them he'd passed, but once again the reporter looked at her, her face alive with curiosity.

'He knew you,' she breathed.

'I've met him…once.'

'Excuse me, but he looked like he hated you,' the girl said.

'Well, that would be a nonsense,' Lily managed. 'He hardly knows me and I hardly know him. Now, if you'll excuse me…'

She turned her back on the girl and joined the slow procession out into the morning sunshine. Only she knew how hard it was to walk. Only she knew her knees had turned to jelly.

She was here for her baby, but all she wanted was to run.

What the hell was she doing here?

Alex shook one hand after another, so many hands his arms ached. His smile stayed pinned in place by sheer willpower. Would this day never end?

And what was Lily doing here?

He'd met her once, for two days only. For a short, sweet time he'd thought it could be different. It could be…something. But then she'd left without goodbyes, slipping away in the pre-dawn light and catching the ferry to Athens before he'd woken.

It hadn't stopped him looking for her—up and down the Eastern seaboard of the United States, searching for the sister of the Queen, who he'd been told was a boat-builder.

He hardly believed the boat-builder bit. When he'd asked Mia she'd simply shrugged. 'My parents separated. I went with my mother, but Lily chose to stay with my father, so I've barely seen her since childhood. Her whereabouts and what she does is therefore not my concern. I don't see why it should be yours.'

Undeterred, he'd kept searching. He'd finally found her employer—an elderly Greek boat-builder based in Maine, who'd eyed him up and down and decided to be honest.

'Yes, I employ Lily, but she won't thank me for admitting she's the Queen's sister. No one here knows the connection except my family. And, as for telling you where she is… In honesty, my friend, I don't know. She left here a month ago, pleading ill health. She gets headaches—bad ones—and they're getting worse. We told her to take a break, get healthy and come back to us. My wife is worried about her. We're keeping her apartment over our yard because we value her, but for now…she's gone and we don't know where.'

So he'd been left—again—with the searing sense of loss that was grief. He'd lost his father when he was five and the old King had torn him from his mother. When finally he'd been old enough to make choices for himself, he'd been reunited with his mother, only to have her die as well.

He'd been gutted. The old King's cruelty cut deep. He'd sworn at his mother's graveside not to get attached again. He'd sworn to have as little as possible to do with royalty.

But somehow the Queen's sister had slipped under his defences.

While they'd made love...while they'd talked and laughed into the night...while he'd held her close and listened to her heartbeat...while he'd felt the wonder of their bodies merging as if they were one...it had seemed then as if she was falling for him as hard as he was falling for her. But in the end, for Lily, it must have been a mere one-night stand. Like her sister, was she just after scalps?

The memory of his useless vow had slammed back, mocking him.

Then she'd phoned.

He'd been back in Manhattan, getting on with his life. It had been mid-morning. He'd just fielded a stressful call. He'd still been feeling ir-ritated that Lily so obviously hadn't wanted to be found. He'd been caught off guard and he'd made a stupid joke.

Okay, it had been the wrong thing to joke

about. It had been crude, but she hadn't given him a chance to apologise. She'd cut the connection. That had been that.

He'd never wanted to fall for her in the first place. Dammit, he did not want to get emotionally involved, especially with someone connected to Mia.

Somehow she'd breached his defences, but that was a mistake. His defences had to get stronger.

So now, for her to turn up here, today…

He was doing all the right things, saying the right things, moving through the crowd with practised ease, but all the time he was looking out for her. A woman dressed in a drab black suit with a crazy scarf…

'Hey, Alex, look at you.' It was Nikos, and Stefanos was right behind him. As a kid, these two had been his best friends. Stefanos was from Khryseis, Nikos was from Argyros.

'When we grow up we'll rule the islands together,' they'd declared. Even as teenagers, they'd dreamed.

Once upon a time the Diamond Isles had been ruled as three principalities; Sappheiros, Khryseis and Argyros—the Isles of Sapphire, Gold and Silver. Then, two hundred years back, the Crown Prince of Sappheiros had invaded his neighbours. He'd taken control and rewritten the constitution.

For as long as he had a direct male heir, the islands would be ruled as one kingdom.

For generations, successive kings had bled the islands dry. Finally came Giorgos, a weak excuse for a monarch. He also had no interest in women, and for years it appeared he'd be the last of the direct line. The islanders had held their collective breath.

Alex and Nikos and Stefanos had held their breath.

Alex had stood to inherit the crown of Sappheiros—as Giorgos's nephew and legitimate heir. Stefanos stood one step back from inheriting the Isle of Khryseis, and Nikos might as well be ruler of Argyros. They were strong men with a common purpose. When the old King died, when the islands reverted to being independent nations, they'd rebuild their economies, they'd stop the siphoning of wealth to the royals and they'd form democracies.

But then, stunningly, Giorgos had married Mia, a woman forty years his junior—and Mia had produced a son. The old rule prevailed. As Giorgos's nephew, Alex could rule, but only as Prince Regent until the baby came of age. The baby would be the next King.

So he was stuck, Alex thought, still watching for Lily, still distracted by his friends but never getting away from his overriding disgust at the way things had played out. He'd be playing father to the child of a man he'd loathed. He'd be playing Prince Regent to a country whose rule he despised, with no authority to change things. And his friends… Behind their smiles there was desperation. They hid it as they'd always hidden it. With humour and false bravado.

'Hey, look at you!' Stefanos exclaimed, clapping his hand on Alex's shoulder. 'One more tassel and you'll be declared a Christmas tree.'

'All you need is some fairy lights,' Nikos agreed, laughing. 'Hey…'

'Mia's sister's here,' he said before they could continue. 'Lily.'

Their banter ceased. They were great friends, Alex thought. If this baby hadn't been born, how much good could they have done?

These two had met Lily. They'd seen how he felt about her. Maybe his feelings were still showing in his face, but he couldn't prevent them.

'Why the hell…?' Nikos demanded, looking round. 'I can't see her.'

'She's playing a drab country mouse—black skirt and jacket, and a scarf over her hair. I guess she thinks it'll stop people recognising her.'

'She has a nerve coming here,' Stefanos said.

'If the people knew... They're aching to lynch Mia.'

'Lily's not Mia.'

'I seem to remember she wound you round her little finger,' Nikos said, still smiling, but his eyes were watchful and tinged with sympathy.

'Yeah, I fell hard,' Alex said, trying to make his voice light. 'I was conned, as Giorgos was conned.'

'Hey, Mia didn't con him. She married him and she bore his child.'

'She married for power and position.'

'And you fell for the sister.'

'It was little more than a one-night stand. Why the hell's she here?'

'Ask her.'

'I guess I must,' he said heavily. 'If Lily thinks she can still play at being part of the royal family...'

'You'll set her right?' Stefanos asked.

'Of course I will,' Alex said heavily. 'And then she'll leave.'

A royal birth, a royal death and a baby abandoned by a royal mother... It had taken Lily most of the day to figure out exactly what had happened.

She'd listened. She'd asked discreet questions of other guests, and she was appalled. She knew enough now to realise the islanders were almost as appalled as she was. There was massive dissent. One more shock might well bring down the monarchy and, for some reason she hadn't figured out, that'd be a disaster.

But it couldn't matter, Lily thought bleakly as the day wore on and she sifted information. She wasn't royal but she wanted the baby. She wanted *her* baby.

Finally she made her way to the nursery. She found it simply by asking for directions from a maid, sounding authoritative, then slipping quietly in without asking.

The nursery was empty, apart from its tiny prince.

Michales was sleeping. He was tucked on his side in his crib, rolled in a soft fuzz of blanket, sucking his thumb in sleep. He had a thatch of thick black curls, amazing for a baby so young. His long lashes fluttered over his tiny cheeks as he slept.

He was…beautiful.

He was hers.

Michales, named after her father, Michael. That was the only promise Mia had kept.

Over the last few weeks she'd wondered how she'd feel when she first saw him, but now, as she gazed at her sleeping son she knew what she felt.

Anger? Betrayal? Yes, both of those, but overriding everything…love. He was perfect, she thought in wonder as she gazed down at her sleeping baby.

Her son. Her baby. Michales.

'What the hell are you doing?'

Alex's voice made her jump. Everything about this man made her jump. He was like a panther, moving with stealth wherever he was least expected. She whirled and found him watching from the doorway, his face impassive.

Twelve months ago she'd found him irresistible. Drop dead gorgeous. Passionate. Even tender.

Now he just looked angry. Regally angry. So far from the Alex she remembered that she cringed.

'I came… I came to see my sister,' she managed.

'As you see—Mia's gone. Abandoning her baby. Abandoning everything to join a man so rich he can buy what she thinks she deserves. Are you saying you didn't know?'

'I didn't.' She fingered the invitation in her pocket, fighting for courage. The anger on Alex's face was enough to frighten a braver woman than she was. 'She asked me to come. She sent me an invitation. I arrived this morning to find her…'

'Gone,' he said bluntly. 'With the son of a

sheikh. Apparently she'd been planning it since her husband died. Maybe before. Who knows?'

'I'm sorry.'

'*You're* sorry?' He stared at her as if she were part of her sister. They looked alike, Lily thought numbly, and he wasn't seeing her. He was seeing Mia, and the way he felt about her was dreadfully apparent.

There was a long drawn-out silence.

She forced her mind back to the first time she'd met him. He'd been here—reluctantly, she gathered—for the King's celebration of forty years of rule. Not knowing the celebrations were underway, shocked by what the doctors were telling her, she'd been frightened enough to try and visit her sister. She'd been stupid enough to hope Mia would care.

Mia hadn't even wanted to listen. *'Lily, please, this is a very important evening. Everyone else is here to party. Here's a dress. Enjoy yourself. I can't listen to your problems tonight.'*

So she'd sat numbly on the edge of the celebrations, trying not to stare into the chasm of her future. But then Alex had smiled at her and he'd asked her to dance.

And here was the result. Michale⋅. Thought by the world to be Queen Mia's ch¹d. Thought, therefore, to be the new King.

No, she thought numbly. Whatever Mia had told the islanders, it was a lie. The true heir was Alex—looking splendid, looking royal, playing his part with ease.

'Have you talked to Mia?' he demanded.

She shook her head. 'That's…that's why I'm here. But I gather she's left…'

'A mess,' he snapped. 'This baby stands to inherit the throne. I'm left in the role of caretaker but I've no power. And here you come… You have no right to be here.'

'I accepted an invitation. I have every right to be here.' She met his gaze calmly, or as calmly as she could manage. Surface calm. Underneath she was jelly.

But somehow she had to break through his anger. She wasn't her sister. He had to see that. 'Alex, last time we met…' she started but his look would have frozen braver souls than her.

'Forget it,' he snapped. 'I don't know what game you were playing…'

'I wasn't playing a game. I was…'

'It doesn't matter.' His anger slashed the stillness. 'What matters now is the future of these islands, and that's nothing to do with you. There are bigger issues. The islanders are enraged. Giorgos and Mia have bled the place dry. I can do nothing to help and I'm stuck with this baby.'

I'm stuck with this baby...

She hadn't known what power he had to hurt her until this moment. Something inside her died, right then.

He was Michales's father. *I'm stuck with this baby...*

It didn't matter. She had to get the baby away.

'So...so what happens now?' she whispered.

'I try and figure a way out of this mess,' he said wearily, as if repeating a tale he was tired of telling. 'The easiest thing to do would be to walk away, but if I do the monarchy will crumble. That'd be a disaster. Giorgos has borrowed to the hilt and most of the island is forfeit if we default. As Prince Regent, I can try and get the economy on its feet. I can service those loans and try to get the land titles back.'

'You can do that?'

'I can try,' he said grimly. 'Do I have a choice?'

'You'd rather be King,' she said and received another flash of anger.

'What do you think?' he demanded. 'I'd like to be King like Giorgos was King? Oh, I'd like his powers. If I was King or Crown Prince instead of Prince Regent, I could restructure the loans and sell royal assets overseas. Did you know Giorgos has properties in Paris, in New York, in London? All over the world. Sold, they'd be worth billions. They'd keep the island-ers safe, but as Regent my hands are tied. And your presence helps nothing. Go home, Lily. I don't need another problem.'

'But what happens to Michales?'

'He'll be cared for. Please leave.'

Dear God…

How could she explain things to him when he looked at her as he did now? And would expla-nations help? If he knew the truth and still made her leave…

She daren't risk it.

Confused, she gazed again at the sleeping baby. That this tiny bundle of perfection could be the result of loving this man…

There was no tenderness now. Alex's voice was implacable. 'Go away, Lily,' he said again, his voice lowering to a growled threat. 'With the way the islanders are feeling, if you show yourself outside these grounds you'll be lucky to avoid being horsewhipped.'

'I'm not to blame for what Mia's done.'

'You're her sister. I have to think you know her better than we do.'

'I hardly know her,' she whispered, touching the soft baby cheek again. There were so many con-flicting emotions playing here. 'Alexandros…'

'I don't think you understand. There is no discussion. You need to leave.' His face was stern. Impersonal.

The man she'd once thought she loved had disappeared.

But what was at stake here wasn't a relationship. It couldn't be. What was at stake was *her baby*. The passion she'd once felt for Alex had to be put aside. It was a memory only, she told herself. It had no basis in fact.

'I want a say in how Michales is raised.' Good, she thought. She'd said it. Maybe in time she'd even manage to tell him the truth. Only not now. Not today, when she felt weak and bereft and torn.

'It's up to your sister to agree to your access,' Alexandros told her. 'If she takes back the role of mother, then of course you can take on the role of aunt.'

'I want more.'

'You can't have more. My people have been betrayed by what your sister has done.'

'So they hate me?'

'They don't know you. But you look like her. So no, you can't have access. Contact your sister instead. Drum some sense into her. Make her be a mother.'

'And meanwhile…' she swallowed '…will you be a father to Michales?'

'Are you joking?' He shook his head in disbelief. 'I didn't like his father and I can't abide his mother. I'll make sure there are good people raising him, but he's nothing to do with me.'

'So he'll be raised how you were raised?'

'How the hell do you know how I was raised?'

'You told me, Alex,' she said flatly and he stared at her.

'I must have,' he conceded at last. 'That one night…I hardly remember.'

It needed only that. A night that had changed her world, and he hardly remembered.

'Look, what is this?' he demanded. 'Lily, we slept together but you left the next morning without even a goodbye. Why bring it up again now? I have to think you got what you wanted.' He sighed again, looking weary of the whole business. Weary of her. 'I'll see you get reports of the baby's progress—even though your sister says she doesn't want anything to do with him. That's all I can do.'

'But he's your…'

She couldn't say it. A maid was standing in the doorway, looking anxious. Looking at Lily in recognition.

'Your Highness, you're wanted downstairs,' the girl said to Alex, but she was still staring at Lily. 'I remember you,' she said. 'You're the Queen's sister.'

'I know I'm wanted,' Alex said grimly. 'I was just saying goodbye to Miss McLachlan.'

'Are you leaving, miss?' the girl asked, looking confused.

'I suppose I am,' Lily said, fighting back tears. 'But… I need to spend some time with Michales. Just a little.'

'Take as much time as you want,' Alex agreed, his tone once again implacable. 'Cradle him all night if you want. See if you can make up for his lack of mothering. But you'll stay out of sight of my guests, and you'll leave by tomorrow morning. Goodbye, Lily. Get off my island. You can return with your sister or not at all.'

And, without another word, he wheeled and walked out of the room, leaving her staring after him.

Feeling ill.

'Did someone give you the letter?' the maid asked tentatively across the silence.

'Letter?'

'The Queen…your sister left only yesterday.' There was awe in the girl's voice, as if she still couldn't believe such scandal. 'She told me you were expected.' She crossed to the vast marble fireplace and lifted an envelope from the mantel. 'I promised I'd give it to you. Oh, but, miss, what was she thinking? To abandon her baby…'

Lily closed her eyes, not even thinking how she could answer. When she opened them the girl was gone. Leaving her with the letter.

What have you done, Mia? she asked herself. Dear God, what a mess.

She flicked open the letter and made herself read. It was like Mia. Blunt, with no emotion.

Dear Lily,

I never wanted your baby. Giorgos was so desperate to stop Alexandros inheriting he decided to adopt a child and swear it was ours. He had it set up—bribing doctors—the works. Then, when you told me you were pregnant and too ill to care for the kid, it was like it was meant.

But now Giorgos is dead. I'm no dowager, Lily, asking for pin money from Alex for the rest of my life. Ben's rich and fabulous and I'm going with him. Now your head's been fixed, the baby will be safe with you.

Mia

Lily stared at the letter for so long her eyes blurred. The blurring was frightening all by itself. The last twelve months had been blurred and more blurred, and then completely blank.

That Alex could look at her as he had…

Once there'd been tenderness but, as he'd said, it had been one night of passion, and one night only. It had been a night of fantasy. Not real.

Her baby was real.

She stared down into the cot and she felt her heart twist. After all the horror, the bleakness that had been her life thus far, this was reality. This tiny being.

She'd thought he was the result of loving.

He was. She thought that fiercely. Even though they'd only just met, she knew she'd loved his father when she'd conceived this child. Yes, she'd been half crazy with fear, but she'd also been in love.

Her baby would be loved.

What had Alex said? *Take as much time as you want.*

The door opened and the maid was there again. 'If you please, miss,' she said. 'It's time for the baby's feed.'

'He's asleep.'

'It's four hours since he was last fed,' the girl said primly. 'We follow rules.'

'I see,' Lily said, swallowing a lump that felt the size of a golf ball. And then she thought, no. No and no and no.

'You heard what Prince Alexandros said,' she

told the girl, her thoughts eddying and surging, then, like a whirlpool, finding a centre. Enabling her to pull herself together and fight for what she most wanted. 'Prince Alex said I can take care of Michales until I leave,' she said. 'Can you bring me his formula—everything he needs until morning—and let us be?'

'What—everything?' the girl said, startled.

'I mean everything.'

'But…we have shifts. We change every eight hours. You can't look after the baby yourself.'

'Of course I can. A baby should have one carer.'

'The rules…'

'Can start tomorrow,' Lily said flatly. 'For today I'm his aunt and I'm caring for him. I'll feed him and then I'll take him for a walk in the grounds. I'll sleep in here with him tonight. Can you let the rest of the staff know I don't need their help until morning?'

'They won't be happy,' the girl said, dubious.

'Their job is to follow rules,' Lily said softly and she gazed out of the window again, but this time she looked towards the sea, where her borrowed boat lay at anchor, gently rising and falling on the swell of the incoming tide.

Dared she?

How could she not?

This boat wasn't big enough for the journey she

had in mind. She'd need help. But then, maybe it was time she called in some favours. What had Mia said? *Ben's rich...*

Her sister owed her big time. That debt was being called in, right now.

'You heard Prince Alexandros,' she said. 'I need to leave. Tomorrow the nursery's yours again, but for today...he's mine.'

It was well into the small hours before Alex found his bed, but still he woke at dawn. He lay staring up at the ceiling, searching for answers.

Trying not to think about Lily.

Thinking about Lily was the way of madness. His life was complicated enough already. He had to find an escape.

There wasn't one. He was locked into a monarchy so out of date that the country couldn't go forward.

And Lily was here.

His head was full already without her. Hell, he had responsibilities everywhere. He was trapped.

But right now all he could think of was Lily. White-faced, big-eyed, thinner than when he'd last seen her. Flinching as he'd said he couldn't remember their lovemaking.

Maybe he'd been too harsh. Telling her she had to leave.

He had no choice. The islanders were appalled at how her sister had behaved. Lily was, at least outwardly, a less groomed, less glitzy version of Mia. Her clothes were built for practicality rather than glamour, but the islanders would still see her sister in her. She wouldn't be tolerated.

For years the islanders had dreamed that with Giorgos's death they'd be able to purchase their homes, their olive groves, their right to moor their fishing boats without paying the exorbitant mooring rents they'd been charged for ever. But with the birth of Michales their hopes had been dashed. And now... For Giorgos to die and for his Queen to walk away leaving such a legacy...

He didn't blame the islanders for their anger. Rebellion was very close but that'd be a disaster, too. He had to find some way through this mess.

To blame Lily wasn't fair. He knew that. But then, he thought wryly, life wasn't fair. He had no choice but to be here, and Lily had no choice but to leave.

Today.

A knock sounded on his door. He hated the servants intruding—in truth he hated the idea of servants—but he had to grow accustomed.

'Yes?'

'If you please, Your Highness...' It was one of the nursery maids, wide-eyed and big with news.

'Yes?'

'The baby's gone,' she breathed. 'I just put my head around the nursery door and he's gone. And so has Miss Lily. The groundsmen say her boat's no longer anchored in the cove. She's taken our baby, sir. She's taken the Crown Prince.'

CHAPTER THREE

IT WAS six long weeks before he found her.

Alex told the islanders he'd given permission for Lily to care for her nephew while Mia decided what to do, but it was a lie. In reality he had a sworn-to-secrecy team working round the clock, making discreet enquiries, searching across the globe.

Finally his enquiries brought up a birth, registered in the United States:

Michales McLachlan, aged five months, son of Lily McLachlan. Reason for not immediately registering the birth: abroad at time of birth and illness after confinement. Father not listed.

She was registering Michales as hers—as a US citizen. Did she think she could get away with it? He was astounded—furious—and, above all, confused.

Was this a ruse so Mia could get her baby back? It didn't make sense. If Mia wanted him she could have taken him. Yes, Michales was the future King of the Diamond Isles, but that wouldn't have prevented him from being raised overseas.

He had to stop it. The one hope the people of the Diamond Isles held was that this baby was a new start. As Prince Regent, Alex could ensure this child was raised with a social conscience. Things could get better.

But things couldn't get better if the baby wasn't on the island where he could influence his upbring.

What the hell was Lily doing? Where was she? And where was the baby?

Mia and her new consort were in Dubai, living the high life.

Lily and Michales were nowhere.

And then he had a call from one of his…researchers.

'Don't ask me how I know, but she's returning to the States by boat,' the man told him. 'The *Nahid* belongs to a corporation owned by Ben Merhdad, the guy Queen Mia's living with. It's due to dock in Maine on Saturday.'

So here he was, in Maine, on the dock, with two of his men plus an immigration official he'd briefed. It'd solve everything if this baby was never permitted legal entry to the United States.

Two minutes before its designated arrival, a magnificent yacht nosed its way into the harbour.

To his astonishment, Lily was making no attempt to hide. She was standing on deck, wearing faded jeans and a plain white T-shirt. Her hair was wrapped in another crazy scarf—a silk confection. Gorgeous.

She was holding a baby.

There was an audible gasp from the guys around him. 'She's not even hiding him,' someone said.

'She's registered the baby as hers,' the immigration official said uneasily. 'She must think she can get away with it.'

'What the hell's she playing at?' Alex growled.

She'd seen him now. Incredibly, she gave him a cheery smile and a wave. She looked like a woman who'd just returned from a pleasure cruise.

She looked…lovely.

Or not. He gave himself a sharp mental swipe to the side of the head. Remember this woman's like her sister. Lovely is surface deep, he told himself. What's inside is selfish, greedy and shallow.

Testosterone was not what was needed.

What was needed was a swift end to this farce.

But she didn't look concerned. She seemed to

be the only passenger, standing calmly on the
deck as lines were secured…as a crewman carried
a couple of bags from below…as Alex gave up
waiting and stepped over onto the deck.

'Hi,' she said, and she smiled brightly again, as
if he was a friend she was pleased to meet after a
casual morning's cruise. 'I thought you might be
here. Good detective work.'

'Are you out of your mind?'

'No,' she said, and kept right on smiling. 'Why
would you think that?'

'You've taken the baby…'

'No,' she said, and her smile slipped a little.
'Not *the* baby. *My* baby.'

'*Yours.*' The word sucked air from his lungs.

'Michales is mine,' she said. She turned to the
crew and her smile returned. 'Thanks, guys.
You've been fabulous. Please thank Ben for me.
I can manage from here.'

'We've organised transport. And security.' One
of the crew—by his demeanour, Alex assumed he
was captain—motioned to the dock, and for the
first time Alex was aware of a limousine. A uni-
formed chauffeur was standing at attention, and
two dark-suited men stood behind.

'Will I need security?' Lily asked, seemingly
of the world at large. 'I'm sure I won't.' She
turned back to Alex and gave him another of her

bright smiles. 'It's up to you, Your Highness. Will I need muscle to protect what's mine?'

'I don't know what you mean.'

She motioned to the men beside him. 'I think you do. You thought you might take my baby away from me.'

'He's not your baby.'

'He is.'

'Miss.' It was the immigration official. Alex had laid the situation before the US immigration authorities, asking for discretion. This man was senior enough to know what to do, and he had the authority to do it. He was wearing a look of determination and gravitas—an official about to lay down the law. 'According to His Highness, this baby is the Crown Prince of the Diamond Isles. He's the son of King Giorgos and Queen Mia.'

'That was a mistake,' Lily said. 'Michales is mine. His birth is registered under my name. He's a citizen of the United States.'

'That's not been proven,' the man said, clearly unimpressed. 'You can't arrive in the States with a baby and claim he's yours.'

'Without proof,' Lily finished for him.

'Registering the baby's birth isn't proof.'

'No,' she said softly. 'But this is.' She handed over a wallet she'd had tucked under Michales's shawl. 'This is confirmation by legitimate medical authorities that I had a baby less than six months ago. You'll see it's indisputable—the French authorities were very thorough when I told them what I needed. Also attached is the report of DNA samples from my son and from me. I'm happy to have the tests repeated here if you wish, but you'll get the same answers. This baby was passed off by my brother-in-law, the King of the Diamond Isles, as his own, in order to prevent Prince Alexandros ascending to the throne. But this baby is mine, and I intend to keep him.'

She wanted this to be over. She was desperate for it to be over. She needed to sound brave, but inside she felt ill. And the way Alex was looking at her…

No. Concentrate on the official. He was the man she had to convince.

She met the immigration official's gaze directly, trying desperately to ignore Alex. The effect he had on her had to be ignored. Everything about him had to be ignored. 'Is there anything more you need from me?' she managed. 'Michales is due for a feed in less than an hour. I want my son settled in his new home by then. If you gentlemen will excuse us, we need to get on.'

The immigration official was leafing swiftly through the papers, his brow creasing in confused recognition.

'These are highly reputable authorities,' he said at last.

'I told you. I've used the best. But of course, as I said, I'm happy for the tests to be repeated.'

'We'll contact you,' the immigration official said, but his tone had changed. 'In view of this gentleman's allegations…' He motioned to Alex, but there was no way Lily was looking there. 'We may well need to have these verified. But on the surface everything appears in order. Welcome home, miss, to you and your son.'

'Thank you.' It was over. Thank God. She took a step towards the gangplank.

Alex was suddenly in front of her.

On the dock, the two men were out from behind the car almost before he blocked her passage, moving purposely towards them. Good old Ben, Lily thought appreciatively. She'd never met her sister's lover, but in the first flush of romance anything was possible. Especially if you had billions and your girlfriend was being threatened with being landed with an unwanted baby if he didn't agree.

She hadn't meant her threats but she'd used them anyway. 'He's your baby until proven otherwise,' she'd told Mia. 'I'll bring him to you and I'll keep on bringing him to you until you help me.'

So Ben's money was at her disposal. She might need it still, she thought. Alex surely couldn't carry her baby off by force but…who knew? He looked angry enough to try.

'Let me pass, Alex,' she said, but his hands fell onto her shoulders and held.

'What the hell are you playing at?'

'I'm taking what's mine,' she said, jutting out her chin. Trying to sound braver than she was. 'Michales is mine.'

'Are you kidding? He belongs to Mia and Giorgos.'

'I just explained that was a lie.' She took a deep breath. Okay. This had to be said some time. What better time than right now? 'Think about why they might have lied, Alex,' she said gently. 'You'll see for yourself what's happened.'

His anger was building. 'The three of you lied? You agreed to it?'

'I was…ill.'

'You mean you were paid,' he snapped, staring around at the luxury yacht as if it had a bad smell. 'I know your family. You don't have a penny to bless yourself with.'

'Let's not get personal.'

'This is nonsense.' He stared down at the baby

in her arms. Cocooned in a soft cream alpaca shawl, Michales slept on, oblivious to the drama being played out around him. 'Of course the baby's Mia's,' he snapped. 'He looks like Mia, and he looks like Giorgos.'

'No, he doesn't,' she said, so softly that no one but Alex could hear.

'He does.'

'Well, maybe a bit,' she conceded. 'But then Mia looks like me. And Giorgos... Giorgos had the Sappheiros royal family features. Who else do I know who might have those features? Work out the dates, Alex. Go figure.'

And, with a faint smile, the result of sheer will-power, she pushed past him.

And that was it. A moment later she was in the limousine. Her baggage was in the trunk and they were moving away.

Alex didn't make a move to follow. He simply stood on the yacht in the warm sunshine and stared after her.

It was done, she thought, shaking with reaction. She'd reclaimed her son.

She could get on with her life.

For days Lily held her breath. She didn't think there was a danger that Alex would try to take Michales forcibly—but she didn't know for sure.

She'd half expected a media frenzy. By reclaiming Michales she was changing the succession of three royal families. The kingdom would dissolve, and the old principalities would take their place. From what she'd figured from reading a potted history of the Isles on the Internet, Alex would now be Crown Prince of Sappheiros. He'd be the real ruler of one island, rather than the caretaker of three.

But it seemed that whatever Alex planned, he wasn't making it public. He hadn't publicised Michales's disappearance either, even though an international hunt might well have blown her cover.

His silence unnerved her, but at least it gave her time to get to know her son. To fall more deeply in love than she'd ever thought she could be.

'It's not the living arrangements you're used to,' she told her tiny son as she introduced him to his new home. Her window looked out over the boatyard. Her boss and his team were at work right under her window, stretching timbers over the frame of a skiff.

She'd soon be down there. The knowledge settled her. Spiros wanted her back and she wanted to be there. If she left her window open she could hear Michales cry, and Spiros's wife would be only too delighted to help.

This could work.

Meanwhile she sat on her faded quilt on her saggy bed and cuddled her son.

She could make him smile, and she was well enough to enjoy him. Life stretched before her, full of endless possibilities. Surely there could be no greater happiness?

Her only cloud? Alex would come, she knew this wasn't over.

Alex—oh, if things could only be different.

They couldn't be different. She forced herself to relax. She forced herself to be optimistic, for there was no going back. This might be Alex's baby, but first and foremost he was hers.

It had taken Alex almost a week to sort things out in his head. Even then they didn't feel sorted. Where to go to from here? He couldn't simply take what Lily told him at face value, tell the islanders they'd been conned and move forward.

But at last, finally, he was starting to accept what she'd told him as the truth.

For the test results Lily had given the immigration official were watertight. Alex had stood by the man's side as he'd rung the French authorities, and he'd heard the outrage that their tests be questioned. Lily had gone to enormous trouble to ensure these were seen as legitimate. She'd organised independent witnesses as DNA samples had been taken. She'd even agreed to have witnesses as she'd been examined to prove she'd borne a child five months ago.

Michales was her baby.

And...*his*? Was she serious?

He remembered the little boy as he'd last seen him, sleeping in his mother's arms. Dark lashes. Thick black curls. Smiling even in sleep.

He was beautiful.

He was his son.

It was too big to take in.

But, believe it or not, this baby was proven to be not the natural child of Mia and Giorgos. There'd been no official adoption—only deception.

The legal ramifications were mind-blowing.

He'd needed help. He'd needed the best constitutional lawyers money could buy, and the best political advisors. He'd consulted them—they'd pored over ancient documents, they'd scratched their heads and they'd outlined facts he didn't want to know.

This was impossible. He needed a magic wand so the past few months could disappear and he could rule without the encumbrance of a baby.

His son.

The more he thought of the lie that had been perpetrated, the sicker he became. That Giorgos and Mia had deliberately deceived the islanders… That Lily had consented…

Had she deliberately seduced him? It had to be faced. Had it been a deliberate plan by the three of them, with Mia pulling out after Giorgos's death only when she'd realised she had no financial independence?

Was Mia's abandonment why Lily had changed her mind and taken her baby back? And what was this illness she'd talked about? She'd been fine six weeks ago at his coronation.

Enquiries to the doctors she'd cited had been stonewalled, citing privacy. Privacy with the succession at stake? Hell, he was almost up to bribing hospital officials to get the answers he wanted.

Not quite. Not yet. He'd ask her directly first.

He'd talked on, privately, to lawyer after lawyer, to advisor after advisor. He'd talked to Stefanos and to Nikos.

He'd thought of one disaster after another…

And when they'd told him the only path that was sure to save the islands he'd felt ill.

Finally, bleak and still unbelieving, he returned to the dockyards, to the address Lily had given the authorities as her permanent home. To the apartment over the boatyard he'd visited once before.

He went alone, slipping in the back way, not wanting to be noticed. Hoping like hell that Lily had rid herself of the bodyguards she'd had with her the week before.

He knocked at the door to her first-floor apartment and he thought this must be a mistake—she'd never live like this. Not Mia's sister.

No one answered. He twisted the doorknob, expecting it to be locked.

It gave under his hand.

Her apartment was one room, simply furnished. There was a double bed, big and saggy, covered with a patchwork quilt that had seen better days. There was a tiny table with a single kitchen chair, a battered armchair, a tiny television, a rod and curtain in the corner constituting a wardrobe.

There was a cot beside the open window. With… With…

Michales? Alone?

No. Ignore the cot. He didn't have space in his head to look at the little person in the cot.

Would he ever?

What sort of a mother was she to leave him alone? Anyone could walk in here.

She was just like Mia.

Concentrate on other things, he thought fiercely. He needed some sort of handle on Lily. Some awareness of who she was.

The apartment was furnished as if the owner

had no money to spare, but it didn't scream poverty. Gingham curtains framed the windows. The windows were open, letting in sunlight and the sounds from the boatyard below. There were pots of petunias on the windowsills, and a seagull was balancing on one leg looking hopefully inside.

It looked…great.

It also looked about as far from a royal residence as it could get.

Where was Lily?

Michales…his son…was sound asleep.

His son.

He could just pick him up and take him, he thought. How easy would that be?

What did he want with a baby? With this baby? With…*his* baby?

He walked over to the window—still carefully not looking at the cot—and glanced out. And there was Lily.

She was right below him, deep in the hull of an embryonic boat. The boat's ribs stretched around her, bare, raw timber. The guy he'd met twelve months before—Lily's boss?—was hauling a length of wood from a steaming vat.

To his amazement, it was Lily calling the shots. She was dressed in serviceable bib-and-brace overalls, workmanlike boots, a baseball cap and thick leather gloves to her elbows. She received the timber from Spiros and her orders flew, curt and incisive.

Her whole attention was on the plank. They had it in place and she was hauling it by hand, pushing, twisting… Two other men were helping, using their brute strength to help her, but Lily was doing the guiding.

He watched on, fascinated. Only when the wood was a fully formed rib, one of the vast timbers forming the skeleton of the new hull, did she stand back and look at it as a whole.

'That's fantastic,' she called. 'Ten down and a hundred and sixty to go? We'll get them done by teatime.'

There was laughter and a communal groan.

She laughed with them. She was…one of the boys? The men were deferring to her with respect.

'I need to check on Michales,' she was saying. 'He's due for a feed. You think you can do the next one without me?' She glanced up at the window.

She saw him.

He'd expected shock. Maybe even fear. Instead, her eyebrows rose, just a fraction. She gave him a curt nod, as if acknowledging past acquaintance, or maybe that she'd attend to him shortly, then deliberately turned her back on him. She strolled over to talk to Spiros.

Spiros was about to lower another plank, but he was looking at it doubtfully. Now he swore and thrust it aside.

'It's not worth it. There's a flaw in the middle and the rest are the same. They'll break before they ever bend. Enough. You go and feed your little one, and I'll send the boys to get more.' He smiled at her with real affection. 'Don't you keep my godson waiting.' Then he, too, glanced up at the window. His smile died.

Spiros stared at Alex for a long minute. What had Lily told him?

Nothing favourable, clearly.

'Hey, look who the cat brought home,' he said, his tone softly threatening. 'It seems we have company.'

His big body was pure aggression. If Spiros had been Lily's father the message couldn't have been clearer. 'You mess with Lily, you mess with me.'

With us. The entire team was gazing at him now. This was hostile territory.

There was a slight noise behind him. He turned and a middle-aged woman was standing in the doorway. Her arms were crossed across her ample breasts. She looked immovable and as aggressive as the men on the docks.

Maybe he couldn't just pick up Michales and take him.

'What do you want?' Spiros demanded from below. 'What the hell are you doing in Lily's apartment?'

'It's okay, Spiros,' Lily said. 'I've been expecting him. Though I shouldn't have left it unlocked.'

'It's okay,' the woman called to Lily. 'I'm here.' She stalked over to the cot and put her body between him and his…the baby.

He couldn't look at…*the baby*.

Unnerved, he looked down at the docks again. Lily was only ten feet under him, giving him a bird's-eye view. She was too thin, he thought. Her bib-and-brace overalls were loose and baggy. Her glorious curls were caught up under a boy's baseball cap, worn back to front. She had a smudge of grease down one cheek.

She looked about fifteen.

But then, 'I'm hoping he's here to organise paternity payments,' she told Spiros, and he stopped thinking of what she looked like.

'He's your baby's father?' Spiros demanded.

'He is. This is Alexandros, Prince Regent of Sappheiros.'

If he'd expected a bit of deference he would have been disappointed. Spiros's aggression simply doubled. Tripled. And the gasp from the woman at the cot was one of indignation and affront.

'So where the hell have you been?' Spiros demanded from below. 'Alexandros of Sappheiros. A prince of the blood, leaving Lily alone with a child… What were you thinking?'

This was crazy. He didn't need these accusations.

He should go down.

Not with the amount of aggression directed at him, he decided. He could talk a lot more reasonably from up here. Especially if he kept his back turned to Madam Fury.

'I searched for her,' he told the boat-builder, trying to keep his voice moderate. Reasonable. 'You know I did.'

'Once,' Spiros said, and spat his disgust. 'You came here once. If she'd been my woman I would have hunted her to the ends of the earth.'

'I'm not his woman,' Lily retorted.

'He's the father of your baby,' Spiros countered, pugnacious. 'Of course you're his woman.'

'Times change,' she said softly. 'You know they do. Spiros, I need to talk to him.'

'Then talk,' he said, glowering. 'Go on. But, prince or no prince, remember he has no rights here. Leave your window open and call us if you need us.' And with a humph of indignation—and a meaningful and warning stare at Alex—he turned his back on him.

CHAPTER FOUR

HE WAS off balance. He shouldn't have entered Lily's apartment. It made him feel like a criminal.

What Spiros had said made him feel like a criminal.

Leaving Lily alone with a child...

How the hell was he supposed to have known?

He heard heavy boots on the stairs. Lily's boots? The door swung open. He turned to face her but she ignored him, making a beeline for the cot.

Michales was still asleep.

Alex waited. He still didn't look at the baby. He couldn't. This was still too big to take in.

Lily though... He could watch Lily. She'd been doing hard manual work. Building boats. He'd heard it before and he'd been hearing verification all week but until now he hadn't believed it.

Mia's sister?

Finally satisfied her son was safe, Lily turned to the woman.

'Thanks, Eleni,' she said. 'I can take it from here.'

Then, as the woman gave him a cold stare and huffed her way out of the door, she turned to him. 'So,' she said, coldly formal, 'what right do you have to walk in here?'

She was angry! There were two sides of that coin.

'I might ask the same of you,' he snapped. 'Entering my palace, stealing the Crown Prince.'

'He's not the Crown Prince and you know it.' She tugged her cap further down over her short-cropped curls. It really was... ridiculous.

'You had no right...' he started, but she crossed her arms over her breasts as Eleni had and glared, lioness guarding her cub.

'I have every right. You can't have him.'

'I'm not saying I want him.'

'No,' she said, and then again, 'no.' Defiance turned suddenly to uncertainty. 'I don't...'

'Know what you want? That makes two of us. Would you mind telling me what the hell is happening?'

'Why should I?'

'For a start, you've implied I'm this baby's father. Am I?'

'Yes,' she said, as if it didn't matter.

It mattered. He'd been working on this, the worst-case scenario, all week, but it still made him feel ill.

Again he couldn't look at the cot. He just... couldn't.

'So you sold him to Giorgos and Mia.'

'I'd never sell him. He's mine, and if you think you're taking him...'

'I'm not here to take him, but I have the right to know what's going on,' he snapped back and she made an almost visible effort to get a hold on her anger.

'Just tell me,' he said. 'You owe me an explanation.'

'I owe you nothing,' she flashed, and then closed her eyes. 'Okay,' she said at last. 'Not that you deserve an explanation, but here goes. I met you, I slept with you and I got pregnant. But I couldn't care for Michales so Mia took him. She and Giorgos told the world he was theirs. I thought they were adopting him. They didn't even do that, which has made my task of reclaiming him a whole lot easier.'

'You're saying you didn't even check what they were doing?'

'That's right,' she said flatly, not even bothering to be defensive. 'I was ill during the pregnancy and I trusted Mia to care for him. I was a fool. Take it or leave it. It's the truth.'

He couldn't believe it. It didn't make sense. 'Mia told the world she was pregnant months before Michales was born.'

'Did she?' She sounded uninterested.

But he was working things out in his head. 'Mia said she didn't want anyone to know of her pregnancy until she was sure she wouldn't miscarry,' he said slowly. 'By the time it was announced, she was five months gone. She was staying in the most exclusive private hospital she could find—abroad, as far from Sappheiros as she could get. Was that so she could bribe people to say your baby was hers?'

'I don't know. I don't care.'

What the hell…? 'Lily, I've had enough,' he snapped. 'To be party to such a fraud…'

'Am I supposed to explain?'

In the cradle behind her, Michales was stirring. Whimpering.

Michales.

He had a son.

He'd known for a week. But he needed more time to take it in. A year or so. More.

And into his jumble of emotions came Lily. She was aggressive and uncooperative. But underneath…

There was a reason he'd fallen for her, he thought. Beneath her anger she looked…vulnerable. And very, very desirable. Despite the overalls and the crazy cap. Despite the steel-toed boots.

She made him feel…

Yeah, that was what had got him into this mess in the first place, he told himself savagely. Leave feelings out of it. Find out facts.

Like why she hadn't told him she was pregnant.

'Did I deserve this?' he asked slowly into the silence. 'That you not tell me you were expecting my child?'

'I tried to tell you.' She sounded tired. Flat.

'I don't believe you.'

'I phoned. Three weeks after we'd…'

'Had sex?' he said crudely and she winced.

'If you like,' she managed. 'Maybe that sums up our connection. Dumb, sordid sex.'

It had been more than that. They both knew it. That was what was messing with his head.

'I tried to find you,' he told her.

'Like I believe that. You only had to ask Mia for my address.'

'I did ask Mia. She told me to leave you alone—she was blunt and aggressive and gave no details. But I did end up here. Spiros has told you. And then you phoned.'

'I did,' she said coldly. 'You can't remember what you said?'

'No. I…'

'If you can't, then I can. It's the sort of conversation that sticks in a girl's mind. You find out you're pregnant. You're sick and confused and scared, but finally you work up courage to contact the baby's father. And his line is… "Lily. Great to hear from you. You're not trying to slap a paternity suit on me as well, I hope.'"

He stilled.

He'd said it. God forgive him, he'd said it.

He remembered, all too clearly.

He was a prince, a bachelor, titled and eligible. He'd made a fortune himself, and as Giorgos's heir he stood to inherit much, much more. As such, he'd endured the most blatant attempts to…get close.

The morning Lily had called he'd just fielded a call from the mother of a Hollywood starlet. Vitriolic and accusing.

'You slept with my daughter and now she's pregnant. You'll marry her or you'll pay millions.'

He'd never slept with the girl. He couldn't remember even meeting her. But obviously the girl was pregnant, and she'd named him as the father.

It happened.

And about ten minutes after that, Lily had called.

He *had* slept with Lily. He'd been angry that she'd left, frustrated that he hadn't been able to find her—and, despite his precautions, pregnancy was possible, though unlikely. So he'd come out with his glib, joking line…

'*You're not trying to slap a paternity suit on me as well...*'

She'd said...what was it? 'Get lost.' And cut the connection.

He remembered staring at the phone, feeling bad, thinking he should trace the call. And then thinking of Mia and how much he disliked her—how much he loathed Lily's connection to royalty. And how much attachment hurt. How love ended in grief. How a sister of Mia's could never be worth that hurt. And it had sounded as if she clearly didn't want him anyway.

And he'd made the conscious decision, there and then, not to make any further attempt to contact her.

'You could have tried again,' he said, but her face was grim now, and drawn.

For over a year now he'd tagged this woman as just like her sister. He'd treated her accordingly. His response to her phone call had been glib and cruel, but if it had been Mia he'd been talking to, maybe it would have been justified.

She wasn't Mia.

And now? She was expecting him to walk away. No, she was wanting him to walk away. With or without paternity payments, he thought. The fact that she wanted nothing to do with him was obvious.

Unbidden, he remembered Lily as he'd first

seen her. Dressed simply in a little black dress. Very little make-up. Those glorious curls.

He'd said something sardonic about their surroundings—the glitz of the royal ballroom—and she'd chuckled her agreement. 'I do like a bit of bling,' she'd said. 'Mind, these chandeliers are a disappointment. I'd prefer them in pink. Plain crystal is so yesterday's fashion. Like stove-pipe pants and shoulder pads.' She'd eyed him up and down—in his tuxedo. 'And tuxedos,' she'd said, and she'd said it like a challenge.

He'd been entranced.

But there was no trace of that humour now. Her gaze was glacial.

'I don't have to tell you more,' she said. 'You're not King here.'

'I'm not King anywhere.'

'Or Prince Regent.'

'It seems I'm not Prince Regent either,' he told her. 'If Michales isn't Giorgos's son…' He hesitated, trying to find words to clarify what he'd figured over the last week. 'If we can get this sorted without calamity, the Diamond Isles will be split into three again. I'll be Crown Prince of Sappheiros and Khryseis and Argyros will be ruled as separate countries.'

'So can you get this sorted?' she asked, but she didn't sound interested.

'Maybe. No thanks to you.'

'On the contrary, it's all thanks to me,' she snapped. 'If I hadn't claimed Michales you'd still be ruled by my sister's lie. So now you can be whatever sort of prince you want and you can get out of my life.'

'There's the small issue of my son…'

'You need to earn the right to be a father. I've seen no evidence of it.'

'I didn't know he was my son!'

'You've known for a week. So what did you do? You disappeared. You went away and did anything rather than come here and say *this is my son and I want him.*'

'I didn't know…' he started, but then he paused, unsure where to go.

'You didn't know what?'

'I don't know how I'm supposed to feel,' he snapped. 'I needed time.'

'Like I needed time when I saw the thin blue line,' she retorted. 'Parenthood isn't something you can think about and then decide *ooh, maybe I'd like a little bit.*'

'Isn't that exactly what you did?'

'I had no choice.' She moved still closer to the cot, putting her body between him and her baby. It was a gesture of defence as old as time itself.

'So why did you give him up?' he demanded,

trying to keep his focus on indignation. Trying not to think how beautiful she was when she was angry. How vulnerable. How…frightened? 'How much did they pay you?'

'Millions!' The word was a venomous hiss.

Okay, not millions, he conceded.

What, then? Had she simply offered her son to her sister instead of having him adopted?

Had she really been ill?

His eyes flew to her baseball cap. She'd covered her curls at the coronation, too.

Cancer? But Lily didn't have that look. Soft curls were escaping from under the cap—short, yes, much shorter than last year, but not regrowth short.

'Just how ill were you?'

'It's none of your business.'

'Your hair…'

'I had an operation,' she snapped. 'I'm fine now.'

He got the message. Ask no more questions. Move on.

Okay, he would. But maybe here there was an explanation.

The consequences of illness, even if relatively mild, might well have been catastrophic. If she didn't have insurance, medical expenses could be huge.

If Mia and Giorgos had paid her expenses and

in return taken a child she could ill afford to keep… A child she didn't really want, until Mia's abandonment had given her second thoughts…

It didn't absolve her from blame, but it might explain it.

Maybe something of what he was thinking was apparent.

'Don't even think about pushing into what's my business,' she told him coldly. 'Let's get this sorted. If you want to deny Michales is your son, that's fine by me. I don't need or want financial aid. If you want access I won't block it—as long as he stays with me. But that's my bottom line. He stays with me.'

'I can't let him stay here.'

'He will stay here.' She sounded blunt and cold and definite. But, underneath, he heard the beginnings of fear.

There was no way he could allay that fear.

'I have to take him back to Sappheiros.'

'You're taking him nowhere.'

'Michales has to be my son.'

'So he is,' she snapped. 'Move on.'

'He has to be my legitimate son.'

That confused her. 'Excuse me?'

'Can you imagine the furore there will be if he disappears? The islanders are upset enough now that you've taken him. For you to keep him…'

'He's mine!'

'The islanders think he's theirs.'

'He's not.'

'He is,' he said. 'You and Mia and Giorgos gave him to the island. The islanders have taken him to their hearts. I won't take him away from them.'

'It's not you who's taking him away.' She was whispering but she might as well be yelling, it was said with such vehemence. 'It's me. He's mine, and he stays with me.'

As if on cue, Michales stirred again, uttering a small protesting whimper. She scooped him from his cot and held him against her. He snuggled into her and her fingers stroked his hair.

The sight…watching her stroke the little boy's hair did something to him he didn't begin to recognise.

This was getting harder. He'd come here fuelled with anger against this woman. He'd come here to try and sort a solution.

What he hadn't counted on was how she made him feel. He'd slept with Lily over twelve months ago and his body still knew why. He was reacting to her as he had then—with a desire that was inexplicable but inarguable.

And Michales…

He'd never thought of himself as a father. This child had nothing to do with him.

Except… He had the look of him. *His son.*

His world was shifting into unchartered territory.

Just say it, he told himself again, feeling cornered. Lay it on the line.

'Lily, this is hard,' he said. 'But you need to listen. The islanders have lived with such uncertainty that when the truth comes out about Michales's parentage their likely reaction will be disbelief. And why wouldn't it be? They've been lied to by Mia and Giorgos. They have no reason to trust me—or you.'

'I don't… It can't matter.'

'But it does matter,' he said forcefully. 'We need to give them reason to believe, and the way to do that is by acting truthfully and acting with honour.'

'Honour…' She filled the word with scorn. 'Honour!'

'I know it's been in short supply, but this is my honour,' he said, ruefully now. 'I need to be seen to do the right thing.'

'Finally.'

'Okay, finally,' he admitted and spread his hands in apology. 'I concede my behaviour until now has been less than perfect. I shouldn't have slept with you. I shouldn't have blocked your phone call with such a response. But we…both of us…need to move on. The islanders need to be told that Giorgos and Mia lied, but they need to accept that the lies are finished. They need to know I'm to be trusted—and that I'm truly Michales's father. Right now the island is on the brink of rebellion, but my advisors believe that it would be reluctant. We can head it off by giving the island stability, good government and hope for the future. The island needs an honourable royal family and it needs an heir.'

Lily stared at him over Michales's small head. 'S-so?'

But maybe she was already seeing where he was going, he thought. She looked suddenly terrified. She was a lot smarter than Giorgos, he thought. Or her sister.

'I'm assuming you know the state of the Diamond Isles.'

'Yes, but…'

'But ruin,' he said forcefully. He couldn't let the shock on her face deflect him from what needed to be said. 'The islanders are poverty-stricken. The islands' land titles are mortgaged to the hilt and there's threatened takeover by outside interests. We're facing destruction of our lifestyle—everything we stand for. That's inevitable, unless these people put their faith in me and in what I can do. The islanders have to accept their new royal family—they can't think I'm inventing this story merely to claim the throne for my own ends. Lily, I've thought about this all week. I've listened to the wisest lawyers and political advisors I can find. And they've come up, over and over, with the one sure answer.'

'Which…which is…'

'Which is that you marry me.'

CHAPTER FIVE

FOR a moment he thought she'd faint. The colour bleached from her face. She stared at him in incredulity. Instinctively his hands caught Michales and held.

She was so stunned she let her baby go. He stood, holding his son. Not sure how to hold him. Not sure where to go from here.

'Maybe I didn't do that too well,' he said at last. Then he said dryly, 'Maybe I should go down on bended knee.'

'Or maybe you shouldn't.' Colour washed back, a flush of anger. Better, he thought. Angry was good.

He could deal with anger.

'I think you need to leave,' she said. 'I'm talking about getting on with the rest of my life. You're talking fairy tales.'

'I'm not.'

Michales wriggled in his arms. He looked up

at Alex and he smiled, a wide, toothless grin that made Alex feel as if the rug was being pulled from under his feet.

He had to keep hold of his anger. He couldn't think while holding…*his son*.

He laid him on the square of carpet under the window. The little boy pushed himself into a sitting position and crowed with delight.

Alex gazed down at him in astonishment. 'He can almost sit up. He wasn't doing that in Sappheiros.'

'As if you'd have noticed.'

'I did notice,' he told her. 'Even before Mia left I was worrying about him. The nursery staff were worrying about him. His mother seemed to be ignoring him.'

'Yeah,' she said, sounding dazed. 'Alex, go away.'

'I can't,' he said soberly, and instinctively he caught her hands. They were cold. Too cold. She didn't pull away, though—she didn't move.

Okay. Get this right, he told himself. Stay logical and unemotional.

'It's politics,' he told her. 'If we leave things as they are, if he stays here with you, the islands will be in a mess. They'll see me as a usurper, and rebellion is a real possibility. But if we marry…'

She tugged her hands back in instinctive protest, but he didn't let her go. He had to impart the urgency of the situation, and at the same time he was trying to figure how to take the blank look from her face.

She looked…battered. It might be a front, but he needed to back off.

He needed to talk a language they both understood.

'You obviously don't understand,' he said. 'But I'm talking money.'

And here it was. He'd come prepared.

'There's a cheque in my pocket for more money than you can dream of,' he told her. 'Call it paternity payment if you like, but it's yours the moment you marry me.' Then, as she stared at him in stupefaction, he ploughed on. 'This is not personal. Think of it as a business proposition. The proposal is that you marry me—a real wedding to reassure everyone that we stand together—you stay on Sappheiros for at least a year so our marriage can't be annulled, and then we can be seen as gradually drifting apart. Once the island is stable we can divorce. You can do what you want. You'll be rich and you'll be free. I can put democratic reform in place so the Crown is titular head only, and you can do whatever you want for the rest of your life.'

And, before she could respond, he produced the cheque and handed it to her.

She took the cheque without saying a word. She stared at him. She stared down at the cheque—and she gasped.

It'd be okay. Money talked. He had this covered. As long as he married her.

He had no choice.

'This…this is for real?' she whispered.

'Absolutely,' he said. 'We've thought of every option and this is the only one we believe can work.'

She was staring at him as if she'd never seen him before. She was staring at him as if he was a lunatic.

'There's more,' he said into the silence. 'We've done a lot of digging in this last week. My researcher knows all about you and the people you work with and we've come up with a package deal. Apparently the only strong connection you seem to have is with Spiros and his team. We've learnt that Spiros's boatyard is struggling. As an inducement—because it would be best for everyone if Michales does stay on the island, and thus you, too—I'm also offering Spiros something he can't refuse. We'll relocate this boatyard to Sappheiros, with every cost taken care of. We'll give him transport of boats between the Diamond Isles and the rest of Europe. We'll give him blanket international advertising. My researchers tell me Spiros has been fighting to make a living here, and he's homesick. He and his wife want to live somewhere they can speak their native Greek. So all you need to do now is agree.'

She said nothing. She was staring at the cheque as if she couldn't believe it.

She was so shocked. She was so…

Beautiful?

Don't go there, he told himself sharply. This was a business proposition—nothing more, nothing less. His lawyers had worked it out as a done deal. 'There's no way she'll knock back this offer,' he'd been told, and for good measure, thinking of Mia's greed, they'd added another zero to the cheque.

As Crown Prince, Alex would inherit all Giorgos's wealth. The lawyers' thinking was that he should use a fraction of this to ensure the island's future. This marriage of convenience was necessary. Michales's continued presence on the island was desirable. So pay her and get it sorted. But…

'Get out,' she said.

He didn't move.

'Get out.' She was breathing too fast, her eyes flashing daggers. 'How dare you…?'

'Propose marriage to the mother of my son?'

'He's not your son.'

'You said…'

'By birth, yes. You want him back on the island

for you? *For you?* Michales hasn't come into this discussion once except as a tool to keep the monarchy safe. Neither have I. For you to manipulate me…to find out about Spiros and use him as a tool… Get out and stay out.'

'Lily, look at the amount on that cheque,' he said urgently. 'You can't possibly knock back what I've just offered.'

'Watch me,' she said and she ripped the cheque in half, in half again and then kept on going until it lay in shreds round her feet. She snatched Michales up and stalked to the door. 'Out!'

'You're being ridiculous. If you want more…'

'*You're* being ridiculous,' she snapped back at him. 'Don't you understand? I have everything I want, right here, right now. I have something you and Mia and people like you can't understand. I have *enough*. I can stay working on the boats I love, and I can raise my son. I have my future and I'm free. Why would I possibly jeopardise that by diving into the royal goldfish bowl?'

Free? How did free come into it? She spoke as if she'd just come out of prison.

He had to make her see sense.

'And Spiros?'

'He's happy here.'

'He's not. Any minute now this business is going to go belly up. Ask him.'

'That's nothing to do with you.'

'It's everything to do with you. You have to marry me.'

'I don't have to marry you.' She opened the door. 'Get out,' she said again.

'I can't,' he said, trying to figure where the hell to take it from here. 'Lily, you have to do this. The islanders are facing ruin. If I don't get this succession sorted, the titles belonging to the Crown will be forfeit to outside business interests. Sappheiros will become an exclusive resort for the rich, and my people will be exiles. The other two islands will face a similar fate.'

Her face stilled. For the first time, she hesitated.

He paused.

Was he going about this the wrong way? Was it possible that this woman had the heart that Mia lacked?

She'd given away her baby. The assumption had been she'd done it for profit, for greed. But now…

She looked pale and sick. And suddenly that was how he was feeling. Sick.

He was starting to feel…smirched. As if he was acting as Mia and Giorgos had acted. Buying her baby. Buying her.

'Get out,' she whispered again, and this time he nodded.

'I'm going. But…' He hesitated but it had to be said. 'Lily, this is too fast. It's urgent but it's not about us. I suspect I've misjudged you, and if I have then I'm sorry.'

'That's kind of you.' She was trying to sound sardonic but her voice was shaking.

She swayed, just a little.

He moved, crossing the few steps to her in an instant, holding her shoulders. Steadying her.

'Don't…don't touch me.'

But she didn't pull away. She couldn't. She was holding on to Michales with one arm, with the other the door handle. 'Please leave.'

Hell, how ill had she been? 'Lily, are you okay?'

'I'm fine,' she managed and steadied. She tugged away and he released her with real regret. She seemed suddenly… frail?

It didn't make sense. Nothing made sense.

He'd walked into this room feeling nothing but anger at the mess this woman had got him into. Determined to act with honour, no matter what the cost. Now, stupidly, all he wanted was to protect her.

It didn't make sense to her either. She was looking at him with a mixture of fear and something else. Something he couldn't pinpoint.

Regret? The word slipped into his mind and stayed.

Regret for what he'd done to her? Regret that she couldn't take up his offer?

Maybe she had used him. Maybe the pregnancy had been planned. But this was…deeper.

He thought of how she'd been little more than a year ago. She'd danced with him, she'd teased him, she'd mocked him and he'd been enchanted. What had happened to knock the spirit from her?

'Lily, I'll leave,' he said and flinched inwardly as he saw relief flood her face. Was she so afraid of him? 'I've come at you too fast, too hard.'

'Yes,' she said blankly.

The pieces of the cheque were still scattered on the floor. There were far too many for her to gather and reassemble after he left.

But she'd seen his glance—and she guessed what he was thinking.

'I won't,' she said, her face flushing with anger again.

'I know you won't.'

'You don't know anything about me.'

He was starting to know more.

From Lily's arms Michales was watching him with interest.

He was his son…

How could he have been convinced that a simple cheque could fix things? It seemed so ridiculous now.

If Lily hadn't been Mia's sister—if he hadn't assumed this had been set up as a con—what would he have done?

Appeal to a conscience he'd assumed she couldn't have?

If she did have a conscience, there was nothing to lose—and everything to gain.

'Do you have access to the Internet?'

His simple question caught her off guard. 'I…yes…'

'Then I'll leave you. But I need you to do something. I want you to look up the websites of our local newspapers.' He pulled out a card and scribbled addresses on it. 'Then contact these men. They'll give you their own references. What they'll do—I hope—is convince you that what I say is true. The islands are facing ruin. Only my marriage to you can save them.'

'But I don't want to be married. I want to be free.'

'Free?'

'Yes, free.' Her colour suddenly returned in force, surging behind her anger. 'I'm free,' she said, sure now. 'For the first time in my life I can move forward, where I want, when I want. You think I'd go from that to *marriage*…' She said the word as if it were some sort of hell. 'How can you ask it of me? You have no right.'

Was the thought of marriage to him so appalling? It didn't make sense.

He wasn't *that* bad. Was he?

It couldn't matter. All he could do was tell her the facts. 'I have no choice,' he said. 'And if you have a conscience, then you don't either.'

Her anger was palpable. Maybe if she'd had a hand free she'd have slapped him, he thought. Maybe it would have made them both feel better. What was between them needed some release— there was nowhere to go with the rising tension.

'Just contact these people,' he said. 'Ask the questions.'

'Go.'

'I'll come back tomorrow. Lily, we're running out of time and you must take this seriously. Combined, you and I hold the fate of the islands, and Sappheiros in particular, in our hands. Whether we want it or not, we need to be married.'

She looked up at him in bewilderment. Anger was giving way to confusion.

'I'm sorry,' he said simply. 'But we have to do this. And maybe it won't even be too bad.'

And then—maybe it was really dumb but he couldn't not—he lifted Michales from her arms. Once more, he set the little boy on the floor.

He took Lily's face in his hands.

And he kissed her.

It was no deep, demanding kiss. He had enough sense for that—almost. But that night a year ago hadn't been an aberration. His body knew what it wanted—and it wanted her.

The kiss was a feather-touch, lips to lips, sweet as honey, and a connection that felt intrinsically right. It was as if a part of him had reconnected that he hadn't known until this moment had been cut loose.

He kissed her and she didn't respond, but neither did she pull away.

Should he take it further?

His body was telling him to deepen the kiss, push past the barriers he could feel she'd erected.

His head was screaming the opposite. He'd pushed her too far as it was. The royal succession hung on this young woman's decision. To push her past the point where she might run…

He shouldn't. But kissing her felt right. It felt entirely natural. Lily…

And things were changing.

Suddenly it was Lily who was taking control.

He'd outlined a business proposition. So why was he kissing her?

She should fight him. She shouldn't let him kiss her.

She was passive, letting him do the running, letting him kiss her…

Why had she done this? Why had she let him?

She knew why. She just had to see…if what she remembered was real.

Like beer. It was a stupid analogy but she'd thought of it a few times over the past months.

The first time she'd been given a glass of beer, it had been after a day spent working in the hold of a sun-baked boat. She'd been hot to the point of exhaustion. She'd been so thirsty her tongue was swollen, and she remembered that beer as almost like nectar.

The next time she'd tasted beer it had been an ordinary day—no heat, no exhaustion. She remembered being deeply, intensely disappointed.

So now…for all these months she'd been convincing herself that what she felt for Alex had to be a combination of time, place and mood. Nothing more.

But she had to see.

So stupidly, dumbly, she let herself try.

Alex's kiss had been tentative, questioning. She felt the first stirrings of regret. This wasn't as she remembered.

She should pull away while she still felt like this.

But she had to push harder. The memory was still too strong to let her release it without grief. She had to take the next step.

She put her hands on either side of his face, she pulled him closer—and she kissed him back.

And here it was again.

Magic.

She'd fallen for this man hard, and she remembered why. No. She didn't have to remember. It was imprinted on her brain, on her body.

Heat. Aching need. Pure animal magnetism.

The crazy conversation of the last few minutes faded—everything faded, there was only this man and his mouth on hers and his body close to her. His taste, his feel, his masculine scent.

She'd remembered this man during the nightmare of the past few months and she'd thought her memories must be imagination born of illness and of loneliness.

But this was real. This was Alex.

Her Prince. Her man.

She felt her lips open and taste as she'd tasted him before. She was kissing him as fiercely as he was kissing her—and maybe consciousness didn't come into a decision like this.

Maybe it just had to happen.

She let herself sink into the kiss. For this one sweet moment she allowed herself the luxury of believing this passion meant something to him. Her fingers twined through his hair and she tugged him closer. Closer.

For just this minute she could savour him, taste him, hold him. Pretend he was really her man, he was her future and everything would fall into place. She'd have a happy ever after.

Maybe ever-after didn't cut it, she thought numbly. Now was the important thing. Now. Here. Alex.

He made her feel so sexy he took her breath away. Desire started deep within, and built.

She wanted him so much.

Her body was on fire, burning with a heat she'd felt once before with Alex, but never before and never since. She was aching for him, hot for him, moist for him, right here, right now, fully clothed, with the only contact being his mouth on hers.

She was helpless in the face of her body's response. She felt herself shift, move closer, so close she was aching to be a part of him.

He could take her here, right now, she thought wildly, regardless of no protection, of no hope for a future, of nothing but burning want. She'd been ill for so long…hopeless for so long…but, within her now, life was surfacing. *She* was surfacing in her response to this man. A primeval need…

Alex.

His body was magnificent. Unimaginably erotic. He was holding her hard against him. His hands were strong and warm, curving into the small of her back, pressing her breasts against his chest, crushing her to him as if he wanted her as much as she wanted him…

If she could just get nearer…

She was out of control and she didn't care.

She let herself go…

But things had changed since the last time she'd let herself love this man. She had a son. And in the end it was Michales who broke the kiss.

The baby was sitting at their feet, gazing up at the adults above him in some indignation. Michales was unaccustomed to being ignored. He needed a feed. He needed attention.

So he did what any self-respecting baby would do in the circumstances. He opened his mouth and he howled.

Michales.

Her baby.

Reality slammed home. She pulled away from Alex as if he were burning her. Which pretty much explained how she was feeling.

She lifted Michales, she hugged him against her and she held him tight, as if he were a shield.

She'd been out of control. Again. After all she'd been through. After all her vows. This man just had to touch her and here she was, tumbling into trust again.

Trust meant heartache. Trust meant betrayal and grief.

Do not trust this man.

This had to stop—now.

Had he messed it up entirely?

He'd come here with a business proposition. He'd never imagined he could seduce her into doing what he wanted.

Was that what she was thinking?

Who knew what she was thinking? She looked dazed.

He felt dazed.

He had to get this back on an impersonal footing.

'That's just what we don't want,' he managed.

'Sorry?'

'That wasn't meant to happen. We need to keep this impersonal or we'll mess this up entirely.'

'Right,' she said, as if she didn't understand a word he'd said. Which was exactly how he felt.

'I'll come again tomorrow,' he said, struggling to sound brisk and businesslike. 'Meanwhile, will you do some research? Discover what I've said is true?'

Her face had become…blank? It was as if she'd

just terrified herself and was struggling back from the abyss. Struggling to hold on to what she knew.

'I don't know why I did that,' she whispered. 'It was crazy. I didn't mean it. I don't want it. I don't want you to touch me.'

She was lying. They both knew it. But there was fear behind her words. He didn't understand it.

She'd come to him last time with joy. Had being pregnant changed something so fundamental that she was afraid of his effect on her?

'I want my freedom,' she said, a flat statement, unequivocal.

What sort of a need was that?

But freedom was the one thing he was more than prepared to give. After all, wasn't that what he wanted himself?

'You can have it,' he said. 'But marry me first.'

'I can't.'

'I believe you can. For Michales's sake.'

'You…don't want Michales for him. You just want him for your island.'

He hesitated, letting himself look at the little boy who gazed placidly back at him. These were his own eyes?

You just want him for your island.

This was way too complicated.

'It's a business decision,' he said flatly, trying

to move on. 'Look, that kiss was an aberration. It has to be. If we let sentiment get in the way it'll never work. I don't want to pressure you but I must. It's not our lives, Lily. It's the fate of an entire country, possible three.'

'Right.'

'It is,' he said. 'Will you think about it?'

'Yes. Just go away.'

Just like that. He had her agreement.

There was nothing else to stay for. Was there?

'If I agree…' she whispered. 'If I was stupid enough to say yes… Could we still be independent? I do not want to fall for you again.'

'Did you fall…?'

'Shut up,' she snapped. 'Fall? Of course I fell. I was an idiot over you. I turned my life into a mess, all because I acted like a lovesick teenager. You kiss me and I turn into that stupid teenager again. If what you say is true…if there really is this huge moral need for me to marry—then we do it as a business deal. Nothing more. I'm not letting you touch me again.'

'I'd rather not…'

'Touch me? Then don't.'

'Lily…'

'Enough,' she snapped. 'I'll think about it. I'll do the homework. And then, if I must, I'll outline conditions. But kissing doesn't come into it.'

'That's a shame,' he said and tried a smile but she glowered.

'Don't you turn that charm on me. I know it. I let you kiss me once to see if what I was afraid of was true, and it is. Now I know where I stand, that's the end of it. If we have to get married then we do exactly what the law requires and nothing more. If I have to do anything that even remotely resembles conjugal rights…'

'Conjugal…' he said cautiously and ventured a smile.

She didn't smile back. 'Enough,' she said. 'Get out. Conjugal or no conjugal, and don't you push me, Alexandros Mykonis—you know exactly what conjugal means.'

'Right.'

She was glowering at him. She'd promised to think about it. There was nothing to be gained by staying.

He'd got what he wanted.

Hadn't he?

She heard his steps fade to nothing. She closed the door and leaned on it, and her whole body shook.

Marriage. Alex.

No and no and no.

Marriage to almost any other man wouldn't be as bad. Because marriage to Alex…it'd be surrender.

He'd kissed her and she'd surrendered, just as she'd surrendered a year ago. Had she learned nothing?

Alex.

She'd have to do the research.

If she was Mia she'd just walk away.

'I want to be Mia,' she whispered, but she knew it wasn't true.

She wanted…she wanted…

Life.

Her body wanted Alex.

She crossed to the window and looked out. He hadn't gone far. He was just below her window, talking to Spiros.

Was he making her boss this crazy proposition already? To relocate Spiros's boatyard to Sappheiros?

Spiros would love it. He and Eleni had come to this country because Spiros dreamed of making his living building the boats he loved, but if he thought he could do it on Sappheiros he'd be there in a minute.

It could happen—if she said yes.

If she promised to marry Alex.

She wanted to lean out of the window, yell at them that this was some crazy proposition by a madman. It was emotional blackmail. She had the right to walk away.

When had she ever had a choice?

She sank onto the floor with Michales and hugged her knees. She felt very tired, alone and afraid.

Alex had kissed her.

And that was what she was most afraid of. He exposed her for what she was. Vulnerable and wanting.

'Love's crazy,' she said. Then, as Michales looked seriously at her, she tugged him onto her knees. 'It only causes trouble. It caused…you.'

Her son would be heir to the throne of Sappheiros. He'd be the legitimate heir, following in his father's footsteps.

It was unbelievable. It was…terrifying.

She rose again and went back to the window. Alex was still there. Spiros was smiling—more than smiling. He was looking incredulous. He was glancing up at her window and she drew back into the shadows.

This was worse than blackmail. He'd placed the islanders' fate in her hands. He'd placed Spiros's fate in her hands.

What if it was a lie? In this day and age, for a marriage of convenience to be the only path to prevent disaster… It was inconceivable.

But she'd promised to do the research, and if it was true…

This was like jumping off a cliff and not knowing what was below. Only knowing that, whatever was at the end, by the time she landed she'd be going so fast the force could kill her.

CHAPTER SIX

Sappheiros Times headlines

14th August:

'Royal Scandal—Secret Baby'
'Queen Uses Sister's Baby to Keep Throne'

16th August:

'After the Lies, Prince Regent Is Ruling Crown Prince'

21st August:

'Islands Revert to Ancient Lineage'
'Three Principalities From One Kingdom: Islanders' Joy'

23rd August:

'DNA Proves Baby Still Heir! Alexandros Confesses Affair'

'Prince to Wed Queen's Sister'
'Prince Declares Lily a Worthy Princess'
'Wedding By End of Month'

Two weeks. It was only two weeks since she'd been hit with this crazy proposition and it had moved from crazy to terrifying. She was standing at the entrance to the cathedral, ready to be a bride.

Was she out of her mind?

Maybe she was, but she'd done the research. Everything she'd read confirmed and reconfirmed what Alex had told her. Giorgos and his forebears had brought the Diamond Isles to ruin. The only way they could be saved was for them to revert to their original states; for their original ruling families to take their care into their hands. But there was such distrust…

She'd looked at it from every conceivable angle and there was no escape. From the moment she'd seen Spiros's face, full of incredulous hope, she'd known what she had to do.

Alex had come back the next day and she had her answer ready.

'Yes,' she'd told him. 'For a year. No more. And you touch me and the deal is off. It's a marriage in name only. Is that clear?'

'It's what I want,' he'd told her. Then, watching

her, clearly unable to figure out her response, he'd added, 'It's a marriage, Lily. It's not the gallows you're walking into.'

'It's a trap,' she'd said. 'I'm doing it but I don't have to like it.'

'It's not a trap of my setting and I don't like it either,' he'd said.

And then he'd left. There was financial chaos in Sappheiros, he'd told her, and he had to sort it out. But the wedding was to take place by the end of the month.

And then the roller coaster began. Or the avalanche. Or whatever it was, but it made her so giddy she thought surely she must still be drifting in and out of the same nightmare world she'd been in before.

Arrangements, arrangements, arrangements. Curt, formal telephone calls with Alex, interspersed by longer calls from officialdom, arranging everything from her bridal gown to a white teething ring for Michales so he could chew his gummy way through the ceremony and still look…bridal?

Yes, the thing was ridiculous, and finally she decided okay, if it was ridiculous she'd simply treat it as a joke gone wrong. She'd close her eyes and get it over with.

And here she was. Her wedding day.

She was about to enter the cathedral where Alexandros had taken his vows two months before. The last time she'd entered this cathedral, she'd slipped in at the rear, wanting to remain anonymous.

Now… Every man and woman was on their feet, waiting for her entrance, and Alex was standing at the altar. The Archbishop was in front and central. Waiting for her.

She was ready to walk down the aisle. Alone.

'Have Spiros give you away,' Alex had told her. 'You can't do this by yourself. Stefanos and Nikos will attend me. You need bridesmaids. At least have Spiros.'

'I need no one,' she'd said. 'I don't see why we can't do this in a government office.'

'It needs to be done with all the pomp and splendour we can muster,' he'd told her. 'The islanders need reassurance that this is real—no one should disbelieve that you're my wife.'

'I'm not your wife.'

'You are,' he'd said gravely. 'You've agreed.'

'Until you have the island stable. No more.'

'Then for the time we have I'll do you honour.' In a different tone this might have been a lovely thing to say but it was said in the tone of a man who knew where his duty lay. 'As the country will do you honour and as you'll do yourself honour.

It's meant as a reassurance to the country that we can move forward. There'll be nothing secret or covert about it. You'll wear full royal regalia, as will I.'

This final decree had left her almost speechless. 'A real royal wedding?' She hadn't attended Mia's wedding—they'd been so distant by then that Mia would never have thought of inviting her—but she'd seen the media coverage and the thought of doing the same left her cold. 'You're telling me what I should wear?'

'My people tell me there's no time to make you a completely new gown but if you'll agree… The royal wedding gowns have been amazing over the centuries, and they've been carefully stored and kept, every one. If we can get you here a few days before the wedding, we can get one altered. You could even wear Mia's.'

And then he'd listened to the silence and conceded, 'Okay, maybe not Mia's. But there will be one that fits you. There's no time to make you one as splendid, and this has to be done right.'

Fine. She was past arguing.

She could do it.

She'd flown here four days ago. The royal assembly line had swung into place the minute she'd arrived. She'd been shown to her own apartment within the palace—an apartment she assumed would be hers for the duration of her marriage. It was opulent to the point of crazy. They'd suggested Michales use the royal nursery and she'd knocked that on the head. There was a cot in the corner of her apartment now; as long as she had Michales she could live anywhere.

So she'd done what was expected, whatever she was told. She'd hardly seen Alexandros and then only when he'd been surrounded by palace officials, lawyers, advisors.

She'd been given her own lawyers. That had surprised her. In all the chaos she'd been given this one sliver of control. The lawyers had been engaged in her name, and they'd been competent and thorough in drawing up a pre-nuptial agreement for her protection. She had no doubt that at the end of her marriage she could walk away— with Michales and with an allowance that made her head swim.

She'd put up a feeble protest about the money but her lawyers had simply ignored it.

'This pre-nuptial agreement may well become public and the Prince must be seen as doing the right thing by you and his son,' she'd been told, and once again she'd subsided.

As she'd subsided in everything. At least Michales would always be well provided for.

But now… The organ blared into its triumphant

wedding march. Reality was suddenly right here. She'd been pushed off the end of the royal conveyor belt and here she was, about to be married.

She wasn't…her. She was inside some creature wearing full bridal gear, extravagant to the point of ridiculous, inside a cathedral, about to be married.

It wasn't Lily who was doing this. It was someone else. Lily was trapped inside.

The doors swung open. At the end of the aisle… Alex.

For two weeks she'd blocked him almost completely from her mind. She was about to be married but this wasn't about Alex. It wasn't about either of them.

Maybe her decision to walk down the aisle on her own had been a mistake. She wouldn't mind Spiros's arm to lean on right now. She wouldn't mind anything to lean on.

She needed to start walking.

Alex was waiting.

No. She told herself that sharply. It wasn't Alex. Just as she was trapped inside someone else, the man at the end of the aisle was a stranger, some prince in his regimentals, waiting to marry a woman in a gown of shimmering beaded lace, with a glorious train trailing twenty feet behind her, with a three-tiered veil attached with a tiara, which had come straight from the royal vaults, the dresser had breathed. Worth a king's ransom.

Her legs felt frozen.

Do this and get it over with, she told herself.

Everyone was looking at her. Everyone was waiting.

Deep breath. Do this and get on with your life.

She looked along the aisle and Alex was smiling at her.

Her prince.

No. If she thought *Prince* her feet wouldn't move.

She had to get a grip on what was reality and what wasn't. This was Alex smiling at her. The father of her child.

This wedding was a fantasy, but the fantasy had a name.

Alex.

She stepped forward and she looked directly at her waiting bridegroom. She forced herself to smile back.

She could do this.

She could be married to Alex.

He'd suggested she have Spiros give her away. But…

'No,' she'd told him. 'Eleni's taking care of Michales during the ceremony. That's all I'll ask of them. If I ever get married for real I want Spiros to give me away then. But not now. Not for a marriage of convenience.'

So she was alone. He hadn't realised quite how alone until he saw the cathedral doors swing open. She was standing quite still, quite calm. She looked as determined on this course as she'd been from the moment she'd agreed to his proposal.

'You know, this could work,' Nikos said from beside him.

Alex was watching Lily walk steadily towards him, regal and lovely, her head held high, the magnificent gown making her look almost ethereal. He was forcing himself to smile at her as the congregation were clearly expecting him to do—but something inside him was twisting. Hurting.

'Why the hell wouldn't it work?' he growled.

'The islanders hated the idea of another Mia,' Nikos whispered. 'But you just need to look at Lily to see she's not like her sister. Mia had twelve bridesmaids. Mia had so much bling you couldn't see her for glitter. Lily's different. Simple and lovely.'

Simple and lovely… They weren't words Alex would have thought appropriate for a royal bride.

But they were right.

Lily was not doing this for money. His cheque remained in its pieces—or maybe it had been burned long since—and it had never been replaced. She'd even tried to refuse the allowance his lawyers had written into the pre-nuptial contracts should they ever divorce. 'You can pay for Michales's upbringing and nothing else,' she'd said.

This wedding…this marriage…it seemed she was doing this for Sappheiros. She wanted nothing from it.

He didn't believe it yet. He couldn't. The anger and disbelief he'd held ever since he'd learned of Michales's true parentage still simmered.

Do this and get it over with.

She'd almost reached him. He smiled and she smiled back, but he knew her smile was as forced as his.

This wasn't the smile he knew from a year ago. This wasn't the Lily he'd made love to. This was a stranger, a woman coerced.

He had an almost irresistible impulse to take her hand and walk out, right there and then. Before this mock marriage could take place. Not because he didn't want it. But because…it felt intrinsically wrong.

She'd agreed to this marriage for all the wrong reasons.

He took her hand and it was icy. Unresponsive.

She looked trapped.

She'd trapped herself by bearing his child, he thought grimly. By agreeing to Mia and Giorgos's great lie.

Forget it, he told himself harshly. Forget the lie. Concentrate on now. Concentrate on the need to be married.

So be it.

Her smile had faded as she'd realised he'd only been smiling for the sake of their audience. He watched a fleeting shadow of something... hurt?...pass over her face.

Why should she be hurt?

This was a formal ceremony and they had to get on.

'Why not ask Father Antonio to marry you?' Nikos had asked, and he hadn't answered. But he knew the answer.

When—if!—he married for real he'd be married by Father Antonio.

This was a royal marriage of convenience. Nothing more.

Lily's hand stayed in his. They faced the Archbishop together.

'We are gathered together to join this man and this woman...'

The formal reception was attended by every person of significance from the Diamond Isles and beyond. In the vast marquee erected in the palace grounds, on the headland overlooking Sappheiros Bay, there were speeches, speeches and more speeches.

This wasn't the simple celebration of a wedding. This was the celebration of three nations finding independence and hope. The islanders' joy had little to do with Lily and Alex.

Lily may have provided this outcome but the consensus among the crowd, the media and by the islanders in general, was that she'd done very well for herself. Where was the need for sympathy?

Or even...civility?

As the day wore on Alex was congratulated by islander after islander, but the eyes that watched his bride were guarded.

She was Mia's sister, and Mia was hated. Like Mia, Lily was suspected as being a woman who'd conned her way into being a part of the royal dynasty.

Alex could do little to protect her. The slurs weren't overt. They were subtle looks, subtle congratulations with the islanders looking only at him, refusing to meet Lily's gaze as hands were shaken.

But, he had to admit, despite the slurs, despite the guarded looks, she was behaving...beautifully. She was a lovely bride—serene and almost breathtakingly lovely. But she was so quiet. He'd pulled her veil back from her face for the obligatory kiss-the-bride, but she hadn't responded as he'd done so and he had the feeling that her veil was down again, metaphorically if not literally.

She hardly spoke through the formal luncheon and the formal reception. She responded civilly to those who spoke to her but her responses were muted.

He'd catch her glance straying over and over to Eleni, who was holding Michales.

She wanted her baby back and her look said she wanted more. She wanted her life back?

The civilities had to be borne—he could no sooner escape than she could. But as the afternoon stretched towards evening he decided *enough*. A band had started playing and a dance floor was laid across the lawns. The festivities would continue into the small hours. But…

'You want to escape?' he asked and saw a flare of hope, unable to be disguised.

'Can we?'

'This party will go on without us. I have a place on the other side of the island.' He'd thought of this yesterday when Nikos had asked about honeymoon plans. They had to be seen as doing something—but this was no time to be away from the island.

He hadn't wanted to take Lily to his own home but unless they stayed in the palace here there was little choice. And the thought of staying in the palace—obligatory appearance on the balcony—prince kisses bride—left him cold.

'A place?' she asked.

'A house. We can be private there.'

'What, for a honeymoon?' It was said wryly. She'd schooled herself to do this, he thought. Maybe if he insisted on his conjugal rights she'd submit as well. To outward appearance she looked beautiful and serene and untroubled. Maybe even submissive?

Maybe submissive was the wrong word. It was definitely the wrong word if this was the Lily he'd met little more than a year ago.

But how well did he know her? Not well, but enough to guess that behind the serenity was quiet desperation.

'We're expected to go away for a bit. I can't go far, but I have a house on the north end of the island.'

'So…you and me and how many servants?'

'Just you and me.' Then, as he saw another fear flare, 'And Michales,' he added swiftly.

Her relief was immediate and obvious. 'I can take him?'

'Of course.'

She closed her eyes and he thought she was trying desperately to disguise what she was thinking. How fearfully out of control she felt?

It didn't make sense. Was she afraid of him? Afraid of the royalty bit? Surely not. She *was* Mia's sister.

'We can go now?' she asked.

'Yes.'

'Then what are we waiting for?'

CHAPTER SEVEN

THEY were to depart in a bridal coach. A gold-painted barouche with the Sappheiros coat of arms emblazoned on the panels, with white leather upholstery and white satin cushions—something straight out of *Cinderella*.

It took only this, Lily thought in disbelief. Alex handed her up into the coach. Attendants arranged her skirts and her train, tucking her in with care.

Alex climbed up and sat beside her.

Eleni handed up Michales.

This had been a crazy day. She was about as far from her comfort zone as she'd ever want to be. But this…this was just plain fantasy. This was every girl's dream—being whisked off in a golden coach with Prince Charming.

In the fairy tales she'd read, babies weren't included. But Michales definitely was.

So… Her Prince Charming was sitting beside her. He looked absurdly handsome—regal and tasselled and armed with sword and all the things a Prince Of The Blood should be.

She probably even looked like a princess, she conceded. All white satin and lace and exquisite beading—and there were diamonds in her tiara, for heaven's sake.

There were four white horses in their traces, heads held high, shiny, sleek, gold harnesses, bits and assorted leather stuff. They had gold and white attachments and white-feathered head-dresses—did horses wear headdresses? These ones did, she decided. They looked fabulous.

Even the coachman looked amazing. His uniform was almost as ornate as Alex's—only he was wearing a top hat.

There were sixteen more horsemen, eight in front and eight behind. Horseguards?

Was one of them carrying a diaper bag? She daren't ask. She hoped someone had thought of it, but the royal princess standing up and asking for diapers…maybe not.

The desire to giggle grew even stronger.

Michales jiggled on her knee. She hugged him. He crowed with delight and squirmed and tried to reach her tiara.

It was too much. She burst out laughing and Alex stared at her as if she'd entirely lost it.

'What the…?'

'Cinderella and Prince Charming—and Baby,' she told him, and grinned and lifted the unprotesting Michales across to his father's knee. 'Here. You hold him. He's not very good with travelling.'

'What do you mean?'

'I suspect you might find out for yourself,' she said and chuckled again at the expression on his face. Then, as it seemed to be expected of her— she'd seen the odd royal wedding on the telly—she turned and smiled broadly at the crowd. She waved!

If he could be a prince, she could be a princess.

'I might find out what for myself?' he said cautiously.

'You'll know it when it happens,' she said sagely. 'Aren't you supposed to be waving?'

'I appear to be needing to hang on.'

'That's all right,' she said magnanimously. 'You hold on and I'll wave for the two of us.'

This was dumb but she couldn't stop grinning. She was so far out of her comfort zone that she ought to be a quivering wreck. But she'd just got through a royal wedding and she hadn't fallen over once. As far as she knew, she hadn't said anything stupid.

She was married.

This was no real marriage, she told herself. She

surely intended staying…well, not married in the true sense of the word. But she was married and she wasn't afraid of Alex. She didn't trust him, but then maybe she didn't have to trust. This was a business arrangement. If she could just keep her cool, keep her independence, maybe she could even enjoy this—just a bit.

Maybe that was hysteria speaking.

Just wave to the crowds, pin your smile in place and try not to think of the man sitting beside you with your baby on his lap, she told herself.

Her baby's father.

Her…husband.

This was crazy. He didn't belong here.

Hell, he had to do this. The islanders needed him to be Crown Prince but every nerve in his body was screaming at him to get out of here, get back to Manhattan, go into his office, slam the door on the outside world and design a garden or six.

For the last ten years garden design had been his life. As a child, his only friends had been the palace servants. An old gardener had taken him under his wing, and the palace garden had become an enormous pleasure.

When his mother had been permitted to return to the island they'd designed a garden, and the two years they had together had seen it become a wondrous living thing.

Then, when he'd joined the army to finally get away from his uncle, to achieve financial independence, he'd kept on designing. He'd sent in an entry to an international competition.

That entry had changed his life.

This wasn't his life, he told himself savagely. It was the last lingering trace of Giorgos's reign. Lily was sister to the last Queen. This woman sitting beside him, waving to the crowd, her smile wide and genuine, was a fairy tale princess. Like Mia, she was playing a part. In time she could move on.

Whereas he…he was stuck with reality.

In the shape of his son?

It wasn't just that, though the sensation of a small robust person sitting on his knee was certainly unnerving. It was the whole set-up.

As an idealistic youngster he'd dreamed of ruling this country, of being able to do what he had to do to make the island prosper. He'd dreamed of being given the authority to do it.

He'd never dreamed of this. He was in a fairy tale coach with a fairy tale wife and a tiny son.

She was looking as if she enjoyed it.

Maybe she was better at pretending than he was.

This was so…fake. The only problem was, though, that when he woke in the morning it would be worse. There were so many problems. He'd take a couple of days out of the frame here to get this marriage thing settled and over, but he had to get back. Two or three days' honeymoon…

It wasn't really a honeymoon.

Lily was waving at the crowd as if she meant it. She was enjoying herself?

Maybe he could use this to his advantage, he thought suddenly. If she was to be accepted by the islanders…she could stay here and play princess. He could still make the important decisions but it might give him time to escape to his other life. The garden designs he loved.

It was worth a thought. Lily as a figurehead.

Maybe…maybe…

Maybe this was too soon to tell. There was no way he was going to trust her.

She was doing okay now. Better than he was.

She was better at pretending. Better at…deceiving?

He looked out over the crowd of onlookers. There were those in the crowd who wished him ill. There were those who wanted this fledgling principality to fail so they could gather the remains.

He had to do this. He had no choice.

His bride was by his side and she was waving. It seemed he was part of a royal family, even if that family was as fractured as his family always had been.

He waved.

'My smile hurts,' Lily whispered.

'My face aches,' he confessed.

'Really?' She swivelled to stare. 'But you're used to this.'

'I'm a landscape architect. Not a prince.' He shook his head. 'No. This is what I wanted. It just feels too ridiculous for words.'

'Just smile and wave,' she said wisely. 'It doesn't matter if no one's at home.'

'If no one's at home…'

'Anyone can be royal. Plan your gardens in your head while you wave.' She waved a bit more and smiled a bit more. 'Look at me. I'm getting good at it.'

'So you…'

'I'm planning boats.'

They'd swung out of the palace grounds now. People were coming out of their houses to see them go past.

They had eight outriders behind and eight in front.

Lily waved to an elderly couple standing in their garden. The old man didn't wave back but

the old woman almost did. She lifted her hand—
and then thought better of it.

'They still think I'm like Mia,' Lily said, sto-
ically waving. 'Just lucky I'm not taking this
personally.'

'Yeah,' he said. He waved and the old man and
woman immediately waved back.

'You must have sex appeal,' Lily said sagely.
'Or something.'

'They know me.'

'They're never going to know me,' Lily said
and it sounded as if the idea was comforting.

He should be reassured by that. But there was
a stab of jealousy. And something more…

The only places Lily had seen on Sappheiros had
been the royal palace and the chapel-cum-cathe-
dral in its grounds. They'd been enough to take
her breath away—all spires and turrets and
opulence in a fairy tale setting, the sapphire coast-
line backed by mountains. The palace and cathedral were way over-the-top for a small country,
she'd thought, but still, royal was royal, and she'd
assumed the whole of the Diamond Isles must be
in favour of a bit of pomp and splendour.

Now she wasn't so sure. The coastal road was
lined with houses that looked shabby, some
almost derelict. From what she'd learned over the

last two weeks, the people had been taxed to the hilt to pay for the kings' follies.

Now Alex told her he was taking her to his private house. He'd been raised as nephew to the King. For much of his life he'd been first in line to the throne, so she assumed his home would be opulent as well.

Their retinue slowed as they came to a curve in a road that had been getting rougher the further they'd travelled from the city. At one time it must have been paved, but the bitumen was cracked now and giving way. The coastal road—a magnificent route set halfway up the cliffs and overlooking the sea—swept around a headland and on, but the coach slowed by a sign that said—discreetly—'Hideaway'.

The coach stopped, as did the outriders.

Alex stepped down onto the track and held out a hand to help her down.

'Um…where are we?' She gazed around her with surprise. They were in the middle of nowhere. A beautiful nowhere but nowhere nevertheless.

'We need to walk,' he said.

'Walk.'

'It's a rhododendron drive. It's too low for the horses to go underneath.'

'These guys can't take off their fancy

headgear?' She gazed round at the impassive horsemen. The horses were standing motionless. There was not a blink from man or horse.

'From this gate we're not royal,' he said, so softly only she could hear. 'This road has been deliberately left so the royal vehicles can't get through.'

'Right.' But it wasn't right. She didn't understand. This was where the fairy tale stopped?

They needed to walk? Fine if you were wearing glossy black boots and a sword to slash the undergrowth. She had four-inch heels and a twenty-foot train.

But she was almost past worrying. Hysteria was carrying her along nicely—as well as her innate sense of the ridiculous.

'Okay then,' she said, and she thought she even sounded hysterical. 'We walk. Did you bring scroggin?'

'Scroggin?' he said blankly.

'Food for serious hikers. You can't go more than twenty miles without it.'

He grinned. 'What about three hundred yards? Or I could bring the Jeep down to fetch you. Sorry about this, but this place is private. We don't want horseguards on our honeymoon.'

'No,' she said cautiously.

Honeymoon.

Right.

Alex had obviously been planning this. Yeah, she could see that about him. A planner.

It made her nervous. Or more nervous. How nervous could she get?

Concentrate on practicalities, she told herself. Here she was, in full bridal attire, stuck in the middle of nowhere.

With a baby. Once again the issue of a diaper bag raised its head.

'There is the small matter of our baggage,' she said cautiously. 'Much as I love being a bride, this look could get a bit over-the-top at breakfast. And you get to look after Michales if there are no clean diapers.'

'Our luggage was brought here earlier.'

She gulped. And nodded. 'Of course it was. So we were always coming here?'

'Did you want to stay in the palace?'

'It all depends,' she said and picked up her skirts. 'On what I find at the end of this rhododendron drive. Thanks, guys,' she said to their escort and waved but they didn't respond by one fraction of a lift of an eyebrow.

She wasn't much good at this princess business.

Just lucky it was temporary.

She looked sideways at her temporary husband.

'Okay,' she said. 'If you didn't bring the scroggin, then we'd better move fast.' She faced up the track and took a deep breath and started walking. She was aware that Alex watched her for a minute without moving. Why? Surely the sight of a bride trudging into a gloom of rhododendrons must be commonplace!

But finally he followed, carrying her son.

She turned and looked—and then looked away again fast. The sight of Alex with Michales had the power to make her feel…hungry?

Hungry for what? She wasn't sure.

'You're good,' he said as he caught up with her. They were out of sight—and out of earshot of their outriders now.

'At hiking? I'd like to see you hike in heels this high.'

'I couldn't,' he admitted. 'But that's not what I was saying. You were great today.'

'I did what I had to do,' she said, stalking on as purposefully as four-inch heels allowed. 'The islanders don't like me, but that's okay. I won't be staying here long enough for it to matter.'

'A year,' he said.

'That's what the deal is.'

'Unless we want more.'

She stopped. Uh-oh. There were things to clear up here before they went an inch further.

'Alex, let's get this straight,' she said, making her voice firm. Or as firm as it was possible to get when her breathing wouldn't work properly. 'There are two things I want in life and only two.'

'And they would be?'

You, she thought, but there was no way she was telling Alex that. She was afraid of even admitting it to herself.

'My son and my boats,' she managed. 'I might be able to squash a marriage of convenience in at the edges but that's all. If anything—*anything*—gets in the way of my two priorities then I'm out of here.'

'You don't want to be a fairy tale princess?'

'That's Mia's department. I'm just me.'

'It's possible to compromise,' he said softly. 'That's why I brought you here.'

'To teach me to compromise. No deal. I told you...'

'Your baby and your boats. Yes, you did. I get that loud and clear. But there's also the fact that we have a country to govern.'

'You, kiddo,' she snapped.

'I need your help.'

'For what? I've done the fairy tale bit. This train is so heavy...'

'I need you to help me create stability,' he said. He took her train from her grasp so he was holding her son and the sheer weight of her gown. He met her look so steadily that she thought for a blind, dumb moment that he was sex on legs and she was married to him for real. She fought a fast internal fight and managed a sensible reply.

'How can I do that when the islanders hate me?'

'They don't hate you. They don't know you.'

'Which is fine.'

'Which would have been fine if I hadn't seduced you...'

She gasped. 'What the...?' Whoa. Where was he going with this?

There was no way she was continuing this hike into nowhere if he stayed believing that. 'If I remember rightly, it was me who seduced you,' she snapped. 'Did I not?'

He looked a bit...stunned. 'I can't remember,' he admitted.

'You said that before. Any minute now you'll tell me you were drunk.'

'I wasn't drunk. I remember every part of that last night.'

'Me, too,' she said. 'It was a truly excellent night. But it wasn't me playing the pathetic part of Sleeping Beauty, leaving the action solely to my prince. I'm your equal in every way and I have rights. We made love once and we were stupid.

We were both stupid. So get over it.' She grabbed her train, turned and walked on a few steps, then swore, removed her shoes and picked up the pace.

He let her go. She was holding her own train again. She looked…free, he thought and was hit by a stab of pure, unadulterated jealousy. And more…

His bride, running under the dark canopy, looking nothing at all like Mia, nothing at all like any woman he'd ever met.

She was still wearing her veil and her head-piece. She was still a bride. If he wasn't holding Michales…

She emerged from the tunnel of rhododendrons, angry and confused.

She saw Alex's house and she forgot angry and confused. She forgot everything.

It was as if a wand had been waved, transforming the world from a dark, threatening place into sheer fantasy. Not fantasy as in the over-the-top royal palace. Fantasy as in sheer delight.

The house had been built into the cliffs. It was a whitewashed villa, built on three levels, with winding steps joining each level. There were rocky ledges between each level, with bench seats and tables so someone could conceivably carry a drink down towards the beach and pause at each bend, to sit and admire the view.

There were flowers everywhere, spilling from every crevice, so the rock face was bursting with colour. Bougainvillea—crimson, pinks and deep, deep burgundy. There were daisies, growing as if birds had dropped their seeds and they'd simply grown where they'd been dropped. A great twisted vine of wisteria seemed to hold the place together, its gnarled, knotted wood adorned with vast sprays of soft, glorious blues.

The house looked deceptively simple, built of stone, weathered to beauty, appearing to be almost part of the cliffs. Tiny balconies protruded from each window, joining the intricate flow of steps down to the beach.

And, below the house, the sea—sapphire, translucent, magic. A tiny cove. A wooden dinghy hauled up on the sand.

There were even a couple of dolphins in the bay.

Lily stopped and stared. It was all she could do not to cry out in delight.

'The dolphins…'

'I pay 'em to do that,' Alex said, coming up behind her. He smiled. 'Welcome home.'

'I… It's not my home,' she whispered, awed.

'You've married me. I guess in a sense it is your home.'

'Does the pre-nup say I get half?' she said

before she could stop herself, and kept right on gazing, eager to convince herself that this was real, that this wasn't some *Cinderella* fairy tale. There was no midnight looming here, for fantasy to return this place to mice and pumpkins.

Or maybe there was but she couldn't think of that right now. This place was seductive in its loveliness.

She could play with Michales on this beach. Maybe she could stay here for the year of their marriage. There'd be no need to juggle work and baby care. The terror in her head was gone.

Here she could be free.

Her eyes filled with tears. She brushed them away fiercely, angrily, but still they came.

Alex was beside her, calmly handing her a handkerchief.

She took it and blew her nose. Defiant.

'What's wrong?' he asked, but he was still smiling and she had to suspect he knew exactly what was wrong.

'This would have to be the most seductive setting in the known universe,' she whispered.

'You're the first woman I've ever brought here.'

She sniffed. She looked at him with suspicion over the top of his handkerchief. 'And that has to be the most seductive line,' she managed, trying to sound caustic—and failing.

'You don't trust me?'

'Would you trust you?' She waved his handkerchief at the scene in front of her. 'Would you trust yourself?'

'It's great, isn't it?'

'You built this garden?' She hesitated. 'Of course you built it. You're a landscape architect. I read about it. You've won prizes.'

'You build boats. I design gardens.'

'Here?'

'Not many,' he admitted. 'I mostly work out of Manhattan.'

That was confusing. 'Are you still working in Manhattan?'

'When I can. As often as I can get away from here.'

Whoa. Panic! 'You mean you're going back to Manhattan?'

'You don't want me here, do you?' He shrugged. 'I'd assumed you'd stay in the palace, play with Spiros and your boats and your son. I need to put some solid work into rebuilding this economy but if I can manage to get that sorted then I'm free to do what I want.'

Where was the problem with that? She stared down at the cove. Thinking. Or trying to think.

There were factors at play here she hadn't thought of. She felt as if she were floating in a bubble—she was precariously safe within, but any minute it could burst. What was outside? Who knew?

'Do you swim?' he asked.

'Of course.' In the midst of confusion, here was something solid.

'I feel a swim coming on,' he said, and why did she feel he was changing the subject? 'We have an hour or so before dusk. Can you bear to take off your wedding dress?'

'I can't wait to take off my wedding dress.' Then, dumbly, she felt herself blushing. 'I mean…'

'I know what you mean,' he told her. 'You'll have a separate apartment here, too.'

Great. It was great. Wasn't it?

'But Michales…' she managed.

'He's almost six months old. Shouldn't he be surfing by now?'

'How long can we stay here?' she asked, staring longingly down at the cove. The dolphins had been joined by friends. They were catching waves, surfing in amazing synchronisation, then performing sleek tumbling turns and gliding out to catch more.

It looked fantastic. How could she think of anything but the sight before her?

'You can stay for two weeks maybe,' he told her. 'I need to go earlier.'

Suddenly she didn't want to know. She didn't want to think past this moment.

'Then we're wasting time. Those dolphins are in my waves. Let's swim.'

CHAPTER EIGHT

HE NEEDED to swim. He needed to get rid of some pent-up energy.

He needed to clear his head.

Half an hour later they were all in the water. Lily was sitting in the shallows, letting Michales kick his delight as tiny waves broke over his toes. Leaving him free.

Which was what he wanted. Wasn't it?

Of course it was.

He was doing backstroke, back and forth across the cove so he could watch her as he swam. He needed to let her be. But he could watch her in the shallows, holding Michales, watching him splash, absorbed in her son.

He didn't have a handle on her. He'd met her once and been entranced. She'd said she'd seduced him, and to a certain extent it was true. Her laughter had seduced him, her loveliness, her vibrancy. Today, standing in the rhododendron drive in full bridal finery, discussing scroggin, he'd seen that part of her again. It was as if it had somehow resurfaced, despite herself.

Resurfaced… That was the problem. His gut was telling him this was the real Lily. Only she'd handed her baby—*his* baby—to her sister. She'd made one phone call to him and then abandoned the idea of telling him.

It didn't fit. The Lily he thought he knew would have appeared on his doorstep, angry as hell, tossing her pregnancy to him as she'd tossed the idea of seduction. It was something they'd shared. It was something they'd taken responsibility for together.

There were two Lilys. The Lily he knew—and either a conniving Lily or some other Lily. He couldn't cope with the idea of either.

Whichever was right, they had to achieve some way of facing the world together. But first…how were they going to get through these first few days?

By avoidance? They'd changed in their separate apartments, and they'd met on the steps coming down to the beach.

She was wearing a plain black bathing costume and another of her lovely scarves.

She'd made him feel…confused as hell.

Dammit, a woman was not going to mess with his head. He couldn't afford confusion. He had to put every bit of energy he possessed into getting this island back on its feet. He needed to get it back to where it just needed a figurehead.

Could Lily be part of that figurehead?

She'd reacted with fear.

He didn't understand what was going on. He didn't understand her.

He swam and swam.

This was the only way to go, he told himself. Get yourself so physically tired you can forget her.

Right.

This place was fabulous. She sat in the shallows with her baby son and the frisson of excitement she'd had when she'd first arrived resurfaced.

Freedom had many guises. Staying here, with Michales, could be a form of freedom. Only Alex's initial statement that this was her home had been quickly rescinded. Two weeks... Then the palace.

There were issues here she hadn't thought about. Alex's work, for one. If he thought she was staying in the palace while he swanned off back to Manhattan...

No deal.

He was swimming back and forth. Back and forth. It was as if he was driven.

He hated royalty. She'd figured that.

Did he plan one day to escape and leave Michales and her to represent royalty in their own rights? When the islanders hated her? Not likely.

But she couldn't trust him.

She closed her eyes. Michales was kicking his feet in delight, splashing them both. Suddenly she was hit by an almost overwhelming longing. For someone to trust.

Her father had been in his sixties when she was born. She'd been his carer. He'd depended on her but she'd always known that when her father looked at her, he only saw echoes of the young, fascinating wife who'd deserted him. He always saw pain. Her mother and Mia had abandoned her. Mia had betrayed her in the worst possible way.

You didn't do trust. Not ever.

But she gazed out at Alex and she couldn't stop the feeling of indescribable pain washing through. He was her husband but she was still alone.

Not alone. Michales depended on her.

She needed to be practical and firm—for Michales's sake.

She needed to remember who she was. A mother, yes. And a boat-builder.

Not a lover. Not a wife.

A boat-builder.

She turned deliberately from watching Alex and looked instead up the beach.

She'd been absorbed in the antics of her small son. But suddenly he saw her attention turn to the old dinghy high on the sand. She rose, cradled Michales against her and strolled up the beach to inspect the boat.

Michales waved his hands indignantly towards the sea, where the dolphins were still cavorting far out. Alex sensed her smile from this distance. She walked back to the shallows and started playing again.

She should have time to look at the boat if she wanted.

He didn't want to go near either of them. The same feeling he'd had in the coach came flooding back. Family, he reminded himself.

He did not do family.

Maybe he could go back to the castle. There was pressure mounting from all sides. If he went quietly back, maybe the press wouldn't discover he'd abandoned Lily here.

Maybe if he left she might feel safer, he thought. He could leave her here to have a holiday in the sun with her baby.

Meanwhile, he could get himself organised.

Get this damned island organised. Meet with Nikos and Stefanos and see what they could figure out.

Leave Lily?

Yeah, that felt good. Not.

They were his family.

He didn't do family.

Love meant grief and loss and heartache.

She wanted to look at the boat. Okay, he could take Michales for a bit. That small commitment wouldn't hurt.

He swam slowly in to shore, catching a wave for the last part, letting the surf sweep him on. He ended up right beside her. Too close.

She rose, stepping away from him, making space.

'Sorry.' He swiped the water from his eyes, kneeling in the shallows. 'I should have been taking turns with Michales.'

'It's your turn now,' she said and suddenly he had his arms full of baby. And, astonishingly, her voice had turned indignant. 'Did you know you have a treasure of a boat up there? She's a gorgeous old clinker-built dinghy, planked in King Billy Pine with Huon Pine and a Kauri transom. What the hell are you doing, letting her rot?'

'I... She's old,' he said, astounded by her sudden passion. 'My father brought her here before I was born. I took her out a couple of years ago and knocked a hole in her on the rocks.'

'So she's been sitting on the beach since then.' Indignant wasn't the half of it. She made it sound as if he'd murdered a puppy.

'She's got a hole in her.'

'You'd have a hole in you, too, if you'd hit a rock. That's a reason for abandoning her?' She was stalking up the beach towards the wreck, letting him follow if he wanted.

He followed, carrying Michales. She had a really cute butt.

Um…think of something else, he told himself. He'd put a hole in the boat. He was the bad guy?

Michales yelled. Lurched his small body back towards the water. Yelled some more.

'He wants more swimming,' Lily said without looking back.

He wants…

He definitely wanted. Michales's full focus was on the waves.

Alex's father had taught him to swim. It was the only memory he had of his father—blurred by time but with him still. He was floating in the water, his father's big hands under his tummy, coaxing him to push off, to see if he could float if his father's hands weren't there.

And when he had…his father whirling him

round and round, spinning with excitement, calling out to his mother, *'He's done it—our son can swim.'*

Now it was…his turn?

He walked slowly back into the water, to just beyond the breaking waves. He dipped his son into the sea. He held him under his tummy.

Michales was far too young to coax as his father had coaxed him. But Michales figured out the basics as if he'd been born to the waves.

Balanced on his father's hands, his legs and arms went like little windmills. He was a ball of splashing, chortling delight. He had no fear. He knew his father's hands would keep him safe.

His son.

Lily was up the beach, inspecting his old boat.

His wife.

The sensations were almost overwhelming.

But then his thoughts were interrupted. Out to sea, a boat rounded the headland. A cruiser. Thirty feet long or more. New.

There were a couple of men in the bow and they had binoculars in their hands. Or cameras.

Hell, he'd wanted privacy. He might have known reporters would try and get in here.

He lifted Michales into his arms. The little boy must have finally had enough. He snuggled into his father's bare chest—and here were more of those sensations he didn't know what to do with.

He strode up the beach to his wife. *His wife.*
She was still focused on the boat.

'Lily, let's go,' he said urgently.

'Why?'

'These people…' He motioned back towards
the cruiser and she glanced at it without interest.
'I suspect they're reporters.'

'So?' To his frustration, her attention was all on
the boat. She'd crouched down to look closer.
'She's looking great for two years stuck on the
beach. Look at the workmanship. All she needs
is a couple of new spars and calking. New expoxy
resin. I could make her fabulous.' The edge of one
side of the boat was half buried in the sand and
she started digging.

'Lily…'

'I want to see if this is intact. I bet it is. I'm
wondering if the sand's been covering her.
Sometimes boats buried in the sand can last for
half a century or so before they start rotting, especially if the sand stays dry.'

'I don't want these people to photograph you.'

'Why not?'

Good question, he thought. Because she
wasn't glamorous? Because she wasn't made-up
for the cameras?

She was wearing a cheap, ill-fitting bathing
costume and no make-up. Her short-cropped

curls clung wetly around her face, escaping from her wetly limp scarf. Did she care?

'Look at the rear thwart,' she said reverently. 'It's gorgeous. That's Huon pine. Tasmania's the only place it grows. It's a dream of mine, to build a boat all of Huon, only of course there's so little left. Those babies take centuries to grow. The Tasmanians flooded a valley last century and they're diving for the timber now. If I could get some…'

She was lost, he thought, fascinated. She had eyes only for the boat.

The cruiser had come into shallow waters. Two men jumped overboard.

With cameras.

They were photographing as they came, as if expecting any minute they'd be noticed and their quarry would run.

Lily wouldn't run, he thought. Not the first Lily he'd met. Not the passionate Lily. Not when she had her hands on a sick boat.

Real Huon pine. Her eyes were shining with missionary zeal.

'Lily…'

She didn't look up. He groaned inwardly but gave up. How could you protect someone from herself?

Did she want protecting?

His protectiveness was mixing with something else now. Pride?

The thought was novel but there it was. She knew the reporters were here, but she wasn't losing concentration. She'd finished digging out the side of the boat and was running her fingers gently round the timbers. Taking in every square inch of the ancient dinghy.

'Can I fix it for you?' she asked.

'It's a wreck.'

'It's not a wreck. Look at these timbers. They look almost as watertight as the day she was made. All she needs is lots of TLC.'

'TLC?'

'Tender loving care,' she said and ran her hands over the old timbers with such a look on her face that he felt…

Jealous?

Whoa, that was nuts.

He was holding Michales. Michales was gazing down at his mother as well.

'You've been usurped,' he told the baby ruefully. 'Your mother's fallen in love with a boat.' But then he figured maybe he'd better pay attention to the press. The two men were getting closer. Their trousers were wet from wading ashore. They were snapping for all they were worth, as if they thought they were about to be thrown off the beach.

He should have brought a couple of security

guys down here. Instinctively, he moved to put his body between Lily and the photographers but, apart from one uninterested glance, all Lily's focus was on the boat.

'Ma'am?' the younger man called and Lily tore her attention from the boat again.

'Lily,' she corrected him. 'I don't do ma'am.' She'd spoken in Greek, almost absently. Now she went back to inspecting the boat.

The photographers were taken aback. Whatever they'd expected of her, it wasn't this.

He'd allowed no press conferences before the wedding. There'd been such hostility towards her that he'd worried she'd get a really hard time—certainly be treated with contempt. Now he thought maybe a restricted conference might have been better—with pre-approved questions. As it was, these men knew nothing about her and they were able to ask anything.

The first question was harmless enough. 'You speak Greek?'

'Yes.'

'Queen Mia didn't.'

She sighed as if vaguely irritated but not much. 'Mia and I were raised by different parents. My father taught me Greek. My maternal relatives were Greek and they taught me boat-building. My boss is Greek and I like learning. Okay?'

'Are you really Mia's sister?'

She didn't answer straight away. Instead, she crawled around to the other side of the boat where the hole was a gaping mass of shattered timber. She touched the fragments of timber as a doctor might touch a fractured arm—with all the care in the world.

'Of course I am,' she said at last, without looking up.

'And the baby… He's really yours?'

'Michales really is mine,' she agreed. 'Prince Alexandros has proved it. Who wants to know?'

'Just about all the world.'

'So how did you feel when you discovered the Queen had stolen your baby?' one of the reporters asked and Alex stopped thinking about language. How could she answer this?

But she didn't even have to think about it. 'There's no need to be melodramatic.' She was using her hands to measure the width of the hole. 'Mia didn't steal him. I was ill and she cared for him.'

'And passed him off as her own.'

'I know nothing about that,' she said. 'Mia cared for my little boy, and when I was well enough I came here to fetch him. Alex supports me. So what else do you want to know?'

She'd said it as if what had happened was an

everyday occurrence. As if there was no contro-
versy at all.

'Prince Alex says he didn't know he was your
baby's father.' The younger man had lowered his
camera and was holding out a voice recorder. Alex
thought about objecting, but then thought *why*?
Maybe Lily's calm pragmatism was just what was
called for.

What the country needed?

What he needed.

She didn't seem to be aware that she looked…
dowdy.

No, he thought. Dowdy was the wrong word.
A woman as cute as Lily could never look dowdy.
Her swimsuit must have been bought before her
illness—it was too big for her. Her nose was
turning pink from the sun. Her scarf was slipping
backwards, and her curls were twisting in damp
tendrils across her forehead.

Cute? More. She was gorgeous. He was
starting to feel…

'Yes, I was dumb enough not to tell him,' she
said to the reporters. She might have been discussing the weather.

'Why didn't you?'

'I had my reasons.' She sounded a bit irritated.
But then she seemed to think about it. She sat

back on her heels and gazed up at Alex, as if assessing him and rethinking her answer.

'You know, the first time I met Prince Alex I thought he was wonderful,' she admitted. 'But I was ill and on medication and maybe I wasn't myself. Alex didn't know I was ill—or pregnant—only a rat would have taken advantage of me and you must know by now that the Prince is an honourable man. Now that Alex knows the truth, he's made me an honest woman. I intend to stay here with my son and my husband, build boats and live happily ever after. I'll start with repairing this one. Is that okay with you?'

What were the reporters supposed to say to that? They were staring at her, open-mouthed. It was so obviously not a rehearsed speech that she'd taken their breath away.

She'd taken his breath away.

She'd been ill.

She'd downplayed it, but suddenly he thought, *how ill*? She'd said it before, but it had been brushed aside. She'd implied she'd had a minor operation. Maybe she'd had morning sickness as well.

But…ill when she'd conceived?

And…she'd made their marriage sound ordinary.

He wouldn't have minded if she'd looked up and smiled at him, formed some sort of connection to make these guys think that their initial attraction still held.

To make *him* think that initial attraction still held.

Hell, what was he thinking? One part of him wanted a marriage of convenience. The rest of him wanted to claim this woman as his.

Which was ridiculous. What had changed to make him trust her?

'Do you have any more questions?' she asked, rising and wiping sand from her hands on the sides of her bathing suit. 'Michales has been in the sun for long enough. I need to take him up to the house.' She lifted Michales from Alex's grasp and waited—politely—for the reporters to leave.

'Are you in love with Prince Alex?' the older reporter asked and Alex drew in his breath. Of all the impertinences…

But Lily didn't seem perturbed.

'I'd imagine half the hot-blooded women in the western world are in love with His Highness,' she said and she grinned. 'Ask your readers.'

'But your marriage…'

'The Prince is an honourable man,' she said again, flatly. 'He's my husband and he's doing right by me and my son. I think he's wonderful. You should all be very proud of him. Now, if you'll excuse me, I really must go. I'll leave you with Prince Alexandros—he can answer any more questions you might think of. Good evening.'

'Can we have a photograph of the three of you together?' the cameraman pleaded. 'One?'

'Okay.'

Alex was too bemused to protest. Mia would never have agreed to a photograph like this, he thought, but Lily seemed unperturbed. How many photographs had been taken of her today? Obviously one more wasn't going to do any harm.

She turned and stood beside him, holding her son. She smiled.

'Can you lift Prince Michales a little higher?' the cameraman called and Alex thought, damn this, he was going to be part of this photograph, too.

He took Michales from Lily's arms and he held him between them.

Michales gave an indignant squeal, twisted and grabbed for his mother.

He caught the tail of her scarf. And pulled.

Maybe if her hair hadn't been wet he wouldn't have seen. But her hair was tugged upward with the scarf.

For a moment, before the curls fell again, he saw a scar.

A huge scar—from behind her ear almost to her crown.

The photographers hadn't seen. But Lily… She knew he'd seen it. Her face stilled.

Don't say anything, her face said. Please…

He didn't.

In one fluid movement he was tight against her, blocking the reporters' view, twisting her to face the camera slightly side on. So the scar was invisible.

He was holding her close, as if he cared.

Hell, he did care. Why hadn't he asked. *Why hadn't he asked?*

He forced a smile. The photograph was taken. He handed Michales back to Lily—still standing as close as he could. He took the scarf from Michales's chubby fingers and tied it gently around his mother's curls.

'I'll not have you sunburned,' he growled.

'It's almost dusk. There's no need to fear sunburn,' the reporter said.

'No matter. It's time you went up to the house, Lily,' he said and gave her a gentle push.

She got the message. She gave the reporters a brief smile and turned and trudged up the beach. Leaving three men gazing after her. Two reporters who thought they'd just gained a scoop.

One Prince who felt ill.

She'd called him honourable, wonderful even…

He didn't feel either.

'You look confused,' one of the reporters said. He tried to get his face under control again. He was watching Lily walk up the beach. What the hell…?

'You look like you'd like to bed her again,' the man said.

Enough. There was only so much a man could take and this was well over the boundary.

'Excuse me,' he said coldly. 'This is a private beach. You have no right to land here. I think we've given you enough. Can you please leave now?'

'We're going,' the man said and then he hesitated. 'She's a bit different from her sister, then?'

This was where he should turn haughty, supercilious, as if reporters were somewhere beneath pond scum. This was where he should produce a dose of royal arrogance.

He couldn't do it. Not when they were saying something he agreed with so entirely.

'Do you think I'd have married her if she was like Mia?' he demanded.

The reporter hesitated. He looked as if he wanted to say something and finally decided he might as well.

'We came here on the spur of the moment,' he said. 'We never dreamed of getting this close. The old King and his bride…they never let us near.'

That was what he should have done, Alex thought. He knew he needed to protect Lily. Standing on the beach, watching Lily's departing back, the reporters with bare feet and soggy trousers, Alex in his swim shorts and bare chest... It didn't feel like a them-against-us situation. It felt like three guys admiring a cute woman. Three men thinking about how this situation affected the country.

'You know what the headlines are going to be tomorrow?' the reporter asked, still not taking his eyes from the departing Lily. 'They're going to be: "Don't Call Me Ma'am. Call Me Lily." I just figured the angle. A Princess of the People. As a question. Like we need to get to know her before we pass judgement. You want to add anything to that?'

'I don't think I do,' he said, thinking maybe that was where he'd gone wrong in the first place. *We need to get to know her before we pass judgement...*

'You want us to say you threatened to throw us off the beach?'

'I want you to say I'll do anything in my power to protect my own.'

'Nice,' the guy said, grinning and scribbling himself a note. 'Now, all you need to say is that you fell in love with her the first time you saw her...'

'For our women readers,' the younger guy said apologetically. 'They want a love story.'

'I'm not buying into that,' he snapped.

'You can't keep your eyes off her,' the older guy said.

'Neither can you.'

'Yeah, well...' They watched as Lily rounded the last curve in the path and disappeared. There was a communal sigh of regret. 'I expect our readers will add two and two...'

'I hope they will.'

'I'm sure they will,' the reporter said cheerfully. 'We've got some great shots here. You know, if I were you, I'd show her off. You need the rest of the island to take her to their hearts.'

'Just like you have,' the younger reporter said and grinned. 'Can I quote you as saying that, sir?'

CHAPTER NINE

HE'D seen the scar.

No matter, she thought. She'd never consciously hidden her illness from him. If he'd asked, she'd have told him.

But…

But she hated him knowing. That was why she'd consciously played it down, blocking his questions. She hadn't lied to him about it, but neither had she told the truth. For the truth still hurt. The memory of her illness was still terrifying. Even thinking about it—how helpless she'd been—left her feeling exposed. Vulnerable. More vulnerable even than she'd felt getting married, which was really, really vulnerable.

Think about the house, she told herself. Think about practicalities.

Think about anything but Alex.

The house was fabulous.

Lily had spent only a few minutes here while

she'd dumped her bridal gear and donned her swimsuit. The beach, the sea, the need to stop being a bride and have a swim, had made her rush. Now she had time to take it in.

Her apartment—a guest wing?—was beautiful: a long, wide room with three sets of French windows opening to the balcony and the sea beyond. The windows were open, the soft curtains floating in the breeze.

Everywhere she looked there were flowers. The boundaries between house and garden were almost indistinguishable.

Fabulous.

So think fabulous, she told herself.

Don't think about Alex.

Was he still at the beach?

Maybe he'd only caught a glimpse of the scar. Maybe he wouldn't ask.

She showered with Michales in her arms. When she emerged, wrapped in one vast fluffy towel, and Michales enclosed in another, birds were doing acrobatics in the vines on the balcony. Finches? Tiny and colourful, they made her feel as if she'd wandered into a fairy tale.

'But this is real,' she told Michales a trifle breathlessly. 'Paradise.'

With Alex?

She thought of his face when he'd seen the scar. He'd looked…numb.

At least she had something she needed to focus on other than Alex's reaction. Michales was drooping. The little boy had been wide-eyed since their arrival, crowing in delight at the sea, soaking it in with all the delight at his small person's disposal. Now he was rubbing his eyes, snuggling against her and beginning to whimper.

He needed to be fed and put to bed. She needed to find the kitchen. She should have checked she had what she needed before she'd gone for a swim, she thought ruefully. She needed to dress fast, but if she put him down he was going to wail.

There was a knock on the door. It swung open—and there was Alex.

He'd moved faster than she had. Showered and dressed, he looked slick and handsome and casually in control of his world.

He was carrying one of Michales's bottles. Filled.

How did he know what was needed?

'I watched the nursery staff feed him a few times before you took him away,' he told her before she asked. 'I know he's a man who doesn't like to be kept from his meals. We knew your formula and…'

'We?'

'Me and my hundred or so staff,' he said and

smiled, and she was suddenly far too aware of being dressed in only a towel, which was none too secure.

She was none too secure.

'Why don't you dress while I feed him?' he said and held out his hands to take his son, and that made her feel even more insecure.

'He'll need it warmed.'

'It's already warmed.'

'By your hundred or so staff?'

'Only me here,' he said apologetically. 'A housekeeper comes here every morning, and a gardener when I'm away. When I'm here the gardener doesn't come. That's it.'

'So you live here all by yourself?'

'I do,' he said gravely, then sat on the bed, settled Michales on his knee and offered him his bottle. Michales took it as if he hadn't seen food for days.

'Greedy,' Alex said and chuckled, and Lily felt her insides do that somersaulting thing again and thought she really had to get a grip.

Her towel slipped a bit and she got a grip. Fast.

'I'll get dressed,' she said and grabbed a bunch of clothes and headed for the bathroom.

But she kept the door open. Just a little. There was so much she wanted to know. And it might buy her time. Maybe it could even deflect questions from the scar.

Asking questions could be seen as a pre-emptive strike. Yeah, right, as if that would succeed. But there was little else she could think of to do.

'How long have you had this place?' she called.

'My father had it built when he married my mother.'

'He planted the garden?'

'He and my mother did the basics. My father died when I was five and my mother was forced to leave. My mother and I rebuilt the garden when she came back.' His voice softened. 'She was passionate about gardening. Like you are about boats.'

She'd been steering the conversation to him. There was no way she'd let him deflect the conversation straight back.

'Your mother died when you were…seventeen?'

'Almost seventeen. She was sick for a long time before that.'

'You told me you were raised in the royal nursery.'

'I was,' he said, latent anger suddenly in his voice. 'My uncle hated my father and when I was born that hatred turned… vindictive. Giorgos holds…held…the titles to the entire island. When my father died he banished my mother from the island. Because I was heir to the throne, he demanded I stay.'

'He loved you?'

'He hated me. But if I was to be his heir, he'd control me.'

'Oh, Alex.'

'Yeah, it was tough,' he said. 'The law supported him, and my mother's pleas were ignored. My pleas were ignored.'

'But…you got her back?'

'I did,' he said and she heard a note of grim satisfaction enter his voice. 'Finally. By the time I was fifteen…well, even by fifteen I'd learned things Giorgos didn't want me to know. I was making his life uncomfortable, and he no longer wanted me at the castle. So finally my mother was allowed to return and he allocated an allowance for us to live on. We came back here to live, for all the time she had left.'

There was an untold story here, she knew. A fifteen-year-old standing up to a King. But instinctively she knew he wouldn't tell her more.

'I'm so sorry,' she said.

'There's no need.'

She was still in the bathroom. She had her clothes on now. Jeans, T-shirt.

There was no reason for standing in the bathroom any longer.

She walked out, cautious. Michales had finished his bottle. Her son was looking up at

Alex, sleepy but expectant. Alex was looking at Lily, expectant.

The resemblance was unnerving. She was unnerved.

She smiled. It was impossible not to smile at these two.

Her men.

The thought was weird.

'Tell me about your illness,' Alex said softly and her smile died, just like that.

'You don't need to know.'

'I do.' His gaze met hers. Calm. Firm. Unyielding.

The time for dissembling was past.

Okay, then. There was, indeed, no practical reason for her to dissemble—apart from increasing her vulnerability—and she felt so vulnerable anyway she might as well toss in a bit more to the mix.

'I had a brain tumour,' she said, so quickly, so softly that she wasn't sure he'd hear. But the flash of horror in his eyes told her he had.

'A brain tumour…'

'Benign.' The last thing she wanted from this man was sympathy, but sympathy was in his eyes, right from the start, wanted or not. There was also horror.

When the doctors had told her the diagnosis

she'd gone to the Diamond Isles to talk to Mia. She'd been hoping for something. Support? Love? Even kindness would have done. But of course Mia had been caught up in her own world. 'Don't be ridiculous,' she'd said when Lily had tried to tell her. 'You've always had your stupid headaches. I won't even begin to think you're right.'

She'd been bereft, lost, foundering. Calls to her mother had gone unanswered. She'd never felt so alone in her life.

Then came the night of the ball. She might as well attend, she'd thought, rather than sit in her bedroom and think about a future that terrified her.

And so she'd met Alex. When Alex had smiled at her, when he'd asked her to dance, she'd found herself falling into his arms. Doing a Mia for once. Living for the moment.

And for two glorious days he'd made her forget reality. He'd smiled at her and she'd let herself believe that all could be right in her world. She'd blocked out the terror. She'd lost herself in his smile, in his laughter, in his loving…

And in his body.

And now here he was, looking at her as if he really cared, and she was lost all over again.

She couldn't be lost. Not when her world was so close to being whole again.

'I always had it,' she said, still too fast, searching for the quickest way to tell him what he had to know. 'Okay, potted history. You probably know my father was a Scottish baronet, a childless widower. My mother was a distant relation of the Greek royal family, fearsomely ambitious. She set her cap at my father's money and title, even though he was forty years her senior. Mia and I were born, two years apart.'

'I know this. The country's been told this.'

'Yes, but as Mia's story. This is mine.'

'Okay,' he said, cradling the almost sleeping Michales. His eyes never left her face. 'You want to sit down and tell me the rest?'

She cast him a scared look. Scared and resentful. Sure she wouldn't be believed.

'No one's pushing you into a chair,' he said gently. 'There's no naked bulb swinging eerily above your head as you spill state secrets. Just tell me.'

She nodded. She closed her eyes. She opened them again and somehow found the strength to say what needed to be said. 'When I was six I started getting headaches,' she told him. 'I was diagnosed with a tumour, benign but inoperable.' She shrugged. 'I guess that was the end of my parents' marriage. My mother loathed that I was sickly. It was almost an insult—that any daughter of hers could be less than perfect. And then Dad's money ran out.'

She paused. This was too much information. Dumb.

She didn't want this man's sympathy.

Alex's silence scared her, but she had to go on.

'So my mother left, taking Mia with her. Dad and I muddled through as best we could. When Dad died my mother's uncle, a man as different from my mother as it was possible to be—took me in. He was a boat-builder in Whitby in the north of England, and I learned my passion for boats from him. When he died, Spiros, my uncle's friend, persuaded me to go to the States and work for him. So that's what I did. My headaches were a nuisance I'd learned to live with. I made great boats. I was…content.'

'You didn't come to Mia's wedding.'

'I wasn't invited. We'd hardly seen each other since our parents separated and, believe me, I wasn't fussed. Would you have liked to be Mia's bridesmaid?'

She tried a smile then, but she didn't get one in return. His gaze made her feel he was trying to see straight through her. It left her feeling so exposed she was terrified.

Get on, she told herself. Just say it.

'Then the headaches got worse,' she said, trying

to get to the point where Alex could stop looking…like he scared her. 'I was getting increasingly dizzy. Increasingly sick. Finally I had tests. The doctors told me the tumour had grown. They thought…unless there was a miracle I had less than a year to live.'

His eyes widened in shock. 'Lily!' His hand reached out towards her but she shook her head. She stepped even further back.

No contact. Not now.

'So I was in a mess,' she said, trying to sound brisk and clinical and knowing by the look on his face she was failing. 'My mother didn't want to know about me. I didn't want to burden Spiros. You've already figured his boatshed looks prosperous but it's struggling. But I had to talk to someone. So, stupidly, I came to the palace to try to talk to Mia. I arrived just in time for the King's celebrations to mark forty years on the throne. That's when I met you.'

Her words had the power to change his world. That was how he felt. As if his world had shifted.

The first time they'd met they'd been surrounded by glittering royalty, the royal ball in full swing. Giorgos had been flaunting his young glamorous wife, taunting him. Telling him there was no way he'd inherit the throne.

But as his uncle had walked past Lily the King's corset had creaked. Lily's lips had twitched. They had, it seemed, a shared sense of the ridiculous.

Intrigued, he'd asked her to dance.

She'd laughed about the chandeliers. She'd gently mocked his tuxedo.

She'd felt like a breath of wind against his heart.

That was the start. They'd laughed and talked for two days. They'd become as close as two people could get.

That she'd had this threat hanging over her...

'So...' He was struggling to find his voice.

'So I slept with you.' Her chin tilted upward in that wonderful, defiant way he was learning to know. 'It was crazy, but crazy was how I felt that night. Crazy wonderful. Yes, we took precautions but maybe I wasn't as careful as I should have been. It was like nothing was real.'

She smiled then, a real smile, with real humour. Making him remember why he'd wanted her. Making him remember why he'd thought she was different. 'It's okay,' she said softly. 'It was great that night. It was fantastic.'

He didn't feel like smiling. *I wasn't as careful as I should have been,* she'd said. How careful had he been?

Not careful enough.

'I got you pregnant.'

She nodded. 'You can't imagine how I felt when I found out. I couldn't work. I had no money. I was having a baby and the headaches were getting more and more frequent. Nevertheless, even after I phoned you… I couldn't consider abortion. I had tests and it was a little boy and he was so real. I wanted… I so wanted…'

She shook her head, seemingly shaking away a memory that held nothing but despair. Moving on. 'Well, finally I contacted Mia again,' she whispered. 'She gave me the same dumb line. It was my business. Not hers. But then she phoned back. Excited. It seemed Giorgos was infertile. They'd been quietly trying to arrange an adoption, but they'd so much rather it was my baby. I know her reasons now—Giorgos's reasons. But by then I was so sick I couldn't enquire and even if I'd known maybe I wouldn't have cared. All I could think was that Mia would give my baby a chance of life.'

He didn't respond. The audacity of the scheme still left him dumbfounded. Mia and Giorgos using Lily's desperation for their own ends… How could Lily have guessed their intention?

And of course Lily had accepted their offer. It was the child's best chance. In a royal household, she knew the baby would at least be well taken care of. Like Lily, the alternatives seemed unbearable.

He looked down at the almost sleeping Michales. His son. To not bring this little boy into the world... The child of two mature parents, conceived in what could almost be taken as love...

He thought again of the call she'd made to him in early pregnancy, and of his response, and he felt sick.

There was a drawn-out silence. Silence and silence and more silence.

She hated it. He could see it. She hated anyone knowing, but to tell him... It was making her feel exposed and frightened and very, very small.

'But you survived?' he said softly, finally, into the stillness.

'So I did,' she said humourlessly. 'You think I'm lying?'

'I didn't say that.' He shook his head. Definite. 'My God, Lily...' Once again he put a hand out towards her but she backed even further. Standing against the French windows as if preparing to flee.

'Let me finish.' She hesitated, then forced herself to go on. 'Part of this I've only heard from others,' she said. 'But I need to tell you. Mia and Giorgos paid for me to be admitted to a private hospital in France, a place known for its discretion. Mia arrived as I was getting really ill. I know now that her plan was to tell the people back on the Diamond Isles that she was pregnant and suffering complications. If my baby survived to term she'd take him as hers. Giorgos would bribe anyone who needed to be bribed.'

'But how did she…?'

'I can't tell you what I don't know,' she said bluntly. 'I gather I ended up in a coma. I gather Michales was born. I also gather one of the nurses in the hospital became really troubled that I was lying untreated. Apparently, until Michales was born, Mia acted concerned, but after she took him I was left alone.' She took a deep breath. 'The nurse saved my life. She risked her job and contacted a doctor she knew who was doing groundbreaking surgery. He checked me out and figured he had nothing to lose if he tried operating. Mia had left my mother's contact details for when I died. The surgeon contacted her for permission to operate—offering to do it for free.' She managed a smile again. 'Even my mother couldn't knock that back. So finally I woke. The tumour was gone. Unbelievably gone. I had my life.'

He didn't know what to say. He just gazed at her in awe.

'Unreal, isn't it?' she said, half mocking.

'Unbelievable. Parts of it I didn't figure out myself until I arrived here at your coronation, and even now I'm having trouble coming to terms with it. But it's okay. I'm not asking for belief. I'm not asking for anything. I just want to build boats and care for my son. I want to live.'

Her chin tilted forward again, pugnacious, defensive.

How could he believe such a story?

But then he thought of Mia. He'd been present at the wedding, and he remembered Mia's mother as well. They were two of a kind. Grasping, greedy, social climbers. Flaunting their connection to the Greek royal family and to English aristocracy.

They were about as different from this woman as it was possible to be.

'I won't impinge on your freedom,' he said softly and she nodded.

'Good, then.'

'But…no one came near you?'

'Spiros and Eleni would have if I'd told them. I didn't tell them.'

'I would have if you'd let me.'

'Would you?'

'You can believe it. It's true. Hell, Lily, you could have died.'

'That's what I expected,' she said. 'I guess

nothing will ever be so bad again. Drifting into unconsciousness, knowing there was no return ticket. Knowing I had to leave my baby in Mia's care.'

'If I could get my hands on her…'

'There's no joy down that road,' she said simply. 'Being angry just makes everything worse. Anyway…' she shrugged '…now you know. We can get on with it.'

'With what?'

'With our sham marriage. With doing what we have to do before I can go home.'

'Where's home?'

'Where Michales is,' she said simply. 'I don't care about places. I care about my baby. That's all.'

CHAPTER TEN

SHE'D lied.

I care about my baby. That's all. She'd known it was a lie before she'd uttered it but she wasn't about to add her other...care.

Alex.

He looked appalled. It helped, she decided, that he looked appalled at what she'd gone through. When she let herself think about it, she was pretty appalled herself.

That he was horrified on her behalf... It did something to her insides. There was a warmth forming inside her—a glow that was starting to build.

She looked down at the bed, where he still sat holding Michales on his knee.

Her men.

Her family.

She'd never had family. Her mother had been entirely uninterested in her sickly daughter. Her father had been elderly when she was born and their relationship had been built on Lily's role as carer. Mia simply didn't want to be a part of her life.

But here…this man didn't want her to care for him, she thought.

This man cared.

Um…no. He'd been horrified at an appalling story. Nothing more.

So don't get your hopes up, she told herself severely.

Michales was starting to grizzle. After his swim and shower and feed he should be drifting into sleep.

So be a mother, she reminded herself sharply.

She lifted Michales from Alex's arms, held him to her shoulder and rubbed his back.

He emitted one very satisfactory belch.

Alex's brows hiked in amazement. 'Is he supposed to do that?'

As an ice breaker it was great. The tension inside the room fizzled and died, and she found she could smile, too.

'Better out than in, wouldn't you say?' She was laying Michales into his cot. He'd had a very busy day for a baby. A wedding, a reception, a first ever swim… He snuggled down, his eyes closing almost before he was tucked in.

She stood gazing down at him. When she looked up, Alex was standing beside her.

The tension zoomed in again.

'What?' she said, suddenly breathless.

'You're beautiful,' he said on a note of discovery.

'Yeah, dressed to kill.' Jeans and T-shirt. Her standard uniform for life. She'd left the scarf off. Why bother?

'Lily…'

'Let's not,' she managed.

'Not what?'

'Whatever you're about to say. Like paying compliments. I don't like it.'

'You don't like compliments?'

'Mia gets the compliments. You want Mia? You need to line up behind a guy called Ben.'

'You're nothing like Mia.'

'Well, there's the truth. Can you excuse me? I need to unpack.' She made to go past him but his hands caught her shoulders and held.

'Lily, can we start again?'

'I don't know what you mean.'

'Wind the clock back,' he said softly. 'So we don't have baggage between us.'

'By baggage I guess you mean Michales.'

'He's very noisy baggage,' he said and smiled as he glanced into the cot. 'I doubt he fits the description. But in a way…he complicates things. Your illness complicates things. All sorts of things complicate…things.'

'What do you mean?'

'Between you and me.'

'There's nothing…'

'You see, that's where we differ.' He moved so he had a hand on each arm. His hands were on her bare skin. They felt big and warm and sure. In his hold she suddenly felt…safe.

'Alex, don't,' she murmured but still he held her, his eyes asking questions.

'Don't what?'

'H-hold me.'

'You don't want to be held?'

'I'm scared.' It wasn't true, but it was what she ought to feel. She should be running a mile. But she could give herself to him.

The idea was suddenly there, and it was so overwhelming that *scared* was the right description. To give herself to this man…

She'd married him, she thought, frantically trying to get her hormones under control. But to fall in love with him… To give her heart…

She already had.

Sensations were sweeping in from all sides.

And suddenly she was remembering how she'd felt during those last appalling months, as the tumour in her head had threatened to overwhelm her. She'd had times when she was dazed, confused, disoriented. The sensation of being out of control was terrifying.

Gazing at Alex now, that was how she felt. As if her body wasn't her own. As if her head wasn't her own.

'Lily, what is it?' He was gazing at her in concern. Something of what she was feeling must have shown in her face, for the grip of his hands changed. It was a subtle shift. Not a withdrawal exactly but… From the beginnings of passion, it had changed to a hold of comfort. 'Lily, I won't hurt you.'

'I know you won't.' But here was a shift again. She didn't want him to look like that. She didn't want this man's sympathy.

The night Michales had been conceived had been a night out of frame. She'd emerged from plain, frightened Lily to being someone else. She'd been seductive, wild and free.

It had been imaginary.

It had been fun.

The memory of that fun was with her now, like an itch building within. Goading her. Go on, Lily. You know you can be like that again. If you dare…

'Alex, are you suggesting…that you want this marriage for real?' she whispered.

'What do you mean?'

'I know it's not love at first sight or anything

like that,' she said hurriedly. 'But we've…we've got this attraction thing going.'

'We do.' He sounded puzzled, but laughter was replacing sympathy. Which was what she wanted—wasn't it?

No. She wanted a serious discussion.

'I'd prefer it if you didn't laugh,' she told him, and he schooled his expression to gravity.

'Of course. I'm not laughing. So you're saying we might be attracted to one another. I agree. So where might that be taking us?'

'See, here's the thing,' she said, fighting for courage. But suddenly she was sure she was right. Mia wasn't the only one who could fight for what she wanted, she thought. All her life she'd let events shape her course. Now…she had her life back. She had a beautiful baby, and before her was the most gorgeous prince in the known universe and he was her husband. Whatever the reason for the marriage, marriage it clearly was.

So here was the idea. What was the harm in asking for more?

'When we made our wedding vows, did you mean any of them?' she asked quickly, before any more qualms raised their heads.

'You mean keeping me only unto you for as long as we both shall live?' he asked, and the laughter in his eyes had suddenly gone. 'Lily…'

She hadn't meant to get this serious; it was scary. 'I didn't mean that,' she said hurriedly. 'I wouldn't ask that. For as long as we both shall live… This is only for a year. And you've known me for what—two minutes?'

'I've known you for over a year.'

'But in real time. Two days and a couple of meetings in between. Not enough to base a whole life on. But what I'm asking…' She faltered, fought to find the right words and then forced herself to say them. 'It's just the first bit. It's the keeping yourself only unto me.'

'Keeping myself faithful to you, do you mean?'

He had it. She nodded, relieved it was in the open. 'That's the one.'

'Are you suggesting you might want to keep a couple of gigolos on the side while we're married?' It was said lightly but his gaze said this wasn't a light question. His gaze was locked onto hers, as if he were trying to see inside her.

'Of course I don't,' she said. Unconsciously her chin tilted again, assertive. Or trying to be assertive. Inside, she was jelly. 'Alex, I'm willing to swear that for the whole time I'm married to you I will be faithful.' Deep breath. Just ask, she told herself. Do it. And she did. 'Will you do the same for me?'

And there was no hesitation at all. 'I will,' he

said, and he might as well have said *I do*, there was such gravitas.

Her eyes widened. Just like that, she had his promise.

She didn't know where to take it from here.

He was watching her, concerned now by her silence. 'You don't believe me?'

'It's just…you're a royal prince, you could have anyone. I didn't think you'd want to be…'

'Monogamous?'

'That's the one.' She was practically stuttering. She felt as if she was tying herself in knots. 'What makes you different?'

'I wouldn't mind seeing if it works,' he said, so softly she thought at first she'd got it wrong. But the way he was looking at her said she had it exactly right.

I wouldn't mind seeing if it works… That was an implication that he wanted something more than a marriage of convenience.

Don't go there, she thought. She wasn't ready. She wanted her freedom. Or she thought she did. Alex was…fabulous. But to be sucked into the royal goldfish bowl for ever…

Think about that later, she told herself. Later was truly scary. Think about here. Think about now.

Right here, right now, her prince was promising to be faithful. To her. While they were married.

Starting now?

'You're beautiful, Lily,' he said softly. 'You've had such a tough time…'

'See, that's just what I don't want you to think,' she snapped, confusion fading. 'That's what I suddenly realised. Last time you took me to bed… did you do it because you felt sorry for me?'

'Of course I didn't.'

'Then that's what I'd like to revert to. I remember lying beside you and thinking it was magic. Thinking your body was scrumptious.'

'Scrumptious,' he said blankly and then he grinned. 'I believe that's what I thought about your body as well,' he said and the laughter had slammed back.

Shared laughter… That was what had attracted her to him in the first place. A whole lot of other sensations had fallen into line behind that initial attraction—a body to die for, sensations like tenderness, passion and wonder. But laughter had come first and it was laughter that was a refuge here. If they could laugh… Scary emotions could be left for later.

She could be free later on. She could be free when she had to be free. For now… Maybe this was dumb, but his sympathy, his concern, had seemed to unlock something inside her that had never been touched. From swearing she wanted to keep her life for herself and for her son, suddenly she was thinking what if…what if…

'So you're promising to keep yourself only unto me all the time we're married,' she ventured.

'I am.' Flat. Definite. Absolute.

'So…' She swallowed. 'If we're to be faithful…'

'Mmm.'

'And if we're to be…chaste…as well, then we might have a very monastic type of year in front of us.'

'I'd make a very bad monk,' he said promptly, laughter returning. He seemed to be willing to go where she was leading. More than willing. 'I don't think a tonsure would suit me.'

She looked up at his thick black curls. She tried to imagine what he'd look like with a neat ring of hair and a bald crown.

She chuckled.

'Not a sexy look,' he said, smiling his agreement, and she smiled back at him. And wham! Here they came again. Hormones and hormones and more hormones.

But there were things to be said—things that must be said if those hormones were allowed to hold sway.

'If…if we were to sleep together we'd need to take a lot more precautions than last time,' she managed, trying not to sound as breathless as she felt.

'I've changed my brand of condom.'

She blinked. He was smiling. He was with her and beyond.

Two could play at that game. 'I've taken precautions, too,' she said, and watched his eyes crease into surprise and appreciation—and then darken to something more.

'You've taken precautions,' he said softly.

'That's what I said.'

'You've taken precautions already?'

'Seeing as I was getting married. Seeing as I didn't trust myself.' Seeing also as she hadn't trusted him not to demand his conjugal rights. She'd never dreamed the advance could come from her.

'I see.' His hands took hers, gripping warmly, strongly, surely, and the laughter was back again. Laughter and something deeper. 'So let me get this right. You're in my house on your wedding night—*our* wedding night—you look so lovely I can't believe it and you tell me you came prepared.'

'That's not necessarily an invitation,' she managed, but of course it was. And he was playing her game.

'It'd be a prince without chivalry who thought it was,' he said and he tugged her closer. 'But if it was a prince who was to issue the invitation…'

'What…what sort of invitation?' she managed.

'A very proper invitation,' he whispered. His mouth was against her hair. She could feel his breath. It was unbelievably erotic. Unbelievably sexy. 'Something like: His Majesty, Prince Alexandros Kostantinos Mykonis, Crown Prince of Sappheiros, requests the pleasure of the company of Her Majesty, Princess Lily Mykonis…'

'Princess…' It was practically a squeak. She swallowed. 'Um…princess?'

'That's what you are as my wife,' he said into her hair. 'Whereas Mia is now Queen of nowhere, as the Kingdom of Diamas no longer exists. She's about to get a very legal letter telling her she has no further right to use the title.'

She gazed at Alex—*at her husband*—in awe. Thinking of Mia's reaction.

'I think you're wonderful,' she said before she could help herself, and the world stood still.

His eyes darkened once more. She saw passion flare and burn. 'So this invitation I'm thinking of issuing…' he murmured.

'When?' she asked, still breathless, but no longer worrying about an irrelevant thing like breathing.

'I'm getting to that,' he said reprovingly. 'Patience, my love. Official invites take time. I need to melt the wax for the seal… Oh, I'll have to find some wax. You don't happen to have a candle about you?'

'I don't believe I do. And I certainly don't have time to search for one.'

'You don't?'

'Not the way I'm feeling.'

'So…' His hold tightened. 'If I were to send this invitation without an official seal… If I were to request an RSVP by return post…'

'You might get it faster than you expected.'

'Really?'

'Really,' she whispered. 'Right about…now.'

'Now?' His hands were in the small of her back, tugging her closer, closer. 'Now, my love?'

'Maybe,' she whispered.

'And what might this RSVP say?'

'Ooh,' she whispered. 'I'd have to think about it.'

'Think fast.'

She thought fast. She could think without breathing. 'I guess it'd say something along the lines of: Her Majesty, Princess Lily Sophia Mykonis, is delighted to receive the very gracious invitation of said prince and accepts with pleasure.'

'Does she just.' She could feel his pleasure. She could feel his heat. The world outside had ceased to exist. There was only each other.

How had they done it? How had they turned a sedate domestic scene—feeding her baby—into passion, just like that?

But there was no mistaking what had happened. Her knees felt distinctly wobbly, but there was no longer a need for them to stay firm. Alex was sweeping her up into his arms, holding her against him, his dark eyes possessing her, loving her, wanting her.

Her prince.

'About place and time…' he murmured.

'Subject to negotiation, wouldn't you say?'

'Okay, let's negotiate. First factor—time. Is now okay with you?'

'I don't believe I have any pressing appointments.'

'Excellent.' His dark eyes gleamed. 'Place?'

'Maybe not here,' she said, somewhat reluctantly.

'We might corrupt our son,' he said, and those two words…*our son*…were so sexy that her insides felt quivery along with her knees. All of her felt quivery.

'See that adjoining door?' he murmured, and she looked up and saw the door and her eyes widened.

'You don't mean…'

'I do mean.' He was laughing again. She loved it when he laughed.

'You had this planned!'

'I did not,' he said, wounded. 'But, as a good father, I thought I might be expected to take a turn at night duty. I thought if I was to lie awake at night listening for my son then I'd need to be near. Really near. So I allocated you this apartment.'

'You're saying your bed is right through that door?'

'Right through that door. If it's grand enough for you.'

'I can make do,' she said serenely. 'But I don't mind a bit of glitz. The last time I... The last time we made love, I believe you were sleeping at the castle. Under a chandelier, if I remember correctly.'

'I was there as my uncle's heir,' he said. 'He liked glitz. He also expected me to act as his deputy, so I was on duty.'

'But you're not on duty now.'

'I'm delegating responsibility to my son.' He grinned. 'I like the idea of delegating. If there's armed insurrection before the morning, Michales is responsible for waking me up and ringing the newspapers.'

She choked.

'I love it when you laugh,' he whispered and it was so much what she was thinking that she gasped.

'What?' he demanded.

'I guess…laughter from you is a real turn-on as well,' she admitted.

'You like it when I laugh?'

'I love it when you laugh.'

'So we should find ourselves a good piece of slapstick on television?'

'We could,' she said cautiously.

'But I can think of something better,' he growled and he walked across and kicked the door open. It wasn't even properly closed, Lily thought, and she couldn't figure whether she was shocked or delighted.

But then she thought again. Definitely delighted. For Alex was carrying her across to his bed and laying her on the counterpane as if she were the most exquisite thing he'd ever touched.

'I'm sorry there's no chandelier,' he whispered.

'I can cope. As long as there's laughter,' she said, breathless again. When he looked like that…

It was still too soon, the sane part of her brain whispered. Sense said she needed to taste freedom first.

But not now. Not when the rest of her brain was disagreeing. Not as he was tugging his shirt free, baring his chest, making her gasp…

'Laughter,' he said, agreeing. Smiling and smiling. 'Okay, my love, here we go. Two sausages in a pan. One turns to the other and says, "Gee, it's hot in here." What does the other one say?'

He was loving her with his eyes. He was smiling down at her with that wicked, laughing smile—and he was waiting for an answer to his dumb riddle. 'I don't know,' she whispered, choking with laughter and something else entirely. 'What does the other one say?'

'"Bless my soul, it's a talking sausage!"' he said, and he grinned like a seven-year-old cracking his first riddle. It was so ridiculous she found herself laughing with him.

While hungering for him with every nerve in her body.

And then he was beside her on the bed, lifting her T-shirt over her head. Unclipping her bra.

'But it's not just the sausage who's hot,' he whispered, laughter fading, his strong, skilful fingers moving to cup her breasts. 'Lily, you're the most beautiful woman in the world. You give yourself to me and I can't believe that you do. I'll never let you forget it. But now, my love… Now is for us. Now is for laughter. Now is for loving. And if we try very hard…' He closed his eyes and she had a feeling he was taking a mighty step forward. 'Now might just end up being forever.'

* * *

Only forever had a habit of being not as long as expected.

In Athens, a plane was landing. A private jet. A woman emerged. She stood on the tarmac and surveyed the scene before her. Deeply displeased.

There was no one to meet her. Olivia had needed to barter with her daughter to get this flight. Mia had grudgingly arranged for Ben's plane to bring her here. The negotiations had made her seethe. While her daughters lived in splendour, she had to fend for herself.

Okay, maybe she would have done the same if she'd been her daughters' age, she conceded. Maybe she had. But for Lily to forget she was her mother... Not even to invite her to her wedding...

Some things were unconscionable. Sometimes a gentle reminder was needed.

Or a big one.

She made her way into the terminal, went through Customs— like a mere mortal, she thought savagely—and then thought of what to do next.

A private plane to Sappheiros was out of the question. Unless...

Unless the press came to the party. Which they would. She simply had to open her mouth and tell them who she was.

Mother of the Queen. Mother of the Crown Princess.

She'd done very well for her girls.

She now intended Lily to acknowledge it.

CHAPTER ELEVEN

FOR three days he made her laugh, he made her love, he made her live.

She'd never felt so alive. She'd never thought life could be so magical.

She wasn't to know that Alex had posted guards to prevent more intrusions into the little cove beneath the house. There were roadblocks set up to stop intrusions from the road. She thought this was normal, this was what life could be like, married to this man and living happily ever after.

And he was learning to love his son.

Of all the seductive turn-ons, this was the most powerful. For Alex's delight—his infatuation and wonder with his infant son—were impossible to disguise. He made Michales laugh, and every time he did she fell deeper and deeper in love with him. He swam with Michales in his arms, and she watched them and ached with happiness. She loved it that when Michales murmured it was Alex who'd scoop up the little boy and bring him back to their bed. He'd heat his bottle and they'd feed him together, and then Alex would take him back to his cot and tuck him in.

He told his son stories. She wasn't supposed to hear—he thought she was sleeping—but she lay and listened to him telling Michales all about this island, all the things they could do, all that life offered.

When Michales wouldn't settle they lay and told each other stories of their past. They were telling Michales of his history, they said solemnly to each other, but in reality they were growing closer and closer to each other.

She learned of Alex's childhood. She learned of the aching void left by his father's death, the desperation when his mother had to leave the island, leaving him with an uncle he loathed.

She even heard briefly of his desperation when his mother died. He skimmed over it but she heard enough to know he'd cared for her on his own, that Giorgos had let no one come near, that her death had changed who he was for ever.

He'd been known as a man who walked alone. She understood it now—a little. A tiny part of her was starting to think that maybe she could change it.

But now wasn't for resolutions. Now was simply for…now. For listening and learning and loving.

She learned of his friendship with Nikos and Stefanos. The 'guardians', they'd called themselves, and it seemed they might now all be in power; they'd hold government of each of these, the Diamond Isles. They had plans.

She listened to those plans. Alex could achieve them now. He lay beside her, he played with his son, he let his big body curve against hers and he told her his ideas for financial restructure, economic growth, tourism, wealth for this island he loved so much.

The stories weren't one-way. In turn he probed her childhood. He grew silent as she told him, and she knew his silence was anger. The sensation was incredible. No one had ever been angry on her behalf.

Her mother had deserted her. Her father had leaned on her, and her sister… Well, Mia was to be forgotten.

'Though I'd love to think of something else we could do,' Alex murmured. 'Stripping her of her title isn't enough. That she left you for dead…'

Michales had just been fed. Cradled between his mother and his father, he was sliding fast towards sleep, with the look of one very contented baby.

When he went to sleep... Lily was already tingling in anticipation of what would happen when he went to sleep.

She needed not to think about that, she told herself, trying to be severe. She needed to listen to what Alex was saying.

'I'm thinking of some sort of permanent memorial,' he said. 'We're opening a new refuse station on the far side of the island. How about we call it the Mia and Giorgos Garbage Dump? By royal decree.'

She grinned. 'You're a wonderful man, Alexandros.'

'I know,' he said humbly. He looked at Michales. The baby's eyes were closed. 'Our baby's asleep,' he said with deep satisfaction.

'Well, then...'

'You want to make love or go for a swim?'

'I...'

'More indecision,' he said and sighed. 'There are royal decrees all over the place this morning. Okay then, here's another. Lovemaking. Followed by swim. Followed by more lovemaking. And later... I intend to make you dinner.'

It was a dream time. It was a time of wonder but it had to end. He could ill afford three days. The island's grim financial situation couldn't wait any longer. There were decisions everywhere that needed his attention.

He had to leave.

He couldn't bear to tell Lily this had to end, but end it must.

He'd use this last night to good effect, he decided. He wouldn't talk about leaving.

Up until now they'd lived on what was in the refrigerator. His staff had stocked it well, but it was all ready-made stuff. He'd told his house-keeper to stay away. But this night had to be special.

When had she had someone cook for her? Never, he thought.

In the afternoons she'd taken to sleeping with Michales. She hadn't taken the time she needed after the operation to let her body recover fully, he thought. He insisted she take it now.

She thought he slept beside her, but instead he lay and watched them.

His wife. His son.

They slept while he watched over them.

Things were changing inside him. He was ac-knowledging a hunger he hadn't known he had until it was being assuaged.

His wife. His son.

So on this, the last day of their honeymoon, he left them while she slept and headed into the town.

She woke as he was unpacking in the kitchen, and came to investigate the sounds.

'Dinner,' he said, smiling at her, his beautiful wife, dressed in only a loose sarong. His beautiful Princess. 'I've decided you need feeding and it's time I lent a hand.'

'I can feed myself.'

'Not tonight.' He flipped her a disc and motioned to the sound system. 'Here's our music. You listen while I cook.'

So she sat and played with Michales and watched her husband cook her dinner.

He took over the whole kitchen. He was so large. So overpoweringly male.

So wonderful?

He upended a bag. Fat, juicy scallops with their lips still intact spilled out onto the table in a luscious heap.

Since her illness she'd been having trouble eating. Trauma, depression, shock—she didn't know what had caused it. She had to eat, but she couldn't remember a time when she'd last felt hungry.

She suddenly felt really, really hungry. And really, really…

Hungry, she thought again, but not for food.

Alex was piling the scallops into a bowl and unpacking the next parcel. Coriander, Lily thought, smelling the pungent herb. Mmm.

'Would you mind not looking like that?' he demanded.

'Like what?'

'You know very well like what,' he said. 'Like I need to sweep you up and carry you back to my bedroom right now. Or take you right here, among the coriander. But no. I'm a man on a mission. No distractions, woman. Listen to the music and let your Prince of the Kitchen do what he's here for. That's an order.'

He was setting out to make her smile and make her eat. Life had been bleak for this woman for a long time but right now, if he tried hard enough, he could make her smile.

He'd brought Abba. She'd put on the disc expecting—what—something classical? But instead there was Benny and Bjorn and Agnetha and Frida belting out their toe-tapping harmonies with passion. He could practically feel their Lycra.

It was impossible for her not to smile as she toe-tapped with Abba.

He cooked the scallops, searing them fast, then serving them on lettuce cups with a light dressing of coriander and lemon. Lily ate six while she listened to 'Dancing Queen'.

He watched her eat in quiet satisfaction. This was what he'd set out to do—have her eat without thinking about it.

Maybe she was thinking about the food, but the whole setting was confounding. He could see that. Him. His cooking. The music.

Excellent.

He would have liked to give her a really hefty steak as the next course, but in the end he'd opted for temptation rather than substance. So, instead of steak, he served slivers of fish caught that morning, coated in tempura batter and lightly fried. He accompanied them with tiny potatoes, parboiled and crisped in the oven. A salad of witlof, asparagus, mango and herbs.

'Fernando' started as he served the main course. It was one of Abba's slowest, finest songs and it meant Lily could lose herself in the music and eat again without thinking. She ate three slivers of fish, three tiny potatoes and a good serving of salad.

He cleared the plates with the same satisfaction he might have felt if his company received top place in the Chelsea Flower Show.

She seemed…bemused.

She really was beautiful, he thought as he watched her enjoy herself. When he'd first met her he'd thought her hair was glorious. Now, with her mass of drifting curls replaced by an almost boyishly short crop, he thought her hair had been a distraction. Her eyes were huge in her pale face. Her face was alive with emotion and enjoyment as Abba launched into 'Take a Chance on Me'.

Beautiful didn't begin to cut it.

He'd taken this woman to bed. She'd borne his son. He'd married her. Now, weirdly, he was starting to regret it. He'd like to start this again, without the baggage, without the tentative twelve-month time line, without the feeling that she'd been coerced into marrying him.

He'd filled her wineglass but she'd drunk a mere inch. She was still wary, he thought. She was giving in to the moment but she was still…afraid? Maybe that was too harsh a word, but behind her laughter there was always the echo of knowledge that this had to end.

He didn't want her to think this had to end. He didn't want her to be wary. He wanted her to laugh.

He wanted her to be free, he thought. Free to decide to love him?

Would she want a real marriage?

Would she want to be tied to him?

More and more, it was what he wanted. With Lily by his side, he could do anything, he thought. They could change this island together. They could truly be Sappheiros's ruling couple.

The thought was so exhilarating that he wanted to shout it. He wanted to tell her, to hold her in his arms and say it just like he'd thought it.

But he had to be wary here. There were loose ends. He'd left them loose because…because he hadn't wanted to commit himself. Only now he did.

But he wasn't going to pressure her. This was too important to mess with.

And he had things to sort out. He'd leave tomorrow and get it sorted—get it all sorted. Then he'd come back and woo her as she deserved to be wooed.

Meanwhile…dessert. He'd sweated over the dessert, wanting to present her with something irresistible. But the thought of her still pale and thin face had given him pause.

He'd cared for his mother when she'd been ill that last time, and he'd learned a little about invalid appetites. Lily was still recovering. A big dessert, a slab of luscious chocolate cake, for instance, could serve only to make her feel queasy.

He'd learned the hard way that tiny amounts were far more tempting.

So he'd lashed out on a really special dessert. Now he spent ten minutes arranging it, while Lily listened to 'Mamma Mia', 'Rock Me' and 'Take a Chance on Me'.

She didn't talk. The only way to get her to talk was for him to push, but he wouldn't push.

What he was trying to do… Well, to be honest, he was still trying to figure it out for himself, but he knew it behoved him to behave as if he were balancing on eggshells.

This was precious.

That would do as an adjective, he decided. He didn't know what to do with it, but he knew it had to be protected.

Lily.

Michales.

Lily.

His family?

Where was he going?

He knew where he was going. Maybe it scared him, but the alternative was far, far worse.

Family was what he wanted.

The dessert was irresistible. It was served on an antique platter, delicate china etched with faded rosebuds, pink and cream. On the plate…six tiny desserts. A tiny chocolate éclair. A thimbleful of chocolate-orange mousse. Crystallized ginger. A strawberry sponge cake, exquisite in miniature. A gold-burned baked caramel, two spoonfuls at the most. Grapes, frosted with sugar and glistening.

Yum.

Maybe she could relax a bit more, she decided, and took another sip of his lovely wine. Just a little. Just enough to enjoy the desserts.

He'd bought the desserts from the best cook on the island. Marika had had to close her restaurant tonight to prepare them, but what the heck? What was the use of being royal and rich if you couldn't be indulgent? Watching Lily try and resist the last grape—and fail—Alex thought it'd have been worth it if it had cost half his fortune.

She had him fascinated. More.

He'd wanted her the first time he'd seen her, and he wanted her so much now it was like a hunger, starting deep within and refusing to be sated. Wary of commitment for so long, he knew now what the truth was.

He wanted her on whatever terms she cared to name.

She popped the last grape into her mouth and smiled at him. 'All finished. And our son's fast asleep. What to do, what to do…'

'I'll show you,' he told her. And did.

He needed to get his business over and come back here. They slept in each other's arms but he woke before Lily and gently disentangled himself. He showered and dressed and she woke to find him standing over her with a mug of coffee, toast and an apologetic smile.

She sat up fast, drawing the sheet up to her chin.

She'd changed in these three days, Alex thought. She'd blossomed. She glowed from the inside out.

His Lily. He'd known she was beautiful but he couldn't have guessed how beautiful.

She held his heart in the palm of her hand.

'What do you think you're doing?' She sounded a little bit scared, he thought, but she was covering it with indignation. 'Dressed, sir, when I'm not.'

'A man has to have the advantage some time.'

'Well, I don't like it,' she said. 'Come back to bed.'

'I need to go back to the palace. I have things to do. I may need to make a fast trip to Manhattan.'

Her face stilled. 'Of…of course.'

'Will you stay here until I come back?'

'You'll be back…when?'

'A week? Maybe less. I can't say.'

'As long as that?'

'I can't help it, Lily. There's pressure from all sides. But now that you and Michales are settled…'

Her face grew even more expressionless. 'You've sorted us out and now you can move on?'

'I didn't mean that.' He looked down at her and she was so lovely… He should sit down here and now and tell her his plans. His dreams. His desire to fit her into his life so she'd never leave.

But if she reacted badly… If she took fright… The need to go was imperative, and if she didn't agree… He wouldn't have time to retrieve it.

Better not to say anything until he could return and stay.

And maybe she understood. 'I know you didn't,' she said, contrite, schooling herself to look calm. 'I know you need to go. I need to catch up with Spiros as well. I haven't even seen his boatshed.'

'It's great,' he said, grateful she'd moved on so easily. 'He and Eleni are in a house by the harbour—my people set it up for them. As far as the boatyard goes, Spiros is using a small one for now but in the long-term he'll tell us what he needs and we'll build a bigger one.'

She tried to get her head around this. Alex sounded businesslike. She needed to be, too.

Their honeymoon…was over?

'I thought you said this country was poverty-stricken.'

'It is, but if I pay bills and do nothing else we'll be bankrupt in no time. I'm organizing to rationalize our debts and work our way through them. Now I'm Crown Prince I can sell our overseas assets, and I can also access royal funds. I can get Spiros's boatshed working, employing locals, and that's just the beginning. I can get this whole island working.'

He bent and kissed her solidly—so solidly that her coffee slopped onto the sheets. 'Uh-oh,' he said and took her coffee, placed it on the side table and started kissing her again. 'Don't worry about a little stain,' he said. 'We've practically worn this set of sheets out anyway.'

'There's an ego,' she said, and he smiled.

'There's a lot to boast about,' he said. 'You've given me this, Lily. By agreeing to marry me... There's nothing I can't do.'

She smiled at his enthusiasm. But... But... She kissed him back but, for the first time in days, she knew doubt.

By agreeing to marry me...

He could have had all this without marrying her, she thought. Couldn't he?

Maybe not.

Of course not. She knew that.

How could she have forgotten? She'd agreed to marry him to secure the Crown so he could save this country. Not because he wanted to wake up beside her for the rest of her life.

He was moving on. He'd stepped back now, and she saw the latent energy in him, her Prince about to achieve his goals for this nation. He'd achieved what he needed here. It was time to move on to the next challenge.

She was being fanciful, she thought, but she couldn't stop a shiver starting deep and growing.

'Lily, you're beautiful,' he said, sensing her doubt and looking as if he didn't know how to quell it. Looking as if he didn't have time to quell it. 'You know you are. But…' he glanced at his watch and grimaced '…I'm meeting a group of international bankers at the palace in two hours and there are figures I need to check first. I've stayed with you for as long as I can. You'll be okay on your own?'

'Of course.' There was no *of course* about it, but a girl had some pride. 'Go slay 'em, my love.'

'I've organized a car for you. It's in the garage and the keys are on the bench in the kitchen. There's a baby seat in the back for Michales. Go down to the harbour if you want, and find Spiros. Just keep a low profile and stay away from the press.'

'You don't want me talking to the press?'

'It'd be better if we did it together.' He bent to kiss her again—hard, possessive, claiming his own. 'You and I stand together. We're a team. Remember that.'

He touched her lightly on the cheek. He strode

into the other room and bent over Michales for a moment—a silent farewell to his son.

And he was gone.

We're a team, Lily repeated softly to herself. A team.

Only…what sort of a team was it when one member was free to come and go as he pleased? The other…had been told not to speak to the press. Had been given permission to visit Spiros.

He's not promising you a real marriage, she told herself, fighting against sudden, inexplicable desolation. This is a marriage of convenience. The fact that we enjoy each other's bodies…

She enjoyed more than his body.

No. *Enjoy* was such a miserly word.

She loved.

A woman who's ruled by her heart is a fool.

Where had that come from? It was a saying of her mother's. She remembered her mother explaining why she had to leave.

'We've run out of money and your father wants to move to a cottage on the coast. I can't live that life. You say you love your father, but love isn't in my vocabulary. It shouldn't be in yours either. Mia and I are going. Come if you want but don't whinge about your headaches if you do. I can't bear it. And if you stay…don't blame me if you end up unhappy. Make decisions with your head, Lily. A woman who's ruled by her heart is a fool.'

Maybe she was a fool. She was so deeply in love.

What was she doing?

She rose and crossed to the windows looking over the driveway. Alex was driving a Jeep. Until now she hadn't even known he had a car here.

Her sense of unease deepened.

And then…as his Jeep approached the rhododendron drive she saw two men in suits step out of the shadows. Alex stopped to talk to them. He motioned towards the house—up to her window—and she shrank back against the curtains.

When she looked again his Jeep had disappeared and the men were melting back into the shadows.

Security?

What had she got herself into?

She needed to get out of here. If he thought she was going to sit here calmly and wait for him…

She wouldn't speak to the press. She'd go and find Spiros. She could have fun helping him set up his boatyard.

It'd be more fun than sitting here waiting.

Maybe that was what royal princesses did—sat and waited for their men to have time for them.

Not this one.

CHAPTER TWELVE

By the time Lily had figured out the car, the baby seat, the logistics of getting the garage roller door raised, she was more than flustered. She was fuming.

It was all very well for Alex to buy her a car and blithely say *go visit your friends if you want*. But he didn't have to juggle strollers, baby bottles, diaper bags and a baby who decided just as she strapped him into the car that he had other plans. Which necessitated taking him out of the car, heading for the bathroom, then figuring out a whole new wardrobe for both of them.

'Though it's just as well we weren't halfway down the coast road,' she told Michales ruefully. 'I want Spiros to be pleased to see me.'

But at last she was ready.

As she swung out into the rhododendron drive, a grey saloon swung in behind her. It stayed about a hundred yards behind, speeding up when she speeded up, slowing when she slowed.

Was this something she had to get accustomed to?

'These'll be your father's heavies,' she told Michales. 'Where were they when you needed changing or when I was trying to fold up the stroller?' She glowered into the rear-view mirror. 'If you guys intend to stick with me, your job description's about to change.'

But, inexplicably, her mood was lifting. The morning was gorgeous. The sun was sparkling off the ocean like the diamonds that had given the isles their name. The islands of Khryseis and Argyros looked mysterious and wonderful on the horizon. They were nations now in their own right. When she had a boat she could explore them.

'With my bodyguards chuffing along behind me,' she reminded herself and managed a grin.

Defiant, she slowed, opened the sun roof and hit the sound system. Hey! Alex had set Abba on for her.

He was a very nice man, she decided. And so sexy he made her toes curl. Her very own prince!

She hit 'play' and sang along at the top of her voice, grinning at Michales in the rear-view mirror.

Happy—yet defiant.

That was how she felt. Not a princess, she thought. Just…normal.

So what did Alex think he was doing, supplying her with a luxury car and a couple of bodyguards, then going off to play banker?

Maybe she was being unfair.

This was what Mia and her mother had spent their lives trying to achieve, she thought. Fame. Riches.

Lily's aim of independence came a very poor third.

But I don't want to be independent any more, a small voice whispered in the back of her head.

Just as well, she thought. When she was followed by security men. When she wasn't allowed to talk to the press.

Her vague sense of unease deepened. Was what had happened over the last three days a fantasy?

She slowed as she passed the palace. Somewhere within that vast confection of turrets, towers and general ostentation was Alex. Trying to sort things out.

Without her.

So he still had his independence. While she stayed…where she was supposed to stay.

'I don't want to stay in the palace,' she told Michales but she knew she was lying.

Where you go, I will go, and where you lodge,
I will lodge, your people shall be my people...

Ruth had it right, Lily thought. Where her love went, there was her home.

She'd fallen so deeply in love that if Alex needed to live surrounded by chandeliers—or if he needed to live in Manhattan—then that was where she should be, too.

He didn't want her. Not like that.

She couldn't sustain her happiness. The unease was too great. For the last three days she'd allowed herself to believe in happy endings.

Today was the beginning of reality.

Alex pulled up in the castle courtyard. Nikos was waiting. He'd asked his cousin to be here.

'Hey,' Nikos said, strolling across the forecourt to grasp his friend's hand. 'How goes it?'

'Fine,' Alex said. And then he grinned. 'Maybe even great. I'm thinking we have a chance of getting this sorted. Thanks for doing this for me. I didn't want to face these vultures alone.'

'I thought you had Lily here,' Nikos said.

'She's over at the hideaway.'

'She didn't want to be here?'

'This is nothing to do with her.'

'Right,' Nikos said. Then he shook his head. 'Nope. Not right. Aren't you two married?'

'Yeah, but…'

'Then she's supposed to be here.'

'You think Lily will understand one part of what these guys are saying?'

'You think I will?'

'You're here for moral support.'

'Right,' Nikos said again, dryly, contenting himself with a quizzical look without further comment. He took his friend's arm. 'Okay, let's go. But, before we do this, there's something you should see.'

'What?'

'Lily's mother is in Athens. Mia's mother. She's been talking to the press. If you and Lily aren't having problems already, I suspect you're about to now.'

Okay, she wasn't speaking to the press but Alex hadn't forbidden her to shop.

Feeling strange and self-conscious and more than a little nervous, Lily swung the big car into Sappheiros's main shopping square.

She was feeling ever so slightly defiant. She might do something really shocking. Like…like buying sexy lingerie.

There was a thought.

She found herself grinning, shoving the unease aside. Do it, she told herself.

She parked. Her grey shadow parked two cars up, and two grey-suited men climbed out.

She emerged from the car and waved to them. They looked taken aback.

'Can one of you guys unfold my stroller?' she called, hauling it out of the trunk and looking at it as if it were a weapon of mass destruction. How could a stroller be so complicated?

The men hesitated. Clearly they'd been told to stay in the background.

'Are you guys paid to look after me or not?' she demanded, and they looked at each other and finally the oldest shrugged.

'Yes, ma'am.'

'Hooray,' she said, unclipping Michales from his car seat. 'Then we'd appreciate some help. His Highness, Prince Michales, has no transport until his stroller is erected.'

Two minutes later she had Michales in his stroller. She was wandering along the shop fronts.

Everyone was looking at her.

She wasn't half obvious, she thought dryly. Young mum taking baby for a walk, with two beefcakes following about three feet behind.

She stopped. She turned. 'Do you guys ever back off?'

'We're not permitted to let you out of our sight,' one said.

'Fine,' she said and glowered and, before they knew what she was doing, she'd pushed the stroller back to them. 'I'm off to buy a newspaper and then find somewhere to buy a coffee. You can stare at me through the café window if you must. Take care of His Highness.'

She'd meant it as a joke. She was going to buy herself a newspaper and then return to Michales before she bought her coffee.

Only… Only…

Thanks to her father's love of scholarship, she could read Greek. Not well, but enough.

The photograph caught her eye before she'd even purchased the paper. She picked it up numbly.

Grey Suit Two was suddenly beside her, pulling out his wallet. 'We pay,' he said.

'Like hell you do,' she muttered, still staring in horror at the front page. But then she realised she had no choice. She'd had not a moment since she'd arrived on the island to arrange currency conversion. 'Okay. Pay for them all,' she said, motioning to the array of newspapers on the counter. 'I'll pay you back later. And, while you're at it, kindly give me enough money for a coffee. Then leave me alone. Look after Michales and don't come near me.'

And then she thought she sounded like Mia. She winced. Royal arrogance was so not her thing.

'And buy yourselves coffee,' she called after him. 'And something to eat. Whatever you fancy. I'll reimburse you for that, too.'

Feeling a tiny bit better, she found a coffee shop. It looked nice and dark in its recesses—a Diamond Isles version of Ye Olde Nautical Coffee Shoppe. The patrons were shadows. It was so gloomy the girl behind the counter didn't recognise her.

Which was excellent. She was starting to crave anonymity.

She found a seat at the furthermost table and started reading the papers.

And stopped feeling better.

The girl brought her coffee. She swallowed the first mouthful so fast she burnt her mouth.

She had three papers spread out around her now. Their headlines shouted, in sequence:

'My Triumph: Two Royal Daughters.'

And:

'My Clever Lily—Taught to be a Princess From Birth.'

And:

'Alexandros Never Stood A Chance Against My Princess Lily.'

Here it all was, laid out for the world to see. Her mother's naked ambition. Her mother's connivance, her ruthlessness, her fight to get the glory for her daughters that she felt she'd been cheated of herself.

Her mother was the second daughter of the second daughter of a princess. If only she'd been the first son of a first son of a king… She spelled it out. Her anger and humiliation at being raised as second-rate royalty. Her betrayal by her husband, who should have been richer, should have enjoyed the limelight his aristocratic birth entitled him to. Her fight to get Mia to where she should be in the world and her pride that Mia had gone from being Queen to being fabulously rich as well.

And now…and here was the implication… through incredible planning, forethought, cunning, here was Lily, her second daughter, claiming the throne in turn. Not as Queen but Crown Princess. Almost as good as her sister.

This, according to her mother, was the culmination of a family dream. She was travelling now to be with her. Her clever daughter.

Lily felt sick.

The girl came up to collect her coffee cup. She stared at the papers and then she stared more closely at Lily.

'It is,' she breathed.

'It is what?' Lily said dully.

'You're her.' The girl pointed to a picture of Lily, inset on a much larger picture of her mother looking triumphant. 'You're Princess Lily.'

'I'm not a princess.'

'Oh, but you are,' the girl breathed. 'I'd love to be a princess. I read the papers after your wedding. There was a picture of you on the beach with your baby, and I thought you looked lovely. You looked like it could even be a marriage for love.' She sighed theatrically. 'But now your mother tells us how it really is…' She clasped her hands over her heart. 'My Carlos is a fisherman and he's poor, but even if a prince offered, I'd give him up for my Carlos. Your prince has to marry you for honour. I see that. But my Carlos will marry me for love.'

She carried away Lily's empty cup with her moral high ground, and Lily was left feeling even more sick.

She went back to the papers.

There was no condemnation of Alex. Alex was seen as virtuous for having done the right thing

under extraordinary circumstances. He was
morally fine.

Michales remained heir to the throne. He was
okay, too.

But she wasn't. Lily was now being portrayed
as another of these women who sold themselves
to the highest bidder.

There was resigned acceptance. Alexandros
was a good man, the editorials advised. An honourable man. The country was counselled to put
their distaste for Lily and her family aside and get
on with life.

Outside, Bodyguard One and Bodyguard Two
were pacing the pavement with the stroller, taking
smaller and smaller circuits of the shopping strip.
They were staring in at her with increased hostility.

Had they read the newspapers as well?

This was what they expected of her, she thought
dully. That she might abandon Michales, too?

She read on, feeling worse and worse. At the
end of the last editorial was a comment, almost
an aside:

This newspaper has heard rumours that
Prince Alexandros has been asked to take part
in a prestigious gardening project in the US.
If Alexandros decides to leave any of his royal
duties to this woman, we wish to register a

very strong protest. Princess Lily has made an extremely advantageous marriage. Let her be content with that. We note the Prince has not brought this woman to the palace. So be it. Let this woman and her objectionable mother stay out of our lives.

And finally... There was a picture of three rings—the caption labelled them the rings of the Diamond Isles. The Sappheiros ring was sapphire with three diamonds. The Argyros ring was silver with three diamonds. The Khryseis ring was gold, again with three diamonds.

Apparently they'd been locked in a bank vault for generations, only for use by the Crown Princess of each country.

They were...exquisite.

The editorial went on:

Let the women who wear these rings be truly deserving of the honour. They've sat in the bank vaults since Giorgos's forebears dissolved the principalities. We note Alexandros did not use the Sappheiros ring on the occasion of his marriage. Now we understand why.

She stared down at the plain gold band on her finger for a long time—then twisted it off and shoved it to the bottom of her jeans pocket.

Her cellphone rang. She answered it absently, still staring at a full face photograph of her mother. Her mother? The woman who smirked up from the photograph didn't deserve the title.

'Lily?'

Alex. Of course it was Alex. She was out in the public eye, disobeying orders. It was a wonder her phone had stayed silent this long.

Let this woman and her objectionable mother stay out of our lives.

'Have you seen the papers?' he demanded.

'I'm reading them now. What "prestigious gardening project"?'

'That's nothing. Your mother…'

'Is being objectionable. Of course. What project?'

'Can you ask her to shut up?'

That was it. No apology. No thought that this might hurt.

'I haven't spoken to my mother for five years.'

'She's still your mother.'

'So she says.'

He got it then. The anger. She heard him register, regroup. Even turn placatory. 'What she said…it doesn't make any difference,' he told her.

'Of course it makes a difference.'

'If she's nothing to do with you. .'

'I'm still her daughter. One of her two daughters, both of whom are on the take. Do you think I'll sit back and let your country think that of me?'

'It's nonsense. Lily, they'll see you're different.'

'While you go back and forth to Manhattan and keep on with your very prestigious project. That you haven't talked to me about.'

She heard a sharp intake of breath. Then...

'Lily, I need to organise...'

'Of course you need to organise,' she cut in. 'I don't need an explanation.'

'Lily, what is this? The guys tell me you're sitting in a public café. Can people hear?'

'Of course they can hear,' she said, looking around as she spoke and realising that every person in the café was listening. The waitress had turned off the radio. Her words were being broadcast to an audience.

Whatever she said now would be carried from one end of the island to the other by nightfall, she realised. So be it. If she was intending to be resolute, the time was now.

'I'm on my way to Spiros's boatyard,' she said, speaking distinctly in Greek so every occupant of the café could understand. 'And then I'll talk to the local realtors. I need a house somewhere down by the harbour.'

There was a stunned silence. Then, 'Lily, what are you talking about?'

'My future. As a boat-builder.'

'We'll be living in the palace.'

'You'll be living wherever you want to live, but I want a home for me and Michales. I'm not talking money. A bedsit will do fine. I'm not my mother's daughter, Alex, no matter what the press says.'

'I never said you were.'

'It doesn't matter what you said. It's what the islanders believe. But I'm *not* her daughter.'

She was getting loud. Good. She felt like yelling. She felt like picking up chairs and flinging them through windows.

For the last few days she'd been exploring this wonderful new sensation of having a life. A future. Michales and Alex both.

But marriage to Alex was a fairy tale. She'd been kidding herself. Fairy tales were for children's books. What Alex was planning for her was no fairy tale. Living in the palace as a princess, with the islanders hating her and Alex coming and going as he pleased. Or being left in his hideaway while he did…whatever he wanted to do.

'I've married you so Michales can stay as your legitimate heir, and so you can govern,' she said, feeling cold and sick but knowing she had to say this. 'But that's all. I'm not a princess. I'll live in a house by the harbour. You can have all the access you want to Michales, as long as he comes home to me every night. But the royalty bit is yours. Do whatever you want but don't factor me in. Now, if you'll excuse me, I need to find Spiros. We have a future together. You and I don't.'

Alex had another meeting scheduled, in what…three minutes? Nikos couldn't handle this alone.

He needed to get down to the docks and talk to her.

'She can build her boats while she lives here,' he muttered but he knew this was a deeper problem.

The butler entered, carrying iced water in an exquisite crystal glass on a silver tray. The elderly servant raised his brow in a question, thinking he'd been talking to him.

'Sir?'

Hell, he had to talk to someone. 'The Princess Lily,' he snapped. 'She stays here.'

'Of course,' the man said. 'Will her mother be staying here, too, sir?'

'No!'

'Queen Mia's mother has her own apartment here.'

'Board it up,' Alex snapped. 'It won't be needed. That woman comes here over my dead body.'

'And…the Princess Lily?'

'She's saying the same thing about herself,' he growled. 'Which is a nonsense.'

'The country wouldn't mind if she didn't live here,' the man said diffidently. 'The islanders understand this is a marriage of convenience.'

'That's what she thinks.'

'It's what everybody thinks,' the man said, and then gave a discreet cough and glanced at his watch. 'Your meeting, sir.'

'Damn my meeting.'

'It's the bankers from Switzerland. They hold the titles to…'

'I know damn well what they hold the titles to. Nikos can take over. I need to go…'

'To the docks?' the man said, raising his brow politely again.

'Yes. And I won't need a chauffeur,' he snapped. 'This is between Lily and me.'

'Yes, sir,' the man said woodenly and stood, waiting.

'What are you waiting for?'

'To collect your glass.'

'How much are these glasses worth?' Alex said, in a voice his friends would have recognised as dangerous.

'They're antique,' the man said. 'Priceless.'

'So if I tossed it into the fireplace…'

'You could well create a scandal.'

'Use plastic ones.'

'Pardon?'

'Or, better still, jam jars. I can smash jam jars.'

'I don't know if…'

'Of course you have jam jars,' he snapped. 'You have jam for breakfast, don't you?'

'King Giorgos favoured smoked salmon.'

'Well, here's my first household order as new ruler,' Alex growled, sounding like a man driven. 'I want jam for breakfast. In jars. This might be a palace but it has to be a home as well.'

'Yes, sir.' Not a muscle quivered. 'But, sir, the meeting… I don't believe Nikos can…'

'I don't believe Nikos can either,' he said and sighed and set his glass—carefully—on the silver tray. 'I'll deal with the titles. It'll take hours but they have to be sorted. But Lily straight after.'

'Yes, sir. I'll tell them you're ready.' He walked out of the room in stately style—but paused at the entrance. 'And the Princess Lily's mother? She's contacted the staff to say she'll be here on the afternoon ferry. Did you…er…mean it about your dead body?'

'I guess not.'

But then he hesitated. Something told him he

needed to get this right. Lily's mother. He thought for a minute. He thought of what this woman had done. Lily's mother? Did she deserve the title?

'Or maybe…yes,' he said slowly. 'Maybe I did mean it. Where is it that Mia's living now?'

'I believe she's still in Dubai.'

'Dubai.' He grimaced. 'Damn, I don't have time…'

The man coughed. Discreetly. This discretion was like another language.

Maybe he ought to listen.

'Yes?' he said.

'If I may venture a suggestion, sir,' the butler said. 'If you're under pressure… There are some things you can't delegate but you have a full staff here waiting to serve you. Until now you've used us reluctantly. But…' he met Alex's gaze square on '…but it would be a privilege for us to actually serve you.'

Alex stared at him, bemused.

A full staff…waiting to work for him.

He was royal.

It would be a privilege for us to actually serve you.

He hadn't figured it until now. Until right now.

It cut both ways.

'I have a palace secretary,' he said slowly.

'Yes, sir.'

'Giorgos's man?'

'I believe he would wish to serve *you*,' the man said, still discreet but his message was crystal clear. 'As you wish to serve the islanders.'

'And the Princess Lily?'

'If she's truly to be your wife, then that service would, of course, extend to her.'

'Then send him in,' Alex said slowly. 'Tell the Swiss guys I'll be with them in ten minutes… Give them something stronger than water in those ridiculous glasses—and yes, I'll need a fast car and a chauffeur as soon as the meeting finishes. But dammit,' he added, 'I meant what I said about the jam.'

The man's wooden countenance cracked, just a little. He allowed himself an infinitesimal echo of a smile.

'Yes, Your Highness. Certainly, Your Highness,' he said and left, closing the door carefully after him.

It took five hours.

Five hours spent beginning to sort out the mess that was the island's financial affairs might not seem long, but they were the longest hours Alex could remember. But finally he was free. Finally he could drive down to the harbour. Or be driven. Fast. By a driver who looked as if things were finally slotting into the natural order.

But Alex didn't have time to think about order. He strode into Spiros's boatshed and stared in astonishment.

Lily was underneath a boat.

He'd had this place set up for Spiros. It was a great little shed, right on the main Sappheiros harbour. Last time he'd seen it, it had been empty, waiting for its new tenant.

Now it contained six men, two women and one baby. They were clustered around what he recognised as his boat. He could see where it had been towed in—sand and bits of rotten timber had trailed in its wake.

How on earth had she got it here so fast?

Lily was at work already. She'd wriggled under the bow of the dinghy and was prodding each plank in turn, while everyone else watched from the sides.

'It's a great project to start with,' she was saying to Spiros. 'This'll keep us happy until we get the materials to start bigger projects.'

'Lily.'

She hadn't seen him enter. He saw her freeze at the sound of his voice. Her expression became almost defiant—and then she went back to what she was doing.

'We can restore it exactly as it was,' she said,

only the faintest of tremors acknowledging his presence. 'See these joins? See how they slot together? That's real craftsmanship. The guys who built this really knew their stuff. I need to do some research before we start.'

'We have an Internet connection at the palace,' Alex said loudly into the silence.

'That's right,' she responded, as if he were just another voice from the outside. 'I'll need an Internet connection at my house.' She was being as businesslike with him as she was with Spiros.

'You won't need anything at your house. We need to live at the palace.'

He was ignored. 'My laptop's a bit old but it should be okay. Can we get broadband at the harbour?'

'I said we'll live at the palace.'

Finally she acknowledged him. She hauled herself out from under the boat, pulled herself upright and dusted herself off.

'No,' she said simply, 'I'll not live at the palace.'

'Why not?'

'My mother's living at the palace. Haven't you seen the papers?'

He shook his head. 'She won't be.'

'She said…'

'No matter what she said.'

This conversation should be private, but first he had to break through this icy indifference. 'There's a generous lifetime allowance allocated to Mia as Giorgos's widow,' he told her. He told them all. 'I'm the administrator. This morning I converted part of it into a permanent travel fund for your mother. She's been handed first class air tickets to Dubai, and hotel vouchers. The travel allowance will be ongoing. Wherever Mia moves, the funds will pay for flights and luxurious accommodation so your mother and Mia can stay together for ever.'

There was a deathly hush. The onlookers didn't understand.

Lily understood. Her anger faltered. She gazed at him in awe. And…magically, the beginning of laughter.

'They'll kill each other,' she whispered at last.

'Excellent.' He ventured a smile.

Which was maybe a mistake. 'Don't you dare smile at me,' she snapped. She was obviously trying to haul herself together. Remembering where she was—remembering her grievances. 'What you've done for my mother…it's all very well, but if you think you can buy me…'

'I never thought I could buy you.'

'You're going to Manhattan. While I stay in the palace? No way.'

'We need to talk about that.'

'We don't,' she said crossly.

'I have to talk to you.'

'So who's going to make me?' she said softly.

There was a stifled laugh from the onlookers. This was an impossible conversation to have in public.

'Please, Lily. I need to talk to you alone.'

'I'm busy.'

'Mending *my* boat.'

'Don't you want it mended?'

'Yes, but…'

'There you go then. Can we send you the account? Spiros, this can be our first local commission.'

'Lily!'

'Yes…Your Highness?' she said, raising her brows in mute enquiry. 'Was there anything else you wanted?'

'I want you!'

'I don't see why.'

She turned her back on him, talking to Spiros. 'Let's write up a list of materials we need,' she said. 'You want to do it in your office? Eleni, can you take care of Michales for a few more minutes? If you'll excuse us…'

He moved, barring her way. She was back in her bib-and-brace overalls and her baseball cap. Did she have any idea how cute she looked? Did she have any idea how desperate she made him feel? Or how inadequate. 'Lily, I need to talk to you. Now!'

'Maybe you'd better listen,' Eleni said uneasily. 'His Highness has been very good to us.'

'To you. Maybe not to me.'

'He brought you to this place,' Eleni said. 'He's making you a princess.'

'I don't want to be a princess.'

'Every girl wants to be a princess,' Eleni said.

'Would you want to be a princess?' Lily demanded, rounding on Eleni. 'If it meant not being married to Spiros.'

Eleni gazed at her in confusion. 'Spiros is… different.'

'How different?'

'He's Spiros,' she said, looking at her rotund and balding husband with affection. 'He loves me,' Eleni said. 'This isn't a fair comparison.'

'It's not, is it,' Lily agreed. She turned back to Alex. 'See? Spiros loves Eleni. There's no negotiation there. They went to America together. They came here together.'

'You're saying you want to go to Manhattan?'

She shook her head, looking angry. 'You don't want me in that part of your life,' she said flatly. 'And the islanders don't want me in their face either. But it's okay. The realtor's been here and he's shown me the perfect house. Two bedrooms, so Michales and I don't have to share unless we want, and it overlooks the harbour. We'll live happily ever after. Now, if we could get on…'

'Lily, talk to me,' he said through gritted teeth, and Eleni grinned and gave Lily a push in the small of her back.

'Go with him before he explodes,' she advised. 'He's very close to exploding. I can see this.'

'It doesn't matter if he does explode.'

'It'd make a mess,' Eleni retorted. 'As did hauling in this boat. Why you had to tell Spiros about it today… You knew he wouldn't rest until he had it. So off you go, the pair of you. Spiros,' she said sharply, 'help me.'

And suddenly Spiros was behind Alex, Eleni was behind Lily and they were being propelled out of the boatshed. They were outside before they had a chance to argue, and the boatshed doors were slammed shut behind them.

So they were suddenly out on the docks. The berths were all empty. A lone seagull was preening itself on a bollard. Water lapped against the pilings.

There was no one in sight.

'Where…where are all the fishing boats?' Lily asked, sounding desperate, looking desperate.

'Out fishing. Lily, you can't do this.'

'I can,' she said gamely. 'I will. My house is over there.' She pointed across the harbour. 'It's the one with window boxes. It's not only you who'll have a garden.'

'Do you really want to live alone?'

'With Michales. But yes.'

'Why?'

'Because I'm not about to follow my mother's and my sister's example. I hadn't realised it until I saw the newspapers—how much damage they did. But do you think I can stay around as your wife now?'

'Of course you can.'

'When you're not here?'

He was trying his hardest to figure this out.

He'd thought he had it figured on the way here. He did have it sorted. He loved this woman. They could do this. But the explanations he'd prepared seemed to have disappeared into confusion.

'I will need to leave you sometimes,' he said slowly. He wasn't about to lie to her now. 'If you have your boat-building… I need something. I can't only be a prince.'

'That's just it,' she said, indignation fading. 'I have no right to expect anything. It's a token marriage.'

He shook his head. 'How can it be a token marriage when we share a bed? When you've asked me to be faithful and I've taken the same promise from you?'

'I shouldn't have done either. Alex, please, I've been out of control for too long. What I want is to get my life together. I had this notion back at your lovely house that I could sink into your life—make it my own. Only, of course, that's dumb. I don't want the people of the Diamond Isles looking at me the same way they look at Mia and my mother. I have to carve my own way.'

'And I fit in where?'

'Nowhere,' she said forlornly. 'Not as your wife. I've been trying to figure it out and I can't see it. For you to be a part-time prince and leave me as a full-time princess...'

'You do want me to stay here all the time?'

'I don't want you to do anything.' She was close to tears. 'I have no right to want anything of you, other than support for Michales. I need nothing.'

'You deserve everything.'

'I have everything,' she said, flatly but surely. She tilted her face so the sun shone full on it. 'I have my son. I have my life. I have a career I love, in one of the most beautiful settings in the world. What more can I ask for?'

'Me.' It was an egotistical answer—maybe

dumb—but it was what he needed to say. He wanted her to want him.

He wanted this woman.

But she was shaking her head. 'I daren't ask that,' she whispered. 'Because if I let myself ask…'

'I might just give?'

'Would you?' she asked. 'How much would you give?'

He was struggling here, trying to work out where she was going. Trying to understand. This morning he'd woken up beside her and the world had been at his feet. But now…

He'd pushed it too hard. He knew he had. But how to get it back?

She looked…scared, he thought. Angry and defiant but, deep down, terrified.

Should he back off?

How could he back off? What would happen if their marriage was simply in name only?

He'd be gutted.

A marriage of convenience…

What the hell was he doing?

A memory came back, piercing into his conscience from a time he'd tried desperately to block. His mother, lying on a bed of pillows on one of the ledges jutting out from a rock path leading to the sea. She'd been back on the island for such a short time before she'd become ill. They'd planned their garden together, and he was building it. It was all he could do for her.

He'd been planting the rock wall with scented geraniums. She'd called down to him. He'd looked up, his hands covered with loam—filthy, happy, the sun on his face, where he most wanted to be in the world.

'Mama?'

'I love you,' she'd said, so softly he hardly heard. 'No, don't stop what you're doing. It's just…I thought it and I needed to tell you… It's the only important thing and you need to remember it. I love you.'

Two months later she was dead, and somehow the message she'd given him had been…not forgotten exactly, for it had helped mould who he was. But he hadn't thought of that love as extending from what he and his mother had shared.

Only of course it had extended. As love must.

Loving. He had it, right here, in this woman before him—his Lily, looking at him now, troubled, battered by her mother's betrayal, confused and hurt by what he'd done this morning but, even in her confusion, looking to the future. Trying to make the best of what he'd given her.

This woman was his wife. What was he doing, messing with it?

Start with Lily, he told himself, feeling dazed.

'Alex, what is it?'

'I wasn't going to Manhattan to work on a project,' he told her. 'I never was.'

'You were going…'

'To wind up the company. To put it into the hands of a couple of competent employees, and to offer to keep a role as offshore consultant. I thought I might be able to go over occasionally…but not often.'

'There's no need…'

'There is a need,' he said softly. 'I should have told you. And I should have asked you, too. Lily, will you marry me?'

Marry…

He obviously wasn't making sense. She stood in the afternoon sun and she stared at him as if he were speaking an unknown language.

Maybe he was.

'I've already married you,' she whispered.

'Yes, but it wasn't right.'

'I don't know what you mean.'

'I think you do.' He caught her hands and held. 'It wasn't true. This time I want to stand before a priest I know and love, beside a woman I know and love, and I want to make my vows and keep them.'

'But…why…?'

'Your illness…'

'No,' she snapped and the sudden flare of hope in her face disappeared to nothing. 'Don't you dare feel sorry for me.'

She tried to drag her hands away but he wasn't releasing them.

'No, Lily, wait. I'm not saying this because I feel sorry for you. How can I feel sorry when I'm so proud I'm close to bursting with pride? That a woman like you would stoop to marry me... Lily, we did this the wrong way round. I married you as a royal bride. I stood before the islanders and said you were my wife. And then I took you home to a place which can't be our home. It's a place where we can stay hidden, it's a place for time out, but now's not the time for hiding.'

'But I don't want...'

'You don't want to be a princess by yourself,' he said, still sure that he was right. 'But what if you weren't by yourself? What if you were half of a whole...half of the ruling royal couple of Sappheiros...?'

'The islanders would never agree.'

'They never will if you stay hidden. Lily, I'm asking you again. I want to marry you, but this time I want it to be between us. I want to declare my love for you. And then I want to start making reparation for both of us.'

'Both...'

'We've been robbed,' he said slowly. 'It's taken me a while to see it but now I do. Royalty robbed me of my childhood. My mother had to leave me behind and I've blamed more than Giorgos for that loss. I blamed this role. I blamed royalty. I wanted desperately to help the islanders, to rule so I could set things right, but I didn't want to commit myself. That's how I married you.'

'So what's changed now?'

'You,' he said softly and tugged her in so her breasts rested against his chest. 'I nearly had it. I thought this morning that I'd head to Manhattan and close things up there, then come back and see what I could do. Only I should have told you, asked you to come with me. I had a hell of a day with financiers and that was daft, too. You know why? Because I had Nikos there, trying desperately to be a friend, to understand. Only he has problems of his own on Argyros. You know who should have been there? You.'

'You think I could understand financiers?' She was bewildered, he thought. He wasn't explaining this right.

'No,' he said lovingly. 'No one could understand that lot. I've set my lawyers onto them. But they had to talk to me first and I came away hornswoggled…'

'Hornswoggled…'

'Hornswoggled,' he repeated. 'Great word. Pity it's not Greek. But I wanted to be hornswoggled with you, and the only person I had was Nikos—and he was busy telling me I'd done everything wrong. But, Lily, I'm losing track here. I love you. Will you marry me?'

He was holding her at arm's length so he could watch her face. He was watching her confusion. He was aching for it to disappear.

'I guess I don't have to ask you to marry me,' he conceded. 'Not officially, for you've already done that. But what I want now… I want more. I want you to trust me.'

She nodded. The confusion was fading. She was as serious as he was. 'That's a very different thing.'

'So?'

'I think I already do trust you,' she whispered but he shook his head.

'You don't trust me to care for you. You don't trust me to be beside you, whatever life throws at either of us. You've been alone all your life. You expect more of the same. You say you want to live down at the harbour. Do you really want to live on your own?'

'No, but…'

'But if you live with me, you'll be fearful that it'll be on my terms.'

'That's reasonable. You don't want…'

'It's not reasonable,' he said. 'I've just figured it out. I want you to live with me, but on your terms.'

'Alex, you're a prince.'

'I am a prince,' he said softly. 'But what does that mean? I need to earn the respect of my people, as I need to gain your respect and trust. Can I start with you and work my way out? Can we marry for real?

'For we're not properly married,' he said. 'You didn't walk down the aisle with Spiros to give you away. We didn't get married in front of Father Antonio. And we didn't go straight to the palace and stand on the balcony and wave and kiss each other in front of the whole island and I didn't say to the world I'm so proud of you that if anything, anyone, even implies that you're not totally perfect I'll have them tossed into a good deep dungeon for high treason.'

'A dungeon,' she said faintly. 'Do we have dungeons?'

'I'll have them dug on the off chance,' he said grandly. 'Lily, what do you say?'

'I…'

'I love you, Lily,' he said hurriedly, before she had a chance to answer. 'This is the most important moment in my life. I stared at those newspaper headlines this morning and I thought that if I were you I'd walk away and never come back. And I wouldn't blame you. I might have known you'd do the noble thing instead. Move out, stay married, take the flak but get on with your own life as best you could. Lily, please, could you include me?'

'Um…okay,' she ventured and he held her back at arm's length so he could look into her eyes.

'Just okay?'

'Okay, Your Majesty?' she tried.

'Not…okay, my love?'

'You want me to be a princess.'

'Not *a* princess. *My* princess.'

'You'll be my prince.'

'That's the idea.'

'Does that mean I have to take off my dungarees?'

'For the wedding, maybe, but afterwards… I see us as the people's prince and princess,' he said and he pulled her against him and was holding her so their hearts were suddenly beating in synch. She could feel it. Magic.

Magic!

Move over, Cinderella, she thought. This prince is mine!

'So where does that leave us?' she whispered.

'It leaves us planning our future,' he said, awed

by the vision. 'In between government duties I'll design gardens from one end of this island to the other. When I finish here I'll start on the gardens of Argyros and Khryseis. And, as for you… The fishing fleet on the three islands is in shocking condition. Shocking!'

'Really?' she whispered, starting to smile.

'You'll be appalled when you see. I think you have a job for life.'

'I love you,' she said.

'You do?'

'I do.'

'Will you say that in front of Father Antonio?'

'I'll say that in front of the world if you want me to.'

'So you'll marry me? Properly? With your heart?'

There was only one answer to that. 'When?'

'How about now? If I can get Father Antonio away from his fishing, if there's no funeral and if he has a clean cassock… Why not now?'

'Just…just us?'

'And Nikos to hold me up,' he said promptly. 'He'll never forgive me otherwise. Stefanos is in New York, but we're not waiting that long.'

'We need a photographer,' she whispered, her eyes alive with laughter. And something else. A joy so great he could see it.

'Why would we want a photographer?'

'Because this is a real wedding,' she said and, astonishingly, she was starting to sound efficient. 'I need photographs to show our grandchildren.' Then she paused—and blushed. 'I mean…eventually Michales might have children. I might even be a grandma. I might…'

And he watched her eyes widen as the implication of what they were about to do sank in.

He laughed. He felt as if the weight of the world had shifted from his shoulders.

They could do this. Together they could face their future and plan and laugh and love.

'What if we let the two reporters who met us on the beach know what's happening?' he suggested. 'A scoop.'

'Wow,' Lily said and she was smiling. A chameleon smile—from anger to laughter in seconds. 'Okay. Deal. Can I tell Spiros and Eleni? They'll have to come.'

'I suspect they've guessed,' he said wryly and glanced at the boatshed door—which closed very quickly. 'Spiros will give you away? What about in three hours? Seven o'clock. Right on sunset. The photographs will be fabulous, for us or for our grandchildren. If I can find Father Antonio.'

Her smile didn't fade. 'You'll have to do the organisation,' she warned. 'I have sawdust under my fingernails. A girl has some pride. You go find the priest and I'll go let Eleni turn me into a bride.'

'Lily…'

'Mmm?'

He kissed her gently on the lips. Tenderly. Then he set her back from him again. There was still something he needed to say. 'Lily, I want the islanders to know the truth about you.'

'The truth…'

'I will not let them go one minute more than I must, thinking you abandoned your son. Please… will you trust me to tell them?'

'I don't like…'

'I know you don't like,' he said. 'But the time for protecting your mother and your sister is past. We need to move forward and the only way we can do this is with truth. Do you trust me to tell your story?'

He was looking at her with such gravitas… Her Alexandros.

'I trust you with my heart,' she whispered. 'With my life.'

'It's the greatest gift a man can be given,' he said and pressed her hand to his heart. 'And I'll honour it as long as I breathe.'

CHAPTER THIRTEEN

Alex left.

The door of the boatshed opened.

Maybe she had to move. Maybe she had to speak.

'Eleni?' she ventured but the word came out a squeak.

Eleni was the closest thing to a mother Lily knew. Alex had brought Spiros and his family here as part of her future. These people were her future.

She couldn't do this without them.

'What is it?' Eleni demanded, looking torn between awe and fear. 'Lily, what's happened? You haven't sent him away?'

'Just for a bit,' Lily confessed. 'Until seven.'

'What's happening at seven?'

'That's something I thought I might talk to you about,' she said, suddenly feeling absurd. Dumb. Crazy.

'What?'

She walked back into the boatshed. She had the attention of everyone, including the men who worked for Spiros.

'I thought I might get married,' she said, and the silence was deafening. 'Sort of like last time,' she added, sounding defensive. 'Only different. Only…' She gasped and could hardly go on. 'Only for ever.'

More silence. More and more silence.

And then… 'At seven,' Eleni said at last, and this time it was Eleni's voice that came out a high-pitched squeak.

'I need a dress,' Lily told her.

'The one you wore last time?' Eleni said.

'That was everybody's dress. The royal bridal gown. I want my own.'

'In three hours.' Eleni was squealing for real now. 'In three… Look at you!'

'Don't I look like a bride?'

'You're making fun, no?'

'No,' she said, and got serious. 'This is for real. But I want you all there.'

Another long silence. Then, 'Spiros,' Eleni said, rounding on her husband. 'Take a bath.'

'Whaa…?'

'Take a bath,' she ordered. 'Now. It'll take until seven to get the grease off you. You can sit right up the back and…'

'I want Spiros to give me away.'

There was another of those deathly hushes. She was getting used to them.

She looked round at their faces—at their open mouths—and she giggled.

It was either giggle or faint, she thought. She was hysterical, either way.

'Can we do it?' she asked Eleni, and Eleni stared at her for another full, long minute. Lily could practically see lists being written. And then she nodded.

'Yes,' she said at last. 'Shops first. A dress. A dress so fast. Ooh, I want to see the faces of the shopkeepers.'

'They don't like me,' she said.

'You're a princess. They'll love you. They don't know you, is all. Spiros, bath. Boys, get into town. I want flowers. Soft and romantic—tell the florist what it's for and she'll break an arm to get it right. Bouquet for Lily, sprays for me, and single roses for the men…' Eleni was already on item three on her list and working down.

This wedding was going to happen.

Nikos was still at the castle. He was deep in a pile of paperwork, looking put upon.

'I'd rather be fishing,' he said soulfully as Alex entered. 'This ruling business has knobs on it.'

'You need a break,' Alex said. 'How about a wedding?'

Nikos had been entering figures in a ledger. His hand paused mid-pen-stroke. He turned and looked at his friend, long and hard. 'Have you been out in the sun?' he asked slowly.

'No,' Alex said and then he grinned. 'Actually, come to think of it, I have.'

'So whose wedding?'

'Mine.'

'I thought we just did yours.'

'This is sort of a rerun. We're doing it properly this time.'

'I…see,' Nikos said, nodding to hide any confusion he just might be feeling. 'So…you're thinking of marrying…Lily?'

'How can you doubt it?'

'When?'

Alex glanced at his watch. 'In two hours,' he said. 'Sorry it's short notice. Father Antonio was fishing!'

Nikos nodded. Bemused. 'He likes to fish, does our Father. So… You've interrupted him to marry you?'

'That's right.'

'What a truly excellent way to avoid these figures,' Nikos said and grinned and threw his pen aside. 'A wedding, you say. Okay, my Prince. Lead the way.'

* * *

The leading reporter for the *Sappheiros Times* was halfway through an article on the Princess Lily's astounding outburst in a local café when the call came in.

'It's the palace,' the receptionist mouthed to him.

The man sighed. He'd been one of the two men on the beach on Alex's wedding night. His instinct then had been to warm to Lily, but the reports coming in were damning. Her mother's outburst and then Lily's declaration that this was a marriage of convenience were going to cause problems that might even unseat royalty.

The palace secretary would be ringing to attempt to put a different spin on it, he thought. He was accustomed to being bullied by palace officials. Giorgos's threats had made this newspaper almost puppet media.

So what was new?

He picked up the phone with distaste. 'Yes?'

'This is Prince Alexandros. If you can be at the palace in fifteen minutes I have a story for you. A very long story. How soon can you get the presses rolling?'

He didn't like rushed weddings but this...this was different.

Father Antonio glanced into the mirror and

thanked God his cassock was clean. There were probably fish scales on his boots, but at least they were covered. He gave his cassock a last twitch, then stepped out into the church proper.

Prince Alexandros was waiting. To his astonishment, Alex was dressed almost casually for a prince, in a simple dark suit, crisp white linen and a tie with boats on.

He'd last seen Alex a little less than two hours ago when he'd hailed him from a friend's boat. He'd been dressed in jeans—this was the Alex that the old priest had known from childhood.

The Alex who smiled at him now was the same. He's a prince no matter what he wears, the old priest thought emotionally. This is as he's always been. He's a man with a good heart.

Nikos, too. He had high hopes for these islands with men like these as rulers.

He looked out over the church. His congregation was tiny. One Greek lady he knew already— Eleni, cradling a sleeping Michales. They were in the front pew.

In the second pew were the lads from Spiros's boatyard. They looked scrubbed and uncomfortable in their hastily hired suits. They looked as if they'd never worn a suit before.

These boys needed to be introduced to his church, Antonio decided, thinking already which nice girls he could introduce them to.

And then he forgot them. Sophie Krykos had interrupted her evening by the television to play, and play she did. The organ blared out the wedding march.

And at the church door...Spiros and Lily.

Lily's dress was simple. Maybe it was not fit for a princess, the priest thought, but then what did he know of princesses? His job here was to marry this man to this woman and, simple or not, this dress made a man sigh with pleasure.

If he'd been privy to the hysteria in a local dress shop over the last three hours maybe he'd have chuckled but there was no sign of that chaos now. The dress clung to Lily's slight frame as if it had been sewn on her—as, actually, it had been. It was a shimmering lace confection, held by butterfly straps, the bodice arching softly over each breast, clinging to her waist and then flowing outward to form soft folds falling to the floor.

She wore no veil. There were tiny rosebuds threaded into her short-cropped curls. She carried a trailing bouquet of roses and ferns.

She was beautiful.

The priest watched Alex's face and felt his heart swell within him.

He did love a good wedding. A wedding where love was all that mattered. And the look on Alex's face right now...

Love was all that mattered, he thought. Everything else would fall into place.

She was about to be married. For real.

'Ready?' Spiros asked, patting her arm.

Her prince was at the end of the aisle, waiting to marry her.

But it was Alex...simply Alex.

Spiros was nervous. Beads of sweat were building on the boat-builder's brow.

They couldn't both be whimpering heaps. A girl had to have courage. But who needed courage when this was just Alex? Her Alex.

The man she loved with all her heart.

She took his hand and steadied. 'I'm ready, Spiros.'

'Than let's see you married,' Spiros whispered. 'Before I collapse in fright.'

'You don't need to be afraid,' she said. 'It's as Eleni said. When you marry for love it's different. It's as it should be. It's as it is.'

She was a bride in a million. His Lily.

Home was where Lily was, he thought with a flash of insight and he found himself smiling. That she'd agreed to this...

'You still need to go to Manhattan?' Nikos whispered.

He couldn't drag his eyes from Lily. How could she be so beautiful?

'What?'

'Your business,' Nikos teased. 'Is it so important?'

'I can't even remember what it is.'

'Funny about that,' Nikos said, watching Lily start the slow walk up the aisle. 'I believe you're not alone in falling for Lily. I think there's not a man or woman in this church who wouldn't die protecting her. And I suspect the islanders are about to follow.'

But Alex was no longer listening. He was watching his bride walk steadily towards him and he had eyes for no other.

Nikos smiled, fingered the ring in his pocket and decided okay, enough of the talking, he needed to turn into a best man.

With this ring I thee wed. With my body, I thee worship. All my worldly goods, with thee I share.

She blinked at that. Alex, giving her half his wealth?

This was hardly the time to argue. The priest was waiting for her to repeat the words, as Alex had just repeated them. She'd have to let the wealth thing go.

Now she'd have to let everything go, for Alex was smiling down into her eyes, sliding a ring on her finger, holding her hand for longer than he needed to.

There was that teasing smile. Half laughing but half serious.

The ring… It was the Sappheiros royal ring. A sapphire surrounded by three exquisite diamonds—breathtakingly beautiful.

It was on her finger.

It seemed she was a princess.

As long as we both shall live…

CHAPTER FOURTEEN

ALEX had told one reporter.

He hadn't expected him to share, but share he had. He emerged from the church with his bride on his arm and was confronted by a crush of media.

'Thanks for the heads up,' the reporter he'd talked to called. 'I got the release out. The papers are already on the streets.'

Thus there were even reporters here from Athens. Television crews. Palace staff were appearing, slipping into the crowd. Islanders from all over. Their private ceremony was being gate-crashed.

So be it, he thought. He'd give an even bigger party some time in the not so distant future, when everyone who wanted to be here would be here, when they did the full royal bit and declared Lily to be Crown Princess.

There had to be some really dignified ceremony

for that, he thought, and if there wasn't then he'd
make one up.

Actually…he hadn't been crowned Crown
Prince yet. That meant a double ceremony. A
ceremony to share. A life to share. But first…

'We need to go to the palace balcony,' he told
his bride. 'We're doing this properly or not at all.'

'It's too late for not at all,' she said, smiling and
smiling. 'So I guess the balcony it is.'

It took them half an hour to get back to the
palace. The whole island was out to see what was
happening. Their chauffeur drove them but they
had to drive slowly through the crush.

A woman taking photographs through the car
window had a newspaper tucked visibly in her
bag. Alex put a hand through the window and
snaffled it.

'May I borrow this, ma'am?'

'Keep it,' she called. 'It's my wedding present.
Why didn't you tell us about Princess Lily?'

And there it was, emblazoned on the front page.
'Our Princess's Secret.'

Lily all but snatched the paper from his hands. He
watched as she read—he watched her face change.

From joy to bewilderment.

'This…this is my story.'

'It is,' he said gently and he wondered if he'd
done it wrong.

'I need the islanders to know who you are,' he said gently. 'I can't bear our people not knowing how wonderful you are. I love you and I need our people to love you, too.'

'They'll feel sorry for me,' she whispered, scanning the story he'd told the reporter.

'Maybe for a while,' he said. 'But then they'll be as proud as I am. They'll know they have a princess in a million.'

'Alex…' Her face twisted in distress.

'It's a price,' he said to her softly, holding her close. 'A responsibility. It's why I wanted to keep you at our hideaway a bit longer. But events took us over. Maybe it would be better if the way your mother and sister treated you was never known. But their actions tainted us, and they'll continue to taint us until the truth comes out. I love you, Lily. I'll spend my life protecting you, but we can't hide lies.'

'It's that important?'

'I believe it is. We're going into this marriage proudly,' he said. 'We'll rule this island with pride. With love. With honour.'

'Properly or not at all?' she whispered.

'That's the one.'

'Then I guess properly it is,' she said and she kissed him.

And he kissed her.

To the roar of the crowd, he kissed her all the way to the palace.

Then, to the applause of the palace staff, they ran, hand in hand, up the great staircase to the main balcony overlooking the forecourt.

'Can you do this?' Alex asked her, holding her tight.

'Just hold me,' she whispered. 'Hold me for ever. If you hold me, I can do anything.'

Palace protocol was that the Prince kiss his Princess.

Protocol be damned. She kissed him first. And then it was a moot point as to who was kissing who.

Sappheiros had its new royal family.

What followed was a year of wonder…

On the morning of their first anniversary, Lily woke to laughter. They were at the hideaway. Michales was an early riser, but so was Alex. Father and son were out on the balcony, watching the finches in the vines, watching the sea, chuckling at inane manly jokes. The standard hadn't risen past the sausage joke, she thought sleepily. How a girl could love the pair of them was a wonder in itself.

What a year. How could she ever have imagined it would be so good?

This life they'd chosen was unimaginably wonderful. They spent most of their time at the palace, but the palace had changed. Was still changing.

The island had had practically no public buildings. Thus some of the vast palace was now set aside as a truly magnificent library. Meeting rooms. Mothers' clubs, patchwork, anglers' clubs…whatever the islanders needed. The gardens had been made public. The island had been desperate for a new hospital so the palace summer house overlooking the sea was now its base.

She and Alex had worked together to make these things happen. They were a team. His enthusiasm fed hers and vice versa. They lay in bed late at night and made plans. And made love.

There was still a section of the palace retained by them, for their exclusive use. They'd made it a wee bit more of a home. They'd removed a score of chandeliers. They'd introduced jam for breakfast. They'd accepted that it needed to be their permanent home.

For the islanders had taken their royal couple to their hearts. They loved them living in the palace. Finally, they had a real royal family. They had continuity and pride.

She'd accompanied Alex to Manhattan twice now. But Alex drew his plans here, he asked for soil samples to be analysed and the results sent here, he worked on the Internet and constructed plant lists here.

Sappheiros was his home.

As Sappheiros was her home. Lily worked on her boats as Eleni and Spiros played grandparents. Their boatyard was going from strength to strength.

So… She and Alex had their separate careers, but whatever they did, they did where they could come together at nightfall. Where they could stay together as a family.

Family was the best thing, and the times they could escape to the hideaway were delicious.

She was languorously drowsy. Deeply content. Tonight they'd have dinner here, on the balcony, to celebrate their first year of marriage. Alex had wanted to do something special but special was here. And a restaurant with spicy food…maybe not.

'Are you staying in bed till noon?' Alex was standing in the doorway, smiling in at her. He set Michales down and the little boy toddled over to his mother. She tugged him into bed and he crowed with delight.

'We have a gift for you,' Alex said. 'Michales and I. Only you have to get out of bed for us to give it to you.'

'Bed,' Michales said and beamed.

'Can I dress first?'

'Nope,' Alex said. 'Okay, you can put on a wrap. And sandals. That's all. We're too impatient.'

She was intrigued.

He'd been doing something. Part of the cliff between here and the beach had been blocked off for the past year. 'We're worried it's eroding,' Alex had told her, but he'd been here too often for a simple erosion problem.

Something was brewing, she knew. He'd looked mysterious when she'd probed, but definite that she should not go down there.

'Let's go now,' he said and held out an imperious hand. Then, as she didn't move, he strolled over to the bed, bent and kissed her. Deeply. Strongly. Thoroughly. Then he took her hand and tugged her to her feet.

'Come,' he said in his best born-to-rule voice and she giggled and grabbed her wrap and came.

Sure enough, the path that had been cordoned off was now un-cordoned. It led to another cove, just around the cliff from the bay where they swam.

She'd been down this path once when they'd just married but it had been cordoned off straight after.

And now…

She could see why.

This was a garden. Only…what a garden.

It was a waterfall, rock, rough and tumbled, as if tossed together by nature. As she reached the first set of steps, Alex flicked a switch set in the rock—and the waterfall came alive. Water tumbled from above, cascading over rock formations so wonderfully natural she'd have sworn they'd been placed by the gods themselves.

'You made this,' she gasped.

'The water's pumped from the bay with solar power,' he said in quiet satisfaction. 'The sun comes out, the waterfall runs. Water comes from the bay and goes back to the bay.'

She choked with wonder.

'It's my anniversary gift,' he said and held his hand out again. 'Come on. There's more to show you at the bottom.'

The cove at the base of the waterfall was tiny— a miniature version of the cove where they swam. It was a natural harbour formed by two outreaches of cliff. The waterfall ended as a rippling creek that ran beside an ancient boathouse, then over the sand and out to sea.

She'd seen this boathouse twelve months before. It had been dilapidated—about to fall down.

It wasn't dilapidated now. It was gleaming with new paint, pale blue and crisp white, bright and welcoming in its ocean setting. A tiny jetty reached out from the boat doors. Alex's newly restored dinghy was tied at the jetty. The setting was…exquisite.

'Our own boathouse,' Lily breathed. 'Oh…'

'There's more,' Alex said in satisfaction and handed her a key tied with a big blue bow. 'It's from Michales and me. See the soggy end of the bow? It's been sucked personally by the Prince Michales. It should have a royal insignia, but we ran out of time.'

She gazed at her two boys in wonder—her men—and she unlocked the doors.

And drew in her breath.

'Happy anniversary to us,' a sign said inside the door. The banner hung the full length of the boat-house.

And behind it… There was a pile of wood, as wide as it was high. Dressed timber. Tons of it. Enough wood to build…

A boat?

She walked forward, scarcely able to breathe. She touched the nearest plank.

'You haven't,' she breathed.

'I'd like to say I personally dived for it,' Alex said modestly. 'But I'm lousy with a snorkel. I figured you'd want me alive to hold hammers and stuff.'

'It's Huon Pine,' she gasped. 'It's... Alex, there's enough here to build...'

'A yacht?' he asked, hopeful. 'Would you like to build one?'

She was running her fingers from plank to plank, her mind already seeing what she'd build. Twenty-five feet... She stood back. No, thirty. A half cabin. Oh, she'd sail like the wind.

'I'd like something that sails like the wind,' Alex said and she turned and gazed at her husband in astonishment. He was holding their son and looking at her with such eagerness that a bubble of laughter built within her.

'Hey, is this my present or your present?'

'Both,' he admitted. 'I figured you could build it and teach Michales and me to sail. That could be your anniversary present to us.'

'I already have an anniversary gift for you.'

'You have?' He set Michales down on his feet. 'You have a gift for me?'

'Mmm.'

'Then why are we down here when we could be back at the house opening presents?'

'This one's a work in progress,' she said. 'Like your boat.'

'A work in progress...'

'One might interrupt the other,' she said. 'I can't build two things at once. At least I don't think I can.'

'You're already building me a boat?'

'Guess again.' And she smiled at him with all the love in her heart. 'I've been building it for a couple of months now. Give me seven months more…'

He got it this time. He stared incredulously at her—and then he surged forward and lifted her high. He whirled her around and around, while Michales looked at his parents as if they'd lost their minds.

He toddled forward and Alex had to stop swinging or he'd have bowled his small son over. He set his wife down, gathered his son into his arms and then held them both. He simply held them, a man holding his family. A man granted everything he wanted in life—and more.

The terrors of the past were done. The fears. The injustices and their bitter legacy. Dispersed by love.

He loved this woman in his arms so much…

'The dolphins are watching,' Lily murmured, glancing out through the boatshed doors to where a pod of dolphins had glided into the cove, seemingly to check out what was happening.

'Let 'em look,' Alex said. 'As long as they don't have cameras. This is no time for paparazzi.'

'I wouldn't mind the odd paparazzo,' Lily murmured. 'There should be someone to document how happy I am right now.'

'There'll be enough documentation at the royal reception tomorrow,' Alex said, gathering her even more tightly into his arms. 'Meanwhile, I'll remind you every time you ask. You're asking now? I'm telling you. I love you. You're my wife. You're the mother of my children. You're my own beautiful Princess. You're my Lily and you're my love.'

EXPECTING
MIRACLE TWINS

BY
BARBARA HANNAY

MILLS & BOON®

First published in Great Britain 2009
Harlequin Mills & Boon Limited,
Eton House, 18-24 Paradise Road, Richmond, Surrey TW9 1SR

© Barbara Hannay 2009

ISBN: 978 0 263 86964 4

Set in Times Roman 13 on 14¼ pt
02-0909-46888

Harlequin Mills & Boon policy is to use papers that are natural, renewable and recyclable products and made from wood grown in sustainable forests. The logging and manufacturing process conform to the legal environmental regulations of the country of origin.

Printed and bound in Spain
by Litografia Rosés, S.A., Barcelona

BABY STEPS TO MARRIAGE...

**A brand-new duet by RITA® Award-winning author
Barbara Hannay**

*Pregnancy is never predictable, and these two stories
explore the very different experiences of two friends,
Mattie and Lucy. Follow their steps to marriage
in these two very special deliveries...*

**This month Mattie's expecting twin trouble!
EXPECTING MIRACLE TWINS**

**Next month
THE BRIDESMAID'S BABY**
When old friends Will Carruthers and Lucy McKenty
are thrown together again as best man and bridesmaid at
Mattie and Jake's wedding, unresolved feelings resurface.
Their biological clocks might be ticking—
but a baby is the last thing they expect!

CHAPTER ONE

MATTIE was grinning as she turned into the driveway at her new address. She couldn't believe her good luck. The block of flats was so much nicer than she'd expected, with charming white-washed walls, Mediterranean-blue doors and sunny balconies that overlooked the bay.

Her flat—number three—was on the ground floor, which meant she wouldn't have to climb too many sets of stairs in the later months of her pregnancy, and Brutus would be able to run in and out to the garden to his heart's content.

As she parked on the driveway, she saw a welcoming pot of bright pink geraniums beside the doormat and the garden was filled with sunshine. Mattie could already picture her life here. In the mornings, she would bring her laptop outside and watch the sun sparkle on the water while she worked. She could put Brutus on his lead and take him for walks along the path beside the bay.

The flat was close to the hospital and it had all the right vibes. If she stood on tiptoe, she could even see the tip of Sydney Harbour Bridge. She was going to love living here for a whole year.

Everything about her new venture felt good. She'd talked to the doctors at length and she'd thought about the project from every angle, and she knew she was doing the right thing.

It was green lights all the way and, if all went well, by the end of the year she would deliver to her best friends the precious baby they both longed for. All she needed now was a successful implantation and the surrogacy would begin.

Humming happily, Mattie reached for the door key in her handbag, scooped up Brutus from his basket and opened the car door.

Wham!

A blast of strident music burst like a machine gun from number three and Mattie's happy smile disintegrated. Stunned, she checked her key tag, but there was no mistake—number three was definitely the right flat—*her* flat. Gina had assured her for the hundredth time when she'd handed over the keys this morning.

'It's yours for as long as you need it,' she'd said.

Everything was arranged. Gina's brother Will owned this flat, but he was working on a mine site in Mongolia and, as Mattie had refused any kind of monetary exchange for the surrogacy, Gina had settled on the use of the flat instead.

The last thing Mattie had expected was to find another tenant here, playing music—loud heavy metal music that set her teeth on edge. She clutched Brutus more tightly as she stared at the blue door.

Had squatters moved in? Were they throwing a party?

She almost returned to the safety of her car, but her sense of justice prevailed. She'd been assured many times that this was *her* flat. Gina and Tom were excessively grateful that she was willing to help them in their quest for a baby. Justice was on her side.

Mentally gathering her courage, she marched up the path, up the two stone steps and knocked.

And knocked.

And then thumped with her fist.

At last the volume of the music was lowered and the door opened, and Mattie took a hasty step backwards.

The man who suddenly filled the doorway did not look like a squatter. Far from it. But he did look like a pirate.

At least, that was Mattie's first thought, which was no doubt prompted by his rather wild dark hair and his scruffy jaw—and the fact that his shirt was unbuttoned to reveal rather a great deal of dazzling tanned chest. Mattie tried very hard not to look at his chest, but it was an incredibly eye-catching sample of male anatomy.

He propped a bulky shoulder against the door frame and studied her from beneath disconcerting half-lowered lids, and he managed to look both annoyed and bored by her intrusion. 'How can I help you?'

When he spoke, Mattie stopped thinking about pirates. For a moment she stopped thinking altogether. His voice was rich, dark and smooth, like an extremely sinful chocolate dessert. Combined with his gaping white shirt, it sent her mind completely blank.

She forced her gaze up and away from his chest and looked him bravely in the eye. 'I… um…think…there's been a mistake.'

A dark eyebrow lifted lazily. 'I beg your pardon?'

Mattie tried again. 'There seems to have been some kind of mix-up.' She waved her door key. 'This is my flat. Number three. I'm supposed to be moving in here today.'

He cast a quick, assessing glance that took in Brutus, curled in her arms, and her little car, crammed to the roof with her worldly possessions. Then he glanced back over his shoulder into the living room and, for the first time, Mattie saw his companion—a long-legged blonde, reclining on the sofa with a glass of wine in her hand.

'What's she want?' the woman called.

Ignoring her, the fellow narrowed his eyes at Mattie. 'Did the real estate office send you here?'

'No.' She straightened her shoulders. 'I have a…a private arrangement…with the owner. He knows all about it.'

'Does he now? And would you mind telling me the owner's name?'

'Excuse me?' Mattie was incensed. 'What right have you to ask that? I can assure you, my claim on this flat is legitimate. Is yours?'

To her annoyance, he chuckled. Mattie almost stamped her foot and Brutus, sensing her distress, licked her hand. And then the woman on the sofa uncurled her long legs, set down her wineglass and joined the fellow in the doorway. She draped an arm around the man's massive shoulders. 'What's going on, Jake?'

'Just a minor border incursion.' The man, whose name, apparently, was Jake, watched Mattie with a look of faint amusement.

'A what?'

'A territorial battle,' he told the blonde without taking his dark diamond-bright gaze from Mattie.

An unwelcome ripple of heat fluttered over

Mattie's skin. She glared at Jake for causing it, and deliberately turned her attention to his sulky companion and rattled the keys again. 'There's been an unfortunate mistake about the flat. I'm supposed to be moving in here.'

'When?' asked the other woman in a tone as unhelpful as her boyfriend's.

'Today. Now. This afternoon.' Mattie pointed to the number three on the tag. 'I have a key.' Again, she glared at Jake. 'Do you have a key? Or did you break in?'

His response was to fold his arms and favour her with a withering look.

In desperation, Mattie said, 'Look, I told you I have an arrangement with Will Carruthers.'

'Will Carruthers sent you here?' Jake's eyes widened with surprise. 'Why didn't you tell me that in the first place?'

Mattie was surprised too. 'Do you know Will?'

'Of course I know him. I work with him in Mongolia. He's my best mate.'

'Oh.' She gulped unhappily. 'So I suppose he knows you're here?'

'Absolutely. I'm on leave. I had a week in Japan and now I'm in Sydney for a week and Will insisted I use his flat.'

Mattie clung to the faint hope that Jake's week was almost up. 'When did your week start?'

'Day before yesterday.'

Deflated, she dropped her gaze to Brutus, and he made sympathetic doggy noises and tried to lick her chin. 'There's obviously been a mix-up with the times.'

She tried not to sound too disappointed, but if she and this Jake fellow both had a claim on the flat, and if he was here first, she supposed she had no choice but to find somewhere else to stay for the rest of this week.

She wondered despondently where she should start her search for accommodation. It would have to be somewhere cheap and she didn't know Sydney very well.

'Rotten luck for you,' chirped the girlfriend and she grinned smugly at Mattie as she rested her chin possessively on Jake's shoulder.

'You haven't explained how you know Will,' Jake drawled.

'I've known him all my life,' Mattie told him and it was perfectly true. Even though she hadn't seen much of Will Carruthers in recent years, they belonged to a circle of friends who'd grown up together in Willowbank in Outback New South Wales.

'Will's sister, Gina, is my best friend,' she explained. 'And Gina and Will organised between them for me to live here for twelve months.'

Jake frowned as he digested this and then he shrugged. 'In that case, I guess there's no reason why you can't move in. After all, there are two bedrooms.'

His companion let out an annoyed huff.

Mattie's mouth opened and shut, then opened again. She really didn't want to have to start searching for somewhere else, and this pair would only be here for a few more days. 'Are you sure you don't mind? I don't want to intrude.'

He uttered a gruff sound of impatience. 'I've offered, haven't I? Anyway, I don't plan to be around much.' He turned to the girl. 'We may as well hit the town now, Ange, while—' He paused and gave Mattie the briefest flicker of a smile. 'What's your name?'

'Matilda Carey.' She held out her hand rather primly. 'Mostly I'm called Mattie.'

'Jake Devlin,' he said, giving her hand a firm shake.

'Pleased to meet you, Jake.'

He indicated the small, silky terrier-cross in her arms. 'Who's this?'

'Brutus.'

Jake chuckled. 'Oh, yeah, he's a real brute, isn't he?' Then he remembered his companion. 'This is Ange.'

Mattie smiled at her. 'How do you do?'

'Oh, I'm fine,' Ange responded sulkily.

'Would you like a hand to bring your things inside?'

Jake's courtesy surprised Mattie, but its effect was offset by the predictably dark look on Ange's face. 'Oh, heavens, no,' she assured him. 'I can manage easily. I only have a canary cage and a few suitcases.'

'A canary?' Jake looked both amused and puzzled. He scratched his head and the gesture caused all sorts of muscles in his chest to ripple magnificently.

Mattie was about to explain that she'd inherited the canary from her grandmother but, once again, his chest distracted her.

'Jake.' A warning note had entered Ange's voice. 'We're heading off now, right? I'll get my things.'

'Sure,' he said and he began to close the buttons on his shirt.

Mattie watched as the two of them hurried away to find a taxi and then she went into the flat. It wasn't quite the exciting introduction to her new home that she'd pictured. The unpalatable music, although diminished, still throbbed from the stereo and she quickly switched it off.

She crossed the lounge room, skirting the

coffee table with the abandoned wine bottle, bowl of nuts and glasses, and went through to the kitchen. The sink was littered with dirty dishes and the dishwasher door hung open, as if someone had intended to stack it but had been distracted by a better idea.

Down the hallway, she found the bathroom and she was not surprised to see wet towels dumped on the floor, as well as a pair of black lace knickers. Mattie had shared flats before and some of her flatmates had been untidy, so she was more or less used to this kind of scene. It was weird, then, that the sight of those knickers depressed her.

The next room was a bedroom, dominated by a king-size bed—unmade, of course. The bed's tangled sheets told their own story, as did the empty champagne bottle on the bedside table.

An inexplicable hollowness in Mattie's stomach sent her hurrying on till she came, at last, to a neat bedroom at the back of the flat.

It was much smaller than the main bedroom and there was no view of the bay, but it was perfectly clean and tidy.

And mine, Mattie thought. That was something. Actually, when she gave it further thought, she realised that she would probably have taken this room for herself anyway, and kept the front room with the view for visitors.

Then again, she mused, mulling over this as she headed back to unload the car, she probably wouldn't have too many visitors this year. Gina and Tom would want to visit from time to time and so would her parents, now that they'd recovered from the shock of hearing what she planned. But she'd agreed with Gina that they should keep their surrogacy arrangement very private, so she'd told her other friends very little about her move to Sydney.

Mattie's decision to move to the city had not been made lightly. She and Gina had talked it over at length. They both knew that if she'd stayed in Willowbank, they couldn't possibly keep the surrogacy under wraps. And Gina had been sensible enough to recognise that her constant vigilance of Mattie's pregnancy would be stifling, so they'd agreed it was better this way.

In some ways, however, it was going to be a lonely year. That was the one thing that had concerned the psychologist when she'd explored Mattie's motivations and commitment to the surrogacy process. Mattie had managed to convince her that she was perfectly happy with her own company. As a children's book author and illustrator, she was used to spending long hours lost in her work.

'Do you have a partner? A boyfriend?' the psychologist had asked.

Mattie had told her there was no special man in her life. She didn't add that there hadn't been a special man in her life for almost three years.

'What if you meet someone in the next few months?' the other woman had prompted. 'A pregnancy will restrict your social life.'

Mattie had thought it best not to mention that her social life had been on hold for quite some time. 'It's only one year out of my life,' she'd said with a shrug.

'But you're going to need support.'

'The baby's parents will come to Sydney for regular visits,' she'd responded with jaunty confidence. 'And my friends and family are only a phone call or an e-mail away.'

She'd wisely avoided announcing that she hadn't asked for support, but the truth was that Matilda Carey made a habit of giving support to others, rather than receiving it. Her impulse to help and rescue had begun so far back in her past it was as vital to her nature as her heartbeat—and that wasn't going to change in a year.

It was past midnight when Mattie heard the front door open and the sound of heavy footsteps on the terracotta tiles. She expected the murmur of voices or laughter, but all she heard was a thump and a muffled curse, as if someone had tripped, then more footsteps and, eventually, taps turning on in the bathroom.

The footsteps continued on to Jake's bedroom and Mattie pulled a pillow over her head. If those sheets were going to be tangled again tonight, she didn't want to listen to the sound effects.

She was washing up her breakfast things when Jake stumbled into the kitchen next morning, bleary-eyed and unshaven—like a bear with a sore head, her mother would have said.

'Morning,' Mattie said breezily, flashing a careful smile over her shoulder.

He replied with a grumpy monosyllable.

'There's tea in the pot and it's still hot, if you'd like some.'

Jake shook his head and scowled at the sparkling clean kitchen benches. 'What's happened to the coffee plunger?'

'Oh, it's up here.' Mattie reached into the overhead cupboard where she'd put the plunger pot after she'd washed it last night.

She handed it to him and he scowled at it as if he didn't recognise it. 'Did you wash this?'

'Well…yes.'

He scowled some more. 'And you've cleaned up the kitchen.'

'I didn't mind. It didn't take long.'

He shook his head and winced and she wondered if he had a headache. She thought about offering to cook bacon and eggs. Most guys seemed to find a big breakfast the best cure for a hangover.

But this morning she had the distinct impression that Jake Devlin would bite her head right off if she made such an offer. And, anyway, he had Ange to fuss over him, didn't he? She supposed his girlfriend was still in bed, sound asleep after her late night.

'I'll get out of your way,' she said. 'I'm going into town. I have an appointment this morning.'

Jake flashed a brief, keen glance in her direction. 'So have I.'

'Right.' Mattie inhaled sharply, surprised that he'd shared even this much about himself. 'I…um…hope it goes well, then.'

He looked faintly amused and, for a moment, she thought he was about to smile and say something friendly, but then he shrugged and turned his attention to the kettle.

Mattie hurried away and told herself that she didn't care if he was unsociable. He would be gone in less than a week and it didn't matter if he never smiled. His grumpiness was his problem, not hers.

But, as she went past the open bedroom door, she caught sight of those sheets again. She quickly averted her gaze—she didn't want to spy on Ange. Except…

She couldn't help taking another hasty glance and she realised then that she wasn't mistaken. The bed was empty. Clearly, Ange had not come home with Jake, which perhaps explained his bad mood.

CHAPTER TWO

THE woman at the nursing home smiled at Jake. 'Come this way, Mr Devlin. Roy's up and dressed, ready and waiting for you. He's very excited about your visit.'

'Glad to hear it,' Jake replied, but a small coil of dread tightened in his stomach as he followed her down a narrow hallway. This place was as bad as he remembered from his last visit. It smelled like a hospital and the walls were lined with pastel paintings of butterflies, flowers and fruit bowls. Roy wouldn't like them. Not a horse or a gum tree in sight.

As Jake passed doors, he caught glimpses of white-haired old folk in bed asleep, or nodding in their armchairs, and his feeling of dismay settled like cold stones in the pit of his stomach. He hated the fact that a great man like Roy Owens, who'd spent his entire life on vast Outback cattle stations, had to spend his twilight years shut away in a place like this.

His throat was already tight with emotion even before he entered Roy's room. But then he saw his old friend.

It had been six months since Jake's last visit and the changes in Roy were more devastating than ever. The tough and wiry hero Jake had idolised throughout his boyhood had all but vanished and had been replaced by a pale and fragile gnome. Jake tried to swallow the fish bone in his throat but it wouldn't budge.

Throughout Jake's childhood, Roy had been the head stockman on the Devlin family's isolated Outback cattle property in Far North Queensland. Until a few years ago, Roy had been a head taller than Jake's father and as strong as an ox. He'd taught Jake how to ride a horse and to fish for black bream, how to leg rope a calf, to fossick for gold, and to follow native bees back to their hives.

At night, around glowing campfires, Roy had held young Jake entranced as he spun never-ending stories beneath a canopy of stars. No one else knew as much about the night sky, or about bush lore, or the adventures of the early Outback pioneers. By the age of ten, Jake had been convinced that Roy Owens knew everything in this world that a man ever needed to know.

Roy could turn his hand to catching a wild scrub bull, or leading a search party for a lost tourist, or baking mouth-watering hot damper in the coals of a campfire. Most miraculous of all, Roy had endless patience. No matter how busy he'd been, or how hard he had to work, he'd always found time for a small lonely boy whose parents had been too occupied raising cattle, or training their racehorses, or pursuing their very active social lives.

When Jake had questioned his parents about Roy's transfer to a Sydney nursing home they'd claimed that they hated that he had to go away, but they had no choice. Roy needed constant care and regular medical checks.

'But have you visited him down there?' Jake demanded. 'Have you seen what it's like?'

'Darling, you know how terribly busy your father and I are. We will get down there, just as soon as we can spare the time.'

So far, his parents hadn't found time.

But Jake's affection for Roy had never wavered. It pained him that the old stockman, who'd been like a second father, was now a frail and lonely old bachelor with no family to support him. It tore at Jake's guts to see him waiting docilely in his postage-stamp-size room. He was fighting tears as Roy's face broke into an enormous smile.

'Jake, how are you, lad? It's so good to clap eyes on you.' With a frail hand Roy patted a chair. 'Take a seat, son. They'll bring us morning tea in a minute. Come and tell me all about Mongolia.'

Roy's body might have betrayed him, but his mind was still alert and, unlike most people who asked Jake about Mongolia, he was genuinely interested. He knew that horses were as important to the people there as they were in the Outback. And in the same way that many Outback kids learned to ride when they could barely walk, so did children on the steppe.

Roy was more than happy for Jake to retell the same stories he'd told last time. But, as Jake talked, he was painfully aware of the reversal of their roles. Now he was the one spinning stories and Roy was the grateful listener.

Two hours later, however, as Jake re-emerged into fresh air and sunshine, he knew that a few stories had not been enough. He was plagued by a gnawing certainty that he was letting the old guy down.

Mattie was in a very good mood when she came home from the doctor's. Everything for the surrogacy was set to go. Gina and Tom's frozen embryos had already arrived at the clinic and in two weeks' time, when Mattie's cycle was right, she would begin taking pre-transfer hormones. With luck on her side, she would be pregnant within a month.

She could hardly wait to get started.

Gina and Tom were an amazing couple and if anyone deserved to be parents they did. They'd been childhood sweethearts and their deep love for each other had remained unshakeable. These days they ran a farm on the banks of Willow Creek and Gina's house was always warm and welcoming, always filled with baking smells, a pot of tea at the ready. But there was a little yellow and white room at the end of the hallway, still waiting for the baby Gina longed for.

Mattie had seen Gina on the day she'd been told she needed a hysterectomy. She'd found her friend huddled in an unrecognisable ball in a corner of the lounge, red-eyed and shrunken— shut down—as if someone she loved with all her heart had died.

Of course, that was what had happened really, because now the baby Gina dreamed of would never have the chance to live.

For Gina, of all people, this was the cruellest blow. Mattie and Gina had been planning their families since they'd played with dolls in the tree house Gina's dad built.

Mattie was an only child and she'd thought two

children would be nice, but Gina came from a big family and she had been adamant she wanted five. Her husband was *always* going to be Tom and they would have two sets of twins and then a single baby at the end, a baby girl for her to spoil and cuddle when all the twins had gone to school.

It was unthinkable now that Gina couldn't have at least one baby, and as Mattie had dumped any dreams of a family of her own after the truly toxic break-up with her fiancé, she hadn't taken long to come up with her surrogacy proposal.

For her it was a perfect solution. Gina and Tom could have their baby, and she had the chance to do something positive and life-affirming—the perfect antidote to heartbreak.

This way, Mattie figured, everyone was a winner and she'd wasted no time before putting the idea to Gina and Tom.

They'd invited her for Sunday lunch, a simple, relaxed, happy meal of roast chicken and winter vegetables, followed by berries and ice cream. After the other guests had gone, Mattie had stayed behind to help with the cleaning up. The three of them had been in the kitchen, Mattie washing wineglasses at the sink while Gina stacked the dishwasher. Tom had just brought in freshly chopped wood for the fire.

At first Gina hadn't understood.

'A surrogate pregnancy,' Mattie had clarified.

There'd been a momentary flash of shock in Gina's face, but it was quickly outshone by hope and excitement. Then Gina had seen her husband's grim frown and doubt had crept into her eyes.

'That's a huge ask, Mattie,' Tom had said. 'Have you thought this through? You'd be carrying another woman's baby, fathered by another man.'

'I know, I know. But you're both my best friends.'

Tom had tried to smile and failed, and he ran a distracted hand through his spiky red hair. 'I can't get my mind around the fact that a woman other than Gina could give birth to my child. That's off the wall. Even when it's a wonderful friend like you.'

That discussion had taken place six months ago.

Mattie had thought the subject was dropped and she'd been disappointed. The idea of carrying her friends' baby had filled her with a sense of purpose, which she badly needed. After the break-up with Pete she'd cared for her grandmother but, since Gran had passed away, her life had felt... blank and not very meaningful.

She'd kept busy, of course, had created another

book and that had been fun and worthwhile, but she'd still felt vaguely restless and empty. And then Gina and Tom had called.

Could they come around for a chat? Tom had changed his mind. They'd considered adoption, but it wasn't their first choice and if Mattie really was still willing to carry their baby they'd be deeply and eternally grateful.

Now, in Sydney, after receiving the doctor's re-assuring news, Mattie was in the mood for a minor celebration, and she stopped on the way home and bought a bottle of wine. After all, she wouldn't be able to drink any alcohol once she was pregnant. She also bought the ingredients for one of her favourite meals, a scrumptious potato and mushroom pizza.

If Jake Devlin was still in an irritable mood, or if Ange was hanging about the flat, giving out sour looks, she would ask them to share the pizza. It was amazing how often a nice meal cheered people up.

Back at the flat, she sent a quick, excited e-mail to Gina and Tom and then she took Brutus for a nice long walk. She was extra-patient when he wanted to sniff at interesting smells every few metres or so and when she got back, happily wind-blown and refreshed, she put one of her own CDs in the player—a very popular movie soundtrack.

She opened the wine and poured a glass, which she sipped while she sifted flour and kneaded dough and chopped vegetables for the topping.

The pizza was almost ready for the oven when she heard the sound of a key in the front door. Her skin flashed hot and cold.

For heaven's sake, it was such a silly reaction. What was the matter with her? As Jake Devlin's footsteps sounded in the hallway she concentrated on adjusting the oven's temperature setting, but she knew it wasn't the stove's heat that made her face bright and hot when he came into the kitchen.

'How's it going?' he asked casually.

Mattie flashed a nervous smile in his direction. He looked as devastatingly sexy as ever.

'Fine,' she said.

'You've been busy.'

'Not really.' She tried to sound offhand. 'I've made plenty of mess, but it's just a pizza.'

He came close—*too* close—and stood looking down at the pizza, with his hands resting lightly on his lean hips. Today his shirt was respectably buttoned and there was absolutely no reason for Mattie to feel weak at the knees.

While Jake studied her pizza with surprising interest, she drew a calming breath. At least, her deep breath was supposed to be calming but it didn't seem to help her. She was still distinctly fluttery.

'That looks really good.' He spoke with every appearance of sincerity. 'I've never seen potato used on a pizza.'

'Oh, you should try it. It's delicious.'

Great. Now she sounded breathless.

'I'll bet it's terrific.' He smiled at her and his smile was more dangerous than his bare chest had been.

Mattie's movements became jerky and nervous as she began to tidy the cooking mess. Without looking at Jake, she said, 'It'll be ready in twenty minutes.'

'I'm afraid I can't hang around that long. I've already made plans.' He slipped his sleeve cuff back and glanced at his wristwatch. 'I have to leave again almost straight away, and I need to shower first.'

Mattie smothered her ridiculous disappointment with an extra-bright smile. She supposed Jake was going off to meet Ange.

'Enjoy your dinner,' he called over his shoulder as he left the room.

'I will.'

It was a warm evening so Mattie ate her pizza slices and drank another glass of wine out on the balcony with Brutus at her feet. The balcony faced the east, but the sky reflected the pinks of the sunset from the western sky and the light turned the water a pretty pearlescent grey. She enjoyed the meal immensely—despite the dull cloud of tension and disappointment that had settled over her.

She was very annoyed with herself for feeling low. Yesterday morning she'd been over the moon with excitement about living in Sydney alone. This evening she longed for company.

It didn't make sense. When she'd started preparing this meal, she hadn't really expected to share it with anyone and the sudden slump in her spirits was irrational. How would she cope with nine months of pregnancy and the ups and downs of her hormones if one unpleasant man she hardly knew could send her moods swinging like a seesaw?

She didn't even like Jake Devlin!

Her low spirits lingered as she went back inside, cleaned up the kitchen and covered the canary's cage. She asked herself disconsolately, *What now?*

Of course, there was one thing that she could always rely on to lift her mood. She fetched her art block, pens and paints and set them on the coffee table.

Humming to herself, she found a flat cushion, then sat cross-legged on the floor, ready to sketch an opening scene for her new book.

The idea for this story had been bubbling inside her for the past few weeks, but she'd been too busy planning her move to get started. This evening was the perfect time to let her ideas for the artwork come to the surface and spill onto the page. At last.

As always, her children's story would start in her young heroine's ordinary world—an old-fashioned house in an inner-city suburb, where the little girl lived with her mother and father, her cat and a canary.

In this new book, Mattie would begin with a bathroom scene.

She selected a pencil and sharpened it carefully, took a deep, happy breath and made the first mark on the fresh white page. Within moments, she was completely absorbed, lost in the enchanting world of her imagination. Thank heavens it never let her down.

The flat was in darkness when Jake arrived home some time after midnight. Last night he'd tripped over something in the dark, so he turned on a light this time and he blinked as the living room came to life, blinked again when he saw the clutter on the coffee table.

Surely Mattie, the neat freak, hadn't left this mess?

Curiosity got the better of him and he moseyed over to take a closer look.

Blow me down.

The table was covered by a painting, which Mattie had obviously left to dry. It was a pen and ink sketch, coloured with pretty watercolours in a soft wash, and it showed the corner of a bathroom.

A little girl peeped out of a sea of bubbles in an elegantly curved, claw-footed bathtub. Bright rainbow-tinted bubbles drifted over the edge of the bath and onto a white fluffy mat on the floor, where a pair of pink-and-white-striped socks with lacy frills lay abandoned.

The long sleeve of a blue jersey hung over the edge of a wicker laundry basket and the cheeky face of a black cat peeked out from behind the basket.

It was such a simple little scene, drawn with an economy of lines and coloured delicately, but there was something utterly fascinating about the picture. Jake looked again at the little girl's mousy-brown curls and beady blue eyes and he chuckled softly. She looked incredibly ordinary and yet unexpectedly appealing. Not unlike her creator.

Mattie woke next morning to the unexpected sound of pots and pans being rattled in the kitchen, and when she opened her bedroom door she caught the distinctive aroma of mushrooms frying.

She'd slept in, after staying up much longer than she'd intended last night. When she'd finally finished work on her painting she'd lain awake for ages, thinking about the rest of her book, but she hadn't heard Jake come in, so he must have been very late. How extraordinary that he was up already.

She dressed quickly, pulling on a T-shirt and jeans, and she made a hasty stop in the bathroom to wash her face and tidy her hair, then she entered the kitchen cautiously.

Jake was whisking eggs and he turned and grinned at her. 'Morning.'

'Good morning,' she returned carefully.

'I let Brutus out into the garden,' he said.

'Thanks.' She blinked with surprise when she saw that he'd also filled Brutus's bowl.

'How did such a tiny mutt end up with a name like Brutus?' Jake asked as he watched the little dog crunch miniature biscuits.

'I've no idea,' Mattie admitted. 'I guess his former owners had a sense of humour, even if they were careless.'

'Former owners?'

'I have a good friend, Lucy, who's a vet.

Someone dumped Brutus on her doorstep and she needed to find a new owner.'

Jake stopped whisking eggs. 'And you offered.'

'Yes.'

For a long moment, Jake watched her with the slightest hint of a smile lurking in his eyes, then he pointed to the frying pan. 'I found some leftover mushrooms in the fridge so I'm making an omelette.'

He looked rather pleased with himself, but Mattie refused to be amused or impressed. Last night she'd been shocked by her reaction to this man and she'd vowed to remain unimpressed by anything about Jake Devlin. With a little willpower, she could rise above the attraction of his broad manly chest, his sexy smile and his flashing dark eyes.

There was simply no point in getting hot and bothered about him. Apart from the fact that he already had a girlfriend, or possibly several girlfriends, he brought back memories of the one time she'd fallen disastrously in love and she'd vowed never to put herself through that kind of agonising heartache again.

Besides, no matter how attractive Jake was, he would be gone in under a week. And, very soon after that, she would be pregnant with someone else's baby.

No man on earth would be interested in her then.

Not that she minded. This was her year for living chastely. She was dedicated to a higher cause, to Gina and Tom's baby. When she was old and she looked back on her life, she would see this gift to her friends as one of her greatest triumphs.

With a breezy wave of her hand, she smiled at Jake. 'You're welcome to the mushrooms.'

'Would you like to share this omelette?'

'No, thanks. I'm allergic to eggs.'

He shot her a sharp, disbelieving glance and Mattie shrugged. 'I usually have oatmeal.'

He looked momentarily disappointed, and she couldn't suppress a spurt of triumph. *Touché, Mr Devlin.*

But then he gave an offhand shrug. 'Bad luck for you. My omelettes are legend.'

As Mattie spooned boring oatmeal and water into a bowl and stuck it in the microwave, she asked, over her shoulder, 'So where did you learn to cook?'

'In Mongolia, on the mine site.'

She turned to him. 'Really?' In spite of her vow of indifference, she was intrigued.

'We have this fabulous cook—a French Canadian called Pierre—and, whenever I'm at a loose end, I pop into the kitchen to lend him a hand.'

'I don't suppose there are too many ways to spend your free time on a mine site in Mongolia.'

'Not unless you can get a lift into the capital, Ulaanbaatar.' Using a spatula, Jake skilfully folded the omelette in two.

'Are you a geologist like Will?'

He shook his head. 'I'm an enviro.'

'What's that?'

'An environmental scientist.'

'So it's your job to make sure the mining companies don't wreck Mongolia?'

He grinned. 'More or less.'

'I guess that must be rather satisfying.'

'It's not a bad job.' Jake lowered the heat beneath his frying pan.

The microwave pinged and Mattie gave her oatmeal a stir.

'What about you?' he asked casually. 'What do you do?'

'Oh, I haven't been to university, and I don't have what you could call a career. I tend to drift from one situation to another.'

'But you paint.'

'Well…yes. I suppose you saw the mess I left last night. Sorry.'

'Don't apologise. I was actually glad to see stuff lying about. Now I know you're normal.'

His sudden smile was so charming that Mattie

felt a dangerous flutter inside and she was grateful when a burst of song from the cage by the window distracted them both.

She darted across the room and removed the cover from the cage. 'Morning, Pavarotti.'

Jake snorted. 'Pavarotti?'

'That's his name. Like the opera singer.'

He shook his head as he skilfully tilted the pan so that the omelette slid smoothly onto a plate.

At the cutlery drawer, Mattie fetched him a knife and fork and got a spoon for herself, and then they sat opposite each other at the small kitchen table—and Mattie knew she was in trouble.

Her insides were twittering in time with the canary's warbling.

Jake nodded towards the bird cage as he cut into his light and fluffy omelette. 'So you're a fan of opera?'

Remembering the heavy metal music he'd played, she almost said yes, just to provoke him, but her habitual honesty prevailed.

'My gran was the opera fan,' she explained. 'She named the canary. I wanted her to call him Elvis, but he was her bird so of course she had the last say.' Mattie realised that further explanation was necessary. 'My grandmother died last year and I inherited Pavarotti.'

Jake nodded slowly. 'You were close to your grandmother?'

'Oh, yes. I lived with her and looked after her for the last two years of her life.'

Across the table, his dark eyes registered surprise and then, eventually, an unexpected sadness. He scowled and looked more like the gruff man Mattie was used to and the flutters inside her settled. She was much more comfortable soothing other people's worries than dealing with her own fluttery insides.

They ate in silence for several minutes. Eventually, Mattie said, 'Do you have something interesting planned for today?'

'I was thinking of taking in a movie.'

'On a lovely day like this?'

His jaw stuck out as if he didn't appreciate her implied criticism. 'I've missed six months' worth of movies. I've a lot of catching up to do.'

'Of course.'

'Do you want to come?'

The question was so unexpected that Mattie's mouth gaped unbecomingly. Her mind whirled. She wanted to ask Jake if Ange was his girlfriend. Or was he a free agent who hooked up with the nearest available woman whenever he was on leave?

She didn't have anything planned for the day,

but if there was even a slim chance that Jake was actually asking her on a date, she should say no.

'I'm afraid I can't come today,' she said quickly and decisively, before she could be tempted to change her mind. 'I have another appointment.'

If Jake was disappointed he didn't show it, but after he'd gone Mattie sunk to a new low. She couldn't believe how restless and just plain miserable she felt. The flat felt hollow and empty and she seemed to rattle around inside it—like a pebble in a tin can.

In a bid to think about something else—*anything* else besides Jake Devlin—she rang around the local hairdressers until she found one who had a cancellation.

Two and a half hours later, she grinned with delight at her reflection in the salon's mirror. Chestnut and copper streaks had transformed her mousy hair, and an elegant bob flattered her jawline and gave a nice emphasis to her cheekbones.

She told herself she was doing this as a pre-pregnancy ego boost. The new image had nothing to do with Jake. But when she got back to the flat, she took a long bath and she changed into her best dark grey trousers and cream silk blouse and she put garnet studs in her ears.

She looked fabulous, but she felt foolish. Wouldn't Jake wonder why she'd dressed up?

She was still trying to decide if she should change again when she heard the front door open, so she dived into the kitchen and pretended to be busy in the pots and pans cupboard.

Jake came down the hall, then paused in the doorway. 'Excuse me,' he said, a small smile playing at the corners of his mouth. 'I think I'm in the wrong flat.'

To Mattie's eternal embarrassment, she blushed.

'I guess you're going out?' he said. 'You're all dressed up.'

'Yes,' she lied. As she closed the cupboard door, she hoped he couldn't see through her fat white fib. 'I'm meeting a friend for dinner.'

Jake nodded slowly, then said quietly, 'Have a good evening.'

'I will. Thanks.'

He was about to head down the hall when he turned back. 'By the way, Mattie.'

'Yes?'

'The new hair looks fabulous.'

She was really mad with herself as she set off on foot down the street. Ever since she'd met Jake she'd lost her grip on her common sense. Now, she'd lied about her plans for this evening and here she was, wandering the streets of Sydney like a lost waif, looking for somewhere to eat. The really silly thing was she'd stocked the refrigerator with the ingredients for a perfectly good supper.

She decided to eat at the first place she found—a café a block away. It was a simple place with bare concrete floors, metal tables and chairs and selections of Asian-style noodles and stir-fries scrawled in chalk on blackboards.

Most of the customers were wearing jeans and T-shirts and Mattie felt distinctly overdressed, but she took a seat and was determined to enjoy herself.

She placed her order and asked for a glass of white wine and all went well for about ten minutes. Then Jake strode in.

CHAPTER THREE

MATTIE'S heart began a ridiculous thumping. Jake was dressed in black and his unruly hair was tousled by the wind as he stood at the café's front counter. Framed by the doorway, shoulders back and feet planted wide apart, he looked unbelievably gorgeous.

She wasn't sure if he'd seen her, but it could only be a matter of moments before he did, and even if she could come up with a plausible explanation, he'd probably realise that she'd lied about meeting a friend. Talk about embarrassing!

His dark eyes scanned the café and she quickly dropped her gaze, letting her smooth new hairstyle swing forward, hoping that it would hide her face. Perhaps she could pretend she hadn't seen him.

Within a heartbeat, however, strong, confident footsteps rang out on the concrete floor, and they stopped at Mattie's table. Holding her breath, she lifted her head and there he was, standing before her.

He looked directly into her eyes and he smiled.

Mattie swallowed. What could she say? It would be pathetic to trot out a feeble excuse about her friend being delayed. Somehow, she just knew that Jake would expose her as a fraud.

While she sat there, feeling silly, Jake held out his hand. 'How do you do?' He smiled with effortless charm. 'I'm Jake Devlin. Do you mind if I join you?'

She expected to see a teasing glint in his eyes but, to her surprise, she could only find genuine warmth. Nevertheless, she hesitated.

'Come on, say yes,' Jake urged. 'Otherwise you'll force me to try my pick-up lines.'

'Are they corny?'

'So bad you could feed them to chickens.'

His confession was accompanied by a lopsided self-deprecating grin that melted Mattie on the spot. She suspected that Jake had seen right through her, but it somehow no longer mattered. He was wiping their slate clean. Starting again. And she was enchanted. Caught. Hook, line and sinker.

'You're welcome to sit here, Mr Devlin.'

'Thank you.' He pulled out a chair and sat opposite her and happiness fizzed inside Mattie like soda pop.

Following his lead, she held out her hand. 'How do you do? I'm Matilda Carey.'

'Pleased to meet you.' Jake's expression was deadpan. 'Do your friends call you Mattie?'

'Quite often.' She gave a little shrug and added rather recklessly, 'At times they've been known to call me Florence Nightingale.' She didn't mention the other tag that she hated—Saint Matilda.

'Is that accurate? Are you a caring type?'

''Fraid so.'

The skin around his eyes crinkled and he cocked his head on one side. 'Let me guess. You're probably the kind of girl who cares for sick grannies.'

Mattie's sense of fun faltered. Was he teasing her? Uncertain, she quickly changed the subject. 'I've already ordered. I'm having the chicken noodle soup.'

'I think I'll try the beef stir-fry.' Jake waved to a waitress and, when she came over, he gave his order. 'And I'll have a beer.' Turning to Mattie again, he asked, 'Would you like another glass of wine?'

She tapped the side of her glass. 'This is fine.'

When the waitress left, Jake leaned towards Mattie, hands linked on the table top. His smile faded and, with it, all pretence dropped away. 'Seriously, Mattie, I've been thinking about what you did for your grandmother. That was a huge gesture, to spend two years looking after her.'

She took a quick sip of her wine to cover her surprise, then set the glass down.

'Did it feel like a big sacrifice?' he asked urgently.

'Not at all. Those two years were rather lovely. Gran was always so sweet. So grateful for my company. She never complained about her health.'

'Was she very ill?'

'She had a weak heart, so she tired easily and she couldn't take proper care of her house, but I was happy to help.'

'What do you reckon would have happened if you hadn't looked after her?'

'She'd probably have gone into a nursing home. My parents run a hardware store in a little country town and they were too busy to give her the care she needed.'

'They were lucky you stepped up to the plate.'

'I was happy to help,' she said again. 'Anyway, it was tit for tat. When I was little, my gran nursed me through the chickenpox and the measles and umpteen bouts of tonsillitis. Mum was always too busy helping Dad in the store.'

Unexpectedly, Jake frowned and he looked deeply pained as he rearranged the salt and pepper shakers in the middle of the table.

'What's the matter, Jake? Have I said something wrong?'

He let out a heavy sigh. 'No. You're just confirming my worst fears.'

'Really? How?'

Exhaling another deep sigh, he rested his chin on his hand, and suddenly he was telling her about an old stockman he knew, someone from his childhood called Roy, who was now in a nursing home here in Sydney. As Jake talked about how strong and tough this stockman used to be and how shockingly weak and shut-in he was now, Mattie could see how deeply he cared for the old man.

'My parents and I have let him down,' he said quietly. 'We should be doing more for him.'

On impulse, Mattie reached out and touched the back of Jake's hand. He stiffened as if she'd burned him.

'It sounds as if you've visited Roy whenever you can,' she said softly. 'There's not much else you can do if you're working in Mongolia, but I'm sure your visits mean a lot.'

His gaze met hers and his dark eyes were shimmering and vulnerable and something shifted inside her, almost as if a key had been turned in a lock. *Oh, help.* She'd been trying not to like Jake Devlin, but now she feared she was beginning to like him very much.

Too much. Was she falling in love?

Surely not. She mustn't fall in love. Not again. Not ever. Certainly not now.

Gently, she removed her hand from his. 'Did you take Roy with you to the movies today?'

'No.' Jake looked angry as he shook his head. 'I didn't even think of it. How selfish am I? Roy would have loved a movie. It was an action-adventure flick and they're his favourite.'

'There's always tomorrow,' Mattie suggested gently.

His brow cleared. 'Yes, of course. It's my last day, but that's a good idea.'

'Actually,' Mattie said, warming to this subject, 'if Roy's an outdoor type, he might prefer to be out in the fresh air. You could take him on a ferry ride on the harbour. Do you think he'd be well enough for that?'

'I reckon he might be. That's a *really* good idea.'

The waitress brought Jake's beer and Mattie couldn't help watching the movements of his throat as he took a deep draught. Every inch of him seemed breathtakingly male and dark and sexy. She was beginning to think she'd never met such an attractive man.

Apart from her fiancé, the guys she'd dated had all lived in her home town and she'd known them since they'd first grown baby teeth. She'd gone to kindergarten and school with them. They'd belonged to the same pony club and Sunday school. There were no mysteries there.

Jake, on the other hand, was a man surrounded by mystery.

Pink rose in Mattie's cheeks and Jake watched the telltale colour with mounting dismay.

His reasons for following her to this café weren't crystal clear to him, but he supposed he'd been hoping for useful tips on how to help old Roy. One thing was certain—he wasn't here because she looked cute in those sleek grey trousers, or because her new hairstyle looked terrific and brought out the blue in her eyes.

Hell, no. He wasn't interested in Mattie as a *woman*.

She wasn't even close to his type. She was small and serious and mousy. Well, maybe she wasn't mousy exactly, certainly not now, but she was most definitely small. And *earnest*.

The heat that had scorched him when she'd touched his hand a few minutes earlier was *not* what he'd first feared. He couldn't possibly have experienced hot, pulsing *lust* for her.

On the other hand, Jake didn't want to think too hard about why he'd ended it with his latest female companion, Ange, or why he'd started hanging about the kitchen in the flat in the mornings, or why he'd casually asked Mattie to the movies today.

None of his recent behaviour made sense, and Mattie was giving out confusing signals too. It was as if she was trying to impress him and avoid him at the same time and, like a fool, he'd followed her here. He wasn't in the habit of following women, but he'd convinced himself that she would be able to give him good advice about Roy. That was the only reason he'd come here, wasn't it?

He wished he felt surer. It was a relief when their meals arrived and he could concentrate on eating.

Mattie declared that her soup was delicious—so full of noodles and vegetables that she ate most of it with chopsticks.

Which caused a tiny problem. Jake found himself watching the way she deftly used the chopsticks. Her hands were pale and delicate and graceful, possibly the prettiest hands he'd ever seen. He pictured her holding a pen or a paint-brush as she created her whimsical works of art.

He thought about the way she'd touched him a few minutes ago. Imagined—

'What's the food like in Mongolia?' she asked.

Jake blinked, dragged his mind into gear. 'Er…do you mean the traditional food of the locals, or what we eat on the mine site?'

'Both, I guess.'

'Our cook serves mainly western food, but the Mongolians eat mutton. Loads of mutton. They even drink the mutton fat. It's no place for vege-tarians.'

Mattie wrinkled her nose. 'I rather like Mongolian lamb.'

'The meals in Asian restaurants here in Sydney are nothing like the mutton eaten out on the steppe.'

Mattie accepted this with a shrug. 'Do you live in barracks, or one of those little round tents?'

'I have a tent. They call it a *ger*.'

'It sounds rather primitive.'

'Actually, *gers* aren't too bad. The walls are made out of layers of felt and they're quite snug. In winter we have a stove for heating and in summer we can roll up the sides for ventilation.'

'It's a very different world, isn't it?' she said, glancing out through a window to the city lights.

'That's part of the attraction for me. Then again, I grew up in a remote part of the Outback, so I suppose that made it easier for me to fit in.'

Her blue eyes challenged him. 'Why do you work there?'

Jake had been asked this question before, but suddenly, when Mattie asked him, he wished he had higher motives. There was no point, however, in trying to pretend he was a paragon of virtue.

'I'm footloose and fancy free,' he said, aware that his jaw was jutting at a defensive angle. 'And the job offered a chance to see a really different part of the world. But the big drawcard is that it pays very well.'

He expected to read disapproval in her eyes. To his surprise, she smiled. 'And when you're on leave you can party hard.'

'Mostly.'

The obvious fact that he'd been partying when Mattie had arrived on his doorstep and the equally obvious fact that he was nowhere near a party right now was not something Jake wanted to analyse too closely.

'Tell me more about your paintings,' he said quickly to change the subject.

Mattie dismissed this with a graceful wave of her hand. 'They're just illustrations for a children's book.'

'Do you plan to write the story as well?'

She nodded.

'Have you been published?'

'Uh-huh. I've had three books published so far.'

'No kidding?' He knew his eyes were wide with surprise. 'That's terrific. I've never met an author.'

'Most people don't think of me as a *real* author. They assume that children's stories are incredibly easy to write.'

'How could they be easy, when they're created entirely out of your imagination? And you don't just write the stories, you do the illustrations as well. Aren't children supposed to be the harshest critics of all?'

She nodded and smiled, clearly pleased by his enthusiasm.

'What are your stories about?'

Now Mattie looked embarrassed. 'Nothing you'd be interested in.' She poked her chopsticks into the noodles at the bottom of her bowl.

'Try me.'

'Don't laugh,' she ordered.

'Wouldn't dream of it.'

'They're about a little girl called Molly.' Carefully, she laid the chopsticks across her bowl and sat back, arms folded.

'And…' Jake prompted.

'Molly's actually a white witch and, when her parents aren't looking, she has all sorts of adventures. She goes around doing secret good deeds and terrific acts of heroism.'

Just like her creator, Jake thought, and suddenly he was struggling to hide his amusement.

Mattie's eyes blazed. 'I knew you'd laugh.'

'I'm not laughing.' Why couldn't he stop smiling? 'Honestly. I'm seriously impressed. I'm sure Molly's stories are very popular.'

'They seem to be.' Mattie sniffed, then rolled her eyes, as if she hoped he would drop the subject.

To make amends, Jake said quickly, 'Would you like to go somewhere for coffee?'

She almost glared at him. 'Don't you have other plans?'

Across the table their gazes met, and held. Mattie's eyes were very blue and steady and Jake had the distinct impression she was about to decline his invitation. Which was wise, wasn't it? After all, they weren't planning to hook up. To go on somewhere else for coffee implied taking another step—in completely the wrong direction.

Before he could think of a way to extricate himself from this trap of his own making, Mattie smiled slowly.

'Coffee sounds good,' she said and her smile deepened, revealing an enchanting dimple. 'Your place or mine?'

He couldn't help returning her smile. She was cleverly letting him off the hook, placing them back on their correct footing. As flatmates. For one more day.

'Try my place,' he said smoothly. 'It's very handy—just around the corner.'

A breeze was blowing in from the harbour and it buffeted them as they walked home, making it hard to talk. When they reached the flat, Brutus was as eager to see Jake as he was to see Mattie.

Jake laughed as he gave the little dog a scratch behind his silky ears.

Mattie offered to get the coffee started, but she wasn't at all surprised when Jake announced that perhaps he would go into the city for a bit, after all. She wasn't surprised, but she was disappointed, which was utterly silly. She knew she didn't want to get involved with him. But she also knew she was the kind of girl men left behind when something better came along.

She waved him off with a bright smile. 'Have a good evening.'

'You too.'

'And if you take Roy out tomorrow, I hope you have a good time.'

'Thanks.'

Jake paused on the front step and looked back at her as she lifted a hand to hold back her wind-blown hair. She twisted a strand lightly around one finger and tucked it behind her ear. There was nothing flirtatious about the gesture, but Jake seemed to be transfixed. His gaze scalded her as he stared at her hand, and then at her hair, at her ear.

His interest was so intense that Mattie couldn't breathe. She swayed against the door frame and her legs threatened to give way. She'd never really understood what swooning involved, but she was certain that if Jake had touched her at that moment she would most definitely have swooned.

But Jake gave a slight shake of his head and the possibility vanished. 'Would you come?' he asked.

'Pardon?' Mattie felt dizzy and confused. What was he asking? Surely he wasn't inviting her to go out with him for a fun-filled night on the town?

'Tomorrow,' he said with a smile. 'When I take Roy out, will you come too?'

Whoosh! It was like having a bucket of cold water dumped on her head. A chilling dash of reality. Now Mattie knew without a shadow of a doubt that Jake hadn't followed her to the café tonight because he liked her new hairdo, or the way she looked in her best silk blouse. He hadn't shared a table with her because he fancied her.

And he wasn't interested in taking her out now. The unflattering truth was—Jake was the same as everyone else in Mattie's life—he needed her help.

Sooner or later, everyone turned to Mattie Carey for help, but this time, for her emotional health, she knew she must say no. She shook her head. 'Sorry.'

He frowned at her. 'Don't tell me you have another appointment. What is it this time? A manicure?'

She looked down at her hands. 'I...I need to get on with my book.'

'Couldn't you spare just one day, Mattie?'

His dark eyes were shining with sincerity, but she refused to be taken in. After one meal with him, she was already a mess. If she spent a whole day in his company, she would fall completely under his spell, and that was unwise. It was worse than that. It was ridiculous. Perilous.

She'd tried one long-distance relationship and she was still flinching at the memory almost three years later. She never wanted to embark on another, especially not now when she was on the verge of becoming pregnant with someone else's baby.

'It would be a pity if you couldn't make it,' Jake said, watching her closely. 'I know Roy would really enjoy your company.'

At the mention of Roy she started to weaken. Poor old fellow. Was she making a mountain out of a molehill? Jake was simply asking for help to entertain an old man. How could she try to read romance into that?

And, after all, helping people was what she did best.

Behind her back, she crossed her fingers and hoped she wasn't making a really bad mistake. 'All right,' she said. 'I'll come for Roy's sake.'

As soon as Jake left, Mattie spread out her art things and started on another illustration for her book. This was to be a double-page spread and she wanted to create a scene with Molly at her bedroom window, looking out at the city at night.

She would show Molly and her cat silhouetted against the yellow light of the bedroom window. There would be houses dotted through the night, all with brightly lit windows. Through the windows, she would show glimpses of people who needed Molly's help. A sick child, a lonely old woman, a lost kitten.

In her head, Mattie knew exactly how this illustration should look, but tonight something wasn't gelling. She couldn't slip into the 'zone'— into the happy, creative space that usually cocooned her from the rest of the world while she lost herself in her work.

Tonight Jake Devlin-size thoughts kept intruding. She couldn't stop thinking about him, kept seeing the way he'd looked at her when she'd innocently fiddled with her hair. She was sure she'd never forget the heart-in-mouth connection she'd felt, as if they were suddenly, perfectly in tune.

She was sure that if she'd been any other girl Jake would have kissed her then, but of course he hadn't. Instead, the astonishing vibe that passed between them had remained unacknowledged. And there wasn't much point in trying to read anything into it. Even if there had been a momentary spark with Jake, Mattie had learned not to trust such feelings.

For years she'd wondered if she would ever fall in love. There'd been a high school crush, but that had only lasted one term before she'd been unceremoniously 'dropped'. She'd taken a long time to get over that blow to her self-esteem and, in the years that followed, she'd dated the occasional local boy but there'd been no one special.

Then, three and a half years ago, a hot-looking stranger had arrived in Willowbank.

Pete from Perth had a cute smile and he'd ambled into her parents' hardware store and set his cap at Mattie and swept her completely off her feet. She'd been crazy about him and when he'd returned to Western Australia she'd taken the long flight over there to stay with him. She had done this every month for seven months and Pete had helped to pay for her fare. She'd felt very worldly and sophisticated. And needed.

Pete had promised her the world…well, a diamond ring and a white wedding, a house in the suburbs plus two children…which was everything that Mattie had wanted. But then the day had come when Pete had rung from Perth and Mattie had heard the difference in his voice.

Something had happened.

When he'd suggested that the air fares to Perth were too expensive for her to keep flying over, it had been dead easy to start putting two and two together. But she'd been too scared to ask the crucial questions. She hadn't wanted to hear the answers.

Finally, however, Pete had sent her a text message:

Sorry, I need to check out of this wedding. It's not you, baby, it's me.

She'd rung back in a blind panic and heard the truth she'd desperately feared. Yes, he'd found someone else and could she return the engagement ring by registered mail?

That had been nearly three years ago.

Mattie's heart hadn't just broken, it had shattered and bled. And she'd felt such a loser. So ashamed. Ashamed that she'd fallen for a guy so cowardly he'd called off his wedding via a text message.

And she was ashamed that everyone—yes, literally *everyone* in Willowbank—had known about her wedding plans. From the mayor down to the butcher's apprentice, the whole town knew she'd been dumped. Not only had her pride been hurt, however. She'd lost faith—in men, in herself, in the romantic twaddle everyone called love.

Her friends had tried to tell her that she shouldn't see this as a failure. Easy for them to say. They hadn't been a hair's breadth from happily-ever-after and then discarded by remote control.

Mattie thought it was perfectly reasonable that she'd given up on her foolish dream of a husband and family. Utterly logical that she'd retreated from the dating circus and hadn't had a boyfriend since. It was far safer to care for people and find countless ways to be helpful than to risk another train wreck for her heart.

Next morning, however, Mattie was pleased she'd agreed to visit Roy. She took one look at his twinkling blue eyes and she liked him instantly. He had thinning hair, carefully combed over his sun-spotted scalp, a wiry body and thin legs, bandy from a lifetime spent astride a horse, but there was something lived-in about him that made her feel very comfortable as they shook hands.

Impulsively, she gave him a hug. Then she saw the shining joy in Roy's eyes when he greeted Jake, and a fresh coil of happiness warmed her heart.

'You must be keen to get out of here, mate,'

Jake told Roy lightly. 'You came bolting out of that door like a racehorse out of the starting gate.'

'I didn't want to waste a minute.' Roy's pale blue eyes were shining with the wicked glee of a schoolboy planning to skip school. 'The nursing mafia ganged up on me,' he told them. 'They reckon I can only stay out for two hours.'

'What happens if you're not back in time?' Jake asked. 'Do you turn into a pumpkin?'

'More likely Prince Charming.' Roy laughed and gave Mattie a wink.

He wasn't walking too steadily, and she quickly offered her arm for support as he made his way to the car.

'Thank you, sweetheart,' he said, but then he shot a gimlet glance Jake's way. 'How did a black-hearted rascal like you find this lovely lass?'

Mattie held her breath and watched Jake's face. She wondered how he would answer this. He would be as keen as she was to make sure that Roy didn't jump to the wrong conclusion about them. He was unlikely to say, Oh, Mattie turned up on my doorstep. Or, We're sharing a flat. But how else could he explain?

She needn't have worried. Clearly, Jake was more practised at coming up with smooth answers to awkward questions than she was. 'Mattie and

I met through a mutual friend,' he said with a slow smile that did not include her. 'One of my mates from Mongolia comes from the same country town as Mattie.'

'Where's that?' Roy asked and Mattie silently congratulated Jake for managing to steer the conversation in a safe direction.

'A little town called Willowbank,' she told him. 'West of the Blue Mountains.'

Roy was delighted. 'So you're a country girl.'

'Born and bred.'

'I knew it.'

Roy might have waxed lyrical about the superior charms of country girls, but they'd reached the car. Mattie suggested that Jake should drive and that Roy should have the front passenger seat because it was easier for him to get in and out, and she insisted that she was perfectly happy in the back.

As Jake drove out of the nursing home's carefully manicured grounds he said, 'Mattie and I planned a ferry trip on the harbour, but I don't think we'll have time for that if you only have a couple of hours. Is there somewhere else you'd like to go?'

They'd emerged onto the busy main road and Roy peered through the windscreen at the expanse of red-roofed houses with television aerials and powerlines. He squinted at the busy lanes of traffic zooming up and down. 'I don't s'pose there's a park nearby? Somewhere with a little patch of bushland?'

'Sure to be,' Jake asserted confidently. 'We'll keep our eyes peeled.'

'If all else fails, we could go to the Botanical Gardens,' Mattie suggested. 'But, I must admit, I don't know much about the parks here. I'm not very familiar with Sydney.'

'Now, if you were looking for pubs,' said Jake, 'I'd be your man.'

But they were in luck and they found a leafy park quite quickly.

Pleased with themselves, they helped Roy out of the car, and the old man stood with his hands on his hips and looked about him at the smooth sweep of lawns dotted with picnic tables and chairs, at the gas-fired barbecues and big shade trees, carefully pruned to give a clear view beneath them. He looked at the ornamental lake, where young mothers and toddlers were feeding ducks. Then he tipped his head back and stared up at the clear blue sky and drew in a deep breath.

'What do you reckon?' Jake asked with a hopeful smile.

Roy looked about him again and he nodded slowly. 'It's nice.'

Mattie could see the wistful sadness in his face.

'But it's not what you hoped,' Jake suggested carefully.

Roy's face pulled into a worried grimace. 'It's…it's all very tidy, isn't it?'

Mattie laughed to ease the tension. 'You want proper bush—straggly gum trees with fallen branches and knee-high dry grass, don't you, Roy?'

He smiled sheepishly. 'S'pose I do.'

'And you want to be able to smell eucalyptus leaves.'

Roy nodded.

'And to boil a billy over a campfire.'

'Don't get carried away, Mattie,' Jake warned, signalling frowning looks over Roy's head. 'There's no way we can do all that here.'

But Mattie was already thinking ahead. This was her very favourite situation. She was never happier than when she detected a need in someone—an almost impossible need—and then figured out a way to meet it. The impulse had begun as a game when she was very young—anticipating a simple need her mother might have, like knowing, without being asked, whether to pick beans or peas from the garden.

It had been easy for Mattie because she knew her mother's habits—beans with beef and peas with lamb—but her mother would exclaim with delight when she discovered the peas in the colander, already shelled, or the beans topped and tailed.

'My amazing little mind-reader,' she would say and sometimes she would hug Mattie, making her feel loved and secure and needed.

'I'm going to scout around for gum trees,' she told Roy and Jake. 'You guys sit over at that picnic table and I'll be back in two ticks.'

Halfway along the path that circled the ornamental lake, she found a clump of gum trees and she knew the familiar skinny white trunks and dull khaki-coloured tapering leaves would gladden Roy's heart. Soon she was back with an armful of fallen twigs and gum leaves.

Jake was smiling and shaking his head at her. He looked puzzled. Roy looked delighted.

'They've dried out but they still smell good,' she told Roy as she dumped them on the slatted timber table top.

With a shaking hand, Roy reached out and picked up a twiggy branch. He crushed the brittle gum leaves between his fingers and leaned in to smell the distinct aroma of eucalyptus. 'Perfect,' he whispered with a blissful sigh.

'It's only a little way around the lake to see them,' Mattie said. 'And I think we can organise billy tea too.'

'No way,' Jake protested. 'We can't have an open fire in a public park.'

Mattie laid a placating hand on Jake's arm. Big mistake. High-voltage tension zapped through her. She retracted her hand, took a shaky breath.

'I…I know we can't have a fire here.' Her voice was thready and soft. She took another breath and told herself that this morning was all about Roy. Her focus was Roy. Jake was a minor distraction she must ignore. 'But we could boil a billy over a camping stove at our place,' she said. 'And we can even stir the tea with a gum tree twig. That would be authentic enough, wouldn't it, Roy?'

Roy was looking a tad dazed, trying to keep up with Mattie and with the undercurrent humming between her and Jake, but he nodded happily.

Jake, however, was still protesting. 'But we don't have the gear.'

'We can stop off at a camping store on the way home. It'll only take a minute to buy a little stove and a billy and they're dirt cheap.'

Jake shook his head but his eyes were warm as he smiled at her, and she could feel that warmth all the way to her toes.

CHAPTER FOUR

JAKE had to hand it to Mattie.

Single-handedly, she had given Roy a perfect two hours. The old guy had been deliriously happy, ensconced in an easy chair in their front garden with Brutus snuggled in his lap, while Jake boiled a billy on a small gas ring.

The morning had been filled with laughter and a huge sense of fun, part of which involved making the billy tea with as much formal ritual as a Japanese tea ceremony.

Summoning immense dignity, Roy threw a handful of loose tea leaves into the pot. Mattie gave the brew a flourishing stir with the mandatory gum tree twig and Jake swung the billy in a wide arc to mix the brew, pleased that he hadn't lost the knack.

They drank their tea out of tin mugs, which Mattie had found in the camping store, and they ate scones, which she'd bought from a bakery and warmed in the microwave, serving them liberally smothered with butter and golden syrup.

'Next time I'll make you proper damper,' she assured Roy.

Jake wanted to tell her that she needn't worry about next time, that Roy wasn't her responsibility. But he sensed the advice would be water off a duck's back for Mattie Carey. She'd taken Roy under her wing in the same way she'd saved Brutus from the animal refuge, and she'd cared for her grandmother and, no doubt, countless other people.

It was clearly the way Mattie was wired. She bent over backwards to please people, to find ways to make them happy. Jake wondered how many people went out of their way to make her happy. Who went to great lengths to make her face light up with the same happiness and amazement he'd seen in Roy this morning?

By the time Roy returned to the nursing home, he was a very different old man. He was walking more confidently and grinning from ear to ear, and Jake could have sworn he saw more colour in his face.

But it came as a shock to realise that Roy wasn't the only guy who'd changed in Mattie's company. Jake felt different too. This morning, buzzing about Sydney in her little car, hunting down camping stores and mucking about with that tiny gas ring, he'd felt more relaxed than he had in years. He'd been more optimistic too, less cynical and not nearly as self-absorbed.

He really liked the person he became when he was around Mattie. He was beginning to think that if he'd had more time, he would like to get to know her better, to let their acquaintance deepen into friendship. Not that he was in the habit of developing friendships with women.

His time in Mongolia was so unbearably long and his leave so annoyingly short that he usually spent most of his leave trying to meet as many different women as possible. A deep and meaningful friendship with one woman was not and never had been on his agenda.

Meeting Mattie, however, had thrown him off balance. He was sure he should do something about that, but he had no idea where to start.

'That was fun, wasn't it?' Mattie punctuated her comment with a happy sigh as they headed back into the city, with Jake still behind the driving wheel. 'Roy's a darling.'

Jake chuckled. 'He'd be red as a tomato if he heard you calling him a "darling". As far as I can remember, he's always been shy around women.'

'A lot of those Outback guys are.' Mattie shot him a cheeky sideways glance. 'Present company excluded.'

Jake shrugged this aside. 'Roy certainly took a shine to you.'

'Maybe…but he's *very* fond of you, Jake.'

'Yeah…well…I guess he looks on me as the son he never had.'

'That's nice.'

The tone of Mattie's voice made Jake glance at her. Her smile had turned inward, as if she was thinking about something personal, something that made her pensive and slightly wistful.

When the silence lingered, he wondered if he'd said something to upset her. He'd merely mentioned that Roy looked on him as the son he'd never had… How had that plunged Mattie into such deep contemplation? Clearly, whatever absorbed her did not involve him.

To Jake's dismay, he realised he wanted her attention. Wanted her animated company. Wanted *her*.

There it was—the crazy truth.

Without making a single overt advance, Mattie had crept under his defences. She was so not his type and yet he was attracted. Madly.

He wanted to know more about her. Wanted to know everything, while there was time.

'Have you always gone out of your way to help people?' he asked.

She smiled. ''Fraid so.'

'I should have said people and animals,' he amended.

'Well, yes, it probably started with kittens.'

'Really? When was that?'

A reminiscent gleam crept into her eyes. 'Oh, I was about ten. There was a group of us who always used to hang out together. We'd play cricket, go swimming or riding and have picnics down by the river.'

'Sounds like fun.' Jake was thinking of his lonely childhood on an Outback cattle station, with no brothers or sisters, only his busy parents and a string of indifferent governesses.

'One time, we went swimming in the local creek,' Mattie continued. 'And I found a bag of half-drowned kittens that someone must have dumped just before we arrived. I was devastated.'

A warm ache flowered deep inside Jake as he pictured ten-year-old Mattie, her blue eyes stricken by the pitiful plight of a bunch of kittens.

'I raced back to my place,' she went on. 'My parents weren't home—they were busy at their shop. So I quickly organised my friends, drying the kittens off with bath towels and feeding them bits of sardines soaked in milk. Then I hid them in the bottom of my wardrobe.'

'I hope you didn't try to keep them there.'

She made a scoffing sound. 'I was too smart for

that. The next day I piled them into the basket on the front of my bike and pedalled them all over the district. I reckon I must have visited just about every family from Willowbank to Nardoo.'

'And you found safe homes for all those cats?'

'Every one,' she said with a grin.

Jake smiled too. 'So…what do you have planned for the rest of today?' he asked her.

Mattie blinked and bright colour rushed into her cheeks. 'Oh…um…I should be getting on with my book.'

'But you'd rather not,' he suggested, sending her his most charming smile. 'You'd rather come to the movies with me, wouldn't you?'

She didn't answer and Jake's spirits took a downward dive. She was sitting very still, staring directly ahead.

'I could throw in lunch as well,' he said.

'But we're very casually dressed.' She frowned down at her T-shirt and faded jeans.

'No worries. There's a terrific fish and chip joint just around the corner from the cinema.'

A corner of her mouth twitched, then her lips curved upwards into a fully fledged grin. She turned to him, offering a full-frontal view of her beautiful smile. Her blue eyes danced. 'How did you know I can't resist fish and chips?'

'I'm a deeply intuitive guy.'

'Sure.'

He pretended to be hurt. 'Haven't you noticed my sensitive side?'

Still smiling, she shook her head, but then, with the speed of a light switch, her smile vanished. 'This wouldn't be a date, would it?'

Jake felt the fun go out of his day. He stopped at a red light and turned to her. 'I simply want to thank you for helping out with Roy.' To his surprise, he found himself adding, 'But would it be so terrible if we went on a date?'

'Ange might think so. Won't she mind?'

At first, Jake thought Mattie was joking. What had Ange to do with this? She was already a fading memory, joining the long list of other women he'd dated.

Mattie, however, was looking distinctly concerned.

'Don't worry about Ange,' he said.

'Have you broken up with her?'

'She wasn't really a girlfriend.'

Her mouth opened as if she was planning to say something, but then apparently changed her mind. As the lights changed and they took off again, she said, 'So…what movie are you planning to see?'

Grinning with relief, Jake bravely named a romantic chick flick that he knew was showing that week. He usually avoided them like the plague, but he was pretty damn sure it was the sort of film Mattie would love. Most girls did. And it was the least he owed her after this morning.

To his surprise, she screwed up her nose. 'I can't believe you want to see a soppy film like that,' she scoffed. 'I prefer crime thrillers. Any chance of catching a good one?'

He was sure she was just being Mattie, trying to do and say the right thing, but this time he wasn't going to argue.

Mattie sat in the popcorn-scented darkness, super-aware of Jake's presence beside her. She tried to concentrate on the screen—it was one of those complicated spy films where you needed to stay focused at the beginning or you'd be hopelessly lost—but Jake's proximity and the darkness were conspiring against her.

She was almost bursting out of her skin with lust.

Good grief. She felt as if she'd overdosed on hormones. How on earth was she supposed to sit still for almost two hours when Jake Devlin was so close?

She was terrified of making a fool of herself, of bursting the bubble of happiness that had seemed to enclose them today. She'd had such a wonderful time this morning with Jake and Roy.

And lunch had been perfect, eating crunchy fish and chips, sprinkled with salt and lemon juice, straight from the paper it was wrapped in.

Now, however, her lusty thoughts were making it impossible for her to relax and enjoy the movie. She kept stealing glimpses of Jake's hunky profile, lit up by the glow of the screen. He was gorgeous. She was deeply, helplessly attracted to him.

There, she'd admitted it. Whether it was sensible or not, it had happened, and her desire felt like a bushfire rapidly burning out of control.

She allowed herself to wonder how it would feel to trace the line of Jake's profile with her lips, to kiss his forehead and his dark brows, then his slightly beaky nose, his rough jaw and, finally, his yummy, sensuous mouth.

Crikey, she was really getting carried away. She tried again to concentrate on the movie. Jake might expect her to talk about it later. He might be the kind of movie-goer who liked to analyse and dissect the plot.

She'd told him that she hadn't wanted to see a romance movie, which was totally untrue. She loved them, but she knew guys would rather have their teeth drilled than watch soppy movies. Now, however, an unexpected romance was unfolding on the screen and Mattie found herself drawn in.

The spy had met a mysterious beauty, a brunette

with a waiflike, vulnerable quality. Mattie decided she was almost certainly a double agent. It was obvious, wasn't it? Why couldn't the hero see that the woman wasn't telling him the whole truth? He was obviously smitten. Fool.

Half an hour later, Mattie had changed her mind about the double agent. She was deeply absorbed in the film, desperate for the good guy to win and for the lovers to get together, when out of the blue the lovely heroine started her car and it exploded in a burst of garish flames and flying metal.

Mattie screamed.

Jake reached for her hand and gave it a reassuring squeeze. 'It's only a movie,' he whispered, nuzzling her ear as he did so.

'A-a-ah…' It was the most articulate response she could manage. The on-screen heroine might have gone up in flames, but Mattie was on fire too. Her earlobe and the side of her neck were burning from the gentle brush of Jake's lips. Their arms were linked now and she was ablaze from her elbow to the tips of her fingers.

Hot desire pooled in the pit of her stomach. Man! She'd never felt so turned on.

A desperate sigh escaped her, but it sounded like a moan and she blushed with embarrassment.

Thank heavens for the darkness.

* * *

Jake was still holding Mattie's hand when they came out of the cinema. They both blinked at the bright daylight outside and Mattie hoped Jake didn't expect her to recall every twist and turn in the movie. For the entire second half she had been unable to concentrate on anything except the mesmerising pressure of his thumb gently stroking the back of her hand.

'So what did you think of that?'

'It was pretty good.' She held her breath, expecting more questions.

He smiled at her and his dark eyes smouldered. 'Would you like to go home now?'

Was this code for something else? Jake was still holding her hand and she felt as if so much had changed since they'd left the flat this morning. This was their last night together. Tomorrow, he was flying back to Mongolia.

'Home sounds good,' she said and she knew there was every chance she would have agreed if he'd asked her to swim across Sydney Harbour.

The short journey to the flat seemed to take forever and the whole way Mattie worried. Did Jake feel the same as she did? She was astonished by the force of her attraction for him. She thought she might expire if he didn't want to make love to her the minute they were inside the front door.

She thought briefly—very briefly—about her

surrogacy plans. But that was in the future—
almost a fortnight away—and Jake was only here
for this one last night. Right now, at this moment,
she only wanted to think about him. She wanted
to stop being careful and to simply let go.

They parked the car and tension hovered above
them like a private thunder cloud as they walked
together to the front steps. Even before Jake put the
key in the door, they could hear Brutus barking a
greeting. The little dog jumped around their ankles
and then darted outside to explore the garden.

Mattie dropped her shoulder bag onto a lounge
chair. Jake set the keys on the coffee table. They
looked at each other. His eyes were intense and
yet warm. The muscles in his throat rippled.

'Mattie,' he said softly.

'Yes.'

He looked at her with a slightly puzzled smile.
'That sounded like an answer.'

'I think it is, Jake.'

He drew a sharp breath, but he didn't speak.

Mattie knew he was waiting. This was it—an all
or nothing moment. Bravely, she said, 'I thought
you might be asking if…if I'd like you to kiss me.'

Before she could say anything else, he closed the
gap between them. With a soft sound that might
have been a groan, he drew her in and kissed her.

Oh, *how* he kissed her.

His lips were as eager and scorching and greedy as Mattie needed them to be. In a matter of moments, she and Jake were stumbling down the hallway together, laughing a little with surprise that this was really happening, stopping to lean against the wall while they exchanged feverish kisses, stopping again while Jake's hands stole under her T-shirt, sending a rush of sweet anticipation over her already sensitised skin.

In the doorway to Jake's bedroom, however, Mattie froze.

'No, not in here,' she whispered. Not on those same sheets he'd tangled with Ange. 'Come to my room.'

With a soft wordless cry, he scooped her up and carried her down to the little back bedroom and together they tumbled onto the bed, hungry, urgent, eager.

Lips, hands, bodies sought each other—kissing, touching, nibbling, caressing.

Jake lifted Mattie's T-shirt over her head. She heard his swift gasp of surprise and she felt obliged to confess her secret weakness for low-cut sassy lingerie. But she didn't mention that she'd kept up the tradition even though there'd been no one to admire the effects.

He chuckled softly. 'I'm so glad you have a vice.' With reverent fingers, he touched the lacy trim on her bra. 'This is a weakness you should never, ever try to give up.'

Mattie was amazed by how uninhibited she felt with Jake, as if being with him took her straight into her natural element.

She loved everything about making love with Jake. Loved the way he tasted and the way he smelled. She adored the daring ways that he kissed her and touched her, sometimes gentle, sometimes fiery.

Always, always he knew exactly what she needed and before she even knew that she needed it.

When they neared the point of no return, only one thing worried her. If Jake wasn't prepared, she would have to raise the touchy subject of protection. With the surrogacy about to begin, she couldn't afford to take any risks.

But she needn't have worried. Jake was well and truly prepared and he was as keen to avoid any risks as she was.

Later, as afternoon sun streamed through the window, Jake reached for Mattie's hands. He lifted them to his lips and kissed each of her knuckles. 'Has anyone told you that you have beautiful hands?'

She laughed with surprise and held out her hands so she could study them in the deepening sunlight.

'See how white and dainty they are.'

But Mattie was looking at Jake's big, wide hands and the darkness of his skin. She trembled deliciously as she remembered the incredibly intimate way his big hands had touched her.

'Compared with yours, my hands are tiny.' She giggled softly. 'To be honest, I prefer yours.'

'No, no,' Jake protested, his voice turning playful. 'Your hands are gorgeous.'

'Yours are gorgeous-er.'

'I could eat your hands.'

He began to nibble her fingertips and Mattie gasped as the warm intimacy of his teeth and tongue sent ripples of heat straight to the pit of her stomach.

'I…I suppose I should take more care of my hands,' she murmured. 'When my friend Gina was single, she used to slather cream on her hands every night and wear gloves to bed.'

Jake laughed. 'No gloves in this bed, please.'

'You won't know. You won't be here. You'll be in Mongolia for the next six months.'

'I'm here now.' Jake took her hands again and held them above her head. With a soft chuckle he lowered his mouth to hers. 'Make the most of me.'

'Oh, don't worry. I plan to.'

* * *

The magic afternoon rolled into an equally magic evening. Dusk fell, filling their room with purple shadows, and Mattie and Jake realised they were ravenously hungry. They went through to the kitchen to make pasta, deciding they would concoct a brilliant sauce from whatever ingredients they could find in the fridge and the pantry.

Together they investigated Will's collection of CDs and agreed on a middle-of-the-road rock 'n' roll number and, while the flat throbbed with its beat, they cheerfully chopped bacon and vegetables and supervised the pasta boiling on the stove. The whole time, their newfound happiness bubbled through them, erupting into sudden bursts of unexplained laughter or melting into blissful lingering kisses.

The meal turned out surprisingly well, and they found half a bottle of wine to wash it down. Then, knowing they had the luxury of one last long night ahead of them, they took Brutus for a walk.

Salty wind plucked at their clothes and at their hair as they walked hand in hand, stealing kisses and sharing jokes, grinning madly at the moon and feeling very much at one with the entire magnificent, beautiful universe.

* * *

It wasn't until Jake looked back on their behaviour the next morning that he realised they'd carried on very much like lovers. Like idyllic fairy-tale lovers who could look forward to a happy and long-lasting future. Not at all like a couple on a one-night stand.

It was a worrying discovery.

As dawn broke, he lay awake beside Mattie, fighting to resist the temptations of her delectable body and to hold at bay the tantalising memories of last night—the heady scent of her skin, the sweetness of her lips, the seductive sounds of her laughter and her soft whisperings.

Last night, every inch of his body had been on fire. He'd never spent a night like it, but now he needed to clear his thoughts, to sort out exactly what had happened to him and to Mattie and what it meant now. Had he made a terrible mistake?

His normal reaction to having bedded a new woman was a sweet feeling of conquest, a subtle boost to his ego that left him tingling with anticipation for repeat performances. But, last night, he'd experienced something more. So much more. And it left him this morning feeling quite shaken.

Making love with Mattie had been beyond beautiful, beyond amazing—but what had caught Jake completely by surprise was the deep sense of inner contentment he'd felt afterwards. He'd lain here, with this heavenly woman in his arms, and he'd been filled with an astonishing sense of well-being, a nudging awareness that Mattie Carey was completely and absolutely right for him.

The experience was totally new, and he found it more than a little frightening. He'd never felt this close to anyone since…

For a devastating moment he was a small boy again, locked on the outside of his mother's bedroom, afraid and lonely and lost. Understanding nothing…

No, he couldn't think about that or the following years when his mother had shut him out. He never allowed himself to think about it.

His priority now was to work out what to do about his worrying desire to stay with Mattie, to protect her.

To protect her from what, exactly?

It seemed he wanted to protect her from everything—falling buildings, colds and chills, other men…

Get real, Jake…

It was his usual style to put distance between himself and the latest girl, to keep her guessing. Normally, he would go surfing, or ring up a mate and down a couple of beers at the pub, anything to avoid getting too involved with any one woman.

Today he would be leaving Sydney and he knew he had to shake off this sense of deeper connection to Mattie Carey. He hadn't planned on starting a relationship. There was no point. He could never promise anything long term and it was only fair that Mattie understood that.

But it was too hard to think about this while lying beside her. Carefully, Jake eased out of bed without disturbing her. He padded down the hall to the kitchen, where Brutus was waiting to be let out. He opened the door and watched the little dog dash off into the garden.

He put water on to boil, removed the cloth covering Pavarotti's cage, topped up the bird's seed and gave him fresh water. While his coffee was brewing, he went to the bathroom to shower.

Naked, beneath the hot water, he thought about the tedious journey back to Mongolia—the long flight to Beijing, followed by another flight to Ulaanbaatar and then a journey by truck out to the mine site.

If he was honest, he had to admit that he'd never really minded his current lifestyle. Even though he'd complained at times about being stuck in Mongolia for long stretches, he quite liked the isolated blokeish world of the mine.

It was almost an extension of his boarding school days.

He got on well with his workmates. They filled the long evenings with chess or poker, backgammon or Scrabble, and he'd also made friends with a few of the locals and managed to go horse-riding at least once a week.

He certainly liked the money he earned. Given the current mining boom and the constant need for environmental monitoring, anyone with his qualifications could make a small fortune if they were willing to work on the remote mines scattered around the world. Jake was prepared to do just that.

His ambitions were important to him, mainly because he had something to prove to his parents. OK—it was a clichéd young bull/old bull struggle, but he'd grown up determined to make his way in the world by rejecting the life his parents had planned for him.

His father had never had much time for him. Admittedly, Jake and his mother had been close before her breakdown, but from the age of nine, he'd been left in the care of a succession of governesses, or to be entertained by Roy. Then there'd been boarding school.

His parents had focused on raising their cattle and training their racehorses, or throwing lavish parties after race meetings. Jake had spent a solitary childhood, never feeling that his parents needed him, and in response he'd chosen to make his own way.

It was vitally important to prove to his parents that he could become successful in his own right, so he had no plans to change his job in the near future. But, this morning, the thought of going back to Mongolia for six long months left a chasm in his gut so big a truck could pass through it.

He was going to miss Mattie.

But he wasn't right for her.

He couldn't give her the steady commitment she needed and deserved. If he was halfway decent, he should tell her that. Now, this morning, before he left, before it was too late.

He was leaning against a kitchen bench, coffee mug in hand, when Mattie came in, wearing a white towelling bathrobe tied at the waist. Her feet were bare and she hadn't bothered to brush her hair. Jake wondered if she'd deliberately left her hair in that just-out-of-bed disarray because she knew it looked so damn sexy.

Her soft skin had a peachy sleep-warmed glow and he had to fight a fierce urge to pull her in for a deep and meaningful good morning kiss.

Hell. Hadn't he decided it was time to back off?

'Morning.' Mattie sent him a shy smile, then looked around the kitchen. 'Oh, I see you've taken care of Brutus and Pavarotti. Thanks.'

'No problem.'

Jake watched the upward tilt of her soft, full lips as she smiled again. He watched the way she tucked a wayward curl behind her ear and he forgot every one of his good intentions in his need to taste her, to let his hands slip inside her towelling robe to explore once more the exquisite softness of her slender waist, the silken roundness of her breasts.

Right at this moment, there was only one thing he wanted and that was to take Mattie straight back to bed.

His lips dipped to meet hers. Ah, yes…he could spend the whole morning just kissing her…

'Um.' Gently Mattie broke the kiss and she pushed her hands against his chest, easing out of his embrace. Her eyes were serious as she dropped a light kiss on his chin. 'I think I'll take a shower.'

'Sure,' he said, disappointed. 'Will I…er… start breakfast?'

She paused in the kitchen doorway. 'Don't you have to pack this morning?'

'I'll take two seconds to throw my few things in a bag.'

Mattie gave a shrug. 'Cook whatever you like,

but don't worry about me. I'll fix tea and toast when I've showered.'

'Let me know if you'd like a hand in there.'

She smiled, but there was no coy come-hither message in her eyes and she left without replying.

Jake took a moment to collect his thoughts. He'd almost made a serious mistake, carrying on with Mattie like a lover, instead of a guy who was about to walk out of her life.

He'd never enjoyed the morning after, letting women know that they couldn't hope for a long term future. He'd had some bad experiences with women who were clinging and possessive and he supposed he should be pleased that Mattie was letting him off the hook so easily.

He should be very grateful. And he was. Of course he was.

CHAPTER FIVE

MATTIE was towelling her hair dry when she heard the phone. She'd been trying to decide if she should use the blow-dryer to try to turn her hair into the sleek bob the hairdresser had achieved, but she abandoned the challenge and hurried into the kitchen, damp hair in a tangle.

Jake had already answered the phone and, when he turned and grinned at her, her tummy flipped.

He was so beautiful. She longed to hurl herself into his arms, but he was leaving today and she had to be brave. The last thing he would want was a clinging vine.

'It's for you,' he said.

'Who is it?'

He handed her the phone. 'Your friend Gina.'

'Oh.' Mattie's stomach stopped flipping and tied itself in knots instead. If Gina had spoken to Jake, her friend would be agog with surprise and brimming with questions. Mattie took a deep breath. 'Hi, Gina.'

'Mattie, how's life in stunning Sydney?'

'Stunning.'

'I'll bet it is.' Gina's voice was rippling with undertone. 'If the man answering your phone's deep, sexy "hello" is anything to go by, you've been having a *ball*! Crikey, Mattie, it didn't take you long to find Jake.'

'I didn't *find* him. He's a friend of Will's from Mongolia and he's been staying here this week.'

'Oh, I remember now. Will mentioned a friend called Jake. Bit of a ladies' man, I take it. Gosh, Mattie, has he been staying there in the flat with you?'

Mattie glanced over her shoulder to check if Jake was listening. He'd made scrambled eggs and now he was piling fluffy spoonfuls onto a piece of toast.

'It seems Will mixed up the dates, but it's worked out OK,' she said.

'So you've been sharing Will's flat with this Jake guy?'

Gina's own voice had risen by several decibels. By contrast, Mattie kept her tone deliberately calm.

'I just told you, Gina. It's worked out fine.'

From the other side of the kitchen, Jake winked

at Mattie, then he pointed with his thumb to indicate that he was taking his breakfast out onto the balcony.

She waved to him and smiled her gratitude.

'Is he hot?' Gina asked.

'Yes, actually.'

'From what I've heard, he's dangerous.'

'Not really.'

'Oh, my God. You've fallen for him, haven't you?'

'Not fallen…exactly.'

'Oh, Mattie, you have. I can hear it in your voice. Oh, no! I know what this means. You're madly in love with this Jake guy and you want to marry him and have his babies and you don't want to do the surrogacy any more.'

'Gina, for heaven's sake, calm down. Of course I'm still going ahead with it.'

'Really? You're sure?'

'I'm absolutely sure. I couldn't be surer. Do you really think I could let my best friend down?'

'But will Jake mind when you're pregnant?'

'He's not going to know.' Mattie's hand tightened around the receiver. She lowered her voice to just above a whisper and prayed that Jake couldn't hear. 'He's going back to Mongolia today.'

'So you haven't told him about the surrogacy?'

'Of course I haven't. I promised you and Tom

that I'd keep this completely private. Why would I discuss it with one of Will's friends?'

Right from the start, Mattie had planned to keep this project under wraps, but Tom had been particularly anxious that their plan must remain strictly secret. He'd been terrified they'd end up as a double-page feature spread in some women's magazine.

'But it must be hard to keep a secret from a boyfriend,' Gina said.

Mattie answered quite firmly. 'He's not exactly my boyfriend. I only met him a few days ago.'

'But you're involved with him, aren't you?'

Mattie gulped. She couldn't possibly answer that question. Gina knew her history with Pete and she would probably get defensive. Besides, it sounded so brazen to admit that she'd slept with a guy she'd only met a few days ago.

But it hadn't felt brazen. It had felt totally right and perfectly lovely.

She drew a quick breath. 'Everything's very… up in the air.' To her horror, her eyes filled with tears. 'Gina, I'll ring you tomorrow. OK?'

'I'm so sorry, Mattie. I just get so intense about this baby. Now I've got you crying.'

'I'm not. Honestly. But I've got to go now. I'll ring you soon. Or I'll e-mail. I promise.'

The tears began to stream down Mattie's

cheeks as she replaced the receiver. She couldn't believe she'd dissolved so quickly. What if Jake saw her like this?

She hurried to the sink and splashed her face with cold water, snatched up a hand towel and mopped at her eyes. That was better.

She found a dollop of scrambled eggs in the pot on the stove and a piece of toast sitting in the toaster. She collected a plate, a knife and fork, helped herself to the food and took it outside to the balcony. For a couple more hours, until Jake was on the plane, she had to behave as normally as possible.

Jake had almost finished his breakfast when she arrived on the balcony. He was watching her closely as she sat down and she prayed that he couldn't tell that she'd been crying.

'That was Gina, Will's sister,' she told him.

Jake nodded, but he was frowning at Mattie and she wondered if he'd overheard her end of the conversation. What exactly had she said?

'Gina's my best friend,' she explained.

'Yes.' He was still frowning at her. 'I gathered that.'

What else had Jake 'gathered'? Why was he looking at her so ferociously? He couldn't possibly know about her surrogacy plans, could he? Somehow, Mattie just knew in her bones that he would be very upset if he discovered she was about to become pregnant with someone else's baby.

But it wasn't really any of his business, was it? He was going away for six months and by the time he came back he might have forgotten about her. He'd told her that he was footloose and fancy free and she was quite sure that was how he wanted to stay. Look at how easily he'd dumped Ange.

Just the same, his frown made Mattie nervous as she cut off a corner of toast and loaded it with egg. As she lifted the food to her mouth, Jake's hand shot across the table and he grabbed her wrist.

'Hey!' she cried as the food toppled back onto her plate. 'What was that for?'

'Aren't you allergic to eggs?'

'Oh.' She let out a whoosh of air. What a relief! His frowning concern had nothing to do with her phone conversation.

He pointed to her plate. 'The other morning when I made an omelette, you told me you were allergic to eggs.'

'You're right,' she admitted. 'Sorry. I'm afraid I was lying.'

Jake's relief was evident. 'I hope you had a good reason for lying.' He relaxed back in his chair and watched her with a look of dark bemusement.

'I had a very good reason. You were being mulish and I wanted to be mulish right back at you.'

'I was mulish?' He pretended to be shocked. 'When?'

Mattie thought about it and realised that her grounds for disliking Jake in those first couple of days had been based solely on the fact that he hadn't shown the slightest interest in her. It was an unsettling discovery and she certainly wasn't going to share it with him now.

'I...I can't remember the exact details,' she said lamely. She took another bite of egg and toast, but it seemed to stick in her throat. Suddenly she was thinking about everything that had happened since that morning Jake had made the omelette. How could she have undergone such a huge transformation in such a short space of time?

She hoped she didn't start crying again, but this morning she seemed to be faced by constant reminders of how deeply and swiftly she'd fallen for Jake. Heavens, from the moment she'd set eyes on him, she'd been sinking like a stone. And she'd promised herself this would never happen again!

She was still lost in thought when Jake glanced at his wristwatch and she was grateful for the distraction. 'It's almost time for you to leave for the airport.'

He sighed. 'I should book a taxi.'

'No, I'll drive you.'

'It's a long way and the traffic will be hell at this hour.'

Her eyes were threatening to water again. Damn. 'Jake, please don't argue. I'd like to take you to the airport.' Any time with him felt precious.

His throat made a swallowing motion and he looked almost as upset as she felt. 'Thanks, Mattie.' He picked up his breakfast things.

'Leave them.' Mattie was aghast by how brittle she sounded. 'I'll look after the kitchen. You go and get ready.'

'OK, OK.'

Her hands were shaking as she loaded the dishwasher, and she broke a cup. She'd just finished putting the pieces in the bin as Jake came in with a backpack swung over his shoulder.

She tried to sound relaxed. 'You travel light.'

He smiled crookedly. 'I'm not much of a shopper.'

'I'll just clean my teeth and get my bag.'

In a matter of moments she was back. Jake was holding Brutus and rubbing the little dog's silky ears. Brutus licked him under the chin. 'We're saying goodbye.'

Mattie nodded and bit her lip to hold back tears. 'I hope you said goodbye to Pavarotti too.'

'Oh, I did and he sang me an aria.'

She dug in her bag for her sunglasses and put them on before her eyes gave her away. 'I'll keep in touch with Roy for you.'

Jake smiled sadly. 'I don't suppose there's any point in trying to tell you that I don't expect you to worry about Roy.'

'No point at all. I'd love to visit him now and again.' Quickly, she went on, 'We'd better get going.'

'Yeah.'

She swung the strap of her bag over her shoulder and looked down at her car keys, took a deep breath.

'Mattie, are you OK?' Jake crossed the kitchen until he stood in front of her. He lifted her sunglasses and a soft groan broke from him when he saw her eyes filled with tears. With trembling hands, he framed her face.

She tried to smile and her mouth wobbled out of shape, but then it didn't matter because Jake was kissing her.

Mattie melted into his warm, strong embrace and she kissed him as if her life depended on it. And, afterwards, she felt a little reassured—a little calmer, which was just as well as she had to concentrate on driving in the heavy traffic.

By the time they reached Sydney's International Terminal her eyes were dry, her stomach reasonably composed. She hoped she could stay that way through the final farewell.

The airport was typically busy, with cars and taxis zapping in and out of parking spots, and travellers wheeling overloaded luggage trolleys onto pedestrian crossings.

'Just leave me here.' Jake pointed to a two-minute drop-off zone.

'Are you sure you don't want me to come in?'

He shook his head. 'It's going to take ages to get through security and you won't be able to come past the customs desk anyway. You know what it's like with international flights.'

'I hadn't thought about that. I've never been overseas.'

Jake's eyes widened. 'Really?'

'The furthest I've been is Western Australia.'

His eyebrows lifted in surprise. 'I guess you've been too busy looking after other people. You haven't had time to travel.'

'I guess.'

He smiled. 'It means you still have a lot of adventures ahead of you.'

Something about the way Jake said this made Mattie's heart leap like a flame. In a sudden burst of confidence, she asked, 'Do you have an e-mail address? It must be so lonely in Mongolia. I could write to you if you like.'

'Yeah, sure.' He pulled his wallet from his pocket and dug out a business card. 'Here you go.'

Mattie stared at his name, Jake R. Devlin, on the card and she felt her throat tighten. This small white rectangle was all she would have once Jake was gone, but she was so pleased that he wanted to stay in touch.

He extracted another card. 'You should write your e-mail address on the back of this one.'

'Of course.' She printed the address and handed him the card and he leaned in close, kissed her cheek.

Needing one last proper kiss, Mattie offered him her lips.

Car horns honked all around them and from somewhere above she could hear the roar of a plane taking off, but she wanted to take her own sweet time over this last lovely kiss.

Finally, Jake touched her cheek with a gentle caress of his fingertips. 'Take care, Mattie.'

'You too.'

He tapped the card she was holding. 'It'll be good to stay in touch. I've had an amazing time.' Without warning, his face grew serious. His mouth hardened and turned down at the corners. 'But you do know that I can't promise you a future together, don't you?'

Mattie's heart clattered and bounced, as if it had fallen down a long flight of stairs. 'Of course,' she managed to say, but her voice was very tight and squeaky. 'I wasn't expecting a future with you.'

Even as the words left her lips, she knew they were a total lie, but Jake accepted them with a nod, then abruptly opened the car door. A second later, he was out on the footpath.

'I'll just grab my pack out of the back.' His voice was efficient and businesslike.

Mattie heard the slam of the car boot and then Jake was on the footpath once more, waving and smiling.

Smiling? How could he smile? A scant minute ago he'd taken all the joy out of her world. She lifted her hand to wave, tears blurring her vision.

Huge glass sliding doors opened behind him and he turned away from her and disappeared...

And Mattie's tears fell in earnest.

What a fool she'd been. She'd known from the start that Jake was dangerous and she'd tried so hard to resist him. But he was the most attractive man she'd ever met. North to her south.

Yesterday they'd had such a lovely morning together, but then, after the movie, she'd been stupid, stupid, stupid.

If only she hadn't been so weak. In less than twenty-four hours, she'd fallen completely in love.

With the wrong man.

Again.

Back at the flat, Mattie threw herself into a frenzied session of work and by the end of the day, she'd finished the painting that had given her trouble. This time, amazingly, the old magic was back. It was as if her creative energy was rushing to fill the despairing emptiness inside her.

When the painting was finished, she stood back, cuddling Brutus, and she examined the picture of Molly, the good little witch, silhouetted at her bedroom window, looking impossibly small and lonely.

Mattie was surprised by how poignant the picture seemed, and she smiled, satisfied with the effect. She really liked Molly's vulnerability and she knew her young readers would enjoy the secret knowledge that this skinny little girl was really a good witch, with superpowers that could help all the needy people in the houses below.

She only hoped she could find a similar strength in herself.

Jake sat in the mess hall at the mine site, lost in thought, wondering what Mattie was doing now. In his mind he could see her walking with Brutus along the path beside the bay, with the wind in her hair, her blue eyes sparkling.

He could see her working on a painting, her face serene yet completely focused. He could see her as she'd looked when she'd lain in bed beside him and he could remember the taste of her, the smell of her skin, the silky softness of her hair when he wound it around his fingers.

He could hear her musical voice, see the silver sparkle of her tears…

'Hey, Jake. There you are!'

Will Carruthers came through the doorway and helped himself to coffee, which he still preferred, even though most of the men drank the locally brewed Mongolian tea. Will brought his mug to Jake's table and grinned at him. 'Good to see you, mate. How was your leave?'

'Not bad.' Jake was valiantly trying to shut down thoughts of Mattie.

Will's eyes narrowed. 'Do I detect a distinct lack of enthusiasm?'

'Sorry. I was miles away.'

'Dreaming about the hordes of beautiful women you left behind?' Will grinned again, but when Jake made no response he tried a different tack. 'Was everything in order at the flat?'

'Yes, absolutely.' Finally, Jake remembered his manners. 'Honestly, Will, thanks for letting me use your flat. It was fantastic. Terrific decor. Fabulous location. Oh, and I brought you a gift from the Duty Free. I'll drop it over to your *ger* tonight.'

Will grinned. 'Sounds like it's a bottle of my favourite refreshment.'

'More like three bottles,' Jake said, then he stared into the depths of his tea mug. He couldn't help it—he had to drag Mattie into the conversation. 'I suppose you know there was someone else staying at the flat.'

'Really? Who was it?'

'Mattie Carey.'

Will's eyes almost popped out of his head. 'Mattie was there at the same time as you?'

'She arrived a couple of days after me.'

'But I thought she wasn't due in Sydney until the fifth. Weren't you supposed to be gone by then? You said you were heading off to Japan to go skiing.'

Jake shook his head. 'Other way around. I went skiing first, and then I went to Sydney.'

'Oops.' Will smiled sheepishly. 'Sorry, I got that mixed up.' He shot his friend a shrewd sideways glance. 'So how did it work out? Did you get on OK with Mattie?'

Jake was pleased that he managed to sound offhand. 'She was fine. She's an easy person to get along with.'

'Yeah, she would be.' Will chuckled. 'Good old Saint Matilda.'

Jake's flippancy vanished. 'Is that what you call her?'

'I meant it in the nicest possible way.' Will, watching Jake closely, back-pedalled fast. 'We all love Mattie. She's my sister's best friend, has been since forever. I think Gina and Mattie met in kindergarten.'

In the awkward silence that followed, Will sent Jake another sideways glance. 'I don't suppose Mattie mentioned why she's moved to Sydney?'

Jake shrugged. 'Not really. I thought she just wanted to work on her book.' He noticed the cautious tension in Will's face. 'Why do you ask? Was there another reason?'

Will shook his head, took a deep swig of coffee. When he lowered the mug, his face was as blank as a poker player's.

'So why did you ask if I knew anything?' Jake persisted.

'I was simply making conversation, man.'

Jake didn't believe him. He knew there was a chance that his perspective was skewed, but he was convinced now that Will knew something else about Mattie. A problem.

What could it be? Why else had she come to Sydney, other than to work on her book? Then again, why would she need to come to Sydney just to work on a children's story?

He thought back to when she'd first arrived. She'd said she had appointments.

A cold chill skittered down his spine. 'Mattie's not in Sydney to see doctors, is she? She's not ill?'

'No, mate. Keep your shirt on.' Will rolled his eyes, as if he was clearly convinced that his best mate had lost the plot. 'Mattie Carey is as healthy as a horse.'

'Then what did you mean? Why did you ask if I knew why she'd come to Sydney?'

'I've already forgotten. Chill, Jake. Forget I asked.' Will looked annoyed and he stood and snatched up his cup. 'The deal with the flat is nothing more than a friendly agreement. Mattie's renting it for twelve months and I'm very happy to have such a reliable tenant.'

Five days before the embryo transfer, Mattie began to receive progesterone injections. Trips to the clinic became part of her daily routine, along with working on her paintings and walking Brutus. She also borrowed several books about pregnancy from the library and began to conscientiously prepare super-healthy meals.

She bought a terracotta pot of parsley to grow on the balcony, so she had a ready source of iron.

She wanted to do everything just right, even though she never thought of this baby as hers.

The embryo had already been created in a test tube from Gina and Tom's genetic material and Mattie saw herself as simply a glorified babysitter. Or perhaps a very fond aunt.

Whenever she felt slightly overawed by the task ahead, she focused on the fabulous and exciting moment in nine months' time when she handed a sweet little baby to her best friends.

It was a relief that things were finally happening and, as the date for the embryo transfer drew closer, Gina kept in e-mail contact almost every day. Neither she nor Mattie talked too much about the imminent pregnancy. Instead, they were just happy to keep in touch and to chat about Willowbank gossip, farming news, Mattie's progress on her new book…

Mattie quickly put a stop to any discussion about Jake and so far she hadn't replied to the e-mail he'd sent telling her about his journey and his first week settling back into life on the mine site.

Her reaction to it had been pure confusion. She was trying to 'get over' him and yet she'd been disappointed that he hadn't written straight away. Then she'd been disappointed by the matter-of-fact tone of his e-mail.

She wished she'd never suggested that they write. It would have been so much cleaner if they'd simply parted at the airport.

Whenever she thought about replying, she was frozen by uncertainty. She kept hearing those fateful words.

You do know that I can't promise you a future together, don't you?

She read the e-mail again and again, trying to search for hidden meanings. How crazy. Was she going to go through months of worrying about Jake the way she had with Pete? She couldn't face that again.

If she did decide to reply, it was hard to know what to say. She had to ask herself if it was right to behave as if her life was ticking along as usual, when the surrogacy was about to begin? She hated deceit of any kind.

However, there was a final reason she hadn't written to Jake, one she hardly dared to contemplate, that caught her out at unexpected moments, especially in the middle of the night.

As she lay in the dark, she found herself wondering if her intense feelings for him could pose a threat to the surrogacy. It was foolish to think this way when she knew they had no real future, but she couldn't help it. She'd never dreamed that the psychologist could be right and that she could meet someone like Jake before the baby was born.

And yet, here she was, wishing at times that she could keep her body for him.

But, in reality, if she was to have a man in her life at this point in time, she needed someone who would be there for her, no matter what—not a gorgeous, dangerous playboy.

She needed a man who was prepared to share her with the baby she carried, someone prepared to wait. Unfortunately, Jake Devlin couldn't tick a single box in her list of vital requirements and so she'd better just get over him, for her own sake.

Jake stared glumly at his computer screen. He'd downloaded his e-mails and again there was nothing from Mattie.

He looked at the back of the card, where she'd neatly printed her e-mail address, and for the hundredth time he remembered their farewell and her tears, and the passion in her last kiss. He could have sworn that she'd planned to write to him and he'd anticipated a constant stream of messages filled with typical Mattie-style warmth.

What did this silence mean?

What had changed?

His conversation with Will on his return kept haunting him. He kept hearing Will's harrowing question: *I don't suppose Mattie mentioned why she's moved to Sydney?*

Jake had quizzed his friend about it again, but Will always shrugged it off, claiming that Jake had misinterpreted a casual enquiry.

'What's got into you, mate?' Will had growled. 'Do you realise you grill me about Mattie Carey every time we meet? You need another holiday. You're way too tense.'

Perhaps Will was right. Jake knew he'd never been like this before. It was beyond crazy to be so uptight over a woman. He was usually trying to shake them off.

Ironically, as soon as he stopped expecting to hear from Mattie, an e-mail from her arrived in his in-box.

To: jakerdevlin@miningmail.com
From: mattiecarey@mymail.com
Hi Jake,
Greetings from sunny Sydney to deepest Mongolia.

I wanted to let you know that I brought Roy over here for morning tea today. We didn't make billy tea, but we had damper and lamingtons and I sent him home with a big bouquet of gum leaves and a vase so he can keep them in his room. As you can imagine, he was as happy as a possum in a hollow log.

Oh, and I found a book in a second-hand shop about old drovers and stockmen. It's full of photographs of the Outback and Roy loved it. He said to tell you he's well. Actually, he said he was fighting fit, but I think that's an exaggeration. And he sends his love.

I don't have much other news. I'm slowly knocking over the illustrations for the book and I'm afraid the coffee table never gets used as a coffee table any more.

I hope that French Canadian cook is feeding you well. Are you still helping him out in the kitchen? Perhaps you should show him our recipe for pasta sauce?

Love from Brutus and Pavarotti,

Mattie xx

Jake was so relieved to hear from her that he swallowed his pride and wrote back straight away, but he kept the content deliberately light, just as she had. He told her about the party they'd had in the canteen for one of the team's birthday. And how they'd tried to play Scrabble last night in three different languages—English, French and Russian. He thanked her for taking care of Roy. He didn't mention a word about missing her.

Mattie replied the very next day and when he read her message he grinned. It was a single question:

What does the R in your name stand for? Robert? Roy? Rudolph? Rambo?

He wrote back that his middle name was Richard, named after his grandfather. And he asked about her middle name.

Mattie replied:

Middle name, Francesca, after my grandmother. Aren't we predictable?

After that, they exchanged e-mails almost every day. They kept their messages short, light and amusing, never hinting at anything like deeper emotions, and Jake was happy.

Mattie was pleased, too. After much deliberation, she'd decided finally to reply to Jake's e-mail. After all, maybe they could remain friends, just keep in touch? She wouldn't expect anything more.

It was best this way, Mattie decided, best that neither of them referred to that blissful night they'd spent in each other's arms again.

It made it easier for her to avoid telling Jake the truth.

Problem was, she still felt horribly guilty about that. And she was left with a helpless longing she didn't how to handle.

CHAPTER SIX

MATTIE was grinning as she dialled Gina's number.

'Guess what, girlfriend? It worked.'

'You mean—'

'I mean the tests came back positive.'

'Oh, my God! You mean we're pregnant?'

'Yep. We're pregnant. Very pregnant.'

Gina screamed in Mattie's ear. Then she began to gabble. 'I can't believe it's actually happening. Oh, God, you're so clever, Mattie. I'm crying. I don't know how to thank you.'

'I'm excited too. I'm so glad it's really on the way. There's going to be a baby.'

'How do you feel?'

'OK. Relieved. I've been fairly sure for the last few days, but the doctor didn't want me to say anything to you until he was certain.'

'So do you have symptoms? Can you tell me all about it?'

Patiently, Mattie told her best friend everything, how her breasts had become increasingly tender and she'd been feeling dreadfully tired. At first she'd been worried she was coming down with something, but then she'd started losing her breakfast and she *knew*.

'Oh, Mattie, I still can't take it in. I'm just so excited, but you poor thing. Is it too awful?'

'It's only yuck for about an hour a day. Most of the time, I feel pretty good. And I have the perfect excuse to take a daytime nap. The really good news is, the doctor's very happy. He said the hormone levels are really strong. Like *really* strong.'

'I see.' Gina's voice grew cautious. 'That sounds like it means something.'

'Well, yes. It's nothing to panic about…but… um…there might be more than one baby.'

Gina screamed again. 'Oh, my gosh—*two*! Do you mind if I hang up? I've got to go and find Tom.'

Mattie laughed. 'Off you go. Give Tom my love.'

When she hung up the phone, she sank onto the sofa. Brutus jumped up beside her and she let him snuggle close.

'Two babies, Brutus,' she whispered. 'I'm going to end up the size of a house.'

With her hand resting on her still flat tummy, she tried to imagine it filled with two lively full-term babies. Twins were a risk, the doctor had warned her when he'd transferred two embryos, but at the time she'd been happy to take the chance. One way or another, she'd wanted Gina and Tom to have a family.

But yikes. How would her figure ever recover? She couldn't help wondering what Jake would think if he saw her, swollen and huge, but then she quickly dismissed that question.

Jake had only entered her life for a few short days and this was something that had been decided months ago. It was a private matter between herself and her oldest and dearest friends. Jake had no part in this.

If only that realisation didn't make her feel so desperately lonely and sad.

I'm being selfish...

She tried to remind herself that she'd been perfectly happy before she'd met Jake. And now her focus had to be positive. She had to concentrate on the wonderful gift she was carrying.

It was an amazing privilege to be able to do this for Gina and Tom. They were going to be fabulous parents and she was going to help them have the perfect little family they so thoroughly deserved.

Gina and Tom's babies would have a happy and idyllic childhood on the farm, going to school in Willowbank, making friends with the local children.

A new generation.

Mattie had such happy memories of her own schooldays with Gina and Tom and Will and Lucy. It was too long since the old 'gang' had been together. Perhaps there would be a gathering for the babies' christening?

What fun!

And what about Jake?

Wouldn't it be wonderful if he could fit into that picture?

As always, when Mattie thought about Jake, she felt a painful jolt in the centre of her chest. There'd been no recent e-mails because he was away in the wilds of Mongolia on some kind of expedition, and she was shocked by how much she missed him. But she knew it was foolish to feel so attached when he'd told her in no uncertain terms that he didn't fit into her future. She'd spent a couple of days with him and now they exchanged brief, chatty e-mails—it had been impossible to cut Jake off altogether. But it was barely the beginnings of a relationship.

Even so, she found it ridiculously easy to imagine Jake being absorbed into her circle of friends. He was already good friends with Will. And Mattie knew he would like her other friends and they would like him. She could picture them all sitting around a dinner table—at Gina and Tom's perhaps.

In her imagination, she could picture it all—driving down to Willow Creek Farm with Jake, bringing wine and cheese from her favourite boutique deli, and arriving via the winding road that led through a grove of pines to Gina and Tom's farmhouse.

They would be welcomed by Tom, wearing the black and white apron he always donned when he was helping in the kitchen. Jake, with his handsome looks and flashing dark eyes, would be a huge hit with the girls and the men would like his laid-back humour. Around the table, they would share stories and lots of laughter along with scrumptious food.

Yes, Jake would fit in very well. How perfect it could be.

But it's impossible and I'm a fool to even think of it.

To: mattiecarey@mymail.com
From: jakerdevlin@miningmail.com
Hey there, Mattie.
I'm back at last after spending three weeks out in the wild wastes of Mongolia on a prospecting expedition. Won't bore you with details, but it's very acceptable to be back in a properly built ger with a comfortable bed and a fire at night.

Hope all's well. Would you believe I miss you

and Brutus and Pavarotti and your drawings of Molly?

How are you? A man needs details. How are you spending your days? What colour is your hair now? What movies have you seen?

More importantly, what colour are you wearing under your T-shirt?
Keep smiling,
Jake xx

Mattie read this and burst into tears.

She'd had a shocker of a day. A headache had started mid-morning and, because she was pregnant and couldn't take tablets, there was nothing she could do but lie down with a cool cloth on her forehead. She'd sprinkled the cloth with drops of lavender oil, but now she was sick of the smell of lavender and her headache hadn't budged.

Her waist was expanding exponentially. She felt fat and ugly and tired and miserable…and Jake was fantasising about her in sexy underwear. It was too much!

She let out a moan of pure self-pity and Brutus whimpered and looked up at her with eyes filled with concern.

'Oh, Brutus,' she sobbed, scooping him up for a cuddle. 'What am I going to do about Jake?'

She knew for absolute certain now that she was carrying twins. She'd seen the ultrasound images and there they were—two little heads, two sets of arms and legs, swimming in their own little sacs. So cute! But already she'd had to buy maternity jeans and her breasts were so heavy now she'd had to buy maternity bras—horrid, hefty harnesses, only available in white, black or beige that made her feel like an ageing matron.

Meanwhile, Jake thought he was writing to a slim young woman who wore sexy lace and satin lingerie in a range of rainbow colours, a woman who had no commitments other than her writing deadlines.

She was a fraud, an impostor, a cheat!

With a helpless sigh, she set Brutus down and began to pace the floor, the little dog at her heels. What should she do? Should she reply? How *could* she reply honestly?

Oh, help. She couldn't keep stringing Jake along like this. But should she simply drop the communication and let him assume that she'd lost interest?

She didn't want to let him go.

I have to.

Tears fell again and she snatched up tissues and mopped her face. If only she didn't have this headache, she could think more clearly. She went through to the kitchen and made a cup of camomile tea, which she took through to the lounge room. Curled on the sofa, she sipped the herbal brew and tried to think calmly.

OK. First, she was pregnant but she couldn't tell Jake what was happening to her.

Why?

It's a private matter and, anyway, he's not serious about me. He's already warned me there's no chance of forever.

But couldn't he change his mind? He seemed really keen when he was in Sydney.

Even if he was keen, the pregnancy would douse his passion in a heartbeat. He's a playboy. A woman pregnant with someone else's babies would send him running for the hills.

Too true. Mattie had enough emotional issues just coping with the surrogacy, without letting Jake mess with her head. He would never understand why she was doing this.

Bottom line, she didn't want to be helplessly and miserably in love again. She didn't want to feel vulnerable and endlessly anxious, the way she had with Pete.

After all, how could she expect to share this surrogacy with a guy who'd openly claimed he had an allergy to commitment?

Heavens, why did she even hesitate when she had so many clear answers? Any way she looked at this, she only had one sensible option.

She should stop writing to Jake…let him go…

It was the only decent thing to do. And, given how easily he'd parted from his previous girl-friend, he probably wouldn't be upset.

No doubt thousands of e-mail exchanges ended when one person fell silent.

No doubt the world was filled with thousands of broken hearts.

Jake switched off his computer, poured himself a measure of vodka and downed it in one fiery gulp. He poured another and downed it too, went to the small window and stared out at the other *gers* scattered over the barren ground. He saw lights burning in most of the tents but he wasn't in the mood for company.

That in itself wasn't surprising. He'd always been a loner, a self-sufficient outsider, who'd learned as a child to get along without company. But there was a difference between being alone and being lonely.

Tonight, as he looked out into the desert night, he could feel the almost forgotten loneliness of his childhood creeping back, sneaking beneath his defences. He was remembering again the long lonesome months after his mother's breakdown, when she wouldn't—couldn't speak to him.

He flinched at the memory, working hard to

dismiss the pain of her bewildering rejection. He'd adored his mother but he'd learned even then, at the age of nine, that he could drown beneath the weight of such love.

More than one girlfriend had accused him of emotional bankruptcy, and he knew he'd deserved the accusation, but he'd learned the hard way to keep his heart safely under lock and key.

This was precisely why he'd told Mattie that he couldn't offer any promises for the future.

So it didn't make any kind of sense that his old anxieties were staging a comeback now, simply because he hadn't heard from her in over a month.

He'd sent her three more e-mails and she hadn't replied. He couldn't believe how much he needed to hear from her, needed to know she was OK.

Will Carruthers could shed no light on her silence and in the end Jake knew there was only one thing to do. He had to ring the Sydney flat, had to hear her voice, to know at least that she wasn't ill.

As he dialled through the international codes, then added the flat's telephone number, he was ridiculously nervous—so damn nervous he was sweating. His hands were clammy and he felt sick, like a teenager trying to pluck up the courage to ask a girl on a first date.

When Mattie answered the phone his throat was

dry and his voice as rough as gravel. 'Hello, Mattie.'

'Is that Jake?'

'Yes. How are you?'

'Are you still in Mongolia?'

She sounded shocked and scared. Why did she sound so unhappy?

'Yes, I'm still here.' What could he say now? The light banter of e-mails became downright stupid when said out loud. 'I haven't heard from you for a while, so I thought I'd check in. How are you? Everything OK?'

'Yes, fine.' Her voice sounded anything but fine. 'I…I've been really busy.'

Jake gritted his teeth. How the hell had he thought this call was a good idea?

What now? On the basis of one night of passion, he could hardly demand an explanation for Mattie's silence.

'How are you?' he asked again and he sounded way too tense. 'Are you well?'

'I'm really well, Jake.'

'You sound a bit…' He paused, searching for the right word.

'I'm a bit tired, that's all. I…I've taken on some extra work and it…it's keeping me really busy.'

'So are you enjoying this work? Is it creative?'

He thought he heard a definite sigh.

'Yes, Jake, it's highly creative.'

This time, there was no mistaking her tone. It was most definitely let's-drop-this-subject.

Jake wished he could see her. If he could look into her eyes, he might be able to see what she wasn't telling him. He would know whether she was happy.

'I've been in touch with Roy,' she said. 'I...I haven't had time to visit him lately, but I ring him every week. He's keeping well.'

'That's good to hear. Thanks for keeping an eye on him.'

'How's Will?' she asked carefully.

'Oh, he's fighting fit. Actually, he's on leave at the moment in California. He should be having a great time.'

'Sounds like fun. Are you going somewhere like that for your next leave?'

Jake's stomach hit the floor. This was a brush-off with no holds barred. Mattie was letting him know that she clearly didn't expect to see him.

OK, so maybe he had dropped a strong warning when he'd farewelled her at the airport, but he felt differently now. He'd missed her. Maybe he'd even changed. He certainly wasn't going to give in easily.

Swallowing his pride, he said, 'I was wondering what would happen if I turned up on your doorstep.'

This was met by silence.

Jake held his breath, couldn't believe how bad he felt.

'I...I...' Mattie was obviously flustered. 'Are you planning to come back here?'

Somehow, he forced himself to ask, 'Will you still be there in a month or two?'

Another awkward silence chilled him to the bone. And then, 'Jake, I'm afraid I'm going to be really busy for the next few months.'

Really busy... He bit back a swear word. Felt sick. This was the ultimate rebuff.

'You mean you'd rather not see me?'

'It'll be difficult.' It was barely more than a whisper and yet he heard the break in her voice.

Why? What was going on? He remembered Mattie's tears when they'd said goodbye. He'd been egotistical enough to think they'd meant she was going to miss him, but was there another reason? Something she wasn't telling him?

One thing was certain. This phone call wasn't giving him any answers and there was no point in prolonging the torture. 'OK. Thanks for setting me straight on that,' he said, battling disbelief that he could actually let her go like this...without a fight.

'Goodbye, Jake.'

He heard a click on the end of the line and, just like that, Mattie Carey was out of his life.

But Jake was left with a niggling doubt, a gut awareness that she hadn't really wanted to let him go.

Or was that simply his ego getting in the way of common sense?

In a harbourside café, Gina sipped a coffee latte with a dreamy smile. She sighed happily as she set it down. 'How lucky are we to have a boy and a girl? It's so perfect. I can't believe it. I keep wanting to cry with happiness.'

Mattie grinned and slipped her arm around her friend's shoulders. Having her friends with her for the ultrasound this morning had made such a difference. Seeing the joy on their faces and treasuring the warmth of their hugs had made everything about this project totally worthwhile.

She could forget about the headaches, the heartburn and the tiredness. If she held in her mind this picture of her friends' happy, smiling faces and the cute black and white images of their two little babies, she could blank out memories of Jake Devlin.

She had done the right thing when she'd ended the phone call. It was the only sane way to approach this, wasn't it? After all, if her fiancé hadn't been able to stay in love with her when she'd been younger and prettier and *not* pregnant, how could she possibly expect a rake like Jake to stay interested in her now?

It was a cold, blustery winter's day when Jake returned to Sydney. He stepped out of the taxi and gusts of wind whipped at him. Sharp rain needled his face. Not exactly a warm welcome, but then he hadn't expected one.

On the overnight flight he hadn't slept, but when he checked in to his hotel he went straight to his room, showered and changed and then hurried downstairs again to collect the hire car he'd booked. Rain lashed at the windscreen as he drove out of the hotel car park and joined the steady stream of traffic.

For a fleeting moment he felt strangely disoriented. The busy arterial road in the frantic heart of Sydney was such a bizarre contrast to the moonscape world of the remote mine site he'd so recently left. He blinked to clear his head, changed lanes and took a right turn at the next set of lights. He'd planned to head straight to Roy's nursing home but now he realised too late he was going the wrong way.

He continued on, looking for a suitable place to make a U-turn, and he recognised the camping store where Mattie had bought the little gas ring and billy can for Roy's tea party.

This direction led to Will's flat.
To Mattie.

Knots tightened in his gut and his heart began to thud.

OK, OK. If he was already heading this way, he might as well drive past the flat. And if he saw Mattie's car parked in the drive, he might as well go in. Get it over and done with. He had to see her at least once. Maybe he was fooling himself that she hadn't really wanted to let him go, but he had to know the truth. Had to sort this out, face to face.

In that disastrous phone call, Mattie had mentioned that she was so busy she'd begun telephoning Roy rather than visiting him. That had surprised Jake and he couldn't help worrying that there was a problem. Why would the same girl who'd gone above and beyond in her efforts to please Roy suddenly be too busy to pay him an occasional visit?

He still couldn't shake the feeling that she was in some kind of trouble. At the risk of totally annoying her, he couldn't let her go until he got to the bottom of this mystery.

Mattie was working near a window in the lounge room, listening to the rhythm of the rain as she drew a preliminary sketch for another illustration.

The book was almost finished and she wanted to have everything off to her publisher in the next few weeks—before the last weeks of the pregnancy drained her energy.

She was concentrating hard, trying to capture exactly the right level of simmering excitement in Molly's facial expression, when a sound from the street outside caught her attention. She glanced through the window and saw a sleek, low black car shooting a spray of water from the gutter as it pulled up in front of the flats.

She wasn't expecting anyone, so she paid the car a cursory glance and went back to her drawing. But then the car door slammed and Brutus began to yap.

'Quiet, Brutus!' Mattie glanced outside again, frowning. Her little dog only yapped to welcome people he knew and liked. Strangers were greeted by silence, or by a low, mean-spirited growl.

Curious now, she watched a man make a dash through the sheeting rain. He was wearing a black waterproof jacket and blue jeans and she admired his considerable height, his thick dark hair and broad shoulders.

Oh, God. Oh, help.

No!

It couldn't be Jake.

Her heart stopped beating altogether. The

pencil fell from her nerveless fingers and clattered to the table, then her heart gave one terrified bound and began to hammer again. Painfully.

Jake.

It was Jake.

Too shocked to move, she sat and watched as he flipped the latch on the front gate and dashed up the path, head down against the rain.

She hadn't heard from him since that dreadful phone call. She hadn't expected him to come, had *never dreamed* he would come.

Instinctively, she wrapped her arms over her ballooning stomach. One of the babies kicked, and then the other joined in. A kicking competition began.

Jake knocked on the door and Brutus darted forward, yapping excitedly. Mattie tried to stand, but her knees shook and her legs refused to support her. What would Jake think when he saw her?

He knocked again.

CHAPTER SEVEN

JAKE knew for certain that Mattie was home. Not only was her car in the garage, he'd caught a glimpse of her worried face at the window. But now she wasn't answering his knock.

Terrific. He wasn't welcome.

Stubbornly, he knocked again.

Her little dog yapped madly and scratched on the other side of the door. At least Brutus was happy to see him.

The Mediterranean-blue door remained firmly shut.

He shouldn't have come.

Acid rose in his stomach. After Mattie's clear rejection, coming here was close to the stupidest thing he'd ever done.

Teeth gritted, hands clenched, he turned his back on the flat and scowled at the driving rain. No way would he knock on that door a third time. A man had his pride.

Which meant he had no choice but to get out of here and bid Mattie Carey good riddance. He didn't need this kind of angst in his life, couldn't believe he'd allowed himself to become entangled in this mess.

He turned, ready to make a dash for the car, when the door opened behind him and Brutus leapt out, yapping madly and jumping at Jake's knees in an ecstasy of welcome.

'Sit, Brutus. Down, boy.'

Mattie's voice. Jake looked up and there she stood in the doorway.

Thud.

Her light brown hair was a soft cloud about her pale face and her blue eyes were huge and worried. She ordered Brutus to settle and she bent to pat the dog, then straightened again. She was wearing a voluminous cherry-red tunic over dark grey leggings and black ankle boots. She was the Mattie he remembered.

Even lovelier than he remembered. She had a special glow about her.

She was…

Jake went cold all over.

No.

No way. She couldn't be.

'Hello, Jake.'

He couldn't drag his eyes from the unmistakable curve of her stomach.

No way. *No!*

During her silence, he'd considered many possibilities.

Never this.

What did it mean? Was he going to be a father?

The thought sent blood pounding through him. Dazed, he gestured in the direction of her middle.

'Why?' He gulped, couldn't get the question out. Tried again. 'Why didn't you tell me?'

She shook her head. 'I couldn't. I'm so sorry.'

Couldn't? What the hell did that mean? 'What's going on, Mattie? Why couldn't you have said something?'

She pressed shaking fingers against her lips, looked ready to cry.

'You haven't got a husband lurking in the wings?'

'No, of course not.'

'You are pregnant, aren't you? It's not…something else?'

'I'm fine,' she said, but she looked anything but fine. 'I'm really well. And yes…I'm pregnant.'

'OK. Right.' Jake raised a hand to loosen his tie, realised he wasn't wearing one. 'On to the next question then… Is it mine?'

The sudden eagerness in his voice shocked him. He hadn't planned on fatherhood, had always made certain that he'd avoided any chance of un-planned offspring. But everyone knew these accidents happened. And Mattie would be the world's best mother. And somehow the idea of her—

Again, she shook her head. 'Don't panic, Jake. You're not about to become a father.'

Not the father.

She might as easily have landed a king hit on Jake's jaw. The result would have been the same.

She had another lover.

He was stunned. Flattened. Shocked by how disappointed he felt.

He dragged in a ragged breath, let it out through clenched teeth and jerked his gaze from the dismay in her eyes to the glistening wet concrete on the driveway.

A thousand questions rained on him. If the baby wasn't his, who the hell's was it? When had this happened? Before he'd met Mattie? Afterwards?

Hell.

Could he believe anything she told him? Short of a DNA test, how could he be certain that the child was his or was not his?

He shot a searching glance at Mattie and high colour rose in her cheeks.

Without quite meeting his gaze, she said, 'This is a surprise.'

'Of course it is.'

'I mean, I wasn't expecting to see you.'

'I dare say.' He couldn't hold back the bitterness from his voice.

Her hand fluttered protectively over her middle. 'I know this is a shock, Jake. I'm sorry.' A small huffing sigh escaped. 'It's complicated.'

'How complicated?'

'Quite.' She chewed her lip. 'Very complicated, actually.'

Before he could snap a biting retort, the bright colour in Mattie's face faded, leaving a gravity that disturbed him. She took a step back.

'You'd better come in. You deserve an explanation.'

When he didn't move immediately, she said again, 'Please, Jake, come inside.'

Until now, he hadn't realised that he'd been secretly hoping to spend his leave with this woman. What a mistake. Jake-the-Rake Devlin never spent his leave with the same girl he'd been with on the last leave.

Right now he should have been partying in Paris or skiing in the Snowy Mountains.

But here he was, back in the flat with Mattie. A sinking sense of foreboding chilled him to the bone as he shrugged out of his coat and hung it on a peg by the door, then followed Mattie into the familiar lounge room. Will's lounge room.

Jake almost staggered under the weight of another alarming possibility. *No, please, no. Don't let the baby be Will's.*

It wasn't possible, was it? But Will had been so cagey about Mattie…and she was living in his flat…

But surely they would have told him? A wave of panicky loneliness swept over him, the frightening sensation of loss that he remembered from his childhood.

He shook it off and reined in his galloping thoughts.

'Take a seat, Jake.'

Mattie pointed to one of the leather sofas that faced each other on either side of the glass coffee table. He saw that she'd set a card table by the window and had covered it with her art paraphernalia. He remembered how she'd once sat cross-legged on the floor while she drew the illustrations for her children's book. No doubt her burgeoning figure made that impossible now.

'Would you like tea or coffee?' she asked.

He shook his head. *Just the truth.*

With a worried little sigh, she sat opposite him. *Opposite.* Not cosily next to him, as the Mattie of old would have done.

She looked down at her hands and he followed her gaze, saw that her fingernails had been painted

a deep, glamorous red to match her top. The strong
colour made her pale hands look elegant and sophisticated. Even lovelier than before.

A handful of pebbles lodged in Jake's throat
and he manfully swallowed every one of them.

'I'm really sorry you've found out like this,' she
said. 'It's the last thing I wanted. I know it's a shock.'

Biting back the barrage of questions he longed
to fire at her, he cracked a bitter smile and very
deliberately relaxed back into the soft leather upholstery, legs casually crossed at the ankles.

Mattie watched him and thought how utterly
wonderful he looked. If she wasn't so nervous and
anxious she would have been deliriously happy.
How fantastic it would be to do nothing more
than to sit here and feast her eyes on Jake Devlin.

Oh…it was *so* good to see him again.

He was wearing a cream cable-knit sweater
and blue denim jeans. A five o'clock shadow
darkened his jaw and his hair had been ruffled by
the rain and wind, reminding her of the danger-
ously handsome pirate she'd met on the first day
she'd arrived at this flat.

She wished she could throw herself across the
room and curl up beside him. She longed to feel
his arms about her, to rest her head on his
shoulder and to feel the soft bulky wool of his
sweater against her cheek. She needed to bury her

face in his neck and smell his skin, longed to feel his sexy lips on hers.

Heavens, maybe pregnancy hormones had caused a spike in her libido, but she wanted nothing more than to rip off his lovely sweater and run her hands all over his gorgeous body. Wanted him to want her the way he'd wanted her last time.

But she'd relinquished such privileges. And now Jake looked hard and distanced. The short gap across the coffee table was as vast as the Grand Canyon.

Jake stretched an arm along the back of the sofa and his dark eyes rested on her pregnant tummy. 'So this is why you've been so busy? This is your new creative project?'

With nervous fingers, Mattie smoothed the hem of her tunic over her leggings. 'To be honest, I've actually been more tired than busy.'

'It's rather late for honesty, Mattie.'

'Yes,' she admitted softly.

'You've kept your condition a state secret. Why?'

'I didn't have much choice, Jake. I wanted to tell you, but I'd promised that I wouldn't tell anyone.'

Before he could open his mouth to fire another question, Mattie hurried on. 'I suppose I could have asked for permission to tell you, but I was worried that, even if I did *try* to explain, you still wouldn't understand.'

'I have an honours degree in biological science. I do have a reasonable understanding of how these things happen.'

Ignoring his sarcasm, she tried again. 'This is a particularly delicate situation.'

To her surprise, Jake's skin turned pale despite his tan. 'Please tell me the baby's not Will's.'

'Will's?' Mattie almost choked on her shock. 'Good heavens, no. How could you think that?'

'From where I'm sitting, anything's possible.' As his colour returned, he said, 'I presume all this secrecy is to hide the father's identity?'

She nodded. 'And the mother's.'

'I beg your pardon?'

She patted the firm mound of her stomach. 'This is a surrogate pregnancy.'

Jake's brow creased. His mouth opened and shut, but he didn't speak. He said nothing to reassure Mattie, or to help her through this awkward disclosure.

When the silence became unbearable, she drew a deep breath and dived in. 'My best friend Gina—Will's sister—had a condition called endometriosis and it was so bad that the doctors more or less ordered her to have a hysterectomy. It was just awful for her. She was only thirty, and she and her husband, Tom, who's the loveliest guy, were planning a big family.'

'They could have adopted,' Jake commented dryly.

'Yes, they certainly considered adoption.'

He shot her a withering glance. 'But you had a better idea.'

Mattie let out a gloomy sigh. This was exactly the reaction she'd expected from Jake. He wasn't going to spare her a moment's sympathy or understanding. She lifted her gaze to the ceiling as she searched for the right words.

'I think this is a much better option. It means Gina and Tom can have their own children. The doctors were able to use Gina's eggs and Tom's sperm to grow the embryos.'

'So now *their* baby is growing in *your* body?'

There was no avoiding the clear disapproval in his voice.

'That's right.'

Across the room, their gazes locked. Mattie saw the shocked light in Jake's eyes. He could never understand. He believed she was crazy.

But it was no comfort to realise she'd been right when she'd anticipated this kind of reaction. It was no comfort now to know she should never have become involved with him. No comfort to face the truth that she'd been weak at the one point in her life when she'd needed to be really strong.

Almost wearily, Jake asked, 'So, when did this happen?'

'After you went back to Mongolia.'

'But I suppose you already had the surrogacy planned? You knew on the night you slept with me that you were going to go ahead with this?'

'Yes.' Mattie's chin lifted. 'But I don't see why you're on your high horse, Jake. This pregnancy isn't any of your business.'

'Really?' he asked coldly.

'You know you never planned a future with me.'

His face was suddenly stern and as hard as granite.

'You can't have it both ways, Jake. You can't carry on like a playboy and then disapprove because I want to give my friends the wonderful gift of two babies.'

This time his mouth stayed open rather a long time. '*Two* babies?' he repeated faintly.

'Yes. Twins. A boy and a girl.'

The news sent him lurching to his feet. His throat worked as he stared again at her stomach. He dragged tense fingers through his hair. 'How could you do this to yourself, Mattie?'

'I've already told you. I wanted to help Gina and Tom.'

'Oh, yes, of course. I should have known.' His smile was falsely bright. 'Saint Matilda.'

The words hit her like a slap. 'You've been talking to Will.'

Jake shrugged.

'You have, haven't you? You've been talking to Will Carruthers about me.'

'I had to tell him that we'd met. After all, we were sharing his flat.'

'And he told you he called me Saint Matilda?'

'Appropriately, as it turns out.'

Jake turned his back on her and stared through the window at the rain, hands thrust in pockets, jaw at a stubborn angle, while Mattie smarted. Had Will suggested that she was crazy too? Surely not. He was Gina's brother.

'I knew you would never understand,' she said miserably to Jake's back.

'And you were dead right.' He whipped around to face her. 'I don't understand. I *really* don't understand.'

He began to pace the room, turned abruptly to face her. 'Hell, Mattie, I know you like to help people. You make a habit of going out of your way to help just about everyone you meet and that's fine, but you've taken it too far this time. You're young and single. You should be making the most of your youth. Having fun. You've never been overseas. Why not try that instead of turning yourself into a damned incubator? That's crazy.'

An incubator!

'How dare you call me that?' Squaring her shoulders, Mattie fought to defend herself. 'If you knew Gina and Tom, you wouldn't call me crazy.'

He dismissed this with a shrug and she felt anger rise through her like steam. Righteous anger. This reaction was exactly what she'd expected and feared. It was why she'd remained silent, why she'd told him not to come.

Nevertheless, she was hurt. Why couldn't he understand?

'This was my decision, Jake. It's my body. My business. I'm perfectly healthy and I'm in no danger. I don't need your permission. Besides, you were on the other side of the world.' She dropped her gaze to her hands, clenched tightly in her lap. 'You know you were never planning to be a part of my life.'

She sensed rather than saw the way his entire body stiffened, but when she lifted her gaze she saw something else in his expression that made her heart stand still.

Oh, heavens. What was it?

Fear? Confusion and disappointment? Tenderness? All of these things?

His distress shocked her. She hadn't expected this. Jake was a renowned ladies' man. She'd seen for herself how quickly he'd lost interest in his previous girlfriend. He'd warned Mattie off at their final parting.

Now her throat ached with welling tears as she watched him standing there, shoulders slumped, hands sunk in pockets, throat working as he stared morosely at her drawing of Molly.

Had she been wrong?

Did Jake actually care?

What should she do? What *could* she do or say? Was it too late? How could she find the courage to take the vital step that might bridge the gap between them? She wasn't even sure it was possible now.

Should she tell him that the night she'd slept with him had been the most moving and beautiful night of her life? Should she admit how hard it had been to give him up?

She wondered if she could tell Jake the other truth, the one she'd barely admitted, even to herself. That she'd been scared that her strong feelings for him might have prevented her from going ahead with the surrogacy.

Watching him, Mattie was gripped by a terrible confusion. For the first time in her life, her vision of right and wrong was unclear. Until now, doing the right thing had always felt safe and reassuring, but now doubts flooded her.

She watched his stiff back and his hard, grim profile and she longed to go to him, to reach out, to throw her arms around him and to tell him how utterly gorgeous he was. But could she be sure that he wanted that?

She was still struggling to find the right answer when Jake turned slowly.

His face was cold. 'I'm pleased I called in,' he said icily. 'At least the truth is out now.'

She'd handled this badly. So badly. 'I'm sorry,' she said, but those two words had never sounded so inadequate.

Jake shook his head. 'It's too late to be sorry. It's…it's simply too late.' He began to cross the room, heading for the door.

Mattie stood quickly, and she flinched as one of the babies kicked hard in protest. 'Do you have to go already?'

'Of course. As you put it so clearly—I'm not exactly a part of your life.'

Brutus started to whimper at Jake's feet and he bent down to pat the dog and gave him a scratch between his ears. Mattie wished that she could whimper too. Perhaps, if she cried, Jake would give her a scratch behind the ears. A pat? Any tiny sign?

Get a grip, girl.

He was already opening the front door.

Desperately grasping at straws, she stammered, 'I...I haven't t-told you about Roy. And...and you haven't told me about Mongolia.'

'Give me a break, Mattie. You aren't remotely interested in Mongolia.'

'That's not true. Anyway, wouldn't you like to hear about Roy?'

'I can visit Roy and get the news straight from the horse's mouth.' He pushed the door wider.

She would never see him again.

Her legs almost caved beneath her. She took a shaky step towards the door. 'You're really upset. You're angry, aren't you?'

Jake didn't reply. Without another word, he stepped outside and closed the door quietly but firmly behind him.

She'd lost him.

Mattie collapsed in a shaking huddle on the sofa, unable to stop her tears. She went through almost a whole box of tissues, but no amount of crying could ease the terrible ache inside her.

It had been so dreadfully hard to see Jake again, reminding her of everything she'd given up.

She'd never had a boyfriend like Jake Devlin, might never meet anyone like him ever again.

And now she'd lost him.

She'd watched that door close behind him and

it had felt like a death—more than Mattie could bear—and it was ages before she could think clearly, before she could chastise herself for breaking her heart over another man.

It wasn't as if Jake's departure was anything like the break-up with Pete. She and Jake hadn't been engaged. Not even close. There'd been no *understanding*. Jake hadn't promised forever. He'd never pretended to be anything but a foot-loose and fancy free bachelor.

Heavens, she shouldn't even be crying over him. If she was going to shed any tears over Jake Devlin, they should be tears of anger.

Heck, yes. As Mattie grabbed another handful of tissues, she deliberately stopped feeling sorry for herself and focused instead on all the reasons she should be angry with Jake. There were so many!

First, he had no right to storm in here and throw a tantrum simply because she wasn't available for another holiday fling. Second, he had no right to criticise her when she was doing something wonderful for Gina and Tom.

Third, it was impossible for him to understand why she'd made this choice because he was so jolly self-centred. And, most hurtful of all—he'd refused to show her an ounce of the compassion he'd showered on his old friend, Roy.

All in all, Jake was an opinionated and selfish prig and she was better off without him.

But…heaven help her, he was gorgeous too. She adored everything about the man—his flashing dark eyes, his cheeky smile, his happy laugh, his electrifying caresses, his sensational kisses…

Oh, good grief, she was hopeless.

Why couldn't he have stayed in Mongolia?

Jake tossed his coat onto the back seat of the hire car and slammed the door. Letting fly with a string of expletives, he wrenched open the driver's door, slid behind the steering wheel and pulled that door shut with an even louder slam.

He gunned the engine and took off, charging down the street at a reckless speed—until he saw the shocked face of a pedestrian and rapidly slowed down, chastened.

As soon as he turned the corner out of Mattie's street, he saw a parking space and pulled into it. His breathing was still ragged, his heart still pounding. He couldn't remember the last time he'd felt this angry. Or this scared.

Actually, that was a lie.

Jake remembered all too well.

He knew exactly when he'd felt this way and the very thought of it drenched him in a cold sweat, but it was too late to stop the memories of that terrible night when his baby brother had been born.

He'd been nine years old and thrilled, because after years of nagging his parents they'd told him that at last he was going to have a baby brother or sister.

He'd been caught up in a whirlwind of excitement during the preparations for the baby's arrival—painting the little back bedroom, watching parcels of impossibly cute clothes arrive from city stores, seeing nursery furniture coming out of storage.

Jake had made a rattle for the baby, a pathetic thing really, but at the time he'd been so proud, filling a small plastic bottle with seeds and painting it rainbow colours.

He'd imagined the baby playing with it, laughing and bashing it on the floor, and he'd dreamed of a future when the baby could crawl and the two of them would play hide and seek together.

He had such plans—so many things he would teach the youngster—how to swim and to ride, how to climb trees, catch a ball, keep secrets from grown-ups.

But then that night had come.

His father and Roy had been away mustering and Jake and his mother had been alone in the homestead. In the middle of the night Jake had been woken by the sound of his mother's raised voice. He'd crept out of bed to find her, with her dressing gown clutched about her, crying into the telephone, begging the flying doctor to come.

Terror had struck Jake's heart. His mother had looked so white and ill, so frightening, with tears streaming down her face. She had been shaking, but when she'd put the phone down she'd brushed his worried questions aside and hurried straight to the two-way radio to call his father.

The men had been asleep and it was ages before anyone answered. His mother had broken down while she'd waited and, when she'd finally managed to speak, her words had been obscured by her sobbing.

Jake had hated to see her like this. He'd tried to hug her, demanding to know what had happened.

At last she'd stopped crying and she'd touched his cheek with a cold hand. 'I need you to be a brave, good boy, Jake. The flying doctor's coming. Can you turn on all the house lights and wait on the veranda for him?'

'Yes,' he whispered, even though the thought of leaving her side terrified him.

'When the doctor comes, bring him to me,' she said wearily. Then, with a soft moan, she turned and she swayed dizzily back to the bedroom, one hand pressed against her pale lips as if she feared she might throw up.

To Jake's horror, as he watched through the bedroom doorway, she collapsed onto the bed and lay perfectly, terribly still.

Petrified, he ignored her order to wait on the veranda. He raced into her bedroom and shook her gently, trying to wake her. Crying and sobbing, he shook her roughly, begging her, but still she wouldn't wake.

Then he saw the tiny bundle…

He tiptoed, heart in his mouth, around the bed and saw the tiny face of a baby, wrapped in a shawl, lying so close to the edge of the bed it could have fallen off.

Its eyes were closed and when he picked it up he touched its little face. It was cold and fear leapt inside him like a gas flame.

If only the doctor would come. Or his father and Roy.

His tears fell on the little bundle as he gently placed it in the safety of the crib in the corner of his parents' bedroom. And then he pulled a blanket over his mother and went to wait all alone on the veranda.

Only in the darkest of nightmares had Jake revisited the terror and misery of that long, lonely vigil. But now the shock of Mattie's pregnancy had torn down his careful defences and he couldn't hold back the black memories.

So many times during that night he'd crept back to the bedroom, praying that his mother or the baby would wake.

It was hours before the men had arrived, but at last they'd come. The flying doctor plane's lights had bobbed and bounced on the rough landing strip at around the same time the thunder of horses' hooves signalled the stockmen's return.

The doctor and Jake's father had gone straight to his mother, closing the door, and it was into Roy's arms that Jake had crumpled.

It was Roy who'd finally told him that his mother was going to be all right, but his baby brother had died. It was Roy who'd never left his side throughout the rest of that night or the next day. It was Roy who'd explained about premature stillbirth, Roy who'd assured Jake that he wasn't to blame for any of this. There was nothing he could have done.

A jagged groan broke from Jake and he slumped behind the steering wheel, staring through the windscreen at the pouring rain.

Now, as a rational adult, he knew his mother's experience wasn't common. She'd been a tragic victim of the Outback's isolation. Pregnancy in a huge city like Sydney was a totally different kettle of fish.

But an irrational corner of his heart shrank, chilled by the old fear he'd never quite been able to bury. He never wanted to put himself through that level of turmoil again.

Thankfully he'd had the sense to distance himself from Mattie, to walk out of her flat. If he'd stayed there he might have done something he'd regret, might have asked more questions, got himself more deeply entangled.

But how *could* a young woman get herself involved in something like this? How could she take such risks with her body for someone else?

You know why. Mattie Carey isn't just any girl.

Too true.

That was his problem.

Mattie was so much more than any girl he'd ever known... She wasn't just divinely sexy in silk and lace lingerie... She was warm, vibrant, special... She had a heart as big as...

Damn. If he went down that track, he'd start to feel involved and overly protective and he'd already decided that this was *not* his responsibility. He didn't want to be involved.

Slotting the key in the car's ignition, he started the engine, determined to put distance between himself and Mattie's pregnancy.

At the first junction, however, when he braked for a red light, his mind threw up pictures of Mattie over the next few months. Carrying twins.

The rapidly growing babies were going to be a huge drain on her. And who would be there to support her?

Did she know what could happen? Did she really think she could manage everything on her own? Why on earth was she doing this? Alone?

So many questions.

So many things to worry about.

Jake drove on, but the thought of Mattie going into labour and delivering twins sent his angry fist smashing into the steering wheel.

This surrogacy gesture was going too far. It was a one-way street with no chance to turn back. And now it was too late to talk her out of it. He felt as helpless now as he had when he was nine.

And he didn't want to get involved.

But did he have any other option?

Mattie needed help.

Without consciously making the decision, Jake circled the block until he was in front of the flats again. And then he was out of the car, dashing through the rain once more, this time without his coat.

He knocked an impatient tattoo on Mattie's front door, and the little dog barked madly. Again.

Again, Mattie took ages to open the door but, when she did, Jake felt as if he'd been slugged in the solar plexus.

Her eyes were red and watery and her nose was red too, as if she'd blown it many times. She was clutching a handful of damp tissues and, as soon as she saw him, she gave a hiccupping sob and her eyes filled with fresh tears.

'Mattie, I…'

She shook her head and pressed the wad of tissues against her mouth.

A strangling sensation seized Jake by the throat. He couldn't bear to think he'd done this to her. If anyone else had hurt Mattie Carey he would have cracked them on the jaw.

'I had to make sure you were OK,' he said. 'But I see you're not.'

Instead of inviting him in, she rolled her eyes and the action sent shiny tears spilling down her flushed cheeks. Hastily, she dashed them away with the heel of her hand. 'I've already told you I'm fine, Jake. You don't have to worry about me.'

She obviously didn't want to talk about her crying, so he tried another tack. 'Who's looking after you?'

'I don't need looking after.' Mattie blew her nose noisily and wiped the last of her tears onto her sleeve. 'I'm not ill. Just pregnant.'

'But you're doing all this by yourself?'

'Pregnancy isn't exactly something you can share.'

She was being deliberately stubborn, which meant she was almost certainly angry. Battling his own impatience, Jake tried again. 'What about the next couple of months as the pregnancy advances?'

'When I'm as huge as two houses?'

'You're still going to have to shop and to cook, and to go to medical appointments.'

'Yes, but don't worry. I'll carry one of those warning signs: Oversize Load.'

He groaned in exasperation. 'Mattie, be serious. Don't tell me you're going to try to do this all on your own.'

'Why not? It's the truth.' She was beginning to sound bored by his interrogation.

Jake drew a deep breath and prayed for patience. 'You're expecting twins. Another *couple's* twins. Surely they owe you something? In my book they owe you big time, but it looks like they've abandoned you.'

'You don't know anything about them.' Mattie was calmer now. Calmer and colder. She stood, blocking the doorway, with her arms folded over her 'baby bump'. 'No one has abandoned me, Jake.'

As she said this her face fell, but she quickly recovered. 'It was my idea to come to Sydney. If I'd stayed in Willowbank, the whole town would have been trying to guess what was going on.'

She paused to blow her nose again and gave him a very deliberate, if watery, smile. 'I'm quite capable of managing alone and this is the way I want it. I couldn't handle the constant fussing if I'd stayed near Gina and Tom. They'd always be hovering over me, making sure I was OK.'

And so they should, Jake thought. *Anything might happen.*

He grimaced, fighting flashes of fear. 'But twins, Mattie. Surely you'll get too tired to look after this place and…and everything else?'

'All taken care of. Gina and Tom have sent me a lovely cleaner. She's brilliant. And they've even talked about a home delivery grocery service.'

This was good news at least. 'So they are looking after you?'

'They've showered me with all kinds of pampering.' She held out her hands, displaying her glamorous nails. 'They've sent me vouchers for manicures, facials, massages, pedicures. They're spoiling me rotten.'

'Right.'

Mattie folded her arms again and stood with her head resolutely high and her shoulders back, as if she'd donned armour and could now face any foe. 'Thanks for checking, Jake. It was sweet of you to worry.'

He gulped. 'No problem.'

She reached for the door, as if their conversation had come to a close and she wanted him to leave.

He felt suddenly deprived of oxygen.

'Wait,' he said sharply. He wanted to tell her that she mustn't cry and that he…that he…

What?

Panic gripped him. What was his role here?

Mattie didn't need his practical support. He was anxious to avoid emotional attachment. Seduction wasn't on the agenda. All the ground rules had changed for him. He didn't have a role.

Mattie was watching him expectantly, one hand on the door, ready to pull it shut.

He gulped, didn't know what to do next. It was unbelievable. Jake Devlin, on a woman's doorstep, lost for words. In desperation, he said, 'You've left out the cat.'

'I beg your pardon?' She frowned. 'What are you talking about? I don't have a cat. Only Brutus.'

'No. In the drawing of Molly, the little witch. You usually have a black cat on every page.'

Mattie turned slowly and a small frown made vertical tracks in her forehead as she looked across the lounge room to the table with her art gear. Jake held his breath as he studied her profile.

He could see the dusty fringe of her lashes, the tiny bump on her nose, the warm curves of her lips, soft as petals. The hairdresser's highlights had faded from her hair, leaving it a gentle light brown. Not mousy at all, but exactly the right colour for her.

He was remembering how her lips had tasted, how eagerly they'd parted for him. To his surprise, her ripening body hadn't diminished his desire. He longed to hold her, to touch her.

'You're absolutely right,' she said. 'I've forgotten to put the little cat in the last drawing. I suppose I can blame maternity amnesia.'

She turned to him again, her expression puzzled and wary.

Jake struggled to remember what they'd been talking about. Not her lips. Oh, yeah, the cat. 'He could…uh…he could be hiding under the table.'

Mattie smiled. 'Yes, I could show him half-hidden by a corner of the tablecloth and waiting for Molly to pass him a piece of mackerel.'

Jake nodded. 'Something like that.'

Her eyes glowed with sudden warmth, the heart-stopping warmth he remembered, and he wondered how she would react if he tried to kiss her now.

Should he kiss her now?

'That's a really good idea, Jake. Thank you for

reminding me about that cat. My little readers would have been mortified if I'd left him out.'

'You're welcome.'

She dropped her gaze to her rounded stomach, gave a sigh, then lifted her gaze again. 'Is that all, Jake?'

No!

The urge to kiss her was all consuming. But, in the past, Jake's kisses had almost always led to seduction and now he yearned for something else. Something more, something deeper, better.

He needed Mattie in ways he'd never needed anyone before. Whenever he was with her he felt happy and strangely content. When he was away from her he was dismal and worried for no reason. But he had no idea how to tell her that. More importantly, he didn't want to admit it to himself.

The very thought that his happiness depended on a pregnant woman was beyond terrifying.

Mattie began to pull the door shut and, through the narrowing space, she looked out at him, her blue eyes huge and wistful. 'Give my love to Roy.'

'Sure,' Jake said, but he knew that he couldn't just walk away. Mattie needed him. He had no idea how to care for her but, God help him, he had to try.

Years ago, his mother had exiled him to the veranda. Now Mattie was pregnant and he couldn't contemplate a similar self-imposed exile.

He took an anxious step forward, but Mattie said calmly, 'All the best, Jake. I hope you enjoy your leave.'

And she closed the door.

CHAPTER EIGHT

AT LEAST, Mattie tried to close the door, but Jake was too fast for her.

With the speed of a tackling footballer, he blocked the narrowing gap.

She gave a startled cry. 'What are you trying to do? Lose an arm?'

He shrugged this question aside and shouldered the door wider open. 'I can't leave you like this. You're being far too stubborn.'

'*I'm* being stubborn?'

'You are if you think you can do this without help, Mattie.' His tone edged towards anger.

Mattie was angry too. 'You can't just barge in here and start bossing me around.'

Ignoring this, he strode past her into the flat.

Breathless with surprise, she followed him. 'I don't want you here, Jake.'

He came to a stop in the middle of the room and looked suddenly lost, like a small boy in trouble.

Mattie's soft heart began to melt.

'Look,' he said, running a hand over his face. 'I must admit I'm thinking on my feet at the moment. I don't have a plan, but I can't…I can't…'

His beautiful face was pale and taut but, as he looked at Mattie, his mouth tilted into an uneven smile that did terrible things to the rhythm of her heart. 'I can't just walk out of here as if I don't give two hoots what happens to you, Mattie.'

For a moment she was too confused to speak. What exactly was he saying?

Her only truly coherent thought was that it would be rather nice if Jake wanted to take her in his arms and kiss her. But he wasn't offering kisses and she certainly wasn't going to ask him for one. She had tried that once before and the very thought of where that kiss had led to made her distinctly dizzy and light-headed.

'I need to sit down,' she said, sinking inelegantly onto a sofa.

'Of course.' Jake waited till she was comfortable, with a cushion at her back, before he sat on the sofa opposite.

Leaning forward, elbows on his knees, he clasped his hands and looked at her intently. 'I know next to nothing about women expecting twins.'

He looked so worried, she couldn't help

smiling. 'Does any bachelor know about twin pregnancy unless he's studying obstetrics?'

Momentarily his face cleared and she caught a fleeting smile, but he quickly sobered. 'Listen, Mattie, I don't plan to make a nuisance of myself. I won't hang around here at the flat. I'll find somewhere else to stay and I'll give you plenty of space, but I'm going to be here in Sydney.'

'While you're on leave?'

'Until the twins are born.'

Mattie's jaw sagged.

'Why?' she finally managed to ask.

'I…I want to spend more time with Roy. And I can keep an eye on you at the same time.'

This didn't make sense. 'I don't need a watchdog, Jake. I have a perfectly good doctor.'

Jake was on his feet again, pacing the room like a caged lion. 'Look, I know you want me to keep my distance, so I don't want to crowd you.' He almost glared at her. 'But someone's got to keep an eye on you.'

Too surprised to speak, she sat looking up at him like a small bird hypnotised by a deadly handsome snake.

'I'll stay at the Dockside Apartments at Woolloomooloo,' he told her.

'But what about your job?' she remembered to ask.

'I'll get special leave. I'll resign if I have to.'

'But that's mad.'

He shook his head. 'I'll give you my mobile number and I want you to call me any time.'

'Call you?'

Frowning, he nodded. 'Any heavy lifting, call me. You want the dog walked, I'm your man. If you give me a list, I'll do your shopping for you. Anything breaks down—from the toaster to the air conditioner—let me sort it out. I'm probably better at dealing with tradesmen than you are.'

Mattie opened her mouth but no sound emerged. Why was he doing this? What did it mean? If Jake had been a proper boyfriend, she might have been charmed by his desire to help. But he was a man she'd slept with once, a man who couldn't commit. In fact, he was the man she was trying to forget!

At last she found her tongue. 'This is very kind, Jake, but I don't need to be wrapped in cotton wool.'

The muscles in his throat rippled. 'Just keep well, Mattie. Get plenty of rest and look after yourself. Let me know if there are any concerns.'

'But…I don't understand. Why are you doing this?'

His eyes flashed darkly. 'I don't like to see a pregnant woman trying to manage on her own.' A spasm jerked in his jaw and he clenched his teeth hard. Clenched his hands too.

Was there something deep-seated behind this unexpected urge to protect her? A secret in Jake's past? A pregnant woman in trouble? Mattie longed to ask, but Jake seemed so different now, so stern and masterful, and she was just a little afraid of him.

He exhaled slowly. 'So,' he said, 'I'd better give you my contact details.'

'Oh, yes…right.' Mattie had to wriggle her bottom towards the edge of the sofa before she could stand.

Jake was suddenly beside her, offering a strong hand at her elbow, supporting her as she stood. His touch sent a wave of heat flashing through her.

'Thank you.' Her voice was breathless and faint. 'I'll just get my little black book from the kitchen.'

'Hey, stranger.' Will's voice sounded jovial on the other end of the line. 'I didn't expect to hear from you. How's your leave?'

Flopped on a sofa in his Woolloomooloo apartment, Jake stared at the ceiling as he answered. 'It hasn't gone quite to plan.'

'Don't tell me the world's run out of beautiful, available women?'

'Something like that.' Truth be told, Jake hadn't even tried to pick up another woman—an unheard-of phenomenon. 'I'm staying on here,' he said. 'That's why I've rung. I've told the boss I'm not coming back and I need you to pack up my things, if you don't mind.'

'You're joking. What's happened? Are you OK?'

'Yeah, sure. I just need to stay here. At least for the next couple of months. Maybe then, if there's a position available…' He let the words trail off.

Seconds of silence ticked by. Will said, 'Does this have anything to do with Mattie Carey?'

'Mattie? What makes you ask that?'

'I had a weird e-mail from her.'

Zap! Jake cleared his throat. 'What did she say?'

'It seems she's worried about you.'

'That's a joke, right?'

'Not at all. She sounded seriously concerned. She didn't tell me you'd resigned, though.'

'I'm fine,' Jake said but, even to his ears, he didn't sound convincing.

'So, what's going on between you and Mattie?'

'Very little.'

'Pull the other one.'

Jake let out a heavy sigh. He'd had enough trouble yesterday, steering Roy away from discussions about Mattie.

'I must say I was surprised.' Will sounded as if he was settling in for a lengthy chat. 'I wouldn't have thought Mattie Carey was your type.'

Jake resisted the urge to rise to his friend's bait. His resistance lasted maybe all of five seconds. Then he had to ask. 'So, why isn't Mattie my type?'

Will laughed. 'You know very well how you like your women.'

'You tell me.'

'Ready, willing and able.'

Normally, a comment like this wouldn't have fazed Jake. Today it sent a blast of embarrassing heat scorching the back of his neck. *Damn.* He'd stumbled straight into this trap.

From down the phone line, he could hear the dawning suspicion in his mate's voice. 'Jake, you didn't.'

Jake tried to ignore him.

Will persisted. 'Tell me it's not true. That week when you shared the flat with Mattie, you didn't—'

'Give it a miss, Will.'

'But—' Will whistled softly. 'Not you and Mattie?'

'It's none of your business.' Jake clenched a threatening fist and unclenched it again. Took a calming breath. 'Anyway, it's rather late for you to be talking to me about Mattie Carey.' He spoke in his driest tone. 'You're supposed to be my best mate and you knew she was planning to get herself pregnant with someone else's kids, but you kindly overlooked sharing that minor detail with me.'

'It was a delicate matter, Jake. A private arrangement between Mattie and my sister and her husband. As far as you were concerned, I was working on a need to know basis. How did I know that you needed to know?'

'I asked you enough questions.'

'Yeah, but I thought that was nothing more than idle curiosity. I never occurred to me—I didn't dream you and Mattie were an item.'

'We're not.'

'Then why's she so bothered about you?'

'Because...because she's Mattie. She's bothered about every living thing on this planet.'

'That's very true.'

'Saint Matilda,' Jake growled.

'Or not so saintly, it would seem?'

'Shut up.'

'OK, OK.'

'I'd really appreciate it if you could pack up my things.'

'Sure. No problem.'

Tom thumped Mattie's kitchen table with his fist. 'Jack wins hands down as the boy's name.'

Gina shook her head. 'Jack's too traditional. Don't we want something trendier, like Jasper or

Jake?' She turned to Mattie, who'd almost spilled her cup of peppermint tea at the mention of Jake. 'Don't you agree?'

Mattie shook her head. 'I d-don't think you should include me in a discussion of names.'

To her surprise, Gina and Tom responded in unison. 'Why not?'

She forced a smile. 'They're your babies. The two of you will have enough trouble reaching agreement. If I stick my oar in, you'll never be able to decide.'

Gina was clearly disappointed. 'I can't imagine not including you, Mattie. Gosh, you and I have been talking about babies' names since we were in primary school.'

Mattie patted her protruding tummy. 'But we're dealing with real babies now. Yours and Tom's. And they'll be stuck with the names you choose for the rest of their lives.'

'Of course, I know that.'

Trying to lighten the atmosphere, Mattie said, 'I've been calling them Dot and Dash.' But Gina, who'd obviously lost her sense of humour, continued to look unhappy.

Relenting, Mattie squeezed her friend's hand. 'All right, if you must know, I hope you don't call your little boy Jake.'

'Why? Don't you like Jake?'

Mattie smothered an urge to sigh. Of course she liked the name Jake. She was very fond of Jake. Too fond and way too sentimental. Just hearing the name brought her to the brink of tears.

Jake Devlin was confusing her to distraction. He'd been kind, yes, but she still didn't really understand what was behind his urge to protect her. There were times when she thought that he truly cared about her, but he remained so careful and distant she couldn't be sure.

Deep down, where the scars left by Pete had never properly healed, Mattie had to admit she was scared. And she was probably confusing Jake as much as he confused her. She'd held him at bay so many times he assumed that was what she wanted. Who could blame him?

If neither of them was ready to open up, she might never get to the bottom of what was going on between them. But if Gina and Tom called their little boy Jake, she'd be hearing his name for the rest of her life, an eternal reminder of this painful, puzzling interlude.

Gina, meanwhile, was waiting for her answer.

'Look…this is why I shouldn't be involved,' Mattie said. 'Don't take any notice of me. Jake's a fine name.'

Gina watched her thoughtfully for several seconds and then her expression cleared.

'*Oh*,' she said with dramatic emphasis. 'I should have remembered. That hot guy who stayed with you here last summer—Will's friend—his name was Jake, wasn't it?'

Mattie winced.

'He broke your heart,' Gina announced dramatically.

'My heart's perfectly sound.'

'But you really fancied him.'

Mattie answered with a shrug.

Gina sighed. 'You poor thing. I'm sure Will told me once that Jake went through women like water.' She rolled her eyes. 'Some men have a lot to answer for.'

This discussion was rather more than Mattie could bear. She didn't want to tell Gina and Tom that Jake was back in Sydney, planning to hover in the distance and watch over her like some kind of anxious guardian angel.

They would want details. Answers. She didn't have answers.

With a deliberately casual shrug, she defended Jake. 'Look, it wasn't all one-sided. It was as much my fault as his.'

'Which means we should drop the subject,' said Tom firmly as he gave his wife a warning glance.

'Hmm,' said Gina.

'We don't want to say anything to upset Mattie,' Tom insisted. 'We shouldn't be raising her stress levels over naming the babies. That's why she's come to Sydney—to be spared all that.'

Tom looked so concerned and fatherly that Mattie thought, for a moment, he was going to lean over and place a hand on her forehead to test her temperature.

But, to her relief, he refrained. And Gina took the hint and gave up the discussion of baby names.

Mattie sat at the card table by the window, typing on her laptop. She was supposed to be working on the final version of Molly's story, but she found it hard to concentrate. Jake had called to ask if she was free because he wanted to visit her and, ever since his call, she'd been in a tailspin.

Carol, her neighbour, breezed past on her way back from the letter box and she doubled back to stop at Mattie's window.

She let out a low wolf whistle. 'You're looking swish today. Expecting a special visitor?'

'Not really.' Mattie tried to sound airy about the fact that she was wearing her prettiest maternity top and two layers of mascara, but she promptly spoiled it by blushing.

Carol smiled knowingly, then glanced out to

the street where a car was pulling up. 'This not-really-special visitor wouldn't be male and about six feet three, would he?'

Mattie blushed again. 'Possibly.'

Grinning broadly now, Carol began to fan herself with her mail. 'Call the hospital Emergency,' she panted theatrically. 'I'm having palpitations.'

Mattie laughed, but then she heard footsteps on the front path and, sure enough, it was Jake who was heading her way and her heart began to quicken too.

Carol disappeared and suddenly Jake was knocking on her front door.

'Behave, Brutus,' Mattie ordered and, to her relief, the little dog obeyed her.

She opened the door and saw that Jake had made an effort with his appearance too. He was impeccably dressed in an open-necked blue chambray shirt and dark trousers, and his sleek tan boots were very well polished. She felt a rush of longing. Good heavens. She hadn't thought it was possible to be heavily pregnant with twins and still feel this kind of wanting.

He kept his hands behind his back, as if he was hiding something.

'Good morning, Mattie.' His deep voice rippled over her like sexy music, and he smiled shyly as he brought his hands in front of him to reveal two potted plants—a small rose bush, covered with the sweetest miniature pink blooms, and a cluster of irises, with frilled petals as deep blue as a midsummer sky.

'They're in honour of your babies,' he said with a shy smile.

'They're gorgeous,' Mattie whispered. 'Pink for the girl, blue for the boy.' Her eyes swam with tears. *Stop it. Stop it right now.*

'I thought you might prefer living plants to cut flowers.'

She nodded her thanks, and sniffed. She was overwhelmed. 'I…I'll put the kettle on.'

'No, you won't. You'll stay here and I'll put the kettle on.'

'Jake!' She rolled her eyes at him. 'Honestly, I'm fit as a—'

'Yeah, I know,' he interrupted, smiling. 'You're as fit as three fiddles, but humour me, Mattie. I've been to the library and I've read up on expecting twins. You're supposed to take it easy in the last trimester. So now it's my turn to be the helpful type and you'll have to accept it graciously. Put your feet up and stay on that sofa.'

To cover her surprise, she said meekly, 'All right. I'll have peppermint tea, please. The tea bags are in the blue pot with the wooden lid.'

Taking him at his word, she kicked her sandals

off and made herself comfortable on the sofa with her feet up.

But she couldn't relax.

Jake's behaviour was too bewildering.

It was so hard to reconcile the man in her kitchen fixing her herbal tea with the man she'd first met. She kept seeing Ange's knickers on the bathroom floor and those tangled bed sheets.

And then, no sooner had Ange been out of the picture, than Jake had leapt into Mattie's bed.

She couldn't stop thinking about that awful farewell at the airport: *You do know that I can't promise you a future together, don't you?*

When he'd returned to Mongolia, she'd realised that everything about Jake Devlin had pointed to one dangerous fact—he was a playboy.

Now he was trying to protect her.

It was all terribly confusing.

Anyone looking from the outside might reasonably assume that a man who'd given up his job to hang about, waiting to help and support a pregnant woman, must care deeply about her. Mattie would have liked to believe that too, but it was so hard to believe that a man who obviously loved to play the field would still find her attractive when she was the size of a whale.

Her entire life these days was dominated by the babies. She was sure she could feel her hips actually spreading. She needed to go the bathroom every five minutes and her ankles swelled if she was on her feet for too long.

She now had weekly visits to the doctor and the babies' progress was being strictly monitored, which meant there were times when she truly felt exactly the way Jake had described her—like an incubator.

She'd begun to wonder if she could ever change back into the reckless, happy girl who'd shared this flat with Jake.

That special day when they'd brewed billy tea for Roy and had gone to the movies seemed so very long ago. As for their one passionate night—that perfect, blissful night—it now felt as if it had happened in another lifetime.

Mattie hoped she didn't look too anxious when Jake returned with her tea and a mug of instant coffee for himself.

To her surprise, he didn't sit opposite her.

Looking super-relaxed and totally in charge, he sat on the end of her sofa, mere inches from her bare feet.

The sofa cushion dipped with his weight. His knee brushed her leg and heat rushed over her in a sweeping flash. It wasn't fair! He looked so cool, while she was taking so many deep breaths she was in danger of hyperventilating.

'Have you seen Roy lately?' she asked breathlessly.

Jake nodded. 'I'm a bit worried about him, actually. I don't think he's very well.'

'Really? I'm sorry to hear that. Have you spoken to the staff at the nursing home?'

'They assure me he's as well as can be expected, but to me he looks like he has one foot in the grave.'

'Poor darling.'

Jake's dark eyes rested on Mattie. For the longest time he watched her. 'You look well,' he said softly. 'Actually, you look—'

'Blooming?'

He laughed. 'I was thinking of something more flattering.'

Really?

Mattie held her breath, but Jake had apparently decided to change the subject. 'So what happens to Brutus and Pavarotti when you go into hospital? Who's going to look after them?'

'Gina and Tom will collect them some time next week, in case anything happens early.'

'Early?'

'It can happen with twins.'

'Yes, so I've discovered.'

'At the library?'

Jake nodded. He was frowning deeply and his

eyes had turned stony as he glared at a spot on the carpet.

'Anyway,' Mattie continued, hoping to distract him, 'Gina and Tom will take Brutus and Pavarotti back to Willowbank, and I think Gina's parents will probably look after them.'

He nodded and then reached into his trouser pocket. 'I bought something for your menagerie.' With a smile, he produced a blue rubber fetch-and-play toy in the shape of a bone. He held it out to Brutus. 'This is for you, chum.'

The little dog immediately went into paroxysms of delight, rolling and wrestling with the rubber bone.

'Jake, it's perfect. He loves it.'

Jake dug into his other pocket and pulled out something that looked like a twig with a pretty hanging mobile attached.

Mattie laughed. 'Is that for Pavarotti?'

'Yes. It's a pedicure perch.'

'A what?'

'A pedicure perch.' His dark eyes sparkled. 'Pavarotti can wrap his little claws around this stick and peck at the mobile and have a pedicure at the same time.'

She laughed so hard she almost hiccuped. 'Wow!' she said between giggles. 'That's outrageous, but I love it.'

Without warning, Mattie stopped in mid-giggle. For a minute there, she'd let go of her doubts and fears. She'd been as happy as she had been in those first few days with Jake. They'd packed so much into their short time together. The laughter, the happiness—the passion.

Jake had warned her that it couldn't last.

That was still true. It couldn't last, could it?

She had to ask. 'Jake, why are you doing this?'

'Doing what?'

She held up the perch. 'Why are you here? Why are you being so thoughtful?' She gulped. Oh, heavens. She mustn't get teary in front of him.

For a long moment he seemed caught out, as if he didn't know how to answer her. Mattie could see his mind working and it was almost as if he was asking himself the same question.

He stared at her, his face serious, almost worried. He dropped his gaze to Brutus, pouncing on his blue rubber bone. 'Remember the day we took Roy out and we brewed billy tea?'

'Yes, of course.'

'I realised then that you're always going the extra mile to make other people happy, but I wondered if anyone ever does that for you.'

The little perch trembled in Mattie's hand. 'Is that what this is about? You're trying to make me happy?'

Jake smiled. 'That's the aim.'

'Oh!'

Mattie couldn't help it.

She burst into tears.

In a heartbeat, Jake's arms were around her and she was sobbing against his big solid shoulder. But he didn't seem to mind. He kissed her forehead and stroked her hair and made soothing noises the way a parent might.

She clung to him—she had no choice—she was collapsing beneath the weight of her emotions. She was happy, sad, confused, scared, but, somewhere within the disarray, she knew that she loved this man.

Even though it was dangerous, and he might break her heart, she loved everything about him. Right now, she could smell his skin and his after-shave and his laundered shirt and the combination was wonderful.

'Mattie,' he murmured hoarsely, 'you mustn't cry. I didn't want to upset you.'

There was a sudden knock at the open front door. 'What's going on?'

It was Tom's voice.

CHAPTER NINE

TOM was like a soldier on sentry duty as he stood stiffly in the doorway, red hair standing up in spikes, frowning at them. 'What's happened? Are you all right, Mattie?'

Her face was flooded with tears, her throat was too tight for speech and her shoulders were shaking from the force of her sobbing. All she could manage was to nod her head vigorously.

Tom marched into the flat, jaw at a belligerent angle. 'Are you sure you're OK? What's going on here?' He shot a scalding glare at Jake. 'Excuse me, but who are you?'

Slowly Jake rose from the sofa and the air in the small lounge room was suddenly thick with tension and testosterone. Jake was a head taller than Tom and he looked ready for a battle.

Without smiling, he held out his hand. 'Jake Devlin's the name. How do you do?'

'Jake, this is Tom,' Mattie supplied in a choked voice. 'Tom Roberts.'

The two men shook hands grimly.

Jake said quietly and without warmth, 'So, you're the babies' father?'

'That's right.' Tom squared his shoulders. 'And I've heard about you—Our Man in Mongolia.' He spoke the way a policeman might address a hardened criminal.

Jake slid a smooth, questioning glance Mattie's way.

'Jake's a friend, Tom,' she intervened. 'A...a good friend.'

'But he has a habit of upsetting you?'

'Not at all,' she insisted. 'Jake hasn't upset me.' She pointed to the plants on the coffee table. 'He's brought me lovely gifts.'

Tom eyed the plants suspiciously and Mattie surreptitiously wiped at her tears with the corner of a handkerchief. She noticed black smudges of mascara on the white fabric and she hoped she hadn't ended up with panda eyes.

'I didn't know you were back in Sydney, Tom.' She was pleased she could speak more calmly now. 'Is Gina here too?'

He shook his head. 'I had to come to town for a quick business trip and I couldn't come without popping in to see you.' He looked again at the potted plants and shot Jake a sharp-eyed glance.

'Why don't you take a seat?' Jake suggested dryly and he sat again on the sofa beside Mattie, so close that his shirt sleeve brushed her arm, and her skin flashed hot and cold.

She hoped Tom would stop bristling and be pleasant to Jake, but she was out of luck.

As soon as Tom was seated, he attacked Jake. 'I presume Mattie's told you she's expecting twins?'

'Of course.'

'And has she also told you that many women expecting twins have to spend their last trimester in hospital to ensure they have sufficient rest?'

Mattie didn't dare to look at Jake, but she could feel his tension.

Tom pressed his point home. 'In other words, Mattie mustn't be upset.'

'Tom, I can reassure you,' Jake said smoothly. 'I want nothing more than for Mattie to be rested and well and to have a safe delivery.'

Tom gave a slight nod of acknowledgement, but his expression was still doubtful.

Diplomatically, Mattie asked, 'How's Gina?'

'Fabulous.' At last Tom smiled. 'Apart from the fact that she talks about the babies all day long and half the night and then in her sleep as well.'

Mattie smiled. 'She's a tad excited, isn't she?'

'Excited? There ought to be a better word.'

Jake rose. 'I should go,' he said. 'I'm sure you two want to have a good long chat.'

'There's no need to leave,' Mattie began, but Jake looked determined so she didn't push it.

He turned to Tom, gave a stiffly polite nod. 'Nice to meet you.'

'You too,' Tom replied without conviction.

'See you later, Mattie.' Jake bent down and kissed her cheek. His mouth only brushed her skin briefly, but her heart leapt as high as the moon and she was sure his lips left a scorch mark.

She wanted to tell him that he was welcome to drop by any time, but with Tom frowning ferociously, as if he were guarding her like one of his sheepdogs, she held her tongue.

'Thanks for the gifts, Jake. They're gorgeous.'

'My pleasure. Take care.'

When Jake left she felt as if all the fun had gone out of her day. It took a huge effort to paste on a smile for Tom's benefit.

'I hope he's not going to make a habit of upsetting you,' Tom said even before Jake's footsteps had died away.

'He won't,' Mattie assured him, but she couldn't be sure it was the truth. She was simply a mess where he was concerned.

For the babies' sake, she should snap out of it.

* * *

What a stuff-up.

Jake couldn't believe he'd made such a hash of visiting Mattie. As he stormed to his car he felt so fired up and mad with himself he wanted to kick something.

He'd gone in there all gung-ho and he'd ended up with Mattie in tears. As if that wasn't bad enough, when the babies' father had arrived, he'd very nearly started an argument with him.

Our Man in Mongolia. That was below the belt.

Then again…

Jake slowed his pace as he tried to sort out what had just happened.

Truth be told, Tom probably had good reason to be so upset. He must have had a shock when he'd turned up at the flat expecting to see the woman who was carrying his children resting up safely and serenely, only to find her in another bloke's arms, sobbing her heart out.

Give the man a break.

Yeah, maybe.

Even so, Jake couldn't shrug the incident aside. He'd been on the brink of some kind of breakthrough.

OK, so Mattie had been weeping in his arms, but if they'd been given half a chance, her tears might have broken down barriers and he might have begun to make some kind of sense of the turmoil inside him.

Then good old Tom had barged in like the SAS saving the world.

Jake pressed his car's central locking device and, as he heard the lock's *click-click,* he remembered Mattie's question.

Why are you doing this?

He'd told her that he wanted to help her, but that was only half the truth, wasn't it? And even then he'd made her cry.

Just as well he hadn't told her the rest—that he was starting to realise that he needed to be with her, that she was the best thing that had ever happened to him.

If he'd told her that, she might have expected a promise of some kind of serious commitment—a confession that he loved her, that he was ready for marriage and a family of their own. But how could he be?

That was going too far. Way too far.

It was downright terrifying.

The true answer was that Jake was taking this venture one step at a time. One day at a time. He didn't dare to look any further ahead and how could he tell Mattie that?

Perhaps, after all, he should be grateful to Tom for barging in when he had.

* * *

Jake was asleep when the phone rang. His first thought as he swung out of bed was Mattie. Panic kicked him in the chest. Had something happened to her? He groped in the dark for his phone.

'Mr Devlin?'

'Speaking.'

'It's Sister Hart from the Lilydale Nursing Home.'

'Yes? What is it? Is Roy OK?'

'I'm afraid I have bad news. Roy's had a heart attack.'

Whack! Jake felt as if his own heart had been chopped with an axe. 'How—' His throat was dry and he had to swallow. 'How is he?'

'It's quite serious. He's been taken to hospital, of course, so you'll need to ring the Coronary Care Unit to check on his condition.'

'Right.' Already Jake's mind was racing. He wouldn't simply telephone. He'd drive straight to the hospital. He knew the first few hours after a heart attack were crucial. He had to try to see Roy.

It was the early hours of the morning, still dark, as he drove through the Sydney streets. His hands were sweaty on the steering wheel and fear gnawed at his stomach and clutched at his throat. He loved Roy and he couldn't bear it if he died.

He accepted that Roy couldn't live for ever,

but he felt a nagging sense of injustice on Roy's behalf. The guy was a legend. He deserved a hero's old age.

Jake drove through the hospital's multilevel car park, eyes alert for an empty parking spot. His fear spiralled as he hurried through the maze of disinfected corridors to the Coronary Care Unit. He'd steeled himself for the grimness of the ward, the hushed atmosphere, the frightening banks of blinking lights and the frowning scrutiny of the nursing sister in charge, but he couldn't stop blaming himself.

I should have done more. Please, don't let it be too late.

Mid-afternoon, Mattie's heart leapt when her phone rang and she saw Jake's name on her caller ID.

'I'm sorry,' he said. 'I've only just found all your messages. I had the phone switched off.'

'I forgive you.' She tried to sound light-hearted and failed dismally. The fact that Jake hadn't answered her messages had frightened her.

It brought back memories of dating Pete. So many times she'd tried to ring him in Perth and he hadn't been available. She'd probably developed some kind of complex about men and mobile phones.

'I've been at the hospital all day,' Jake said. 'Roy's had a heart attack.'

'Oh, no.' Mattie was instantly ashamed of herself. 'How is he?'

'They tell me he's holding his own.'

'I guess that's good news, then.'

'I guess. I'll feel better when I can speak to him.'

'Don't worry,' Mattie said gently. 'Roy's tough.'

'Yeah.' Jake sighed. 'Anyway, how are you?'

'Actually—' Mattie bit her lip. She wished now that she didn't have to tell Jake her news. 'I'm in hospital too.'

'What?' That single word echoed like a rifle shot.

'It's OK, Jake. It's not a code-orange alert. The doctor's simply taking precautions.'

'But why? What's wrong?'

'I started having contractions and he was worried I was going into early labour. The contractions have settled down, but I've been ordered complete bed rest.' She wrinkled her nose as she spoke into the phone. 'It means I have to stay in hospital until the babies are born.'

'Right.'

Jake sounded winded and Mattie felt sorry for him. Two medical dramas in one day was a coincidence no one welcomed. 'We want to give

the babies the best possible chance,' she explained gently. 'Twins often come early.'

'Which hospital are you in?'

'Southmead.'

'The same hospital as Roy.' He made a sound
that was almost a chuckle. 'At least that makes it
easier for me to visit you both. Which ward?'

'I'll give you three guesses,' she said, smiling.

'Oh, yes, of course—Maternity. What room?'

'2203. But, Jake, I don't expect you to visit me
when you're so worried about Roy.'

On the other end of the line, she heard Jake's
sigh.

'You don't have a choice, Mattie.' His voice was
deep, dark and insistent. 'I'm already on my way.'

Mattie's room was empty.

Jake stared at the vacant bed, at the rumpled
sheets and the dent in the pillow where her head
had lain. He saw the novel she'd been reading and
an empty tea cup on the bedside table. He knew
this was her room because, apart from its number,
the pink rose bush and the blue irises sat on a
small table under the window.

Everything looked normal but he felt uneasy.
He'd been talking to her ten minutes ago. What
could have happened in such a short time?

Crossing the room, he knocked on the door to

the *en suite* bathroom, but there was no answer so he opened the door carefully. She wasn't there.

His heart began to thud. Hard. He rushed out of the room and down the corridor to the nurses' station.

A young woman greeted him with a beaming smile. 'How can I help you, sir?'

'Mattie Carey,' he gasped. 'She isn't in her room.'

The nurse's eyes twinkled and her face broke into a silly grin. Jake wanted to yell at her that this was serious.

'You must be Jake,' she said.

'Yes. Did Mattie leave a message?'

She nodded. 'She asked me to let you know they've taken her down to X-Ray.'

'Why? What's wrong?'

'Her doctor ordered another scan.'

A soft groan came from the back of Jake's throat and the nurse took pity on him. Her eyes softened. 'Don't worry, it's a routine procedure. Mattie shouldn't be too long.'

'Right.' He closed his eyes briefly and allowed himself to breathe. 'Thanks.' He took another breath. 'What do you suggest? Should I come back in…in about an hour, then?'

She nodded, then sighed. 'That's so sweet.'

'I beg your pardon?'

But the nurse had turned bright red and wouldn't answer him. She simply buried her nose in a bundle of charts.

Mattie lay on her side with her eyes closed, tired after the scan. Not that it had been a big deal, but everything seemed to make her tired these days. The nurse had told her that Jake had come while she was away. Poor guy.

What a rotten day he'd had.

She tried to shift into a more comfortable position.

She was such a sloth these days. An uncomfortable sloth. She was tired of being uncomfortable, tired of the babies kicking and head-butting her insides.

And now, after just one day, she was tired of the doctors and medical staff fussing over her, tired of the thought of spending day after day in this little white room.

Heavens, she'd become such a grouch. It was almost as if she and Jake had traded places. When they'd met, he'd been the grouchy one and now he was being sweet. So kind to Roy. To her.

But the other day, when she'd tried to talk to him about it, she'd asked him one question and then she'd burst into tears. Poor man.

It was strange that she'd leapt into bed with

Jake without a second thought but, when it came to talking about their relationship, she was a mass of nerves. Perhaps that was Pete's legacy. He'd always hated talking about their future.

She was drifting off to sleep when she heard the soft tap-tap on her door, and she kept her eyes closed. She'd missed Jake's visit, but with any luck she might fall asleep and dream of him kissing her. It was so long ago that he'd kissed her. She wanted to remember exactly how his lips had felt on hers, how he'd tasted.

Perhaps, if she pretended to be asleep, the person at the door would give up and go away. So many people had interrupted her today to take her blood pressure, to give her steroid injections to strengthen the babies' lungs, to give her vitamin tablets, to bring her lunch, afternoon tea. Soon it would be time for supper.

She wasn't hungry.

'Mattie.'

Jake's voice.

Her eyes shot open.

He was in the doorway, looking at her with a worried, tender smile.

She struggled to sit up.

'I'm sorry if I woke you,' he said, coming into the room.

'I wasn't really asleep.' Her hair was falling all

over her face and she tucked it behind her ear. 'I'm pleased to see you. Have a seat.'

Jake brought a chair close to the bed. It wasn't quite as nice as having him right beside her on a sofa, but Mattie wasn't about to complain.

'I came earlier,' he told her. 'But you were away having a scan. Is everything OK?'

'Yes, the babies are doing really well.'

'But you look tired.'

'It comes with the territory.'

He was watching her carefully.

'You've had a rotten day,' she said. 'I'm so sorry about Roy.'

'I think he's going to pull through. They're talking about an operation. Something called angioplasty—to open blocked coronary arteries.'

'How does Roy feel about that?'

'Resigned. He's not ready to shuffle off this mortal coil just yet.'

'I'm glad.'

Jake stared into her eyes for an immeasurable period of time. 'I suppose I should be pleased that you're here, where experts can keep an eye on you.'

'Yes, let them worry about me, Jake. You don't have to.'

'I can't help it.'

'Women have babies every day.'

'Of course they do.' He smiled, but she saw

fear flicker deep in his eyes, quick as a fish's tail, then he looked away and pointed to the pot plants. 'You've brought them with you.'

'I had to. They're my good luck charms, although I can only water them with my tooth glass.'

'They're looking healthy so far.' Reaching over, he took her hands in his. 'You must have green thumbs.'

His thumbs stroked hers slowly and he smiled again and Mattie smiled back at him and she could feel her tiredness evaporating. For ages they didn't speak—simply held hands, smiling.

It was so long since they'd touched like this and it might have been awkward, but Mattie only felt a wonderful warmth, a sense of peace and of rightness, as if being with Jake was like coming home.

But he broke the magic by becoming practical again. 'Were you able to make plans for Brutus and Pavarotti?'

'Not yet, it was all so sudden. But thanks for reminding me. That was one of the reasons I was trying to ring you.'

He jumped in quickly. 'I'd be happy to drop over there and keep an eye on them. I can take Brutus for walks.'

'You should move into the flat,' Mattie said,

wondering why she hadn't thought of it straight away. 'It's just sitting there empty.' Already, she was digging the keys out of a drawer in the bedside table. 'I know Will won't mind, and it's handy for the hospital. Easier for visiting Roy.'

'And you.'

She smiled. 'Exactly.'

As she handed Jake the keys he asked, 'So, how's the food here?'

'I...I haven't had much yet. I haven't been very hungry.'

'You should be eating for three, shouldn't you?'

'So I've been told.'

Watching her, Jake's thoughtful frown morphed into a slow smile. 'Why don't you have dinner with me tomorrow night?'

Her jaw dropped. 'I beg your pardon? How can I do that when I'm confined to barracks?'

'I know a terrific restaurant that does great gourmet takeaways. I'll collect it and bring it here. We can have dinner together right here in this room.'

'Oh.'

For a horrifying moment, Mattie thought she might start to cry again. *I mustn't. I mustn't.*

Jake was waiting for her answer. 'What do you say? Do we have a date?'

It was a crime that he had to ask. As if a solitary

meal of bland hospital food could possibly compete with any dinner with Jake. 'Thanks,' she whispered. 'I'd *love* to have dinner with you.'

'Terrific.' He stood, then reached down and gently touched her cheek. 'Now rest up, won't you? I'll see you tomorrow.'

As if she could rest now. She was way too excited.

Jake walked Brutus along the edge of the bay and dragged in deep breaths of fresh, salty air as he tried to relax. Not an easy task, given that he was up to his eyeballs in life and death dramas.

This morning Roy had been at death's door, now Mattie was about to give birth to not one, but *two* babies, and Jake was deeply involved in both incidents. Heavy going for a guy who'd been accused more than once of living in an emotional vacuum.

To cap it off, he'd asked Mattie to have dinner with him, which meant he was dating a woman who was pregnant with babies that weren't his— or hers. It was hard to get his head around.

In front of him now, the sun was melting into a golden puddle in the distant water. Seagulls screeched and squabbled. Small waves lapped at rocks. Jake drew another deep breath.

He should lighten up.

Things weren't so very bad, really. The doctors

had told him that Roy would pull through, even though his face was still so ghostly pale it almost blended into the pillows. His old mate was being kept alive right now by IV drips and wires, as well as small TV screens with alarming green lines, but he was in good hands.

And, for that matter, Mattie was fine too…

He just had to keep taking one step at a time. He really had no other choice.

The dinner date was perfect—a superbly piquant coq au vin, followed by melt-in-the-mouth chocolate truffle cake, and sparkling mineral water in champagne flutes.

Mattie couldn't remember a meal she'd enjoyed more, but the evening went from fabulous to perfect when Jake kissed her.

It was so unexpected. One minute he was sitting beside her on the bed, laughing as they shared a joke, the next he was leaning in to her and his lips were teasing-soft as they brushed her cheek. He whispered her name and his mouth was warm on her skin, trailing kisses so light she could barely feel them.

'I'm allowed to kiss you, aren't I?' he whispered. 'I promise to be gentle.'

At first she was too stunned and breathless to answer.

'Mattie?'

She was shaking, but she managed to smile. 'I...I'm sure a gentle kiss is just what the doctor ordered.'

Indeed, her greedy skin was already shivering and yearning for more. Jake trailed kisses to her mouth and she closed her eyes. With gentle hands he cradled her face and her lips parted beneath him in an eager offering.

She loved the way he tasted.

Loved the texture of his lips.

The sweet mystery of his mouth.

Shyly, she ran her hands over his shoulders, gliding them over his shirt and sensing the hard bands of muscle beneath the cotton fabric. With trembling fingertips she stroked the back of his neck, thrilling to the heat of his burning skin.

'Mattie,' he whispered hoarsely into her mouth and she thought she might die of happiness.

Winding her arms around his neck, she felt every part of her begin to dissolve as she sank into a slow, dark meltdown.

'What's your problem, Jake? You look like you lost a dollar and found five cents.'

Jake flashed a smile at Roy. He'd been caught out, thinking about his parents, about how angry he was because, once again, they were too busy to come to Sydney to visit the man who'd been their head stockman for thirty years. Not that he'd share that news with Roy.

He shook his head. 'Don't start worrying about me, old-timer. I just want you to concentrate on getting well.'

Roy dismissed this with a wave of his hand. 'That's the doctors' job. Anyway, I'd recover a darn sight faster if I knew you'd stopped making such a dog's breakfast of your love life.'

Jake's jaw dropped so hard he was in danger of dislocation. 'Where did that come from?'

Roy gave a defensive shrug. 'I've been meaning to speak to you about it for a long time.'

'And since when have you been an expert on other people's love lives?'

'That's not the point. I'm an expert on *you*, Jake, and I know what makes you tick. I know what scares you about women.'

Something inside Jake cracked, but he did his resolute best to ignore it. 'Scared of women?' he said shakily. 'Have you any idea how many women I've dated?'

'Too many.' Roy's bottom lip protruded stubbornly.

'It's not possible to have too many women.' Jake's response was automatic, a reflex conditioned by years of carelessness, but now he could hear the hollow ring of dishonesty.

Since he'd met Mattie, he hadn't dated anyone else, hadn't even thought about other women, and that was a mighty scary state of affairs for a perennial bachelor.

Roy was watching him through narrowed eyes.

Jake scowled back at him. 'What does that look mean?'

'I'm thinking about that time after your brother was stillborn.'

The air around Jake solidified. He struggled to breathe.

Roy's hand patted Jake's forearm. 'After that baby died, your mother retreated from you, Jake. She pulled back from the world and spent six months lost under a black cloud. I don't know what they call it these days—depression, maybe—but, living in isolation in the Outback, she probably didn't get the help she needed. Your dad was worried sick about her. Neither of them could see what it was doing to you.'

'You're talking too much,' Jake said quietly. 'You're supposed to save your breath.'

'I feel I've got to say this,' Roy insisted. 'You see, I knew how it was before that baby died. You adored your mother. You had a wonderful relationship with her.'

Jake swallowed to ease the ache in his throat. 'Afterwards, she couldn't look at me without crying.'

'Yeah, I know,' Roy said. 'And I watched you pull on your armour, like a brave little soldier. Shielding yourself from the pain.'

Jake's throat was so tight and sore he couldn't speak. For so many years, he'd blocked out these memories, but now Roy had stripped off their protective coverings. It was as if they were there sitting in front of him. Unavoidable.

'Then, just as your mother was recovering, they shunted you off to that boys' boarding school.' Roy sighed heavily. 'Since you were ten years old, you've lived in a world filled with males and you're still doing it, hiding away in Mongolia. Oh, yes, you date plenty of women, but you've never allowed yourself to get close. You don't want to get hurt.'

'Right now, I'm spending half my life in a maternity ward,' Jake said tersely.

'And it's scaring the life out of you.'

The pressure in Jake's lungs grew. His eyes stung. His throat burned. He gritted his teeth and clenched his hands as he fought for control.

'I'm not right for her,' he said stiffly.

There was no need to explain. Roy understood.

'You're perfect for Mattie.'

'Do you believe that? Honestly?' It was pathetic how badly he needed to hear this from the old man.

'I know it, Jake. And I know she's perfect for you. That's why you're so frightened.'

Jake sat very still beside the bed, staring at the veins on the backs of his hands, scarcely daring to breathe.

'You don't want to end up a lonely old codger like me, Jake.'

'But you chose to be a bachelor.'

This was greeted by a groaning chuckle.

'You never wanted to marry, did you?'

'It wasn't for lack of wanting.'

'What stopped you, then?'

'Couldn't work up the courage.'

'No.' The word came on a whispered breath. Jake couldn't believe his old hero had backed away from anything.

'Bravery's a funny thing,' Roy said softly. 'I could face a wild bull without a tremor, but I couldn't give my heart into a woman's keeping.'

His pale blue eyes regarded Jake gently. 'It's a danger, Jake. If you keep your heart under lock and key for too long, you end up terrified to let it see the light of day.'

Jake sat very still, his pulse slamming in his ears, his mind fixed on Mattie.

'She's such a good person.' It was little more than a whisper.

'And you're not a good person?' Roy croaked a disbelieving laugh. 'Come on, mate. Look at how well you've cared for me.'

'But that's because…' Jake stopped, unable to complete the sentence. He tried again. 'You were always there for me.'

'And Mattie will always be there for you too.' Roy's eyes gleamed softly. 'Give that girl half a chance and she'll let you keep her happy for the rest of her life.'

CHAPTER TEN

'BABY needs chocolate?' Mattie's eyes widened as she read the slogan stamped on the side of Jake's latest gift.

'These are special chocolate bars for pregnant mothers,' Jake told her proudly. 'The woman at Ready and Waiting assured me they're stacked with nourishment.'

Mattie laughed. 'The woman at Ready and Waiting must be your new best friend.'

'I'm certainly her new best customer.'

'And I'm one lucky pregnant woman.' Mattie lifted the lid. 'Ooh, the chocolate smells divine, Jake, thank you.'

She couldn't believe how fabulous this week had been.

Since their first in-house dinner together, Jake had visited her daily, sometimes twice daily, between his visits to Roy, and he'd brought all manner of lovely surprises from a special maternity store he'd unearthed in one of the bayside suburbs.

Such lovely gifts—expensive buttery creams for her skin, a silk-covered journal for her to record her memories.

'You're a writer and I thought you'd like to put the surrogacy experience into words,' he said.

A beautiful idea, she agreed. She'd write a journal for the babies to read in the future.

Jake had also brought all kinds of tempting, nourishing things to eat and sentimental movies Mattie could watch on her laptop.

'I know you prefer thrillers,' he said with a sweet, concerned expression that made her insides do cartwheels. 'But, considering your delicate condition, I thought you might prefer something less bloodthirsty.'

Of course, she hadn't admitted that she actually adored these gorgeous, soppy movies, but she wondered if Jake had guessed.

On several afternoons she'd completely lost herself in the lush romantic storylines of these films. Alone in this room, with the door closed, she'd wept and snuffled to her heart's content.

She'd never dreamed that Jake could be such an attentive and thoughtful hospital visitor. And she'd certainly never anticipated that such a gorgeous man could still make her feel attractive when her abdomen was the size of a harvest moon. Whenever Jake kissed her, he had to contend with a baby's knee or an elbow digging into him, but he didn't seem to mind.

If he was still upset about the surrogacy, he didn't show it.

Today, he was completely at ease. He quickly made himself at home, slumping into the chair beside her bed with his shoes off and his feet in socks, propped on the edge of her mattress. Mattie peeled away the paper wrapping on a maternity chocolate bar and took her first bite.

'Oh, yum.' She offered it to Jake. 'Try some.'

He took a bite from the place where her mouth had been. After he'd swallowed, he laughed. 'Thanks. I hope pregnancy isn't catching.'

They talked about Roy's impending operation and his post-operative care. And Mattie told Jake that the latest scan showed that the babies had settled into an awkward position. The doctor was planning a Caesarean section for the week after next, or possibly sooner.

Jake quickly lost his casual pose. His face paled visibly. 'Do you mind having a Caesarean?'

'I can't wait.'

'Really?' His throat rippled as he swallowed and his face tightened into a worried smile. 'I suppose the bonus is that you won't have to go into labour.'

He seemed so nervous about the birth. Mattie supposed it was a guy thing. He'd mentioned that his mother had had pregnancy complications, so perhaps he had lingering fears.

To her surprise, she wasn't afraid at all. From the moment she'd started this project, she'd had really strong vibes that all would be well. 'I've been assured that Caesars leave very neat little scars,' she said, hoping to distract him.

He nodded, but he didn't look happy.

In the awkward silence she hunted for a safe subject, while Jake frowned and rolled a corner of her bed sheet between his fingers. She wondered if he was trying to find another topic too.

Without looking at her, he said, 'Have you given much thought to how you'll feel when this is finished? When you hand the babies over?'

Mattie swallowed a piece of chocolate too quickly. 'I've thought about little else,' she admitted. 'At times, the only thing that's kept me going is imagining the moment when Gina and Tom first hold their babies. I must have pictured their happy, goofy grins a thousand times.'

'But what about you, Mattie? Have you thought about how *you* will feel?'

'I'll be happy for Gina and Tom.'

With a heavy sigh, he let his head fall back and

he stared at the ceiling. 'But how will you feel when Gina and Tom walk away with their babies?' He was still staring at the dull off-white paintwork. 'When they're off in a nursery somewhere, learning all about feeding regimes or whatever they have to learn, how will you feel when you're back in this room, all alone?'

With a flabby tummy and sore milky breasts?

Mattie felt as if the entire chocolate bar had lodged in her throat. She swallowed uncomfortably, but the sharp, tight ache remained. 'I haven't let myself worry about that. I've been concentrating on growing the babies and getting them safely delivered.'

His dark gaze skewered her. 'With no thought at all for yourself?'

'Not really.'

But, now that Jake had raised this question, Mattie found that she already knew the answer. She would feel abandoned, unnecessary, like an empty chrysalis after the butterfly had flown.

There was every chance she would need a shoulder to lean on, strong arms to hold her. But not just any shoulder, not just any arms.

Could she tell Jake that?

They'd made huge progress in a week. They'd talked about their families, their schooldays, their best friends, their pet hates, their favourite foods.

They'd played Scrabble and backgammon and poker. They'd kissed and their kisses had been... unambiguous.

But they hadn't, until now, talked about the future, or where this newly hatched relationship was heading.

Now Jake's question had taken them into uncharted waters, but he'd relinquished the steering wheel. His eyes were shadowed and difficult to read as he waited for her answer.

Oh, heavens, if only she was braver. If only she couldn't remember so clearly how Pete had squirmed whenever she'd tried to talk about their future. In her most depressed moments, she'd wondered if Pete had only promised marriage to keep her quiet.

If she was too forward now, if she sounded the slightest bit pushy, she might send Jake running and she couldn't bear that.

She massaged an uncomfortable spot just below her breastbone where a little foot protruded. 'I guess I'll pick myself up and start all over again.' She forced brightness into her voice. 'Like the old song.'

'The way you did after your grandmother died?'

'Yes,' she said, pleased that he understood.

Jake, however, was watching her with a disconcerting frown. 'You've also had to get up again after being knocked down in a relationship, haven't you?'

Her jaw dropped in surprise. 'Does it show?'

He smiled sadly. 'There has to be a reason why a lovely, generous girl like you doesn't have half the men in Sydney knocking on her door.'

At first she could only stare at Jake while she savoured his compliment, but eventually she gathered her wits. 'Well, yes…I have wasted three years of my life over a boyfriend who said he wanted marriage and changed his mind at the last moment.'

Jake's frown deepened. 'Was it bad?'

'About as bad as it gets. It's pretty awful calling off a wedding, selling a wedding gown you've never worn. Seeing all that pity in everyone's eyes.'

She held her breath as she waited for Jake's response. In the movies she'd been watching, at a precarious moment like this the hero drew the heroine into his arms and told her that he'd fallen madly in love with her, that he would never let her down.

At the very least, Jake could finally explain why he'd given up so much time and effort to entertain her.

But Jake didn't speak. He simply looked

worried and strained, as if he was distinctly uncomfortable with such private revelations.

Mattie was awash with disappointment. This
was his chance to explain why an unquestionably
hunky bachelor, with his choice of thousands of
available women, chose to spend hours and hours
in a maternity ward with a woman who was not
carrying his child.

But, although she waited, Jake didn't continue.
In fact he avoided making eye contact and she
could feel her heart sinking through the mattress.

'What about you, Jake?' She had to try again.
'How will you feel once the babies are handed
over to Gina and Tom?'

'Relieved.'

Sadness lingered in his smile as he stood slowly
and bent to kiss her cheek. His breath was warm
against her ear.

'I suppose you'll be pleased when I'm no
longer pregnant?' she asked hopefully.

With another sad smile, he tucked her hair
behind her ear. 'I'll be very pleased and very
relieved.' He pressed a kiss onto her lips and then
he left to visit Roy.

He couldn't wait to get away, Mattie thought
as she watched him go, but then *she* remembered
why romantic movies always made her feel miserable and inadequate. In her world, the *real*

world, divinely gorgeous men didn't sweep her into a powerful embrace and swear to love her till she drew her last breath.

In her life, the men made every show of loving her and then they moved on. To other women.

The hospital was dark when Mattie clambered out of bed, needing to go to the bathroom, as she did several times every night.

Fuzzy with sleep, she glanced at the bedside clock and saw the glowing green digits announcing that it was four forty-five. She fumbled in the dark for the bathroom door and one of the babies kicked a mean jab, low into her bladder.

Wincing, she pushed the door open, took a sleepy step forward onto the cool tiles.

Without warning, warm water gushed between her legs, splashing her nightgown and soaking her bare feet.

Her heart pounded as she stared at the puddle on the floor. She felt a leap of fear. Had she totally lost control of her bodily functions?

Then she realised what must have happened and her fear was overtaken by a hot flurry of excitement.

It was only just light. Jake was trying to stay in that happy limbo between sleeping and waking when his mobile phone let out a soft vibrating rumble.

Without raising his head, he felt around in the untidy heap of things beside the bed. 'Morning,' he mumbled into the phone.

'Jake?'

He sat bolt upright. 'Mattie, is that you?'

'I hope I haven't rung too early.' Her voice sounded different, as if she was scared or excited or maybe both.

'What is it? What's happened?'

'I'm going to have the babies this morning.'

The words hit him like a grenade exploding at close range. In that instant, he was wide-awake, facing every nightmare fear, every dark memory.

'Isn't this too soon?' he cried, fighting off waves of panic.

'It's a bit early, but my waters have broken so we don't really have much choice. But it's OK, Jake. Most twins come early.'

He was amazed that she could sound so calm. There was even a smile in her voice, an edge of exhilaration, like a climber who'd almost reached Everest's peak.

Jake's stomach twisted with fear.

'So where are you now?' he asked. *Stick to practical details. Keep those other thoughts at bay.*

'I'm still in my room.'

'I'll come and see you.' Already he was heading for the pile of clothes he'd dumped on a chair. 'I'm on my way.'

'But I'm not sure how much longer I'll be here.'

'Doesn't matter. I'll find you.'

He had to be there, had to see her. Maybe if he was there, if he stayed with Mattie, everything would be all right.

'Jake?' Her voice was tiny suddenly, but it shot like a dart straight into his heart.

'Yes?'

'I…' She hesitated and seemed to change her mind. 'Thanks for coming.'

'No worries, sweetheart. See you soon.' He disconnected and his heart pounded as he hunted for clothes.

The drive to the hospital was torture. The early morning traffic was slow and every junction threw up a red light. Pedestrians crossed roads at a snail's pace. Throughout it all, Jake's stomach churned and his skin was clammy with fear. How would he cope if something happened to Mattie?

How could he help her if tragedy struck today? He owed her so much. She'd changed him. Until he'd met her, his life had been one-dimensional—focused on chasing money and good times. The main attraction of his work in Mongolia had been the automatic transfer of large chunks of money into his bank account.

Hell, he hadn't even been a proper environmentalist. He'd had a keen interest in the natural world, but he'd never become impassioned about any particular environmental issue. He'd been as shallow as a kids' wading pool.

No one was more surprised than he was by his behaviour in the past few weeks.

That was Mattie's doing. She brought out the best in him.

But, even with Roy's prompting, he'd still held back from telling her this. He still wasn't sure he could offer any promises. Had he left it too late to tell her how he felt?

Mattie heard the rumble of the trolley that would take her to Theatre and she took a deep breath. This was it.

Very soon she would no longer be pregnant, and Gina and Tom would be parents.

Her task was almost over.

And, somewhere out there in the busy Sydney streets, Jake was on his way.

She thought of the morning she'd driven him to the airport and the tearful farewell, when he'd told her he couldn't promise her a future with him.

How could she ever have guessed he'd be back in Sydney again, visiting her daily, trying to be with her now as she faced this delivery?

Surely that meant he loved her?

How silly she'd been to doubt him. She'd been waiting for him to say the words, but she, Mattie Carey, knew better than most that actions spoke louder than words. Always.

Thank heavens she'd remembered this just in time.

She was smiling as the two orderlies came through her doorway, pushing the trolley between them.

At last Jake reached the hospital car park and, as he rushed along the walkway to the maternity ward, he tried to call Mattie again. His hands were shaking as he pressed her number. The phone rang and rang until her calm voice told him to leave a message after the beep.

It took forever for the lift to climb to her floor. Jake charged up the hall to her room.

It was empty.

He sagged against the door, expelling his breath in a huff of despair.

Where was she now?

A split-second later, he was rushing to the nurses' station.

The nurses on the maternity ward knew him by now and this morning the friendliest one, Beth, beamed at him.

'Where's Mattie?' he demanded.

'They've already taken her to Theatre.'

'Which way?' he cried. 'I've got to see her.'

Beth shook her head. 'I'm sorry, Jake. I don't think—'

'Don't try to stop me. I'm going to her! Please, just tell me the quickest way to find her.'

Beth's blue eyes widened and for several seconds she stared at him, as if she was weighing his demands against hospital protocol.

'I've got to be there,' Jake urged through clenched teeth.

Beth swallowed.

'I love Mattie,' he said in a lowered, desperate whisper. 'But I haven't told her. You've got to help me.'

Her eyes were suddenly shiny. 'Right!' As if her doubts had vanished, she grabbed Jake roughly by the elbow. 'We've got to hurry. Come on, it's this way!'

To Jake's surprise, Beth ran with him all the way.

'You'll have to change into theatre clothes,' she ordered, shoving him through a doorway.

'I have to what?'

Her eyes were huge, her expression significant as she rounded on him. 'You want to be there with Mattie, don't you?'

'Inside? In the theatre?' He flinched from the thought. He'd been hoping to find Mattie in some kind of waiting area. 'I...I...'

For one treacherous moment he almost caved in. If he went inside, he would see the whole procedure—knives cutting into Mattie. Newborn babies.

Fear became a taste in the back of Jake's throat. A picture of his baby brother flashed before him, forcing him to see again that cold, tiny, lifeless face.

A wave of dizziness swept over him, but he knew he couldn't pull out of this now. He couldn't wait through another lonely vigil like the one that still haunted him. He couldn't leave Mattie alone.

Heaven alone knew what ordeal she faced but, whatever happened now, he had to be with her all the way.

Swallowing a glut of fear, he nodded to Beth. 'I want to be with her.' He felt a small explosion in the middle of his chest. 'What do I have to do?'

'Hurry!' Beth shouted as she thrust a green theatre gown into his arms.

Beneath the bright theatre lights, Mattie felt alone and terrified. She hadn't expected to see so many gowned people in here—obstetricians, paediatricians, midwives, an anaesthetist. Not one friendly face, and not one of the people she needed most.

Jake had probably been held up in traffic. Gina and Tom were on their way from Willowbank, but they couldn't possibly make it in time, and not one of the friendly nurses from the maternity ward was here.

It might have helped if she'd been dosed with relaxing drugs, but nothing like that had been offered. Now, everything was happening too fast.

Already, the anaesthetist was asking her to roll over. He wanted to stick a needle into her spine. But it was too soon.

'Could you wait just a minute?' she muttered, but the anaesthetist took no notice. He rubbed her back with something cold and she felt the prick and sting of a needle. She pictured the anaesthetic sinking into her, spreading to her heart, her arteries, her veins. Soon the entire bottom half of her body would be numb.

'What happens now?' she asked, but everyone seemed too busy to answer her. Had they forgotten she was here?

Could someone smile? Please, don't ignore me.

The medical team began to erect a green cloth as a screen around her stomach. Mattie's heart raced. Any minute now the doctor would make his incision. This felt all wrong. It was too clinical. Like an operation. Not a birth.

Behind her a door crashed open.

'Oh, thank God,' cried a voice. 'We're not too late.'

Mattie turned her head and saw Beth's friendly face. And there was Jake!

Oh, gosh. Oh, wow! He looked wonderful. Familiar and yet strangely alien in a hospital cap and gown.

'Who's this?' Dr Smith, the obstetrician, looked up from whatever he was doing and fixed Jake with a steely stare.

Jake's face was unusually pale as he snapped to attention and took a step forward. 'I have to be with Mattie.'

'He's her boyfriend,' Beth announced and then she made a hasty amendment. 'Her partner.'

Dr Smith's grey eyes looked surprised but Jake was already standing at Mattie's right shoulder and he reached down and clasped her hand. 'I'm…I'm the surrogate father,' he said.

Several masked faces turned to look at Jake, amusement dancing in their eyes, but the doctor simply nodded, businesslike once more, as he turned his attention to Mattie's abdomen.

Mattie looked up into Jake's face and saw his

heart shining in his eyes. She tried to speak, but a thousand emotions rose to fill her throat and she could only manage a strangled sob.

He smiled with aching tenderness as he bent down to her. 'Hi there.'

'Hey.'

He squeezed her hand. 'Just keep smiling, sweetheart.'

She was smiling straight into his eyes when she felt the cutting sensation on the other side of the screen. A flash of fear sliced through her, but Jake dipped his head and she felt the reassuring warmth of his lips on her brow.

There was a pulling sensation somewhere in her middle and suddenly a voice cried in triumph, 'It's a boy.'

Gloved hands held a baby high and Mattie saw his gleaming creamy skin, his perfect limbs and his little scrunched face, capped by dark, unmistakably red hair.

Her face broke into a broad grin. 'Oh, the little darling. He looks exactly like Tom.'

She heard Jake's abrupt laugh—half excited, half scared—and felt his hand gripping hers more tightly.

Already, another doctor was pulling out the little girl but, before Mattie could see her properly, she was whisked away.

'What's the matter?' Mattie called after them fearfully.

'Don't worry. She'll be all right,' Beth hastened to reassure them. 'She just needs resuscitation.'

'Can't she breathe?' Jake's voice was raspy and rough, as if he was scared too.

'She'll breathe. But there was always a chance the smaller baby would need help. It's why Dr Smith insisted on a Caesarean.'

'Are you sure she's OK?'

Beth patted Mattie's shoulder. 'I'm sure, honey, but I'll go and check for you. Be right back.'

It was all over.

Mattie's incision had been repaired. She'd been reassured that the baby girl was fine, although she needed careful monitoring and would stay in an incubator for the next twenty-four hours.

Jake had been outside, making the necessary phone calls, and now there wasn't a lot for him to do as he followed Mattie out of Theatre and into Recovery, where a male nurse hovered over her, watching her intently and taking her blood pressure every few seconds.

Or so it seemed.

Mattie looked bright and happy as she held up her end of the conversation with the nurse. It was Jake who was completely lost.

He felt dazed, like the time he'd been thrown from a horse and found himself on the hard ground, totally winded and looking at the world upside down.

It was so hard to believe he'd actually witnessed the successful birth of two brand-new tiny human beings.

They'd survived. Mattie had survived. None of his fears had been realised. He should be feeling euphoric.

Instead, he still felt tense. The excitement was over and the babies had vanished into some distant nursery where perhaps, even now, they were being met by their parents. This was it—the moment when Mattie had to face the fact that she was alone.

Lost? Needing him?

Yeah, sure. Right now she was chatting happily to the male nurse who apparently needed to know every last medical detail of her surrogacy. Jake watched her cheerful smile and the way she waved her expressive hands as she talked animatedly to this other guy and his tension grew claws, took a stranglehold.

He needed to be alone with her. There was so much he wanted to tell her, but he might as well grab a coffee, visit Roy, do anything rather than hang around here like a fifth wheel.

He took a step towards the trolley. 'Mattie?'

She stopped in mid-sentence and turned. Her eyes were shining. 'Hi, Jake,' she said as if she'd just remembered his presence.

'I thought I might push off now.'

'Oh.' The word fell from her lips softly and a flood of pink rushed into her cheeks. She looked worried, held out her hand to him. 'But I haven't thanked you.'

'I haven't done anything.'

'You have. You came. You were here.' The glow in her eyes took on a damp sheen. Her lower lip trembled. 'You were perfect. All along you've been perfect.' She spoke as if the nurse wasn't there listening to every word. 'And I've made so many terrible mistakes.'

Jake was sure he'd swallowed a golf ball. *Mistakes? What was she talking about?*

Beside them, the nurse cleared his throat and Mattie shot him a cool glance. 'Could you give us a moment, please, Ben?'

'I'm supposed to observe you.'

'I know, but this is important. Just for a moment.'

Ben gave a doubtful shrug. 'I'll just be outside, then.'

'Thanks.'

As soon as he'd gone Mattie took both of Jake's hands in hers. Her cheeks were flushed, her eyes too shiny and she was trembling.

'What's the matter?' Jake whispered. 'Should I call the nurse back?'

'No. I'm all right. It's just…I'm scared.'

'About the babies? They said the little girl's fine.'

She shook her head. 'Not that.' She spoke softly and he could barely make out the words. 'I want to apologise.'

This didn't make sense. 'Mattie, what are you talking about?'

She closed her eyes and took a deep shuddering breath. 'I didn't want to get too close to another man.'

'I understand, Mattie. It's OK.'

'But I need to explain why I stopped answering your e-mails. I was afraid of getting involved, then getting hurt again, and then I didn't tell you about the babies and of course you got a shock—and I turned you away. But, in spite of everything, you've been so good to me and—'

Tears trembled on her lashes. 'I'm sorry.'

'Sorry?' He was at once panicky and wanting to dance on air. 'I should be the one to apologise. I'm ashamed of the way I carried on about the surrogacy, but I was dealing with a terrible fear about what might happen.'

'Because of your mother's complications?'

He realised then that the ghost had been laid to

rest and he could actually talk about it. 'My baby brother was stillborn, you see. I was only nine years old and my mother was ill and I…I saw him. I held him.'

'Oh, Jake, you poor darling.' Mattie touched his cheek in the gentlest of caresses. 'It must have been incredibly hard for you to come here today.'

'I'm on top of the world now.' He smiled shakily. 'You've given your friends the most amazing gift. You're the most wonderful girl.'

She raised her face and looked gravely into his eyes. 'But I'm not the girl you met.'

A bubble of laughter burst in Jake's throat. 'I'm not the man you met.' He lifted her hand and pressed his lips to her fingers. 'The babies aren't the only ones who've grown over the past eight months. I feel like I'm twice the man I was. I've learned so much from you.'

At first she didn't respond, but then a small smile played at the corners of her mouth.

'I love you, Mattie.'

How good it felt to say those words out loud. Finally they sounded real. They *were* real.

They made her smile.

Such a beautiful, shining, radiant smile.

He covered her hands with his and felt his confidence grow. 'I've…er…heard you're on the lookout for a new mission now.'

'Oh, yes. I did say that.'

'I was wondering if you might take me on.'

Her eyes widened.

'As an ongoing project,' he clarified.

'As a boyfriend?'

Jake nodded.

'Are you talking long term?'

He didn't miss a beat. 'Very long term.'

'Not forever, Jake?'

He smiled. 'Why not?'

A cough sounded behind them. 'OK,' Ben said. 'I hate to break up the party, but—'

Jake held up his hand. 'Please, mate, give us one more minute.'

'I really need to take Mattie's blood pressure now. And then she's all yours.'

'Can't you take her blood pressure after I ask her to marry me?'

To Jake's relief, the other guy's face broke into a grin.

'Make it quick,' Ben said, still grinning as he backed out of the room.

Jake turned to Mattie. Her eyes were shining. She was so beautiful.

'I love you, Mattie,' he said again, leaning close so only she could hear. 'I need you in my life.'

She smiled.

'I need you as my wife. I promise I won't let you down. I want to keep you close for ever.'

Her smile broadened to a grin. 'That's exactly where I want to be.'

They were back in Mattie's room when Gina and Tom arrived, their arms filled with flowers and their faces split by enormous grins.

'Mattie,' Gina cried, rushing to hug her. 'The babies are so, so gorgeous. Thank you, darling. Thank you. Thank you. I'm afraid I can never really thank you enough.'

The next few minutes were very noisy and busy as everyone spoke at once about the birth and the babies.

'We're really excited about you two,' said Tom and he pumped Jake's hand and slapped him on the back. Then, before Mattie could question Tom, the ecstatic new parents left, hurrying back to the nursery.

Mattie looked at Jake. His hair was untidy, he hadn't shaved and his shirt was in need of an iron. He looked a little scruffy, just as he had on the day she'd first seen him, and she felt a delicious pang of longing.

Suddenly Gina was back. 'I almost forgot. This is for you.' She pressed a white envelope into Mattie's hand. 'As an extra thank you.' She winked and was gone.

Mattie looked at Jake. 'I hope they haven't been terribly extravagant. They've already given me so much.'

'Not half as much as you've given them,' he said with a quiet smile.

She opened the envelope and found a lovely thank-you card and a slip of paper. 'Oh, my goodness.' She gave a shocked little laugh. 'It's a voucher for a holiday.'

Jake grinned. 'Exactly what you need.'

'It's for two, Jake. A room and meals for two at a resort on Daydream Island.'

His grin deepened. 'Even better.'

'But how did Gina and Tom know?' Puzzlement vied with excitement at she pictured a holiday on a tropical island with her gorgeous pirate. 'How did they know about you? About us?'

'Will probably told them.'

'Will?' Mattie's jaw dropped. Now she was completely baffled. 'How does he fit into this?'

With a sheepish smile, Jake sat on the edge of her bed. 'While they were stitching you up, I ducked outside to make phone calls. I rang Roy. He sends his love, by the way. And I rang Will and told him about the babies.'

'But you didn't tell him about us, did you? You hadn't—we hadn't—'

A dark tide stained Jake's neck. 'And I asked Will if he'd—' He pressed his lips together and looked incredibly guilty. 'I told him that if all went well, I was going to need him some time in the next couple of months.'

'What for?'

'To be best man at our wedding.'

Mattie gasped.

'And then Will must have rung Gina and Tom,' Jake said. 'I'm sorry. Are you mad?'

She shook her head. How could she be mad? 'Will is the perfect choice,' she said. Everything in her life was perfect.

'You look tired,' Jake suggested, dropping a light kiss on her brow.

She *was* tired. Tired and a bit sore, now that the anaesthetic was wearing off, but so happy she didn't care about any of the discomfort.

'Stay with me?' She patted the bed beside her.

With a slow smile, Jake slipped off his shoes and stretched beside her. His arms encircled her and happiness flowed through her as he gently kissed the curve of her neck.

'Close your eyes,' he whispered.

She did as she was told and let the tiredness wash through her. 'I love you,' she told him.

'I love you too.' He nuzzled her ear. 'And I'm going to keep on loving you. For ever.'

Mattie sighed happily and she felt Jake's warmth surround her, felt his heartbeat strong and steady against her, and she fell asleep with a smile on her face.

EPILOGUE

WELCOME to Willowbank.

The white-painted sign stood proudly in a bed of blue and white agapanthus on the outskirts of town.

'*Ta-da!* This is my home town.' Mattie grinned at Jake. 'Not exactly a bustling metropolis.'

She drove on down the wide main street, divided in the middle by a strip of well-tended lawn with willow trees and brightly coloured garden beds. Either side of the street, rows of old-fashioned timber buildings housed a mix of traditional shops and trendy new fashion stores and cafés.

'I like it,' Jake said.

Mattie shot him a sideways glance. 'You don't have to be polite.'

'No, I mean it. There's something special about being in the bush. And this is the quintessential Australian country town.'

'Complete with the quintessential clock tower right in the middle.' Mattie laughed, pointing.

Jake grinned. 'And the quintessential old-timers, passing the time of day on a seat in the sun.'

'There's my old primary school,' she said as they passed a playground filled with yelling, laughing children.

'And the School of Arts where you stood on stage to recite *The Man from Snowy River*.'

'How did you know?'

'I went to a country primary school too, you know.'

'Of course you did.'

They shared a smile and Mattie felt the tummy-tumbling happiness that she always felt when Jake gave her a certain look.

They were on their way to Gina and Tom's for lunch. This evening they would stay with her parents and they would discuss wedding plans. It was all incredibly exciting.

'Slow down,' Jake said as they left the main part of town and drove past houses on acreage.

Mattie slowed and felt a catch in her throat when she saw the *For Sale* that had caught his attention.

'That's the McLaughlins' place,' she said, excited by the eager intensity in Jake's face. 'I heard they were retiring to the Gold Coast.'

'Do you know the house? Have you been inside?'

'Years ago. In primary school I was friends

with their daughter, but I lost touch when she went away to boarding school. As I remember, it's a lovely old house.'

From the street, they could see a graceful federation-style home, set well back from the road and fronted by attractive gardens. Stately old gum trees shaded the lawn and a row of liquid ambers provided a screen from the neighbours.

'The land runs down to the river,' Mattie said. 'And there's a little jetty.'

'It's perfect,' Jake announced as if he'd already made a decision.

'Do you mean you'd like to live here?'

He smiled. 'Possibly.' Reaching out, he traced the outline of her ear with a fingertip. 'What do you think? Should we come back tomorrow and check it out?'

Mattie gulped. 'Are you serious? Do you really think we could live here in Willowbank?'

'Why not?'

'Would you be able to find work here?'

He grinned. 'Couldn't we live off the royalties from your books?'

'If you don't mind starving in a garret.'

He chuckled. 'Never mind. Every district has environmental issues. If all else fails, I'll set up my own business.'

Mattie rewarded him with a kiss. It seemed too

good to be true that she and Jake might settle here, close to her friends and family, in this house that she'd always admired.

A new thought struck, making her gasp. 'I've just remembered.'

'What?'

'Oh, gosh. Oh, wow!'

'Mattie, for heaven's sake, what is it? Tell me.'

'There's a little cottage on the property, down near the creek. Old Mr McLaughlin, the grandfather, used to live there. I remember how he used to sit on the porch, looking out over the water.'

They stared at each other, eyes wide, and then they spoke in unison. 'Roy.'

Next instant they were smiling, laughing, hugging each other with excitement.

'Would you really want Roy to live with us?' Jake asked as she nestled her head on his shoulder.

'It would be perfect. I'd love it.'

'God, I love you.' He nuzzled her cheek. 'How did I ever get this lucky?'

Jake kissed her and the kiss was scrumptious and lasted for ages, but eventually Mattie pulled away. 'I'm afraid we'd better get going. We don't want to be late for lunch.'

She turned off the main road and headed down the winding road that led through a grove of pines to Gina and Tom's farmhouse.

As they emerged onto the sun-dappled drive in front of the house, Tom was already coming down the steps with a grin as wide as a watermelon slice and little red-headed Jasper curled in his arms like a sleepy ginger-topped possum.

'So good to see you,' he said enthusiastically, kissing Mattie's cheek and shaking Jake's hand and congratulating them both, yet again, on their engagement.

Mattie gazed fondly at Jasper and found it hard to believe that he'd been inside her for all those months. 'How is he, Tom?'

'Settled at last, thank heavens, but he kicked up quite a stink this morning.' Tom grinned and his eyes glowed with unmistakable pride. 'He didn't want to miss the party.'

'And Mia?'

'Sound asleep. She's the model child.'

'The darling.'

Jake retrieved the hamper of gourmet delicacies that he and Mattie had scoured Sydney's delis to find and they went inside the big farmhouse kitchen, which was fragrant as ever with wonderful baking smells.

More laughter and congratulations followed as they greeted Gina.

'And Jake must meet Lucy,' Mattie said, beckoning her petite blonde friend closer. 'Jake, Lucy is Willowbank's favourite vet but, more importantly, she's going to be one of my bridesmaids.'

Lucy was smiling as she shook Jake's hand. 'Pleased to meet you,' she said demurely, but her eyes were sparkling as she turned to Mattie. 'Very impressive,' she whispered out of the corner of her mouth.

Gina beamed at everyone. 'We only need Will here now and we'd have everybody together.'

'He'll be back from Mongolia in time for the wedding,' Mattie told her. 'He's going to be Jake's best man.'

Lucy's sudden shocked gasp cut through the group's excitement. Everyone turned to stare at her and bright colour flooded her face.

She gave a self-conscious shrug and an awkward smile. 'Sorry. I...I hadn't heard that Will would be in the wedding party.'

'Is that a problem?' asked Jake, looking puzzled.

'No.' Lucy was recovering quickly, but her cheeks were still bright pink. 'No, of course not. It's no problem at all.'

Mattie wished she'd explained to Jake that Lucy and Will had a history. They'd been best friends at high school and they'd gone away to university together. Mattie had wondered if their friendship might grow into something deeper, but it never had.

She had never suspected any unfinished business between them. Now, she wasn't so sure.

Lucy, however, was clearly determined to make everyone forget her slip. 'It's so exciting that the wedding is only three months away, Mattie. I can't wait to help you with the planning.'

'It's going to be fun, isn't it?' Gina agreed. 'I do love weddings.'

'I can just see it now.' Lucy smiled dreamily. 'Mattie will look so beautiful.'

'Jake will look beautiful too,' Gina added with a cheeky wink.

'I say this calls for a drink,' Tom announced before the girls could get too carried away.

'Great idea.' Lucy was back to her usual bouncy self. 'I've brought a bottle of bubbly. Let's crack it open.'

The cork popped loudly, icy wine flowed and glasses clinked.

Happy voices cried, 'Here's to Mattie and Jake!'

Mattie caught Jake's eye. Months ago, she'd dreamed of a lovely gathering like this, where she and her best friends and Jake were together. She'd thought it was impossible.

Now, Jake sent her a smile and she read the clear message in his flashing dark eyes. They were a team and, together, everything was possible.

 **ROMANCE 2-in-1**

Coming next month

BETROTHED: TO THE PEOPLE'S PRINCE
by Marion Lennox

Marrying His Majesty continues. Nikos is the people's prince, but the crown belongs to reluctant Princess Athena, whom he was forbidden to marry. He must convince her to come home…

HIS HOUSEKEEPER BRIDE
by Melissa James

Falling for the boss wasn't part of Sylvie's job description. Yet Mark's sad eyes intrigue her and his smile makes her melt…before she knows it this unassuming housekeeper's in over her head!

THE GREEK'S LONG-LOST SON
by Rebecca Winters

Self-made millionaire Theo can have anything his heart desires. There's just one thing he wants – his first love Stella and their long-lost son.

THE BRIDESMAID'S BABY
by Barbara Hannay

Baby Steps to Marriage… concludes. Unresolved feelings resurface as old friends Will and Lucy are thrown together as best man and bridesmaid. But a baby is the last thing they expect.

On sale 2ⁿᵈ October 2009

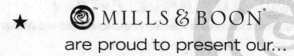

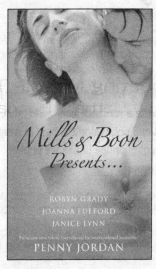

millsandboon.co.uk Community

Join Us!

The Community is the perfect place to meet and chat to kindred spirits who love books and reading as much as you do, but it's also the place to:

- **Get the inside scoop from authors about their latest books**
- **Learn how to write a romance book with advice from our editors**
- **Help us to continue publishing the best in women's fiction**
- **Share your thoughts on the books we publish**
- **Befriend other users**

Forums: Interact with each other as well as authors, editors and a whole host of other users worldwide.

Blogs: Every registered community member has their own blog to tell the world what they're up to and what's on their mind.

Book Challenge: We're aiming to read 5,000 books and have joined forces with The Reading Agency in our inaugural Book Challenge.

Profile Page: Showcase yourself and keep a record of your recent community activity.

Social Networking: We've added buttons at the end of every post to share via digg, Facebook, Google, Yahoo, technorati and de.licio.us.

www.millsandboon.co.uk

2 FREE BOOKS
AND A SURPRISE GIFT

We would like to take this opportunity to thank you for reading this Mills & Boon® book by offering you the chance to take TWO more specially selected books from the Romance series absolutely FREE! We're also making this offer to introduce you to the benefits of the Mills & Boon® Book Club™—

- **FREE home delivery**
- **FREE gifts and competitions**
- **FREE monthly Newsletter**
- **Exclusive Mills & Boon Book Club offers**
- **Books available before they're in the shops**

Accepting these FREE books and gift places you under no obligation to buy, you may cancel at any time, even after receiving your free shipment. Simply complete your details below and return the entire page to the address below. You don't even need a stamp!

YES Please send me 2 free Romance books and a surprise gift. I understand that unless you hear from me, I will receive 5 superb new stories every month including two 2-in-1 books priced at £4.99 each and a single book priced at £3.19, postage and packing free. I am under no obligation to purchase any books and may cancel my subscription at any time. The free books and gift will be mine to keep in any case.

Ms/Mrs/Miss/Mr_____ Initials _____

Surname _____
Address _____

_____ Postcode _____

Send this whole page to: Mills & Boon Book Club, Free Book Offer, FREEPOST NAT 10298, Richmond, TW9 1BR